For everyone who enjoys playing a competitive game,
whether that player is competing against himself/ herself,
as in solitaire, or against another team, as in baseball, or
against a world record, as in sailing. . . .
We could go on and on.
Hey, if you play, this book's for you.

CONTENTS

INTRODUCTION

Games. They bring out the best in us, the worst in us, the thing-we-never-expected in us. From couch potato games on Wii to computer games like World of Warcraft, from church leagues to the major leagues in baseball, from professional bowling to amateur wrestling, from the pankration event at the ancient Olympics to doing a 360 in a skateboard park, human beings just naturally like to test their limits, both mental and physical.

It's not much of a stretch to imagine that supernaturals like to do the same . . . or that otherworldly elements can enter the field of play.

In our latest anthology, you'll find stories that feature ghostly players, bloodthirsty interruptions, and competitions with deadly outcomes. We warn you: this may put you off gaming for a while.

But we don't think that will last long.

CHARLAINE HARRIS
TONI L. P. KELNER

IN THE BLUE HEREAFTER

CHARLAINE HARRIS

Charlaine Harris is the *New York Times* bestselling writer of the Sookie Stackhouse novels, among many others. A lifelong resident of the South, she lives on a cliff with her husband. She has three children, two grandchildren, four rescue dogs, and a rich inner life. She is seldom bored.

During the long drive of the day before, Manfred Bernardo had had plenty of time to reflect on the fact that he would stick out like a sore thumb in a small town. In fact, he'd been rather proud of that certainty. He'd argued mentally with Xylda the whole way from Tennessee to Louisiana. Since Xylda had died the previous winter, that was the only way Manfred could talk to her, but Xylda herself was not so limited. She played games with her grandson, in his dreams. Sending him to Bon Temps, Louisiana, seemed to be the opening move in a new one.

On this sunny, cool afternoon in spring, Manfred scanned the locals around him in the crowded stands, confident in his own street cred. To his chagrin, Manfred observed several people decorated with as much ink as he was, and several more who had facial piercings. Maybe none of them had gone to the same lengths as Manfred, but two or three were in the same ballpark.

The comparison made Manfred smile, because he was actually *in* a ballpark for a fast-pitch softball tournament. According to the schedule a buxom brunette softball mom had sold him when he was paying his entrance fee (and she'd been wearing a T-shirt that read *Softball Mom!*), he was sitting in the stands of Field One to watch the opening game of a two-day tournament.

All around the small complex, uniformed high school girls were dragging or toting bags of equipment to their assigned fields, and coaches and assistant coaches were converging on the officials' table. There were clipboards aplenty, there were baseball caps of many colors, and the concession stand had opened to a brisk business. The stand was the hub in the wheel, and each quarter of the wheel was a different softball field. Each field, of course, had its own set of bleachers, dugouts, and a rudimentary press box. Huge plastic garbage cans were dotted around the venue.

The softball complex was incredibly noisy. Everyone was yelling. A strange green vehicle labeled *Gator* was leaving Field One, driven by two grinning teenage boys, who'd been drawing the chalk lines and raking the pitcher's mound. (Why was it called a "mound" when it was flat? Manfred didn't know, but he'd seen the term on the program.) The wheels on the equipment bags rumbled across the concrete, adding another level of noise, and the loudspeaker at Field One was playing a mixture of music that Manfred could only assume had been selected by the girls of the home team; in this case, the Bon Temps Lady Falcons.

This was the most unlikely place in America for Manfred to be. For the past three nights in a row, he had dreamed of his grandmother, Xylda Bernardo. She had insisted he come here on this day, at this hour, and she wouldn't take no for an answer. He didn't have any idea why she'd wanted him to be here. They'd played games like this as soon as Manfred had become old enough to recognize his own talent and to appreciate Xylda's. Before that, she hadn't been too interested in her only grandson, but when Xylda had discovered Manfred was a psychic, too, she'd done her best to take him over from his mother. His mother, struggling as a single parent, had followed the path of least resistance, figuring Manfred was safer with his grandmother after school was out than he would be at their house on his own.

What do you and Gran do all afternoon? his mother asked.

We play games, he said.

Like Go Fish? Monopoly?

Like . . . Guess why I asked you to do that, or *Tell me what this vision means. You have three tries.*

After that conversation, his mother had driven over to Xylda's by herself and returned flushed and furious. He hadn't been allowed to go to his grandmother's for two days, during which time he'd looked up some porn on his computer, guessing correctly that his mom would check. He'd also made sure his mom would find "evidence" that he'd had someone in the house before she got home from work. Suddenly, his mom and Xylda reached an accord.

The purpose of most conventional games was winning or losing. The purpose of Grandmother's games was to teach Manfred how to make a regular living with a very erratic talent, and how to recognize when he should heed the true compulsions of his gift.

In her disorganized and colorful life, Xylda had experienced moments of true clarity and brilliance as a psychic. She had found lost things and lost people. She had talked to the dead. But those moments had been interspersed with long stretches of making her living by sheer quackery, made credible by her quick and accurate analysis of her clients' desires and needs. After years of this, Xylda's gift degraded. She still had the occasional genuine vision, but it had become almost impossible to distinguish such an event from the flood of canned chatter and vague predictions that made up the bulk of her repertoire.

Manfred's psychic gift was larger, deeper, and truer, but Xylda had taught him how to resort to a certain amount of chicanery to pay his bills. Luckily for Manfred, he had no moral qualms about this expedience.

As Manfred watched the girls warming up out on the field, he realized he was not much older than some of them, yet he felt a decade older in life experience. He tried not to be angry at his grandmother as he calculated how much he'd spent to get to northern Louisiana, both in loss of earning time and in travel expenses. The total wasn't insignificant, especially since he was still paying off Xylda's credit cards. But she had to challenge him in his dreams. "Go down there to see what you can find out," she'd said. "There's a reason you're going. Next time you see me, you tell me what that reason was." In his dream, he'd said, "What's the prize if I'm right?" Xylda had smiled enigmatically, one of her favorite expressions, and she'd said, "You'll know it when you find it." He grimaced at the memory.

"You all right?" asked the woman sitting next to him. The stands had been steadily filling up. He'd vaguely known there was someone next to him because she smelled good. Now Manfred turned to look at her. She was very pretty; of course, he noticed that first. Blond hair, caught back in a ponytail, at least five years older than him, maybe more, which didn't faze Manfred at all. She had remarkable blue eyes and some bodacious boobs, too. But then Manfred spotted a little diamond ring on Blondie's left hand, which (Manfred was fairly sure) meant she was engaged or even married. Too bad. He would have enjoyed flirting with her . . . until he met her eyes the second time.

Those blue eyes were incredibly knowing.

Suddenly, Manfred felt uneasy. There was something weird and different about this woman, and he couldn't relax until he knew what it was.

"I'm fine," he said, forcing a smile. "Just thinking about a dream I had."

"You a fan of softball?" she said, her expression one of gentle inquiry.

Again, he had that uneasy feeling. Though her face and posture were inviting, even benign, Manfred had a strong conviction that she knew what his reply would be . . . if he spoke the truth.

Strong feelings are what psychics are all about.

"I've never watched a whole softball game, or a baseball game, for that matter," he said. "I was never into sports at school."

"Hung out with the Goth kids?" she said.

He nodded.

"I never fit in too well, either," she said, though she didn't seem particularly upset by the recollection. "But I was able to play softball, thank God. I was pretty good."

"So you come to reminisce?" He would have sworn she wasn't the kind of person who'd live in the past.

"I come to watch the home games when my work schedule at the bar permits." That wasn't a direct answer, but as if in recompense Blondie smiled. The effect was so dazzling it made part of Manfred's body jump in a pleasant way. "Also, I help out the coach from time to time if the assistant's out . . . she's pregnant. Today she's fine, but the Softball Moms asked me to help with the tournament."

Was *this* why his grandmother had urged him to come to Bon Temps, to meet this woman? For some kind of love connection? Whoever she was, she was not an ordinary human. Manfred was absolutely sure of that, and his conviction didn't have anything to do with her sunny good looks. In fact, he was sure that she was not for him, that she had already formed a bond elsewhere. But he was curious. This woman had to be significant. *Xylda, a little clue here? Send me something from the blue hereafter?*

That was how Xylda had described her location, when he'd dared to ask.

"Did you have a special reason to come today?" he asked. Maybe if he dug a little, he'd find gold. Then he could go back to his life and livelihood.

"Special reason? Like, is a niece of mine on the team? Nope," she said, trying not to sound like that was a dumb question. "When the Moms called, I volunteered to help set up the concession stand, which I came in two hours ago to do. And I'm going to work a shift or two later. You have a special reason to be here, yourself?"

"Yes," he said, making up his mind. "My grandmother Xylda sent me here, on a kind of treasure hunt."

She looked at him thoughtfully, her head cocked a little to one side. "And she's passed on, Miss Xylda?"

He nodded.

She considered that for a moment. "I haven't had much experience dealing with the human dead," she said.

That was a strange way to put it. "You don't believe that's possible." Manfred was resigned to disbelief and scorn, both of which had come his way since he was a little guy and his talent had manifested.

"Course I believe it's possible," she said, surprised. "That's just not where my talents lie. And if you had a tough upbringing, mine was tough too, buddy."

Feeling ridiculously gratified, Manfred grinned at her. She gave him a decided nod, as if she'd confirmed something in her own mind. She turned to look at the field, unhooking her dark glasses from her T-shirt and slipping them on. A few fluffy clouds scudded across the blue, blue sky. Despite the radiance of the sunlight, the wind made him shiver in his black shirt. Some of the teams had opted to wear their baseball pants and the long socks with their team jerseys, while some had chosen their shorts instead. The ones who'd chosen the pants were far more comfortable.

The Lady Falcons and their opponents, the Lady Mudbugs, had both chosen long pants. The two teams had finished warming up. Each team now huddled before its dugout in a tight cluster. The girls were holding hands. Their heads were bowed.

"What are they doing?" Manfred asked.

The blonde whipped off her dark glasses and looked at him as if he'd asked her why gravity held them to the earth. "They're praying," she said, in a gently pitying tone. After a moment, all the Falcons flung their heads up in unison, gave a yell ("Win!"), and retreated into their dugout. The Mudbugs repeated the process.

"Good afternoon," the announcer said, her voice distorted by the crackling sound system. "Welcome to the tenth annual Louisiana Slam Softball Tournament! The first game will be our own Lady Falcons versus the Lady Mudbugs from Toussaint." There was a lot of cheering.

Manfred leaned forward and looked to his left so he could see into the little hut that passed for a press booth. Sitting behind the microphone was a woman who was surely a former beauty queen. She was perhaps in her late thirties, with honey-colored hair and a smile like an orthodontist's dream. She wore a *Softball Mom!* T-shirt, and she looked as excited as the players. There were a few sheets of paper on the wooden plank in front of her, and she referred to one before leaning to the microphone. "Coaching for the Lady Mudbugs, Head Coach Tom Hardesty, Assistant Coach Deke Fleming." There was polite applause. "Here's the starting lineup for the Lady Mudbugs," the announcer said. "Heather Parfit, pitcher!" Heather, a thin girl with a formidable mouth guard protecting her braces, dashed out of the visiting team's dugout. She took her place on the third base-to-home line.

Eventually, the Mudbug and Falcon players had been celebrated and the seniors recognized.

The girls were all colors and all builds, but Manfred saw they had one thing in common. Their faces were intent, excited, and *ready*.

"And that's our starting lineup for today!" concluded the announcer. "Let's hear it for the home team and their coaches, Bethany Zanelli and her assistant, Martha Clevely." There was a lot more cheering as the

Lady Falcon starters dashed to their places on the field. The announcer continued, "At this time the flag will be presented by the Bon Temps High School JROTC. All rise for the national anthem."

Everyone rose, and kids in uniforms marched out with the Louisiana flag and the U.S. flag. Hands went to chests, hats were removed, and for a moment all Manfred could hear was the snap of the flags in the breeze and the distant shrieks of two children playing tag ("You're *it*!"). After a little crackling from the loudspeaker, a country-and-western star's recording of "The Star Spangled Banner" floated through the air and up into the vast blue sky. People all over the softball park froze in their tracks. Many of them in the stands sang along. The blonde next to Manfred did not. He wondered why.

"Can't carry a tune in a bucket," she murmured, her eyes fixed on the rippling Stars and Stripes. Manfred had an eerie prickling on his arms. He was now absolutely sure that the blonde could read his mind.

". . . laaaaand of the *freeeee* . . . and the home of—the brave!" There was hooting and hollering and clapping at the anthem's end. Manfred felt a thrill of patriotism, something that had never made his hair stand on end before. The announcer yelled, *"Play ball!"*

All psychics learn to be sharp observers, because observation helps to fill in when the gift fails. Manfred could see that his companion reacted physically, viscerally, to the announcer's cue. Her eyes widened, her muscles tensed, her eyes went from player to player . . . he could see the ghost of her former commitment to the game hovering over her head. She wanted to play, even now.

She still looked plenty fit and strong for a woman her age, which he revised upward. He was sure she was in her late twenties.

"Well," she said absently, "I stand up all day, most days, and I do a *hell* of a lot of gardening . . . but I can see thirty coming up in my head-lights." She didn't even bother to look at him; she was scoping out the Mudbugs' first batter, a lanky girl with her hair pulled back in a long braid. The batter put on her batting glove and helmet with a look of determina-tion. She began to swing the bat back and forth to ensure that her muscles were loose. She looked confident and trim in her gold and green.

"You might at least try to pretend you can't hear me," Manfred whispered.

"Oh, sorry." She sighed. "I don't often meet someone who won't have an issue with it. It's a real pleasure to say what I'm thinking."

He considered how difficult it would be to disguise the fact that you knew the private thoughts of everyone around you, every hour of every day. "Hard times," he said.

She shrugged. "I'm used to it. Did you come here to meet me? You think that's why Miss Xylda told you to come? What are we supposed to do?"

She was so guileless that she made Manfred feel old beyond his years.

"I think we're supposed to see what happens," he said, almost at random.

"Easy enough," she said. The top of the inning was clearly a time spent feeling out the other team. The Falcons' pitcher ("She's our number two pitcher," Blondie whispered) got two outs, after a lot of work, and though the third batter hit the ball, the right fielder got it to first in time.

The bottom of the first was nerve-racking, if Blondie's reactions were anything to go by. The Mudbugs' pitcher had gotten one out. The next Lady Falcon had made first base, then made second by the sacrifice of the third batter in the lineup. The Falcon runner turned to look around the field, and Manfred saw that her jersey read *Allen*. She was a skinny girl with curly dark hair, but she was fast and she was alert.

"Georgia Allen, junior," the blonde said.

The next Falcon batter at the plate (*Washington*) was a broad-shouldered girl with her hair gathered at the nape of her neck.

"Hit it out of the park, Candice!" screamed her teammate from the dugout. Three rows down from Manfred and the blonde, a very broad woman said, "You *hit* that ball, Candice!" in a firm voice that implied this was a reasonable command.

Candice Washington's dark face was set in adamant lines. She stood with her feet planted in the batter's box like a statue. The lanky Mudbug pitcher looked nervous for a moment, but then she pinched her lips together, began her windup, and threw a good pitch right at Candice. Because he was intent on the ball, Manfred spotted the moment when it jinked sideways just a little, just a fraction, so Candice's mighty swing smacked it on the bottom instead of squarely in the middle.

"Heads up!" screamed several voices simultaneously. People looked up to spot the ball, and a few covered their heads with their hands. The foul went flying into the visitor stands, to be caught by a boy who seemed to have brought a mitt just for such an event.

"A foul can crack your skull, it hits you just right," Blondie told him. "Did you see that?" She didn't mean the boy's catch.

"Foul ball," called the umpire, a thin woman with brittle auburn-dyed hair. "Ah . . . foul ball," she added in a puzzled voice. She was clearly reviewing the pitch in her head. The ump looked as startled as Manfred felt.

"There's foul play afoot," Manfred's companion said, so darkly that Manfred had to stifle a laugh.

"You must read a lot of mysteries," he said. "And by the way, good play on words."

"I do read mysteries, and thanks. Now let's hush, here's the next pitch." This time, the blonde wasn't looking at the batter, but at the crowd. Manfred watched the opposing team's players; in fact, he tried to watch everyone in that dugout.

Candice watched the ball with her eyes squinted almost shut in grim resolve. Whether by calculation or intuition, she caught the ball square on the bat. The fluorescent yellow orb soared into the outfield. Georgia Allen took off from second like a scalded cheetah, while Candice Washington made it to first before the ball was retrieved by the left fielder. Allen scored, and made a great effort to look nonchalant as she took off her batting helmet. The Lady Falcon fans did a lot of yelling and stomping, and there was a lot of hugging in the dugout.

The next Bon Temps batter in the lineup, a sophomore named Vivian Vavasour, was not as aggressive. Vavasour struck out; whether that was achieved by fair means or foul, Manfred couldn't discern.

"Do you have any ideas?" he said, as quietly as he could and still be heard in the noisy crowd, while the Lady Falcons took the field.

"Well, I doubt it's anyone from Bon Temps," she said dryly. "I was looking at the moms from Toussaint, but I didn't spot any of them doing something witchy."

"What about the assistant coach, Fleming?" Manfred said. "The man in the purple polo shirt, right inside the dugout."

"Why'd you pick him?"

"His fingers were moving funny," Manfred said.

But the man, who was in his fifties, balding, and heavy, didn't do anything odd during the top of the second inning. If he was jinxing the Lady Falcon batters by altering the pitches, he wasn't helping the Lady Mudbug hitters.

The Lady Falcon pitcher struggled but held the Lady Mudbugs at bay. During the bottom of the inning, Jacqueline Prescott (sixth in the Falcon batting order) did something wholly unexpected. The girl, tall and bony and brunette, was obviously nervous . . . so she swung at a ball she absolutely should not have tried to hit. Hit it she did, leaning forward and sideways to do so, while there was an audible chorus of "Oh, no!" from the Falcon stands. The ball thudded to the ground just behind the shortstop and the second baseman, both of whom scrambled for the ball without calling it. In the resulting collision, Jacqueline made it to first. She looked astonished when she realized she was safe. "Yeah, she ought to be surprised," muttered Blondie. Even the Lady Falcons' Coach Zanelli shook her head in amazement, before clapping.

"He looks pissed," murmured the blonde. Following her gaze, Manfred saw that the Lady Mudbugs' assistant coach did indeed look angry.

"He didn't allow for the wild card," the blonde said with some satisfaction.

"I think he'll try harder now; he's mad," Manfred said.

And sure enough, the coach's fingers moved with every succeeding pitch. Jacqueline stole second base, but the next three batters fell by the wayside, and the Lady Falcons took the field at the top of the third with the score still one-nothing. Manfred kept his eyes on the coach, but Fleming appeared to be doing regular coach stuff. He called the batting lineup and kept the team stats. Apparently, the burly man wasn't going to aid his own team, just hinder the opposing one by making Mudbug pitches do unpredictable things.

"He seems to have a code," Manfred said dryly.

"Yeah," the blonde said. "His code is screwing with the challenger. I got to have a word with that asshole."

Manfred could feel the anger rising from her like steam, especially after the Mudbugs scored four runs in the top of the third. The Lady

Falcon pitcher had clearly lost her momentum, and a different pitcher was warming up.

At the coaches' request, the pitcher's circle was leveled out by means of a device dragged by the Gator, which created a short break. The announcer took advantage of the lull to say, "Be sure and visit the refreshment stand! The Softball Moms have fixed popcorn, cold soda, hot chocolate, candy bars, and homemade cupcakes. Hot dogs are going on the grill! Go get yourself a chili dog! All proceeds go to support softball. And now, since we've got an unexpected break, instead of waiting until after the game, we'll take this moment to ask players from the past to take the field."

Manfred's companion rose and clambered down the bleachers, greeting people as she went. She stepped out onto the field with eleven other women ranging in age from sixty-five to nineteen. There was a lot more hugging and back-patting. With a sort of proprietary smugness, Manfred decided his blonde was the prettiest woman on the field, if not the most popular. The other women either embraced her with special vehemence or avoided her.

After all this bonhomie, the women quickly lined up in age order to be introduced. When she came to Manfred's blonde, the announcer said, "And we all remember the *three-years-in-a-row All-Conference, All-State player*, Sookie Stackhouse, one of the best right fielders in the history of Bon Temps!"

Sookie Stackhouse (*What a name,* thought Manfred) smiled and waved like all the others. The people who cheered the loudest were the girls in the dugout.

"She helps coach the team when she can get a few hours off," said the older woman sitting past the spot where Sookie Stackhouse had been.

"Sookie told me something about that," he said agreeably, to prime the pump.

The older woman nodded. She was heavy and plain, but Manfred could see the polished goodness in her. "My son is her brother's best friend," she said, as if her exact connection to Manfred's new buddy were important. "They don't come no better than Sookie. No matter what people say." She gave his eyebrow piercings a cold flick of her eyes, as if to imply he might be one of those gossipers.

Manfred would have been fascinated to know exactly what people had been saying, but he didn't dare to ask.

Sookie did a lot of networking on her way back to her seat, including a brief stop in the booth to have a friendly chat with the announcer, who seemed glad to see her. As the current Lady Falcons took the field, the Gator and its rake having done their job, she clambered back up the risers, giving the woman on her right a cheerful greeting and a half-hug. She turned to tell Manfred, "His name is Deke Fleming, in case you didn't hear it at the beginning. He's the assistant coach, and he doesn't usually travel with the girls' team. He's usually with the boys. The Lady Mudbugs' regular assistant was sick, so Fleming came along. The boys' team has won the state championship in its division the past two years."

"Let me guess, he became the assistant coach two years ago."

She nodded. "So he's a witch," she whispered.

"Not a warlock, or sorcerer?" Manfred asked.

She gave him a raised-eyebrow look that said clearly, *Don't you know anything?*

"No, he's a witch," she said flatly. But she kept her voice very low. This was a woman used to telling secrets. "I pure-D can't stand people who use their special powers to gain unfair advantage," she added in the same low voice.

"So you think you have to do something about it," Manfred said, not really asking a question.

"Course I do. You don't feel that way?"

He shrugged. "This is a small softball tournament between small schools in a poor state. You sure it makes a difference?"

She had a visible struggle with her temper. "*Of course* it makes a difference," she said between her teeth. "Using magic always makes a difference. The person it's used on changes. The person who uses it changes. There's always a price to pay."

"You sound like you know what you're talking about," he said.

"I do. You see the Lady Falcon pitcher? The one who just warmed up?" While the Mudbug pitcher finished the third inning—three up, three down—the Falcon girl kept moving, throwing ceaselessly to a member of her team. Olive skinned and raven haired, she had the look of a warrior: tall, broad, sturdy. The announcer had called her Ashley Stark. He nodded.

"Bethany—Coach Zanelli—was trying to save Ashley for the next game. So she put her second pitcher in this game, which was supposed to be easy to win. Ashley is being scouted by LSU and by Louisiana Tech. Her family doesn't have diddly-squat. If she's signed by either one of those schools, she can go to college without having a huge debt to pay off."

"Maybe the other team has someone in the same position," Manfred argued, simply to see how Sookie would respond.

"If there is such a girl, she has to earn it fair and square," Sookie said vehemently. "Everyone's got to stand on her own merits. With this assistant coach, the boys' team will never get that chance. Today, neither do the girls. The Lady Mudbugs have a reputation for crumpling early. Our girls were sure to win." Sookie glared across the field at Fleming. She said, "There should be *no* magic in softball."

Xylda, did you make me drive all the way to Louisiana to make sure Ashley Stark goes to college? Have I got the answer right, now?

"How the hell do I know why your gran brought you here? My gran seems to remind me of stuff all the time, and it's always to my good. Maybe Miss Xylda just wants you to do the right thing."

"One girl's scholarship?" Manfred felt doubtful, and he didn't try to conceal it. "That just seems weird. Why would Xylda care?"

She gave him a hard look. "Well, don't do anything if you don't want to," she said crisply. "And if Miss Xylda wouldn't care about Ashley, then sadly I think the worse of her. Excuse me. I got to say something to this jerk of a coach." She rose and began making her way down the bleachers again. But people stopped her to talk to her, and a Softball Mom with a clipboard stopped her to go over a schedule, and the fourth inning raced by while Sookie made her way to the Mudbug dugout.

Manfred watched her progress. He was troubled. Xylda—and even his own, more distant, mother—always had a course of action. Part of Xylda's game was making him guess until he got it correctly. He just couldn't figure out what Xylda could possibly want here. Manfred felt he was losing the game. He didn't know the goal he should be trying to reach. And he didn't know the stakes.

Deke Fleming was standing behind the Mudbug dugout going over papers on a clipboard while the Mudbug head coach watched the field. By now it was the bottom of the fifth, and the Lady Mudbugs were sticking with the same pitcher, though her form was suffering. All the girls on the field were encouraging her, their voices a shrill chorus. "*Way to pitch, Heather . . . You can do it, Heather . . . Show 'em what you got . . . You're doing great . . .*"

Manfred was amazed all over again at the concept of working in tandem. Being a psychic was an essentially solitary profession.

The assistant coach looked up from his clipboard as Sookie approached; he smiled since he'd seen her on the field in the little recognition ceremony. The smile faded utterly as she leaned close to him and began to talk. The anger in her straight spine was clear to anyone who happened to look their way, and there were some troubled glances exchanged between a few adults.

After a moment, Deke Fleming actually stepped backward, looking both furious and guilty. Then he caught himself. His back stiffened. (Manfred thought, *It's like watching a pantomime.*) Sookie's finger came up and she shook it in Fleming's face before spinning on her heel and stalking back to the Bon Temps stands. One of the Toussaint moms called out, "Sore loser!" as Sookie walked by, which triggered some anxious laughter. But the umpire, naturally busy at her job of watching the game, wasn't looking happy, either.

"What's the matter, Sookie?" asked the older woman who'd talked to Manfred earlier, after Sookie had plopped down on the bleacher with an angry thud. "Why'd you go lay into him?"

"Maxine, I think he's . . ." she began, and then called herself to order. "I was sure he was playing his roster out of order, and his pitcher is crow-hopping. It makes me so mad! He told me that the ump had already given the pitcher a warning, and that he had just turned in the roster changes to the umpire and the announcer."

"Hmmm," said the older woman. "Well . . . did you check?"

"Yes, he just did turn 'em in," she said, as though she were chewing glass. "And I see he's going to switch pitchers, so no more crow-hopping."

Manfred had no idea what that meant, and Sookie didn't look as though she wanted to explain the game, so he kept silent.

But when Deke Fleming looked up at Sookie in the stands, Manfred watched her tap the area by her eye and then point at the coach, very surreptitiously. Fleming got the point, though. He flushed and looked as though he would have enjoyed something painful happening to her.

The inning was three up and three down for both pitchers, but the tide was beginning to turn for the Lady Falcons, at least psychologically. Not only did the Falcons have Ashley Stark, their star, on the mound, but after the Lady Mudbugs changed their pitcher, the Lady Falcon batters began to relax. Without Coach Fleming's making the pitches go wild, the Falcons were able to hit, and in the bottom of the sixth the bases were loaded.

Manfred was literally sitting on the edge of his seat. For the first time, he understood how exciting sports could be. And though he found himself waiting for each pitch with almost breathless suspense, in the back of his mind he couldn't believe this was the point of his presence. *Team sports? Really, Xylda? All this way to appreciate bats and balls and team spirit?*

When Ashley Stark came up to bat, Sookie directed Manfred's attention to a man in a purple and gold polo shirt sitting right behind the plate, and a woman in khakis and a bright blue polo shirt who was one row up and a little to the left of him. "Scouts," she murmured. "Purple and gold is LSU. The blue is Louisiana Tech." Everyone on the Bon Temps bleachers seemed to catch their breath while they directed their will toward helping their girl to do well. It was their own kind of magic, a natural magic. Ashley was oddly beautiful in the batter's box, her shoulders level, her grip on the bat relaxed and firm, her face a mask of calm.

The Lady Mudbug pitcher watched the signals from the catcher and gave a quick nod. The tension was so great that Manfred found himself absolutely absorbed in watching the girl wind up and pitch, for the first time appreciating an incredibly complex sequence of movements.

Manfred spared a side glance at Sookie. She was intent on Coach Fleming. The assistant coach was glaring back at her, his hands against his thighs as he stood in the dugout. His fingers were motionless.

Manfred's gaze cut back to Ashley as she swung the bat. Ashley smacked the ball a mighty blow, and it flew straight and hard . . . directly into the Mudbug pitcher's mitt. For a second it seemed as though the pitcher would fly away, the ball smacked her mitt with such force, but she seemed to dig her feet into the dirt to stand in place.

There was a collective groan from the Bon Temps supporters, and an ecstatic shriek from the Toussaint fans.

Sookie covered her face with her hands for a second, then straightened up, shaking the dismay off.

"Are you okay?" Manfred asked. "You went to so much trouble . . ."

"All I wanted was for her to have a fair chance," Sookie said. "And the rest, well, that was up to her. Maybe the rest of the game will go better."

Manfred did not comment on the fact that Sookie's eyes were brimming with tears.

The top of the sixth did go better, to some extent, though Manfred watched it alone. Sookie had to leave since it was her turn in the concessions booth, and Manfred told her he'd come say good-bye as soon as the game was over. He'd known her for less than two hours, but he felt he couldn't leave Louisiana without speaking to the telepath again.

Ashley Stark kept her composure and pitched beautifully, getting three Lady Mudbugs out in a row. In the bottom of the sixth, to Manfred's pleasure, the Lady Falcons scored three runs. They were now tied with the Lady Mudbugs. The next inning would be the last. In Sookie's absence, Manfred considered himself bound to keep a close eye on Coach Fleming, and he also felt obliged, in Sookie's stead, to add his wellwishing to the swell of support for Ashley Stark.

He wondered what had kept Sookie from getting similar scholarship offers. It wasn't much of a stretch to understand why she was so invested in the success of the Bon Temps pitcher.

In the bottom final inning, with the score still tied, Ashley got the hit that won the game. With two outs, and no one on base, she swung the bat with incredible precision and power. The softball flew over the fence. Ashley trotted around the bases with a broad smile, happy on many different levels. The other Lady Falcons jumped up and down and ran to meet her at home plate. The Lady Falcon supporters went nuts, hollering and jumping. But all her happiness condensed to one thing: she'd done well, she'd won the game for her team.

Was this why I came here, Xylda? To see this girl's joy at doing something well, something she could only do with the help of others? If I recognize that, do I win, too? He wondered if Xylda was witnessing this moment from the blue hereafter.

On the field, the girls kept their game faces on as they formed two lines and ran past each other, hands held out to touch, chanting, "Good game, good game." And then the Lady Falcons hugged each other, laughing, while the Lady Mudbugs retreated silently to their dugout to gather up their stuff. Their second pitcher was crying, and the first pitcher put an arm around her.

Manfred had never been as lonely as he was while he watched the celebration among the Lady Falcons. Most of the Mudbugs looked as though they were locked in their own private unhappiness, especially the assistant coach. They filed out of their dugout to go to their bus.

Xylda, did you want me to learn that even clever dishonesty can go wrong? Though that didn't seem like a Xylda message. Normally, when Manfred had been able to guess what game Xylda was playing, he'd feel her approval. But he hadn't felt that today, no matter what he did or guessed. He shrugged. Xylda's wiles were beyond him, today. He scrambled down the stands to work his way to the concession booth, a squat cement-block building. He looked back at the field. He figured the booth workers could get a glimpse of the scoreboards but not a good view of the events.

Manfred got in line, since there was simply no other way to speak to his new friend. The woman ahead of him (whose daughter was playing in the next game, from her cell phone conversation) got nachos, and he had to control his disgust as Sookie poured tortilla chips from a bag into a paper dish and ladled liquid "cheese" over them, topping the whole toxic concoction with jalapeño pepper slices.

The very young woman working the concession booth with Sookie looked up at him while she handed the woman her change. "Next?" she said inquiringly. When their eyes met, something in his gut lurched, not in lust but in recognition.

"Manfred," Sookie said, "this is Quiana Wong."

Manfred struggled to absorb many impressions at once. This girl (she couldn't be more than eighteen) was a racial mixture he'd never encountered. Her hair was straight, coarse, and black. Her eyes were slightly slanted and dark brown. Her skin was golden, like the perfect tan. She was short and skinny . . . and she was a psychic. Like him.

Her desperation rolled over him like a blanket of fog.

He glanced around; for the moment, he was the only customer at this window, but that wouldn't last.

"I started thinking about why you might be here," Sookie said, to fill the fraught silence. "So I called Quiana. She's an orphan, so she hasn't got a permanent place to live. She's like you, as I can see you've realized. And she hasn't had any training or 'mentoring,' as they call it now." Sookie beamed at him. She clearly felt she'd solved the mystery of why Xylda had manifested herself in Manfred's dream—so he could rescue Quiana. Manfred spared a moment from his contemplation of the girl to understand that Sookie was a rescuer, and she could not conceive that he might not see himself that way.

"You want to get out of here," he said to Quiana. It was evident in every line of the girl's body. "You want to meet other people like yourself."

"Yes," Quiana Wong said. She had a heavy Southern accent. "I don't fit in anywhere. I do want to meet more people like me. You're the first one."

"Quiana's mom was half Chinese, half African American," Sookie said quietly. "Her dad was no-account white."

Quiana nodded. "He was that and more."

"They're gone?" Manfred said. "Dead?"

Quiana nodded again. "They fought all the time anyway," she said flatly. "Neither of them could rise to the challenge of being together, but they couldn't let each other go, either."

"What do you do now?" Manfred asked her.

"I'm a nanny," the girl said. "I take care of twins."

"I'm not going to be too popular with Tara," Sookie muttered, turning to put more hot dogs on the rotating grill. "Hey, Quiana, can you load up more popcorn?"

Quiana obliged, and then Manfred had to step aside as she became busy. The concession stand was just as noisy as the spectator area, with the background noises from the popper, the chatter of customers, the hum of the crowds, and the crackling of the sound system. Children too young to sit still to watch a game were running and yelling in the space between the back of the stands and the concession stand. While Manfred waited, Quiana Wong and Sookie served a man wanting two bottles of water and a candy bar, a little girl who wanted a hot dog with mustard and pickles, and a boy with braces who wanted a Coke and some nachos. There were also requests for candy bars, bags of potato chips, and sunflower seeds. Two other volunteers were just as busy at the window on the other side.

To Manfred's relief, two plump middle-aged women popped into the stand to relieve Sookie and Quiana, who stepped outside, looking tired. By silent mutual consent, the trio drifted over to an empty area near the fence surrounding the fields, far enough from the entrance booth and the clusters of players to remain unheard.

"I'm eighteen," Quiana said. "I'm free. I graduated high school."

"And you want me to take you when I leave, to find a psychic you can stay with and learn from." Manfred wanted to be sure he understood what was on the plate.

"That's what I want more than anything in the world. I know it can't be you. That wouldn't be right. I need to learn how to control this power, without the sex thing getting messed up with it."

She meant each disjointed phrase, meant it absolutely. Manfred noticed that Sookie was looking at Quiana almost sadly, and he was sure the blonde was revisiting her own teen years in Bon Temps, when she, too, had been on the fringes of everything.

"I'm thinking," Manfred said, when he realized both Sookie and Quiana were waiting for him to speak. Who would take Quiana? If his grandmother had been among the living, his course of action would have been easy. He considered the possible choices in his small community— small in numbers, but spread all across the United States and Canada. To his surprise, a name popped into his mind.

"I do know someone. Marilyn Finn. She's got a going business, real small, but she has genuine talent. She needs some help." She'd told him so via e-mail, not a week before. She'd hinted around that he himself might like a place to stay and work, now that his grandmother was gone. "What . . . are you?"

"Spirits can get into me," she said. "I don't know what to call it."

"You're a true psychic," he said. "That's what I'd call you, anyway. Quiana, let me step away and give her a quick call."

"Great," Quiana said, but her eyes closed and she swayed for a moment. Then she looked at Manfred with an eerie directness, as if she could see through the back of his eyes and into his brain. "I see you in the desert," she said, almost in a whisper. "I see you in an old place, with lots of old things, and people who have amazing secrets." Then her eyes were focused on the outside of Manfred again. "Sorry. Sometimes I have the foreseeing, too."

Manfred took a deep breath and waited for a moment. She seemed to be through exhibiting her talents, and he was profoundly glad. "Ah, thanks for the heads-up on that. Back to Marilyn. You'd have to work hard. I'm assuming she'd have you meeting clients and giving them the procedure to follow during the readings, taking the money, answering the e-mails, and so on. But Marilyn has a lot of contacts in our community, and she's more social than I am. You'd meet a lot of people and you'd learn a lot. She's a good woman, too."

"Anything is better than sleeping in a room with my cousin's two little boys," Quiana said earnestly.

Manfred gave her a quick smile, walked away, and made a phone call, his back to the two women, though he knew as far as Sookie was concerned this privacy was only an illusion. He was relieved to hear Marilyn Finn answer the phone herself.

When he snapped his phone shut and walked back to the thin girl and the robust blonde, he was smiling with relief. "She said okay," Manfred told them. He didn't add that he had been bound to promise to do two large favors for Marilyn in return.

"Thank you," Sookie said sincerely. But Manfred could tell she had reservations. Any sane woman would, at the prospect of sending a girl into a completely blind situation on the say-so of a brand-new acquaintance.

Quiana was openly excited.

"I swear to you, it's on the up-and-up," Manfred told Sookie. She flushed.

"I'm holding you to that," she said. "And Quiana will let me know if it's not." She hesitated, then quietly said, "You're doing a good thing."

In Sookie's eyes, Manfred could see he was cast in the role of rescuer of a fair young maiden. He glanced at Quiana, trying not to smile. He had to admit that he didn't exactly find her fair, and he was pretty sure she was no maiden. But he did have a lot of sympathy for her: that would have to do.

Maybe Sookie is right. Maybe this is why Xylda sent me, Manfred thought. Not to meet Sookie Stackhouse, or thwart the Mudbug coach, but to rescue Quiana. *Have I gotten to the goal, Grandma?*

"So . . . how will this work?" Quiana asked, suddenly getting down to brass tacks. "I've gotta tell the du Rones I'm leaving. The parents of the twins. I owe that to them. Where does this Marilyn Finn live? How do I get there? Am I going to be staying in her house with her?"

"Marilyn lives in Oakmont, Pennsylvania," Manfred said. "It's got a lot of charm. I'll take you to the airport in Shreveport when I leave here, and we'll go in and work out the best route for you. Then we'll call Marilyn, and she'll meet you at the airport when you land. Marilyn and I are splitting your ticket."

"What if I don't like her?"

"Then we'll work out something else," Manfred said. "But I'm hoping you two will get along fine." Manfred tried to keep *You'd better* out of his voice, but Quiana understood. She gave him a sharp nod.

"If it doesn't work out, you call me," Sookie said, and Quiana looked relieved.

The Lady Falcons were clustered under a tree about five yards away, and their coach was giving them a serious lecture, rehashing the things they'd done right and the things they'd done wrong. The lecture ended at that moment, and the girls dispersed, some running to get in line at the concession booth, some meeting with their parents, who'd been waiting a respectful distance away. When Sookie, Manfred, and Quiana walked back to the booth (Quiana had to retrieve her purse), a couple of Lady Falcons approached, obviously wanting to talk to Sookie. One of them was Ashley Stark.

Quiana reached into the little building and grabbed her purse, and told Manfred she was going to her cousin's home to call the du Rones and to pack her things. She pointed down the street from the softball fields to a row of dilapidated houses that had obviously all been built at the same unhappy time by the same inept builder.

With the understanding that he would pick her up in an hour, Manfred tuned in to the conversation Sookie was having with Ashley.

"That was weirdest thing I ever saw," Ashley was saying, and Manfred thought, *Uh-oh*. Though it was wounding to always be regarded as fraudulent, if not worse, Manfred truly believed that the world was better off in general if fewer people believed in the other world, the hidden world.

Sookie said, "It was a fluke, Ashley. You got a great hit in the last inning, Manfred says." She introduced him briefly, but Ashley hardly spared him a glance. She was too worried. Sookie returned to the previous topic. "I just know someone's going to pay attention," she said, hugging the senior.

"I want it more than anything," Ashley said. "If I'm ever going to get out of here . . ." Manfred could read the intensity in the girl, the iron in her.

Sookie jerked her head to the left and said, "Look, Ashley. I think someone's waiting for you."

Manfred turned to look in the direction Sookie had indicated, and he saw a man and a woman who were clearly Ashley's parents, if resemblance was any indication. They were standing with the scout from Louisiana Tech. They were all smiling.

Ashley took a deep, ragged breath. Her back stiffened. She said, "Talk to you later, Miss Sookie," and walked off to meet her future.

Manfred was almost bursting. "Maybe she's destined for great things, or for some spectacular moment, and *that's* why Xylda sent me here . . . to make sure she got that chance."

Sookie Stackhouse laughed out loud. "You got to have one reason?" She sobered quickly. "Seriously, you lead a simple life if things happen to you for only one reason."

Manfred felt himself flush. He couldn't imagine that a barmaid in a hick town could have that complex a life. "Right," he said, and there was an edge to his voice.

She looked at him with a touch of surprise and a little sorrow. "I didn't mean to insult you," she said.

For one of the few times in his brief life, Manfred was ashamed of himself. "Maybe you're right," he said, trying to keep the reluctance out of his voice. "Maybe Xylda wanted me to come here for five different reasons. She loved her little games. She always challenged me. She never made it easy."

"My gran was real different from the way you describe Miss Xylda," Sookie said. "She never played games. She stepped off the beaten track one time, and she regretted that transgression, in some ways, all her days. She was a little superstitious, though. She always thought bad things came in threes."

"Xylda said it was oversimplification to believe that events happen in threes—three deaths, three good things, three bad things. She said it all depended on your time frame." Manfred smiled, trying to smooth things over.

"If you add things up over a year, or over four months?"

"Or an hour," Manfred said. "She thought if you fixed on three, you limited yourself."

"She was quite the psychologist," Sookie said.

"Yes, in her way," Manfred agreed. He allowed himself to feel the sharpness of the grief he'd experienced when she'd passed, far away from home in the cold mountains. "She knew human nature, that's for sure. She wasn't able to control her own," he added slowly. "But she understood how people would react; at least, most often. I don't think she ever met anyone like you."

Sookie smiled and turned to look between the stands at the scoreboard. It indicated that the next game was into its second inning. The Red Ditch Gators were playing a team from Deux Arbres.

"That Deux Arbres team is supposed to be pretty good," Sookie said, her eyes narrowed against the bright sun. There was a chorus of shouts from the bleachers. Manfred knew later they were yelling, "Heads up!" But what he heard in his head was his grandmother's voice, saying, *Look in the blue hereafter.*

His hand shot out above Sookie's head without his conscious decision. For the first time in his life, Manfred Bernardo caught a softball.

He stood frozen in astonishment and delight and horror for a couple of seconds, time enough for Sookie to jump back, looking up at his hand (which stung like the very devil). She lowered her eyes to his face. Her own were full of astonishment and relief.

"Good catch," called one of the Lady Falcons. It was curly-haired Georgia Allen. "Want me to take it back to the field?"

"Sure," Manfred said. "Thanks." He dropped the ball into her hand.

He had a sudden vision of what could have happened, the kind that did no one any good at all. He saw the ball hitting Sookie on top of her blond head. He saw her crumple to the ground, unconscious. He saw the ambulance ride, the bleed into the brain, the blackness. Then that vision evaporated, because that future was not hers anymore. He had changed it by showing up in Bon Temps, Louisiana, on a brisk bright day in early spring.

"So I reckon you won the game," Sookie said quietly. And he understood that she had seen the vision in his head. "Look what you worked into a few hours. You can sure multitask."

"It was my pleasure," he said, trying for a courtliness he'd never aspired to achieve.

"And mine," she said, nodding thoughtfully. "You call me, you hear? You're being real good to help Quiana. But she may not suit your friend Marilyn."

"At least she'll be able to get help to understand how to live with this trait, from Marilyn," Manfred said. "There aren't that many of us."

"And Ashley will get her scholarship. I wouldn't have known it was the assistant coach affecting the pitches if you hadn't spotted him."

"We stopped him for this game." Cheaters kept on cheating. They couldn't resist.

"And my skull is in one piece."

"That, most important of all."

"So I owe you one," she said, and Manfred could tell that this was a serious statement from her. If Sookie Stackhouse owed you one, she stood ready to help you any time, any place.

"No," said Manfred, surprising himself. "I learned a lot today. I think we're even."

"Time for me to get back to work," she said, glancing down at her watch. "You taking off?"

"Yeah, I'll pick Quiana up and head out of town. We'll go directly to the airport. She'll call you when she gets to Marilyn's, I'm sure."

"You let me know when you get to your desert place, the one Quiana thought you should find," she said.

"I will," he promised. "It may not be for a while. I never thought of going to the desert before." He laughed, and she laughed with him.

"Who's to say that a prophecy is not just your inner wishes divined and spoken out loud?" she said. "After all, when you talked to your grandmother about the rule of three, the one she considered so silly, maybe she had another rule in mind—that your good deeds should always outnumber the bad."

She gave him a little hug then, before she returned to the concession stand for another shift. He saw her begin to scoop up popcorn to fill the striped bags.

And Manfred, wondering if the good things he had done would ever outnumber the bad—or even the neutral—went to his car to pick up a girl he hardly knew to take her to begin the rest of her life with a stranger.

He figured that was what Xylda would have wanted. *I don't know what you think, Xylda,* he thought. *I figure I won.*

HIDE AND SEEK

WILLIAM KENT KRUEGER

William Kent Krueger writes the *New York Times* bestselling Cork O'Connor mystery series, which is set in the north woods of Minnesota. His work has received a number of awards, including the Minnesota Book Award, the Loft-McKnight Fiction Award, the Anthony Award, the Barry Award, and the Friends of American Writers Prize. He does all his writing in a St. Paul coffee shop whose identity he prefers to keep secret. He has recently been playing a lot of hide-and-seek at night with his grandchildren, a difficult proposition for him since he's terrified of the dark.

They'd been running forever. He'd kept Billy in front of him the whole way. When he saw that the kid was tiring, Cameron grabbed his shoulder from behind and said, "In there."

He shoved Billy into a recess in a thicket, a place where he knew they couldn't be seen. They were panting, both of them, chests heaving. "Stitch in my side," Billy wheezed, and doubled over.

"Go on and sit down," Cameron said. "We can rest here, but not too long. The game'll begin any minute."

Billy did as the older boy suggested and plopped onto the ground. Cameron sat beside him and stared up at the sky.

It was evening. It was always evening when the game began. The sky was a fading blue, a fragile color that filled Cameron with a deep sadness, and against that canvas, isolated clouds burned with the last light of the dying sun, as if they'd been painted with a brush whose bristles could hold and transfer fire.

"Will they find us?" Billy asked.

"Hush up," Cameron told him quietly.

His small companion peered at the snarl of manzanita and cypress through which they'd run. Billy's eyes were wide, huge whites with dark brown centers like little worm holes. He reached out and held on to Cameron's leg as if he were afraid his friend might desert him. That was something Cameron wouldn't do, not ever.

"I didn't see Rusty," Billy whispered.

"I told you, hush up."

"Do you think he's already been caught?"

"The seeking hasn't even started yet. He's just hiding, like us."

"He's bigger and slower. They'll find him easier."

Cameron hoped this was true. Maybe this night Rusty would be enough.

Billy looked up at him, his eagerness for the game evident in his big grin. "What if we win?" he whispered. "Will they keep their promise?"

Cameron wasn't sure. Usually they did. But adults were strange, unreadable. Best not to raise Billy's hope, he decided. So he simply said, "Be quiet."

He listened carefully, cocking his ear in the direction of the big house, trying to hear if the seeking had begun yet. There was a breeze off the ocean, which was somewhere at his back, behind the thicket. He could smell the brine in the air and knew they would have to be careful. Beyond the thicket and for miles in either direction, the land dropped away in sheer cliff faces, and at the bottom lay great, jagged pieces of broken rock. Cameron had almost fallen over a cliff edge once when he was playing the game. He'd looked down and the rock pieces had seemed to him like sharp black teeth licked by the hungry tongue of a rising sea.

Billy said, "Roast beef. They promised me roast beef. I can practically taste it." His eyes were closed and he was smiling.

Roast beef. That was for the little boys who survived the game. The bigger boys were promised something else, delicious in an entirely different way.

Although Cameron often thought of him as a little brother, Billy was really no kin. Except for Brother Daniel, Brother Ezekiel, and Sister Hepzibah, no one at the house was kin to anyone. Billy was new to the house and new to the game. He was such a sweet, naïve lunkhead that

Cameron had taken an immediate liking to him, a dangerous thing at the house. But everyone needed to have someone to care about, didn't they? That was what Cameron told himself anyway, when he tried to justify this pointless, useless caring.

"I hope they don't find us," Billy said. He quivered like an eager puppy.

Cameron hoped so, too, hoped desperately.

Billy had freckles. They spread across his face like a field of rust-colored flowers. His hair was red and wild. He had a tooth missing, permanently. He wouldn't say how it happened, but Cameron suspected that, like all the boys at the house, Billy had been beaten and neglected before he'd been abandoned. And still, somehow, he'd managed not to lose the goofy grin or childish hopefulness that sometimes made Cameron want to cry.

A minute more, then they'd get up and move again, Cameron decided. The light was fading quickly, and they needed to be farther from the house before the seeking began.

"We should hide in the barn sometime," Billy suggested.

"The barn's always locked."

"No, it isn't. I saw Sister Hepzibah go in there this morning."

"Don't ever go in the barn," Cameron told him harshly.

"Eddie said they'd never look there."

"Eddie's an idiot."

"Eddie got 'dopted," Billy said.

"No, he didn't."

"Did, too. That's what Sister Hepzibah said. And he's gone, isn't he?"

"Nobody adopted Eddie. He just lost the game." The minute he said it, Cameron was sorry. His responsibility was not only to teach Billy how to survive but to keep him in the dark about the game's true nature.

"What do you mean?" Billy asked.

Cameron didn't answer. He heard the baying of the dog and knew the seeking had begun. He leaped to his feet and grabbed a fistful of Billy's dirty T-shirt and hauled him to his feet. "Come on," he said. "We gotta run."

He pushed Billy out of the thicket and back onto the narrow path that wove through the tangle of undergrowth and ragged manzanita and squat cypress, only one of many paths in the maze that surrounded the big house.

"Which way?" Billy panted when they came to a split.

"Left. Twenty yards, then stop," Cameron said.

"Stop? Why?"

"Just do it."

Billy did as he was instructed. When he halted, Cameron pulled up at his side. "Now, back the way we came."

"What?"

"It'll confuse the dog. At least for a while."

Billy turned back but, instead of running, just stood there, as if listening. Then Cameron heard what Billy heard. Far to their right, in the direction of the big house, came a series of screams. They sounded like the cries of an exotic bird in a jungle movie. Cameron knew that wasn't what they were. And a moment later, Billy figured it out, too.

"That was Rusty?" he said.

"Yeah," Cameron said. "That was Rusty."

"He sounded hurt."

And now he sounded dead, Cameron thought as the stillness and quiet returned.

The hound had ceased its baying. Cameron hoped maybe the game was over for the night, that maybe one was enough. But a moment later, the dog, like a hellhound, began to howl again.

"Run!" Cameron said, and shoved Billy roughly toward the place where the path diverged.

This time they took the right fork. In the sky above them, stars had begun to appear, still faint but promising. Through the branches of the cypress, Cameron glimpsed a full moon rising above the barren hills to the east. Night, blessed night, wasn't far away.

They turned a blind corner and Billy stopped suddenly. Cameron ran into him full tilt; they both went down in a tangle of arms and legs. Cameron quickly pulled himself together and stared ahead at what had drawn Billy up so abruptly. There in front of them, not fifty yards away, rose the big house. On the steps of the grand front porch stood Sister Hepzibah. She was turned away from them, looking at the wild hedge that walled the vast expanse of lawn to the south, which was the direction from which Rusty's cries had come. Her long black hair was drawn up in a tight bun. She wore a shapeless black dress that reached to her ankles, but Cameron knew only too well the contours of the body her dress hid. Although he couldn't see her face, he knew those beautiful features intimately, knew the evil her beauty masked.

"We went in a circle," Billy said in a whisper, a quick burst between hard sucks of air.

"Keep down." Cameron pressed Billy to the ground. "And we didn't go in a circle. I know we didn't."

"Well, there it is." Billy jabbed an accusing finger at the mansion, not bothering to hide his irritation at Cameron's confusion.

There were no lights on in the great house. Once night fell, the house would remain unlit, except for the wing that Brother Daniel and Brother Ezekiel and Sister Hepzibah occupied. The doors of the upstairs dormitory would be locked and the boys left in the dark, reminded harshly, if they dared to complain, "We're not made of money here. We all have to suffer a little for the good of the rest."

"Come on," Cameron whispered, and crawled away to where they couldn't be seen. He got to his feet and Billy got up with him. He looked at the path they'd followed, still bewildered at how they'd ended up at the house. At any given time, a dozen boys were kept there, and he was the oldest. He'd won the game many times, knew the maze of paths well and the hiding places. Something was wrong, but he couldn't put a finger on it. "Follow me," he said, and turned and ran back the way they'd come.

They arrived at a place where a cypress much taller than the others stood beside the path. Cameron stopped, dug among the brush at the base of the tree, and brought out a length of thick hemp rope with a loop on one end. He threw the looped end over a long tree limb, threaded the length through the eye of the loop, and drew the rope tight around the branch. He held out the end of the dangling rope to Billy.

"Swing as far as you can that way." He pointed toward a low wall of thorny bramble.

"Why?"

"So the dog will lose our scent. He won't go through all that stickery brush."

"What if I fall in?"

Cameron wanted to say that it would be better than getting caught, but he explained patiently, "You won't fall in. Swing as far as you can and let go."

"What about you?"

"I'll swing next, and I'll be right behind you."

Billy did as he'd been instructed, and then Cameron followed, landing on another path on the far side of the bramble barrier. "Wait here," he said.

He leaped and caught hold of a low branch of the cypress. He moved hand over hand to the trunk, climbed around to the other side, and removed the rope from the limb where it hung. He threw the rope into the cover of the bramble below, shinnied back the way he'd come, dropped from the tree, and landed beside Billy, who looked at him with wonder and admiration.

The dog bayed again, too close for Cameron's comfort, and he said, "Let's go."

He led the way through the gathering dark. He was thinking that not much longer now and Sister Hepzibah would be calling, "Olly, olly, oxen free." That would be the signal that the seeking had come to an end and Cameron and Billy had won the game that night.

But as he turned yet another blind corner, he stopped in shocked confusion. Because there, once again, stood the mansion, with Sister Hepzibah still on the porch. He swung out his arm and caught Billy before the kid could run past him and drew him back under the sheltering boughs of a cypress.

"Brother Ezekiel, Brother Daniel," Sister Hepzibah called in her throaty voice, which always seemed to Cameron the siren call of sinful things. "Have you found our other darlings yet?"

"Still looking for the little bastards," Brother Ezekiel called back from somewhere out of sight.

"One in the bag already and two who present a nice challenge. A good game tonight," she said with pleasure. Then she spoke as if to the sky, "Good luck, Cameron dear. Remember what's waiting for you."

Cameron spun and ran, but turning another corner, he found himself again facing the house across the open yard. Billy drew up beside him but this time said nothing in recrimination. Cameron didn't understand.

He knew every path, every twist and turn, and yet he seemed to be running in circles. And another thing. The light had stopped changing, and the moon had ceased its climbing. Time seemed to be standing still. He felt the cold grip of panic rise and squeeze his chest. He turned and fled thoughtlessly, ran and ran until his lungs burned and he had to stop. Then he remembered Billy. The little kid was no longer with him.

Oh, Christ, he thought. He'd let Billy down. Just as bad, he'd let Sister Hepzibah and Brother Ezekiel and Brother Daniel down. Teaching the new kid how to play the game was his responsibility, a critical one. If they caught Billy, it wouldn't matter if Cameron hid himself successfully. If they caught Billy, there would be no "Olly oxen free." The hunting wouldn't stop until they'd found Cameron, and nobody would survive the game that night.

He ran back, turned another blind corner, and discovered the kid, sitting on the ground, crying.

"What are you doing?" Cameron whispered harshly.

"I'm scared," Billy said. He looked up and, in the sad blue of that awful evening light, Cameron saw that his cheeks were streaked with tears. "I don't want to end up like Rusty."

Cameron sat down beside him. He stared at the changeless sky and thought about the endless circles in which they seemed to be running. The thread of a familiar possibility dangled in front of him. He closed his eyes and took hold of that thread and followed it to a full understanding, which he always did at the end of that last night's game. As always, this final understanding filled him with a stoic acceptance of his situation and, at the same time, put iron in his resolve to keep the little kid at his side from ever having to play the game again.

"You won't end up like Rusty, I promise," Cameron said. "I'll get you out of this."

Billy looked up at him, and Cameron could see that he believed. The kid stood up and waited for the next instruction. Wordless, Cameron rose and waved him to follow.

They distanced themselves from the sound of the dog. Cameron was looking for the place that he'd told none of the other boys about, the place he'd selfishly kept only for himself. He found it along the thicket that edged the sea cliff. It was marked by a single stone on the ground next to the wild hedge, almost imperceptible to the eye. But Cameron knew what to look for. This place had been his salvation during many a game.

He pulled aside a blind of brush that he'd constructed long ago, and he waved Billy into the tunnel it revealed. The kid crawled through and Cameron after him. They came out on the far side of the high wall of brush. A dozen feet to the west, the land dropped away. Cameron crawled to the cliff edge and signaled Billy to come to his side.

Below them, the sea had retreated from the talus at the foot of the long drop. Fifty yards of sand lay between the cliff and the reach of the waves.

"You can climb down," Cameron said. "There are footholds and handholds all the way. You just have to be careful. Promise me you'll be careful."

"Aren't you coming?"

Cameron shook his head. "When you get to the beach, go south." Cameron pointed so Billy would know the direction. "There's a town that way. I don't know how far, but if you keep going, you'll find it. Ask someone for help."

"What about you?"

"I have to stay."

"Come with me, please. I don't want to go alone."

"You always go alone," Cameron said. "And I always stay."

"I don't understand."

"That's because you're not part of the end of tonight's game. You never are. You get away, Billy. You always get away."

The dog howled, the baying much nearer.

"Go," Cameron said.

"Please come with me."

"Go," Cameron ordered, so sternly that Billy flinched.

The kid looked down at the long, difficult climb ahead of him.

"Don't worry," Cameron said. "You make it. You always do."

Billy eased himself over the side and began slowly to work his way down the face of the rock. Cameron watched for a minute—not to be sure; he was always that—but to hold for a moment longer on the image of the kid he loved, the kid who got away.

"Don't forget me," he whispered. "Don't ever forget me."

Then he crawled back through the tunnel in the brush and drew the blind closed behind him so that it was nearly impossible to see where he'd been. He stood a moment, imagining Billy free, thinking of the times he could have escaped himself. But he'd always been so sure of his ability to win the game and so trapped by the pleasures that were his each time he did.

He heard the baying of the hound, which seemed to be almost upon him. He turned and ran in the opposite direction.

Almost immediately, he found himself coming around a blind corner and there was the great house again, with Sister Hepzibah on the steps. This time, he didn't spin and run. He walked toward her, and as he came, she seemed to sense his presence and turned to him.

"Cameron?" She sounded surprised. And then she sounded angry. "Where's the other one?"

"I ditched him," Cameron said.

At his back, a harsh voice spoke. "You were supposed to teach him the game."

Cameron didn't have to turn around to know that it was Brother Ezekiel who'd spoken. And he could hear the pant and the slobber of the hound the man held on a long leash.

"We'll find him," Brother Daniel said. "He's new. He doesn't understand a thing."

"Is that true, Cameron?" Sister Hepzibah asked, with seductive slyness. Her face was blue in the light, like the ice that sometimes formed on the windows of the great house on very cold winter nights.

"The kid's an idiot," Cameron said. "He's out there running in circles."

"Why aren't you out there, too?" Brother Daniel spoke at his back, so near to him that Cameron could smell the brandy on his breath. Brother Daniel always drank a snifter of brandy before the game began.

"I thought I heard 'Olly oxen free.' "

"Oh, Cameron," Sister Hepzibah said. "That's such a shame. I'm going to miss you."

"But," Brother Daniel said, grabbing both of Cameron's arms in his strong grip, "we're going to have such a good time before you go."

Cameron looked into Sister Hepzibah's dark eyes, saw the hunger

there and knew exactly how the game that night would end. He couldn't
help screaming. Screaming long and loud and desperately. Screams that
at a distance might have sounded like the cry of an exotic bird in a
jungle movie.

"What was that?"

It was dusk, and the real estate agent replied, "The night birds,
that's all."

"Night birds?" The husband half of the couple looked skeptical. "I've
never heard a bird like that."

"Relax, Dickie," the wife half said. "This isn't Manhattan. I'm sure
they have lots of wildlife out here that we'll have to get used to."

"Isolated as the house is, the grounds are frequently visited by many
of our native animals," the agent told them with a reassuring smile.
"We've had reports of deer and fox and all kinds of birds. If you're careful and stand at the edge of the cliff, you can see seals on the beach and
even whales sometimes out in the water."

"Whales?" the wife said with a broad grin. "Oh, Dickie, did you
hear that? Whales."

"Now, shall we look at the kitchen?" the agent suggested. She was
in a hurry. She wanted to finish showing the property before the evening
got any darker. She hated scheduling a showing this late, but sometimes
circumstances demanded. The couple from New York seemed eager to
buy and had told her that they were pressed for time and needed to see
the house right away.

She led them back through the broad dining room, which the development company had spent a fortune restoring to its former glory, and
then passed into the kitchen.

The wife caught her breath. "It's magnificent. Simply magnificent.
Oh, Dickie, think of the parties that could be served from here."

The kitchen was lit by the soft blue glow of evening sifting in through
the big windows. Although the agent should probably have flipped the switch
to illuminate the room more fully, she liked the effect of this muted lighting.

Dickie said, "It's nice. The whole damn place is nice." He leveled a
cool eye on the agent. "Why is it such a bargain?"

"The isolation," the agent replied with practiced aplomb. "Not every-one is eager to have this kind of peace and quiet."

"This is just what we've been looking for," the wife told her with a broad smile.

In the next moment, however, another series of cries came from somewhere far beyond the kitchen windows.

Dickie was big and, so far, had remained rather cool in the face of the agent's enthusiasm for the house. But now a look of concern cracked his stone-faced demeanor. "That's no bird. That's someone in pain. Great pain."

His wife, who'd gushed at every turn in the great house, was clearly affected, too. Her eyes grew big, huge whites in the gloom of the evening.

"What's the story?" Dickie demanded. "The straight dope now. Why's this place listed so cheap?"

Full disclosure dictated that the agent, at some point, tell them the truth. She would have preferred to wait until they were in her office, where the familiar and mundane confines might make her story sound less terrible. But they'd asked, here in the fading twilight, and because she was herself eager to quit the property before it got much darker, she took a deep breath and began.

"The house, as I told you, was built in the late eighteen hundreds by Cyrus Brigham, who'd made a fortune outfitting Forty-Niners in the gold rush. He was, by all accounts, a sternly religious man and, apparently, a cruel one. Children came to him late in life, and he raised them in the isolation of this property. There were rumors of, well, mistreatment. What today we would call child abuse, I suppose. At any rate, when Brigham passed away, his three children inherited the property. There were two boys and a girl. None of them ever married, but as the Brigham fortune waned, the result of bad investments by the old man near the end of his life, the children were forced to seek other means of income. They turned the house into an orphanage for boys.

"This was about the time of the Great Depression. Families had migrated west from the Dust Bowl, looking for work that never materi-alized. They were desperate. They often simply broke apart, leaving children abandoned. The authorities of the day were only too eager to send some of these parentless boys here. As I understand it, the care that the Brighams provided wasn't carefully monitored. I suppose it was because of the confusing times. But I also sometimes wonder if it was just that no one really wanted to acknowledge the true horror of what might be going on here. At any rate . . ."

The agent paused. She was never certain how to tell the rest of the story, the really gruesome part. In the silence as she considered, there was another outburst of screams, these much nearer and so clearly the voice of a child in terror, in pain. In the dark of the kitchen, the agent was certain that the faces of Dickie and his wife paled. She hurried on with the story.

"Apparently, the Brighams played a game with the boys. They called it Hide and Seek. But a more appropriate name might have been Hunted and Hunter. They sent the boys out into the grounds to hide, and then, using a bloodhound, they tracked the children. Those who hid successfully were rewarded. Those who were caught—"

The couple waited, and the wife reached out and took her husband's hand as if she needed his strength to bear what was about to follow.

"Well, when the authorities finally came to check on things, they found devices in the barn that could have come directly from the Inquisition."

"You don't mean . . ." Dickie's wife couldn't say it.

The agent nodded. "That's exactly what I mean."

"What made the authorities come here?" Dickie asked.

"One boy finally escaped. He made his way to town and told about the Brighams and the game. No one could ignore it then. The brothers and sister were arrested and tried. The brothers were hanged, but the sister spent the remainder of her life in a secure institution for the criminally insane. The remaining boys here were all placed in legitimate facilities."

Another series of cries broke the quiet of the deepening evening, whose dark blue had begun to feel actually painful to the agent.

"Not birds," Dickie said. He was a man who looked practical and sound, the last to believe in such things, yet he said, "Ghosts. That's why this place is so cheap. It's haunted."

Normally the agent might have argued, might still have tried for the sale, but she was eager to be quit of the place, away from the evil that was so thick in the air she felt she was actually breathing it.

"Fine," she said. "Call it haunted. I suppose you're not interested."

"On the contrary," the man said. "This is just the kind of place we've been looking for. We'll take it."

He and his wife exchanged smiles that made the agent's blood run cold.

"It's perfect, Dickie," the wife purred. "Absolutely perfect." She faced the agent, who saw in the woman's eyes a darkness that was like a deep well, a bottomless hunger. "Shall we come to your office tomorrow? The earlier the better. I'm so eager to move in."

The agent led them from the house, locked the front door behind her, and walked them to their sports car, a sleek little thing, black as midnight. They shook hands, and she felt, as she hadn't when she'd first greeted them, a sense of dread. She stood a moment, watching them leave. The car headed down the long drive east toward the rising full moon and finally crawled from sight like a bug into a basement drain.

Over the years, she'd shown the property dozens of times, with no success. Despite the recent renovation, the evil in this place was obvious, its presence felt in every room. Most prospects left without seeing the entire house; some even refused to enter it. When they departed, they carried with them a chill that no fire could warm, this because they were decent people, repelled by the grotesque energy that abided here. Something monstrous existed in this place, something born of Cyrus Brigham, perhaps, and passed to his offspring. Or maybe it had always been there, waiting for . . . For what? she wondered.

At her back, another scream rose up.

She'd long ago stopped thinking of them as the cries of some exotic night bird. She knew what those screams truly were. This house had made her believe absolutely in ghosts. She wasn't a particularly religious person, but a little prayer came to her lips, a prayer for the souls of the boys who'd died there and whose spirits, night after night, were doomed, God knew why, to replay the suffering. She wondered if maybe the evil sustained itself in that way, with the remembrance of pain, like a jackal gnawing on a meatless bone.

Then she recalled the eagerness of the couple to buy this cursed, isolated place and recalled, too, the hunger she'd seen in the woman's eyes. With a horrible twisting of everything in her that was good, she had a terrible realization. She believed she understood what it was that the house and the grounds had been waiting for all these years, maybe even anticipating: the arrival, one day, of someone who would again feed with real flesh and blood the appetite of the evil there.

For a long, morally agonizing moment, she considered the consequences of transferring the property to anyone actually drawn to it.

But in the next moment a more rational voice spoke to her, one that came from another part of her and out of another kind of evil, perhaps, and the voice said, *It's a sale. And just think of the size of the commission.*

She got into her car and drove away, doing her best to leave her conscience behind.

STEPPING INTO THE DEAD ZONE

JAN BURKE

Jan Burke is the author of *The Messenger*, a supernatural thriller, and a dozen crime novels, which include *Bones* and *Disturbance*. Her books and stories have won the Edgar®, the Agatha, and other awards.

Our changing ideas about childhood, a chilling poem by Goethe (written before he penned *Faust*), and memories of both the fun and misery of grade-school dodgeball are among the inspirations for "Stepping into the Dead Zone."

They both knew this much: when you're a military brat, you learn how to survive entry into that most hostile of all territories—a new school.

On Monday, October 22, 1962, Tommy Montrose was one of two new kids in his sixth-grade class at Grant Elementary. The other one was his best friend, Mike Wilshire. Mike's dad had been transferred here, too. Their dads had arrived at the nearby base before their families did, and both had already shipped out. It made Tommy wonder why they had to move, if his dad wasn't going to be here anyway, but he didn't say so. No use arguing with his mom.

The teacher was nice. She didn't make too big a deal out of introducing them to the class, and best of all, she let them sit next to each other. As usually happened in a new school, the other kids were rubbernecking. Like Tommy and Mike were here from the moon instead of Georgia.

Recess brought the first challenge, which was also the way it usually happened.

A skinny blond kid was walking toward them.

"Rule Number One," Mike murmured.

Rule Number One of being new was that you never accepted the friendship of the first kid to come up to you. That kid was almost always the weirdest kid in the class, so desperate for a friend that he hoped he could fool you into spending time with him before you figured out that his low standing was contagious.

So when Tommy saw Anton Grünwald coming toward them, Tommy pretended he was just this side of deaf, dumb, and blind. Walked right past Anton and his extended hand and his "Hi, I'm—"

Because Anton had *loser* written all over him. On top of being smaller than all the other kids, and a little too beautiful, he was super pale, wore glasses, and spoke with an accent. A *German* accent. Dressed like he thought it was 1955. And he smelled strange. Not stinky, just not right. Kind of like he'd sprayed himself with two types of cologne that didn't mix.

So on that first morning they breezed past Anton—a boy they soon learned some of the other children called "the Kraut"—and looked straight ahead, relaxed, in charge, not anxious. A long time ago, Mike had advised him that you have to treat other kids as if you are walking past a pack of stray dogs. Aloof works best at first, provided you keep the temperature cool, not cold. And being good at games helped.

It didn't take long before they were demonstrating how good they were at tetherball and four square. They both held back a little, but that was on account of Rule Number Two: don't dethrone the schoolyard king, at least not immediately. So the guy Tommy had pegged as recess royalty, Ricky Gibson, was allowed to continue his reign. It didn't take long to figure out that Ricky was a benevolent leader—good-natured, not the class bully. So they didn't win games against him. He soon looked upon them with approval. If Mike decided to mutter a warning to Tommy when he saw him watching Anton—who was making a solitary trip around the inside of the far fence, not looking up, kicking softly at dirt clods—that was Mike's problem. Tommy told Mike he was trying to work on Rule Number Three, but Mike knew that wasn't true.

"You think that scrawny little dipstick is the bully around here? Give me a break."

"Not the bully. The bully's target," Tommy answered. "He'll lead us to the bully."

"Only if the bully is out there sitting on the fence," Mike scoffed.

Rule Number Three actually had three steps. The first step was to figure out who the bully—or bullies—were. The second was to give them the hairy eyeball, which would allow them a chance to just steer clear of you. Step three, depending on the effect of the hairy eyeball, was to pound them after school if necessary. Of course, that only worked with boys. Girls had another way of bullying, but dealing with girls involved a different set of rules anyway.

The bell rang. When they lined up to go back into the classroom, Ricky stood next to them and said, "You lucked out. Bobby Patterson is out sick. Mostly he picks on the Kraut, but he likes to give new kids what he calls his 'initiation.'"

"Thanks for the warning," Tommy said, and out of the corner of his eye he saw Mike grinning.

Rule Number Four was to not raise your hand too much, and not at all on the first day, but each answered politely when called on, so the teacher didn't focus on them too much and after a while, neither did the other students.

At lunch Tommy almost ticked off Mike again by sitting down at a table where Anton ate. But Ricky sat down with them, and so did a couple of the girls. At that point, Anton got up and emptied his half-eaten tray into the trash, then left the lunch room. The girls giggled. Mike smiled at them, but Tommy wished they had picked somewhere else to sit. Mike was more interested in girls than he was, which wasn't saying much, since Tommy wasn't really interested in them at all. Following Rule Number Five, take two weeks to figure out which guys like which girls and vice versa, they mostly ignored the two at their table.

When Tommy finished eating, he looked around the playground for Anton, but couldn't see him.

"What is it with you and that kid?" Mike asked when they were walking back to class.

"I don't know. I think it's kind of interesting that he came from Germany."

"What's so interesting about Germany? His dad could be a Nazi."

"Or he could have come here to escape the Nazis. You don't know."

"And there's that wall there now. They shoot people trying to get out of Germany."

"You've got it mixed up. As usual. The wall divides Berlin. The communists won't let people leave East Berlin."

"Fine, Mr. Know-it-all," Mike said, and walked ahead of him.

Mike never stayed mad at him for long, though. Later in the afternoon, when the teacher announced that they would be playing dodgeball, all tension between them evaporated.

They loved dodgeball.

They ended up on opposite teams, because the teacher had the students count off by twos, with all the ones on one team and the twos on the other. That was okay. Ricky ended up on Mike's team, Anton on Tommy's. The teacher lined up six big red rubber balls on the center line and blew her whistle. Everyone raced for the balls and began to get people out. One of the girls threw a ball at Anton, getting him out almost immediately, which apparently wasn't unexpected by anyone, including Anton. Although Rule Number Two meant they held back a lot on that first day and allowed themselves to be taken out, Mike by getting hit, Tommy by "accidentally" stepping into the dead zone, they were still among the last to go out.

By the end of the game, they were friends again. Mike didn't even mind it when Tommy showed him a map to explain where the Berlin Wall was, and how Germany was divided.

The next day, Bobby Patterson returned to school, and Tommy just missed getting into his first fight during that morning's recess. He would have been happy to knock Bobby flat for the way he picked on Anton, but Mike intervened. Mike was bigger than Bobby, who was about Tommy's size, but Tommy knew that size wasn't what kept Mike out of fights. Mike had this look he could give you that told you directly and sincerely that you would really, really regret throwing the first punch. Bobby was the kind of kid who might have gone ahead and risked it with another kid, but he didn't risk it with Mike.

"About Anton—" Tommy began.

"After recess," Mike interrupted, still giving Bobby the look, "you will be the first person to suggest that people stop calling Anton 'the Kraut.'"

"What?!" Bobby protested.

"I mean it."

That was all it took.

"Thanks," Tommy said, when Bobby moved off sulkily.

"Don't thank me," Mike said. "I only did it to save myself some time. I know you. You would have been in another fight before the end of day, defending that little pipsqueak."

If Anton was surprised that Bobby Patterson was his new champion, he didn't show it. None of the other kids objected when Bobby said there would be no more calling Anton anything but Anton. "Or Tony," he growled at one point, and shot Mike a glance. Mike didn't argue with that, except to say to Anton, "You mind if we call you Tony?"

Anton shook his head.

None of it was the big deal Tommy had thought it might be.

Maybe that was because everybody had bigger problems on their minds. President Kennedy had held a special news conference the night before, about the Cuban missile crisis. Kids at school were talking about the duck-and-cover drill they had been through that morning and looking suspiciously at airplanes that happened to fly over the schoolyard— which was extra dumb, since they were so near the base that planes flew over all the time. The kids were too busy repeating twisted versions of their parents' fears about the missile crisis to get excited about rude nicknames for Anton. Tommy could tell that even the teacher was upset about Cuba.

Maybe all the nervous energy helped that afternoon's dodgeball game seem more intense. Anton got out first, as usual. By the end of the game, it was Tommy and Mike on one team, Bobby on the other. Tommy saw Mike intentionally fail to dodge a ball thrown by Bobby, and do it very neatly, so that it looked as if he had tried to avoid it—the ball just barely clipped him. Tommy was so lost in admiration that he failed to see the next throw coming at him, a throw that got him out.

Bobby apparently wasn't the dodgeball winner very often, because when they congratulated him, he didn't seem to know how to respond.

Tommy slept over at Mike's house that night.

"I think that kid's dad beats him," Mike said from the lower bunk bed.

"Anton's?"

"Naw. Bobby's."

"How do you know?"

"When we were playing dodgeball today, his shirt rode up on his back. He had belt marks."

Tommy lay in the darkness with his fists clenched, wondering if there was a way that he could win a fight against Bobby's dad. He mentioned the idea to Mike.

"Forget it," Mike said.

"I can't sleep."

"You need a scare. Something to take your mind off it."

This, Tommy knew, was Mike's standard cure for troubling thoughts. You did something scary, survived it, and then you ended up feeling not so bothered by anything else.

"I can't sleep either," Mike admitted, when Tommy didn't answer.

"Bobby's dad bothers me more than Cuba."

"I know what you mean."

Tommy drew a resolute breath. "So, we going to hop fences?" He was always sure they'd end up arrested or shot or bitten by a dog when they hopped fences. Serial trespassing as you quickly entered and exited one suburban yard after another had its thrills, but . . .

"No. Let's go through the cemetery."

Tommy shuddered. "That should do it," he said. He climbed down from his bunk and changed from his pajamas into his clothes.

The cemetery wasn't far away. It was a little chilly out, so they wore jackets. They also carried flashlights, although they didn't use them as they made the walk, relying on streetlamps. Leaves tumbled through the air and danced across lawns and sidewalks, as a gentle breeze moved among branches overhead. A faint smell of wood smoke mixed with one of damp earth and grass, the scent of autumn.

The cemetery was surrounded by an old wrought-iron fence with spaces between the pickets not quite wide enough to squeeze through. The pickets were topped with spikes, none of which were really sharp enough to hurt anyone. Mike had found a spot where several of the spikes had long ago been broken off. Mike gave him a boost up, and he was over. He tried to hide his fear that Mike would now just take off and leave him trapped. Mike didn't do that, of course—had never done anything like that—and so Tommy reached through the spaces in the bars and made a stirrup of his hands to boost Mike up in turn.

Tommy turned his flashlight on.

"Careful!" Mike whispered. "Keep it down low and be ready to turn it off if we hear someone coming."

"I'm going to scream my head off if anyone or *anything* comes near us!"

Mike started laughing. He was trying not to laugh out loud, so he was shaking, holding his hands over his mouth as he doubled over. Then he snorted. That made both of them laugh, and trying not to make any noise only made them laugh harder.

Suddenly Mike stood up straight. "Shhhh! Listen!"

Tommy fell silent.

All around them, trees rustled in the breeze, which had grown stronger, but that was all. Tommy looked at his friend and said, "Mike! Stop trying to scare me!"

Mike grinned, then shrugged. "That's what we're here for, right?"

So Mike started telling ghost stories. He told the one about the girl who stuck a knife in the grave of a mean old man on a dare—something Tommy could never imagine doing, even on a dare—and unknowingly pinned her skirt to the grave, so that when she tried to leave she thought the old man was trying to pull her into the grave with him.

And the next day, Tommy thought, knowing the way Mike would tell the story as well as the story itself . . .

"And the next day," Mike said in a voice of doom, "they found her dead on the grave—she had died of fright!"

Even though he knew the story, Tommy shivered.

Then Mike told another one Tommy had heard about a million times before, about someone giving a beautiful hitchhiker a ride, and lending her his jacket, and dropping her off at her house. Came back the next day, and her father told him that his daughter was dead. " 'She died exactly a year ago last night,' he said. 'Right where you say you picked her up.' And the guy didn't believe the dad, but then the dad took him to the graveyard where she was buried, and there on her grave . . ."

Clean and neatly folded . . .

". . . clean and neatly folded was the guy's jacket!"

Tommy shivered again.

They had been walking as Mike told his stories. The cemetery was old and the gravestones took on menacing shapes in the darkness. Tommy figured they were about halfway to the other side and thought it was time to turn back. He started to say so, but Mike suddenly said, "Shhh!"

Tommy froze in place and glanced at Mike. There was a look on his face unlike any Tommy had ever seen.

Tommy's mouth went dry.

"Listen!" Mike said.

But that wasn't necessary.

Tommy heard it too.

A soft voice, making a sad sound. Not a moan but . . . singing a song, a sad song. The sound came from the other side of an elaborate monument.

Tommy was so frightened he felt physically ill, as if he were going to vomit right there in the cemetery. Only the thought of what might rise up from the ground all ticked off at him for barfing on it kept him from shooting his cookies.

The breeze died down for a moment. He caught a few words of the lyrics.

"*Du liebes Kind, komm, geh mit mir! Gar schöne Spiele spiel' ich mit dir . . .*" Suddenly he didn't feel sick anymore.

"Anton!" he yelled, along with a lot of cusswords.

Mike looked at him wide-eyed, then jumped half out of his skin when Anton's pale face appeared around a corner of the carved granite.

"You shouldn't swear so," Anton admonished. "This is a sacred place."

"I wasn't swearing at the place or anybody in it but you!"

"Still . . ."

"What are you doing here?" Mike asked, finally finding his voice.

"I might ask the same."

"I asked you first."

Anton shrugged.

"How did you know it was him?" Mike asked.

"He was singing in German."

"How could you tell?"

"That new show I've been telling you about. *Combat*."

"Was your dad a Nazi?" Mike asked Anton.

"No," he said, looking fierce. "My family had nothing to do with Hitler."

Mike looked ready to challenge him on that one, so Tommy quickly said, "What was that song you were singing?"

"*'Der Erlkönig.'* There are many versions of it. I like that one."

"If you say so," Mike said.

"What's it about?" Tommy asked. "It sounded sad."

"It is very sad," Anton said. "It's about a child and a father and a goblin."

Tommy and Mike exchanged a look. Neither made the *cuckoo* sign, because it was already obvious Anton was crazy.

"Why are you here?" Mike asked again.

"To meet you."

"Now that's just a lie," Mike said. "We didn't know we were coming here until a little while ago."

"Maybe I know things about you. Things you don't even know about yourselves."

"Like what?"

"Do you know of changelings and stolen children?"

"Kidnapped, you mean?" Tommy said.

"Not exactly. Stolen by enchantment."

They both shook their heads.

He studied them for a moment, then said, as if he never intended to answer their questions or even the one he had posed to them, "Let me tell you about the song I was singing. It's taken from a poem by Goethe. It takes place a long time ago, when people lived closer to the real world."

"What do you mean?"

"They lived closer to nature, near forests, and saw wild animals and . . . other things that live in forests. They saw death, too—especially of children. Look around here, at the older stones. Many children are buried here."

"Killed by things that lived in the forest?" Tommy asked.

"Most were killed by disease. Sometimes . . . sometimes by other things. Some were killed by things nearly forgotten but still very real."

"How do you know?" Mike asked, not keeping the scorn out of his voice.

"It is my business to know about children. And the things that harm them."

Mike and Tommy exchanged another look. "You're just trying to scare us," Mike said, with not quite as much confidence as Tommy might wish. "It's dark and windy and we're in a graveyard. We don't need you to tell us lies to spook us."

"Dark and windy." Anton smiled a little. "In the poem I was telling you about, a father rides through the forest on just such a night, holding his son before him. The boy hears the *Erlkönig* calling to him, sees him moving alongside them through the forest, and is frightened."

"Stop it," Mike said.

"His father tells him not to be afraid, it's only a wisp of fog, the wind in the leaves—but the *Erlkönig* keeps whispering to the boy, 'Dear child, come with me! Very lovely games I'll play with you!'"

When he spoke the part of the *Erlkönig*, his voice changed. To Tommy's ear, it sounded deep and soft and . . . wicked. Almost as if the words were carried by more than sound, were spoken somewhere inside him.

He stepped back, as did Mike, but Anton moved closer.

"The boy pleads with his father," he went on, "who gently scoffs at his fears. Then the *Erlkönig* decides that if the boy is not willing, he will use force to carry him away. The boy begins to cry and moan that the *Erlkönig* has harmed him. The father rides faster, at last afraid—but too late. When he reaches his home, his son lies dead in his arms."

Mike and Tommy took off running.

"Pay attention to your dreams!" Anton called after them, except it was as if he had not shouted, but whispered in their ears.

They only stopped running long enough to boost each other over the fence, and then they ran all way back to Mike's street. Just as they came up to the big oak in front of Mike's house, a figure stepped out of the shadows.

Anton.

They were too winded to scream.

"I won't hurt you. I'm only trying to protect you."

"How did you get here so fast?" Mike said, doubled over and panting.

"Pay attention to your dreams," Anton said again, and again Tommy felt his voice all the way through him. Anton stared at him a moment, his eyes sad, and walked away.

Tommy watched him, still scared, still out of breath, but finding himself feeling sorry for him. That kid was strange, but he was troubled, too.

Tommy and Mike didn't say anything to each other, not even once they were in Mike's room, changed into pajamas, and back in their bunk beds.

They had plenty of blankets on each of their beds, but it seemed to take a long time before Tommy felt warm again. He lay in the darkness, eyes wide open. Old neglected toys in the corners of Mike's room suddenly changed from worn, familiar friends into shadowy creatures, the minions of the *Erlkönig*. A J. Fred Muggs chimp looked positively evil, and the silhouette of a Howdy Doody doll made Tommy *really* wish he had never seen "The Dummy," a *Twilight Zone* episode in which a sinister ventriloquist's dummy came to life.

After a while Tommy whispered, "You awake?"

"I'm afraid to go to sleep," Mike admitted.

"Me too."

"How did he get here ahead of us? He had to be moving really fast. He never moves that fast when we play dodgeball."

"*I* don't move as fast as I did tonight."

That made Mike laugh.

Despite his determination not to, Tommy fell asleep and dreamed.

The dream was in three parts. The first was of a castle full of knights. He was training to become one. Tommy was a varlet, a knight's page, as was Mike. They practiced against the pell, a wooden stake as tall as a man, used to learn swordsmanship, and later the quintain—a rotating device with a target or dummy on one end and a sandbag on the other. The object with the quintain was to strike the target true with a weapon and then duck and dodge as the sandbag swung toward you from behind.

He and Mike were among the youngest pages there, and he had a sense of being far away from his family. He spent most of his time running from one place to another, carrying messages, doing errands, cleaning armor, and learning the many lessons that were designed to help him take up his duties when he became a man. There were lessons in manners and religion. He learned about archery, riding, hawking, and hunting. The lord he served taught him about combat—lessons that could be painful but excited him all the same. He learned games of strategy, such as chess.

In the second part of the dream, he was a little older. He was on the back of a galloping horse, with Anton up behind him. Anton, who didn't smell funny in the dream, was dressed in rich clothing, and he was clinging to Tommy. Tommy held the reins as the panicked horse sped recklessly through dark woods on an autumn night, plunging across streams and through brittle brush. Its flanks were lathered and heaving, its ears laid back, and the whites of its rolling eyes glinting in the moonlight. Mike rode beside them, his horse equally alarmed.

They were pursued by something unearthly, a creature in an ebony cloak whose eyes glowed with an icy blue light beneath a hood that concealed its face. The creature effortlessly kept up with the terrified animals, not so much running alongside as floating. It appeared here and then there, on their heels and then suddenly beside them again. Tommy had no clear sense of how they had come to be in this situation, only that they were in danger, that he must protect Anton.

Now the creature leapt from the ground, hurtling itself upon Mike's saddle and clutching at him. All the boys screamed, the horses reared, and Tommy reached to pull Mike to safety. They overbalanced and tumbled to the ground, landing hard, barely avoiding the hooves of the fleeing horses. Mike and Tommy quickly came to their feet and shielded Anton, who cried, "It's me he wants; save yourselves and let him take me!"

Mike and Tommy paid no heed to this but quickly nocked arrows and drew their bows.

Their arrows flew, but the creature eluded them, grinning and making a game of their efforts. He rose onto a high branch, then swooped down upon them, and although the boys drew their daggers, he simply gathered the boys into his mighty hold. Tommy felt a pressure on the hand that held his weapon and was forced to drop it.

The creature did not claw or bite their flesh as Tommy had expected. It whispered into Tommy's ear, its breath warm, murmuring words he could not make out in his dream. The creature's cloak transformed into large black wings that bore them higher, higher . . . Tommy looked down and saw the horses speeding back to the castle, while his weapons lay useless and shining on the dark earth below.

Above him the waxing moon shone bright, only three days away from full, and they climbed so high it seemed for a time that they would be taken to it. He no sooner thought this than the creature dove, causing the wind to shriek in Tommy's ears, and he began to fear that the thing would dash their brains out against the forest floor. But it slowed, and within the blink of an eye they were back down among the trees. Here they were surrounded by bright dancing lights, which seemed to have wings, and to whom the creature spoke in a strange tongue, after which he readily surrendered the boys. To fairies, Tommy thought with a mixture of fascination and dread. He saw the creature take away a bag of gold and disappear into the trees.

Anton seemed to grow as bright as the other lights, whose shapes and faces Tommy began to better discern. Anton moved freely among them, and although Tommy could not understand their language, he thought Anton was pleading on behalf of Mike and Tommy, but without success. Tommy, although warm now, and not in pain, was unable to speak or move, and could see that Mike was similarly afflicted. They were borne away through the forest, and Tommy was soon overcome with a desire to sleep.

He could not clearly remember the final part of the dream. He was in a place of idleness and pleasure, of sweetmeats, soft beds, and eternal springtime. Grass grew green and high. Flowers of unimaginable beauty surrounded them. Over the babble of a brook he heard the laughter of other children and knew this was a place of endless playfulness. Mike was there, and Anton, and he could almost be satisfied enough by that. He had a feeling he owed a duty to them that he must fulfill, and that for now, he was where he needed to be.

And yet he felt unhappy, felt himself fight a kind of drowsiness that seemed to deepen with every breath he took. He struggled as one who wishes to wake, to wake, to wake . . . but was held down by sleepiness. He felt himself to be a captive who could just make out a faraway shore where he would be free, but who had not the least hope of reaching it. Sometimes he heard faint sounds of sorrow in the distance and was troubled by the belief that these were made by his father, standing in the place in the forest from which they had been taken.

He woke feeling bereft. Mike's room was cold and the day outside gray. He looked around him. It was 1962, and he was too old to be afraid of toy chimps or Howdy Doody. He got out of bed and went to his overnight bag and found his toothbrush, which seemed to him, that morning, to be on a long list of great inventions.

As they walked to school together Mike said, "What's a sweetmeat?"

"You dreamed it, too. You know what it is."

"Candy? Some kind of dessert?"

"Yes. Either one."

"There was a blue-eyed creature with black wings."

"Yes." Wanting to think of a happier part of the dream, Tommy said, "You and I—training to be knights."

"Fostered together," Mike said.

The words felt right. Tommy knew what they meant, in this old sense.

"We trained on the quintain," Mike went on. "And Anton was a prince or something. Do you think he made us dream something he wanted to be true?"

"No. I think he made us dream something that *is* true."

"How can that be possible?"

"I don't know. Maybe he put a spell on us."

Mike brooded over this, then said, "I liked the part when we were in paradise, although I was a little restless there."

"I wanted out of it," Tommy admitted. "And I don't know why. It was . . . it was as if I had something important to do somewhere else."

"I don't think we dreamed the same thing about that part. What should we do now?"

"Only one person I know of who might be able to explain it. Let's try to talk to Anton."

But when they found Anton, he only shook his head and said, "I can't talk about it here. After school. Meet me in the cemetery."

It rained that afternoon, so there was no dodgeball, just indoor games, like pairing off to play hangman and board games like checkers and chess. Tommy and Mike chose hangman. Tommy easily guessed Mike's word was *sweetmeat* and Mike just as easily guessed his was *quintain*. They glanced over to see Bobby playing hangman with Anton, and then watched to make sure there wasn't a problem. Bobby was laughing and Anton smiling. Their friendliness seemed to shock the teacher as much as it did their classmates.

The rain let up by the time school was over, and Tommy, Mike, and Anton started to walk to the cemetery together. They hadn't gone far before Tommy became aware that they were being followed. He let Anton and Mike get a little bit ahead of him, then suddenly turned around and shouted, "What do you want, Bobby? We aren't going to let you hurt Anton!"

"I'm not going to hurt him!" Bobby said, affronted. "I promised already, remember?"

"Hello, Robert," Anton said.

"Hi, Tony. Can I come with you guys?"

"No!" said Mike and Tommy, just as Anton said, "Yes."

"Thanks!" said Bobby, hearing what he wanted to hear. He quickly caught up with them.

There wasn't much Mike or Tommy could do, since they were dependent on Anton for explanations. But Tommy still felt irritated and said to Bobby, "You don't even know where we're going."

"Is it to my house? 'Cause we're going the wrong way if that's where you want to go."

"Of all the—no, I don't want to go to your house!"

"Neither do I," he said.

After that, Tommy decided he would keep his big mouth shut.

He thought Bobby might balk when he realized they were walking into the cemetery, but he didn't hesitate at all. Mike said, "You aren't afraid of ghosts?"

"No," Bobby said. "I come here a lot. No dead person has ever done a thing to me."

"There's a first time for everything," Anton said softly, but Bobby didn't seem to hear him.

Anton stopped near a large monument shaped like a curved bench—an exedra, he called it, but the rain had made it too damp. He found a place that was drier—a monument consisting of four tall columns supporting a round roof over a stone block, and they settled in there.

"Robert, I promised Thomas and Michael that I would tell them about children stolen by magical folk," he said. Bobby looked at Mike and Tommy as if this made them the weirdest people he knew, but apparently he had no objections to this program.

So Anton began to talk of two worlds—the mundane, the one they knew as normal. The human world. But there was also a hidden enchanted world—a world of fairies, trolls, goblins, and elves.

"Sometimes," he said, "those in the enchanted world steal human children from the mundane." He told tales of different ways in which each of these races and groups within the enchanted world dealt with the matter. "Some replace the stolen child, others do not. Among the people I—I mean, among the ones I know of—there is a seven-year cycle. A child may be taken for only seven years before being offered a choice. During that seven years, while the child lives among the fairies, he or she does not age."

"What's the choice at the end of seven years?" Mike asked.

"One is to remain among the fairies. To live in a children's paradise, to laugh and play. To be safe and loved. That is the choice we hope he will make."

"And the other choice?" Tommy asked.

"He may choose to return to the mundane world. If that is what he wants, he becomes a changeling. Seven years are taken from his age, and he is exchanged into a new family as a younger child. If, for example, he was taken from the mundane at the age of eleven years and five months, when he returns, he will be a child of four years and five months."

"And that's it?" Mike asked. "He's a regular human from then on?"

"No," Anton said with a smile. "The fae do not give up so easily. When another seven years have passed, the fairies come for him again, and offer him the choice again. Even in the mundane world, he never grows older than the age at which he was first taken, except in one circumstance."

"So if he goes back with the fairies," Mike asked, "he gets to be that age forever?" Tommy thought it was the wrong question.

Anton glanced at Tommy, but answered Mike. "If he chooses to return to the fairies, he never ages. The fairies always want the stolen children to return to them, to stay with them."

"But the children have a choice every seven years?" Bobby asked.

"Yes."

"This goes on forever?"

"No. It may only happen one hundred times."

"Seven times one hundred," Bobby said, doing the math. "So, it goes on again and again for seven hundred years?"

"Yes. Most children decide to remain among the fairies."

"What happens at the end of the seven hundred years?"

"Then the stolen child must choose once and for all. If he returns to the fae, he lives untroubled among them."

"You said he never ages, except in one circumstance," Tommy said. "At the end of seven hundred years, if he chooses to stay with the mundane, does he age, or does he suddenly turn to dust?"

"No, he doesn't turn to dust. If, at the end of all of those years of being parted from those who love him in the fae world—if the stolen child still wishes to remain with the mundane, he will grow older here, and live out whatever days are his. However, if he chooses to stay here, another child must be sent back to the fae in his stead."

"Who wouldn't want to go back?" Bobby asked.

"Exactly," said Mike, staring hard at Tommy.

"No adults in the fae world?" Tommy asked. "No troubles?"

"There are adults, and some children who seem to actually be adults in children's bodies."

"Like you."

Anton lifted a shoulder. "Sometimes you, as well. For all the playfulness of the fae, some have responsibilities. As for troubles, yes, we—they—have their own, but the stolen children are not drawn into them. The children in the hidden world do not worry that their rivers are poisoned, that bombs may drop from the sky while they play, that one day there will be no birds to sing to them. The children do not go hungry or unloved. No harm comes to children in the hidden world. It is very unlike this one."

Bobby and Mike sat looking wistful. Tommy and Anton sat staring at each other, not with hostility, but as if each were trying to study and better understand the other.

After a while, Tommy said, "When?"

Anton said, "All Hallow's Eve."

"Halloween. Figures."

"I need to get home," Mike said. "Bobby, want to spend the night? I'll ask my mom to call yours."

"She's right over there," Bobby said, pointing to a grave.

"Sorry," Mike said.

Bobby shrugged. "I'd like to stay over at your house. My dad might say yes. I don't know."

The four boys began to walk toward the housing tract where Mike and Tommy and Bobby lived. Tommy decided not to ask Anton where he lived. He didn't believe Anton would lie to him, which was the problem, at least while they were within earshot of other people.

They paired off as they walked, and before long, Mike and Bobby were far ahead.

"Are you attached to your parents here?" Anton asked. "Is that why you seem uncertain?"

"They're good people, and I wouldn't want to do anything to hurt them. But there is a sort of distance—I have always believed I was adopted."

"You were, as was Mike. Your parents are waiting until you are older to tell you."

Tommy took a moment to absorb that news, but it wasn't as upsetting as he might have expected it to be. "In the time of the dream—1262, right?"

Anton nodded.

"You were a prince."

"Yes. It is a long story. The short version is that among the fae I am a prince, and in that time, I was stolen by another band of fairies, who exchanged me for a human prince and cast a spell that left me without my powers. My parents are not the sort of beings one should trouble in this way, as the other band eventually discovered. My family is wealthy, and when they learned I had been taken, they offered rewards for my return. I was with my mundane parents on a visit to the noble family you were fostered with when—I don't think there is an English word for this, so let's say, a type of goblin found us that night in the woods. My parents were able, a little later, to return the human prince to his parents, much to their delight. A small enchantment allowed them and any other humans who had met me to believe that the prince they had known was that boy."

"Did he tell them what had become of us? Michael and me?"

"He told them the truth, essentially, by way of an enchantment, one that allowed him to believe he had experienced it. A goblin spirited him away, and the two of you fought for him and allowed him to escape. Alas, the goblin took the two of you instead." He paused, then added, "I know your father grieved for you. I asked my parents to return you to him. But they refused, saying he had given you away to a man who would put you in an army and see you killed. Which was, indeed, what became of most of the earl's forces. Still, I eventually persuaded them to send a healer to your father, so that his grief abated as his other sons and daughters gave him grandchildren. Not a few of those grandsons were christened Thomas."

Tommy found himself wondering about the power of the fairies' spells and how they affected humans. He pondered this, thinking of the dream. "When we first met, you didn't smell funny."

Anton started laughing, and Tommy realized that he knew that laugh, but had not previously heard him laugh here, in this time. It was a wonderful sound, more pleasing than any song. He smiled.

"I have missed you, Thomas," Anton said. "As for my . . . aroma. Over the years, when I have been sent to ask you to come home, I have learned to—put a bit of distance between myself and others. It makes things easier, later on, if no one else becomes attached to me, and vice versa. I find that even children who overlook appearance will judge another by what their noses tell them."

"It works."

"I know."

They both laughed then.

Tommy sobered first. "So you are a prince in this other place? The hidden world?"

"Yes."

"Should I be calling you *Your Highness*, and bowing to you?"

"It's not necessary here." He smiled. "America has no princes."

"How did we end up here? In America, rather than Germany?"

"As other Germans did. Emigration from a set of principalities and duchies beset by wars and famine. We chose families who would bring you here. We sensed you belonged here. We heed such sensations. You seemed to do well in the United States."

They walked in silence. Tommy didn't fail to notice that Anton had stopped giving off his weird scent. As they came around the corner on Tommy's street, all Tommy could smell were the scents of autumn and dinners being made in kitchens all along the block. When they reached his driveway, they stood outside for a while.

Lights were on in the house. Tommy could hear the vacuum cleaner running. He thought of that distant paradise, lit by sun and moonlight, of laughter and dancing and peacefulness. Peacefulness for everyone, it seemed, but him. Mike, he realized, returned to the mundane for his sake. Should he return to the fae for Mike's sake, if for no other reason? But still there was that sense of matters unsettled here.

"I have something I must do here, Anton. I feel it . . ." He broke off, but pointed to his chest.

Anton's eyes filled with tears, but he said, "Then we will do our best to enjoy these last few days together."

"You'll take Bobby?"

"If you haven't changed your mind, yes." He walked away.

In school the next day, Mike and Tommy felt relieved that they had been excused from a hideous assignment. The other students had been told to memorize at least twelve lines of a single poem, or all of two short poems, and each of them had to stand up in front of the class and recite it. The teacher excused the two of them because they were new kids and hadn't had time to pick a poem and study it.

Mostly, it was the usual chance for the kinds who tried to skate through assignments to recite a couple of limericks and the goody-two-shoes types to show off with poems like "Song of Hiawatha," which Tommy could hardly listen to with a straight face. Eleanor Pinksey was into the tenth short stanza of "Barbara Fritchie," right at the good part, when the teacher thanked her and told her that she could sit down.

Everyone was watching the clock because the recitations were being done at the end of the school day. Way too much time left. Most of the students recited their poems in a singsong voice, making Tommy drowsy, and looking around, he wasn't the only one.

Half an hour later, underneath the droning of poetry was the sound that only a classroom full of restless students could make, a symphony of sighs, tapping pencils, shuffling papers, creaking desks, and the scraping noise made by chairs slightly but constantly repositioned on linoleum.

Until Anton went to the front of the class.

There was a little bit of snickering, and then he spoke, and everyone fell silent.

"The title of my poem is 'The Stolen Child.' It was written by William Butler Yeats."

He recited the beginning of the poem, but it was when he spoke the lines that ended every stanza that Tommy and every other student in the class leaned forward, mesmerized:

Come away, O human child!
To the waters and the wild
With a faery, hand in hand.
For the world's more full of weeping than you can understand.

Tommy watched his classmates' faces, and realized that if Anton wanted to lead them away like the Pied Piper, it was in his power to do it. Anton looked at him then, smiled softly, and sat down, releasing the class from his spell.

The bells rang for a duck-and-cover drill, and Tommy dutifully joined Mike under their desk.

It was a world full of weeping, Tommy thought, and it could not be understood.

Over the weekend they learned that an American pilot, Major Rudolf Anderson, Jr., was killed when his U2 plane was shot down over Cuba. It was tragic, and especially upsetting to the military moms.

Despite this and other unsettling reports, though, it seemed the crisis was coming to an end.

Tommy read the papers and occasionally eavesdropped on his mother talking to friends on the phone about the news, but he spent most of that weekend reading a book he had found in the library, a book about knights.

Anton came by and they walked over to Mike's, where they were joined by Bobby. They were going to play baseball but it started to rain again, so Mike's mom popped popcorn for them and they played Chinese checkers and Monopoly before going home. Mike, he noticed with a pang, was becoming good buddies with Bobby. He told himself that this was only right, but he also wondered if Anton had placed some kind of spell on them. He glanced at Anton, who shook his head *no*.

Halloween was a Wednesday, a clear and sunny day. He walked to school with Mike, who seemed more like himself than he had in the past few days. They sat at the same table at lunch, while across the cafeteria,

Bobby, who had come to school with a black eye, sat near Anton, the two of them involved in some intense conversation.

"I wish you would come with us," Mike said.

"I know. But if I do, how many more black eyes will Bobby's old man give him?"

Mike had no answer to that. A little later he said in a low voice, "I remember our time."

"Being a page?"

"Yes. It wasn't always so good."

"No, it wasn't." Tommy smiled. "But we were the best at the quintain!"

Mike smiled back. "You were the best of all of us." His brows drew together. "Do you think it's why we're good at tetherball and dodgeball?"

"Could very well be," Tommy agreed. "I mean, not really fair—seven hundred years of practice . . ."

That one made Mike snort milk out his nose.

When he recovered, Tommy said, "Today we are going to play our best dodgeball game ever. If we're going to have even a small chance of seeing each other again, I need your help."

Dodgeball history was made at Grant Elementary that afternoon. For the first time, Anton was not the first person out. Tommy had delivered that honor to Ricky Gibson, who took it with his usual amiability and good grace. By managing where they stood when the teams were counted off, Tommy, Mike, and Bobby were on the same team, as was Anton.

Tommy played as he had never played before. He found himself moving almost as if he were performing a dance—twisting, leaping, going low to ground. Moving just as smoothly and speedily was Mike. Between them was Anton. They shielded him.

Tommy and Mike caught and dodged anything thrown at them, all the while defending Anton. Bobby saw what they were doing and played a solid offense.

Once Anton was nearly hit but deflected the ball with his hands, and Tommy stretched and caught the ball before it hit the ground, which meant the thrower was out.

Eventually the other team sensed what was going on and tried to focus on Anton, but that only made them vulnerable to hits from Tommy's other team members—Bobby was especially deadly—when they allowed themselves to be distracted.

Near the end of the game, only five players remained: three on Tommy's team, two on the other. Then Mike was hit and was out. Tommy caught a ball thrown at him by one of the two remaining players on the other team, which meant that boy was out. Now there was only Eleanor Pinksey, Tommy, and Anton still on the court. Anton and Eleanor threw balls at the same time. She failed to dodge Anton's throw, and in the instant it hit her, Tommy launched himself to stop the ball headed for Anton. He caught it but lost his balance and ended up on his knees in the dead zone. The teacher blew her whistle to call Tommy out. Anton was the last player still in.

There was a moment of stunned silence, and then all the other students started cheering. Anton moved toward Tommy and reached a hand down to help him to his feet. "Your loyalty never fails to move me," he said softly, so that only Tommy could hear him.

But Tommy didn't rise. Holding on to Anton's hand, he bowed over it, and said, "I would ask a boon, Your Highness."

Anton's eyes widened. "Later," he said, pulling Tommy to his feet as the others began to crowd around them.

They were walking home together, going to Mike's house. Mike and Bobby moved ahead.

"You asked for a boon," Anton said.

"Return for me in seven years."

Anton sighed. "I will try, Thomas, but that is all I can do. I have never heard of such a thing being granted to anyone, and those placed higher than I must agree to it. I'm not sure they will appreciate—dodgeball."

"If you will try, you will have granted me my boon."

They had nearly caught up to the others when Anton asked, "Where did you learn about boons?"

"In this age which fails to enchant you, in this place, all children are encouraged to learn to read and write, and public libraries are built so that anyone may have access to books. I borrowed one about knights."

Anton smiled. "I will keep your lesson in mind."

"Sorry. I didn't mean to be—"

"Impertinent? No apology needed. As I've told you, I'm not a prince here."

"I'm not sure that's true."

"I do tell you the truth, Thomas. For example, regarding this evening's arrangements. I'm afraid things are going to be a bit uncomfortable for you . . ."

The news the next morning shocked everyone except one eleven-year-old boy, whose mother, discovering he had a high fever, had not allowed him to go trick-or-treating with his friends. Thomas Montrose was questioned extensively about the possible whereabouts of his friends, not because the obviously ailing boy was suspected of having a hand in their disappearances, but because the community was so desperate to have any lead that would help them locate Robert Patterson, Anton Grünwald, and Michael Wilshire. None of the many searches uncovered so much as a trace of them.

Over the next few years, Tommy was often told that he was lucky to have caught the flu at just that time. He always replied by asking, "Is it lucky to be without my friends?" That proved to be a stumper for most people.

In 2011, Richard Gibson was retired, no longer the principal of Grant Elementary, but he came back every year for an event that had been started by Tommy Montrose: the Grant Elementary School Memorial Dodgeball Game.

Ricky, as he was still known to most people, felt privileged to talk to the students on Halloween, before the game. He felt he owed this to four friends of his, especially Tommy Montrose.

The story was just spooky enough to grab the children's attention.

He talked to them about safety on this night, and the tale that every child in town knew, of the three boys who disappeared on Halloween.

But it was the second part of the story that meant the most to Ricky. It was of Thomas Montrose, who as a high school student tutored Grant Elementary kids in the public library after school. He somehow roped Ricky and some other friends into doing it, too, which is probably why most of that group became educators.

Tommy Montrose didn't go to college. He enlisted immediately after high school, when he was seventeen, and went to Vietnam when he was eighteen.

On his first mission, he was taken prisoner with three other American soldiers when their Huey was shot down. All three of those men attended these events, every year.

They came to talk about Tommy. Every officer had been killed in the crash, they said, and without even thinking about it, they made Tommy their leader. He was the youngest among them, but he had seemed somehow to have wisdom beyond his years, and skills that went way beyond basic training.

It was Tommy, they said, who gave encouragement to his fellow prisoners, often telling them about the people he knew here in town, and what a fine place he lived in, and even about this dodgeball game. He kept their spirits up, telling them he was going to make sure they would live long enough to name their kids after him, because he was born for this. He wasn't just talk, as they learned, because he also planned their escape.

On the night of Halloween 1969, Tommy broke them out of their prison and led them to freedom. They were nearly back to their own lines when Tommy told them to go ahead, and stayed behind as they made their way to relative safety. He gave them a big smile and ran off into the jungle, making more noise than a rampaging water buffalo. It was the last time any of them saw him alive, although for a time they knew he was out there, because he distracted the enemy—who were much closer than any of them had guessed—with lights he had gathered from heaven knew where and by singing some crazy song in German, drawing the enemy away from his fellow soldiers' position.

Those men also explained why the black-and-white POW/MIA flag was still flying at Grant Elementary, and they swore Tommy Montrose would not be forgotten. Because of him, after the war, they all settled here. Because he had talked to them about how important it was to him that they take care of children here.

One was a state senator now, known for his legislation to protect children. Another a pediatrician. Another taught self-defense. And yes, they all had kids named Tommy, including the senator's only child, a girl.

They had all gone home now, as had the children and the teachers. It was Halloween, after all, and there were preparations to be made. Ricky would go home soon himself, but he lingered just a little longer.

Forty-two years since Tommy was gone, forty-nine since they had all been in sixth grade together. Ricky stood on the court where an amazing game of dodgeball had once been played, and remembered it in detail. The rules of the game had changed a bit since then, and the balls didn't sting the way the old ones did, which was probably for the best. These days, you could watch professionals making moves that nearly equaled Tommy's in YouTube videos. But for Ricky, even though he had been the first man out, there would always only be one dodgeball game worth remembering.

When he thought of it, he found a kind of peace. It was as if he were eleven again, and his friends were nearby, whole and happy and celebrating a sweet victory, cheering for a geeky kid who had always been the first out in every other game. Tommy and Mike had seen to that, too. Ricky smiled, and began to walk home.

One knight guarded the prince and kept him safe in his hidden kingdom. No one doubted his courage or his skill, nor did they fail to see how highly the prince valued him.

"Are you happy, Sir Thomas?" the prince asked him this day, as they approached a mown field.

"Yes," he answered honestly. "I am doing what I was born to do. And you, Your Highness?"

"Oh, yes. I am with the best of my friends. And today, of course, there will be dodgeball."

DEAD ON THE BONES

JOE R. LANSDALE

Joe R. Lansdale is the author of more than thirty novels and numerous short stories. He has written comic scripts and screenplays, including several for *Batman: The Animated Series*. His novella *Bubba Ho-Tep* was made into a cult film. He has received a number of awards, including the Edgar®; nine Bram Stoker awards, among them Lifetime Achievement; the Inkpot Award; and the Grinzane Cavour Prize for Literature. His novel *Cold in July* is filmed, and he was a producer on the film *Christmas with the Dead*, scripted by his son Keith Lansdale and directed by Terrill Lee Lankford. He is a member of the Texas Literary Hall of Fame and the Texas Institute of Letters, is Writer in Residence at Stephen F. Austin State University, and is the founder of the martial arts system Shen Chuan, Martial Science. He is a member of the International Martial Arts Hall of Fame and the United States Hall of Fame. He lives and works in Nacogdoches, Texas, where he lives with his wife, Karen.

It was solid night out there in the woods down by the river, but we had plenty of light 'cause there was a big fire built up in the middle of the clearing for just that reason, and there was a dozen kerosene lanterns hung in the trees. The trees was mostly willows, though there was some giant oaks, and I was under one of the oaks getting ready to clean three catfish that was going to be grilled up for supper.

Uncle Johnny said, "Now you skin them catfish out good," and he gave me a knife and a pair of pliers, then wandered toward the fire to pile on some big-sized logs.

I ain't one to love cleaning fish, but at least catfish you don't have all them scales, like a bass or such. You can hang them up and make a cut around the head and take the pliers and pull the skin off, like helping a lady out of a jacket.

Uncle Johnny got him a bottle of beer out of a tub of ice, sauntered back over. He had on a chambray shirt half buttoned up and some loose pants and boxing shoes he only wore on nights like this. Them boxing shoes had cost him a pretty penny. That was why he kept them stored in the closet most of the time. They wasn't for wearing around, but for boxing only.

He had cut his hair close to his head. He always cut it skin-close on fight nights. The firelight crackling and jumping lit it up like it had been shined with floor wax and a polish rag. I could see cuts here and there where he hadn't been smooth with the razor. It looked like the top of his head had been in a briar patch.

He said something about making sure to look inside the catfish guts when I broke them open, 'cause he had found some stuff in them that was mighty curious from time to time. He even had a pocketknife he said he'd cut out of one of them once, a long one with a yellow-bone handle. That was the one he'd given me to clean the fish with. It was a good knife, and I knew when I got the skins off the fish and touched the point of it to their bellies, they'd split open like a hot watermelon in the sun. I was thinking I'd love to stick it in him, see how he split open, on account of he may have found some stuff inside catfish, but that knife wasn't one of them. He ought to know I knew who it belonged to. I had sharpened it enough.

I don't think he cared. I think he just told that story because he liked to tell it, and maybe he half-believed it himself, and maybe it was just his way of messing with me. That knife had belonged to my Pap. Pap told me someday he was going to give it to me, and I thought about saying something about it, but figured it might not be the thing to do. Not the smart thing anyway.

If Johnny would kill my Pap, I figured he might kill me too. Mama wasn't all that fond of me either, when you got right down to it. She put Uncle Johnny over me and Pap. I guess it could be she was scared of him, and I could understand that. I was scared of him, and everyone else was too.

There was good reason. He was big and strong and in plenty good shape and had a temper like hot water about to boil. I had actually seen him run a wild boar down once, jump on it and kill it with a knife, and it trying to get its tusks in him. It had already killed two of Uncle Johnny's dogs, which is what made him so mad. He didn't care for much, but he loved them dogs. As for Mama, he had wanted her because he didn't have her. Once he got her, he didn't want her, least not all the time. Everyone knew he had other women. Everyone knew he had killed several men and one woman, and there was rumor of a child. A baby that was drowned. One of the men he killed was a lawman that came after him, and the woman that was killed was his first wife. It was pretty well understood, if not proved, that he and Mama had killed my Pap.

Like I said, there was good reason to be scared.

Uncle Johnny stood over me for a moment, a bottle of Jax in his hand, sipping at it like a kitten at its mother's tit, then said, spraying me with beer breath, that I ought to hurry on up, 'cause the grease was hot and the cornmeal was ready to roll the fish in.

I had the three catfish hung up on a limb by a rope run through their gills, and they was huge. I had a kerosene lantern dangling from a nubbin of a limb, broken off by drought and wind, and I was working mostly by that light. I took the lantern down from time to time to hold up next to the fish to make sure I was doing the job right. One alone would have made a meal for five or six, but we had three of them, all of them caught by Uncle Johnny. He had snagged them out of the river that day. They had been kept fresh on lines that let them hang in the water and swim about. I ain't stretching it too much to say them fish was as big as me, and I'm twelve years old and pretty tall and solid of weight. Smaller catfish are supposed to taste better, but when Mama Mooney rolled the cuts of them fat old fish in cornmeal with salt and pepper, put them in a big cooking pot full of boiling, hot grease, it would all come out sweet and tender as the first breath of spring.

While I was working, I could see the grown-ups starting to drive down there in the bottoms. In bad wet weather they couldn't have done that. The river would have been all the way up to the woods and the dirt road, and sometimes over it.

I watched them get out of their cars and trucks and gather around the fire that was too hot for the night but gave plenty of light. They gathered and greeted each other. There was a lot of them, which was how it was expected, this being about the only thing around to do outside of squirrel hunting or drinking potato skin liquor.

Mama was there too, of course. Her long blond hair hung way down her back and she had on a long dress, the way Pentecostals are supposed to wear, but it fit her a little tight, and when she moved she moved like a fish in its skin. I figured there was plenty of Pentecostal men that night would look at her and think of sin, which I figured fit since they was also drinking. Of course, what they had all come to see didn't have much to do with religion either.

There was side dishes brought by all the ladies. Shelled corn, beans and breads, casseroles, pies and cakes, and all manner of fixings. I watched as they stacked them on a row of long plank tables. The men and their wives had also brought gifts for Conjure Man, and those they laid out on a table that had been put away from the food and the fire. The gifts was in brown sacks or wrapped up in newspaper.

I was right seriously scared of Conjure Man, on account of not only how he looked, but because of what he could do. I was scared of Uncle Johnny, but I was more scared of Conjure Man, and nervous about what I was going to be seeing.

When I had the fish cleaned, their guts spilled out on the ground, I checked through their innards by using a stick to push them around, but there wasn't nothing inside them that interested me. Only thing was one of them had swallowed an old white china cup with blue flowers painted on it. It wasn't broke up even a little bit, until Uncle Johnny came over, saw it lying by the bluish intestines of the fish, stepped on it, and smashed it. He didn't like nothing that was whole. Anything like that, a cup, a person, he wanted to break it.

"Ain't them cleaned yet?" he said.

"They got to be filleted," I said, "that's all that's left to it."

"I can see that. Get 'em on over to the cutting table," he said. "Quit messing around."

He took a gulp of his Jax and went back to the fire. Pretty soon I could hear all of them men and women talking amongst one another about this and that, but mostly about the Depression that was going on, and how the president said all we had to fear was fear itself. One man said, "Yeah, that and starving to death."

That might be, but wasn't nobody going to starve this night. I pulled the fish one at a time off their hanging lines and carried them to the cutting table where Mama Mooney was. She was smooth skinned and black as the night. She was meaty and always smelled sweet like honeysuckle. I asked her about it once. She said it was her soap. That it was made with ash and hog lard or bacon squeezings, and sometimes store-bought lye. Said she broke honeysuckles into it when she made it, or mint when she had that, and sometimes both. She said if she didn't do that, the bacon squeezings she used to make the soap would make her smell like breakfast. She said that wasn't entirely a bad thing. Her husband liked it.

Mama Mooney had already started cutting up the catfish when Uncle Johnny came over. He was impatient and nervous, getting ready for what was to come. "You getting it done, auntie?"

"Yes, sir, Mr. Johnny," she said. "I'm working on it right smart."

"Get on it smarter," he said. "We got a crowd here already and more coming."

"Yes, sir," she said, as if she was getting paid a king's ransom instead of five dollars.

I seen then Uncle Johnny had a look on his face that made me feel uncomfortable. He had that Jax half-lifted to his mouth, and was watching the younger girls that had come with their folks and was helping lay out the food. They was maybe thirteen or fourteen.

"Looks like them girls is getting pretty near ripe," Uncle Johnny said.

I felt cold all over. Mama Mooney reached out and got me by the elbow, said, "You come on over here and help me sort out these cuts of fish."

Me and Mama Mooney took the fish she had rolled in her mix of cornmeal and spices, and dropped them carefully into the boiling pot of grease so it didn't splash up on us and burn our skin to the bone. It wasn't hardly no sooner than them cuts was in the grease, than they was fried and Mama Mooney was scooping them out with a wooden ladle long as me.

She dipped the fish out and put them in large bowls on the cook table.

She filled bowl after bowl after bowl. Fact was, we run out of bowls and had to put some of the fish out on a white tablecloth folded up thick on the far end of the table. The chunks stained the tablecloth and filled the air with a sweet, hungry smell. My mouth watered.

It was time to eat, and a little later on would be the Conjure Man.

My Pap was a bad-luck fella, and he wore that bad luck like a suit coat on a bum. He treated me all right, though. He worked hard at the cotton gin, but the job wasn't good like it had been 'cause the cotton crop was smaller, and what things was made from cotton wasn't selling like they once was. Folks didn't have money and were making do with what they had, so the need for cotton wasn't as high as it might have been, least not at the gin where Pap worked. They gave him fewer hours, and this meant he worked a lot of pickup jobs while Mama stayed home, such as it was, and painted her nails and read magazines and was messing around with Pap's brother, my Uncle Johnny.

Now, I didn't know this right away, though I reckon Pap did, but didn't say nothing. I never could understand that. Guess he was so in love with Mama he wouldn't dare to say anything 'cause that would make it real. As for me, I have to say I didn't much care for her, even if she was my mama. She didn't like me neither. I think it's 'cause I look just like Pap.

I found out about her and Uncle Johnny one afternoon when I come in from the river, fishing for our supper. I brought the fish I'd cleaned into the house, heard moaning, the kind you might make when you sat yourself down in a washtub full of clean, hot water.

I saw what was making the moaning pretty quick, 'cause our house wasn't so big you had to hunt for anybody. The door to the bedroom was wide open, and there was Mama and Uncle Johnny on the bed, neither of them with a stitch of clothing on, and what Uncle Johnny was doing to Mama wasn't the sort of thing you'd mistake for a fella trying to help someone get a cinder out of their eye.

I knew enough about farm animals to have that figured, but there I stood, statue-stiff, watching, and then Uncle Johnny looked up and seen me, and smiled. Just smiled like wasn't nothing going on that anyone ought to be concerned about. I took myself and my fish out of there and started walking, and somewhere along the way I just tossed them clean fish and the pail they was in to the side of the road. I don't remember how long I walked. Finally I came back and there was Pap's old car in the yard, him home from work, and when I went in the house he was sitting in a chair, looking as if a rain cloud was right over his head and it was about to blow water and drown him.

Uncle Johnny and Mama was sitting at the table eating some corn-bread with honey, and wasn't neither of them mindful of Pap or me. It was right then I knew Pap knew what I knew. I don't know that he found them in the same way I did, but I think they just told him and said for him to get over it. Pap was like that. He could take a lot and would. He wasn't really a strong person like his brother, Johnny. He just didn't have it in him to be forceful. He was strong all right. I had seen him lift the back end of a car up and hold it while a fella changed a tire, and he could bend a tire iron until it darn near looked like a horseshoe, but in his head and heart he wasn't strong. That part of him the wind could blow away.

Mama finally looked at me, and when she did, the look on her face was so odd it made me uncomfortable. Pap got up slowly, walked over to me, put a hand on my shoulder, and before I knew it he was guiding me out the door and to the car.

He drove us out in the country. The trees were high and green and the hills rose up and were split by the red clay roads. We drove on and on, and sometimes we drove back the way we had come, and on out again.

The night came down and the moon went up and we kept driving, out on the bad clay roads, on through the shadowy woods, and down to the edge of the Sabine River. Pap got out of the car and walked over and stood on the bank. I walked down there with him. The river smelled like wet dirt and fish and rotten things. There was on either side of us some tall reeds growing and there was a little bit of wind. The wind rattled the reeds and whistled in between them in a way that could make your hide stand up off the bone.

Pap stood there and looked at that brown, moonlit water like it was calling to him, like he wanted it to swallow him up and wash him away, as if it were the River Jordan wanting to carry him wet and quick, way on out to the Promised Land.

I reached out and took his hand. His fingers wrapped around mine, and he turned and looked at me. The moonlight glistened off the wet stains on his cheeks and made his eyes glow like a deer's. He smiled. It was a slow smile, and he had to fish for it, but he hooked it and pulled it up.

Without saying a word he went back to the car, climbed into the front seat, stretched out, closed his eyes, and crossed his hands over his chest like a dead man. I got in the backseat and lay there and waited on him to say something, anything, but he didn't say a word. I could hear him breathing, though, so I knew he was alive.

After a time the moon got sacked by some clouds and there was a rumbling of thunder and a skywide slash of white lightning made the sky brighten up. That lightning cracked so loud it was like someone had taken a whip to the roof of the car. When it cracked I hopped up a little and made a noise, and Pap said, "That's all right, son. It ain't gonna hurt you none. You try and sleep."

"Okay," I said.

I lay back down.

Pap said, "You know what's going on, don't you?"

I said I did, and he said, "That's too bad, son. It really is. But you're old enough to know sometimes things are just what they are and not what you want them to be, or what they ought to be, and then you got to decide if you're going to put up with it. I been putting up with it a long time, but today they're telling me to put up with it. It's one thing to put up with it, another to be told to put up with it."

I was a little confused on that at first, but finally it come to me what he meant. I lay there waiting for more, but there wasn't any more. I watched the lightning for a long time, listened to it pop and crackle, listened to the thunder pound and roar, and then there was the rain. It fell down on the car roof, and at first it was loud, but then it got a kind of evenness to it, and that caused me to close my eyes. With my eyes closed I could still hear the thunder and the sizzle of lightning. Now and then there was such a hot blast the light came right through my eyelids.

But I didn't open them. I just lay there, and pretty soon, lightning or no lightning, thunder or no thunder, I was asleep.

In the morning, when I woke and sat up, the rain was gone. Pap was sitting up in the front seat with the window down. The air was turning warm and steamy from the rain, and flies had come into the car and were buzzing around. I waved my hand at them to keep them off my face. Pap shooed them out of the car window, and when they was all out, he rolled up the window and we sat there for a bit. With the window rolled up it was terrible hot, so Pap started up the car and drove us away.

I climbed up front with him as he drove. We rolled down our windows and let the wind come in then, 'cause the flies couldn't, not at the speed we was driving, which was pretty damn fast on wet clay roads. Finally Pap slowed down and drove right. We came off the clay roads and onto a gravel road and rode into town.

Pap drove us to the café, which was something we hardly ever done. We went inside and he ordered up some coffee and breakfast, and while we ate, Pap said, "I once fought your Uncle Johnny. We was both wanting to box. We fought each other all over the place. I had some skill, more than him. I was stronger and the same quick as him, but I didn't have no backbone. Still don't. When it came to the getting place I didn't get any. I gave in because I couldn't stand it and didn't want to stand it. My will wilted like a flower in winter. I ain't one to care much for my brother right now, and haven't cared much for him in a long time, but what I want to say to you is you got to have backbone, not be like me. It ain't got me nowhere in life, not having any. You don't got to be mean or cruel or just wrong acting like your Uncle Johnny, but you might want to get that other part, the backbone, and wear it up tight under your skin."

"Pap," I said, "it's you I want to be like."

Pap didn't seem to hear what I said. He sat there with the coffee still full in his cup, his food untouched. He said, "I tell you what. I'd like one more crack at Uncle Johnny, gloves on, or gloves off. Just a hard, square fight, and not even square, now that I think about it, but a fight to the death, 'cause I think maybe now I could find some backbone."

That was the last real conversation we had, 'cause a few days later they found him dead and dumped out by the river with a bullet in the back of his head. Wasn't no way to prove it, but I knew, and everyone else knew, it was Mama and Uncle Johnny that had done it, Johnny being the one to pull the trigger. With Pap shot in the back of the head I got to figuring maybe Uncle Johnny didn't have all that much backbone after all. But then there were fights, and who he fought went against that thinking, because so far he had fought Bob Fitzsimmons, Gentleman Jim Corbett, and John L. Sullivan, who gave him the best fight, 'cause he was more like a street brawler and strong too. He had fought them all and won, and them wasn't men you fought if you didn't have no backbone; you fought them that backbone had to be made of steel.

No one was at the funeral or the grave burying besides me and a preacher and the colored folks that worked with Pap at the cotton gin. One of the men when he come by me at the grave, said, "Your daddy was all right. He was a good man."

I thought maybe he was too good. So good he didn't have that backbone he said he needed.

Right after that I went home and got to thinking on how I could kill Uncle Johnny. I wasn't feeling all that favorable toward Mama neither. This went on for a year, me thinking, and watching my back, 'cause I didn't know for sure I wasn't next. I didn't stay at home any more than I had to, to sleep mostly, 'cause that's where my bed was, on the screened-in back porch. But I slept nervous. It was like the sheep in the Bible that was supposed to lie down with the lion. He might do that, but I figured he'd keep an eye open, and that was me, one eye open. And maybe like the sheep, I lay there thinking on how to kill the lions in my life. I was thinking on this one night, lying in my bed on the back porch, when Pap came to see me.

He came and sat on the edge of the bed. The front of his head was all torn open where the bullet had come out of it. He said, "I had one more straight-out crack at Johnny, I could take him."

I said, "I know, Pap," though I didn't know no such thing at all. And then he was gone. I wondered was I dreaming. But I felt wide awake. I got out of bed, went to breathe the air through the porch screen. It seemed like real air. The moths that were clinging to the screen wire seemed real. I pinched myself. I was awake all right.

I figured it was Pap come back from the grave, and not a dream. It was easy for me to believe that, because I had seen Conjure Man and what he could do, so it wasn't much of a jump to think Pap had come on out from behind the veil to speak to me.

I waited for him to come back, but he didn't never show.

When we finished up eating the catfish and all the sides we wanted, the men took to whiskey flasks, or pulled Jax Beer from a tub of ice, and everyone set about digesting. I hadn't felt hungry at first, but the smell of that cooking fish had made my belly gnaw, and I had eaten my fill.

I noticed the men was starting to check their pocket watches. It had to be getting along time for Conjure Man and the bout. And sure enough, it wasn't five minutes later that I heard Conjure Man's old truck, its loose parts clanking along the road, its motor grumbling like a hungry lion. As the sound came nearer you could see the women was looking nervous and the men was trying not to. Only Uncle Johnny seemed solid, like that backbone of his, the one Pap had talked about, had latched in tight and was packed with fire.

Conjure Man's old black truck come into view and along with it a cloud of red dust, and the dust crawled around that truck like a dusty snake. The truck drove on past the crowd and parked out by the table with all the gifts on it. The door creaked open and Conjure Man stepped out. Something inside the truck stirred but didn't come out, even though the door was left open.

Conjure Man was tall and thin and his skin was night-sky black. He wore a black hat, black shirt, pants, and coat, and black cowboy boots. It was as if him and that old black truck had peeled themselves out of the dark.

He had a clay jar under his arm, and he come along to the tables smiling. Not like no other colored, the ones that knew they best act a certain way around whites, but in a way my Uncle Johnny said was uppity, but he didn't never say that to Conjure Man.

Conjure Man seemed to float up close to the fire. He had a smell about him, sweet and sharp to the nose, like old flowers dying. Big blue-bottle flies came with him and made a halo around his head. He set that clay jar on the table with the food, and without a word to nobody, got himself one of the metal plates, a fork and spoon, went along picking up a little of this and that, heaping it on his plate. Now and again he'd pick something up and bite into it, frown, and toss it over his shoulder. After he had done that a couple of times, a big black dog with a head the size of a well bucket and a slink to its walk come out of the shadows of the truck, out of the open door, and loped over and took to eating what Conjure Man had tossed.

No one said nothing, just watched. Conjure Man finally had his plate the way he wanted it, and he found him one of the wooden chairs and set down and enjoyed it, got up when the plate was nothing but greasy, heaped some great spoonfuls of banana pudding onto it, sat back down and ate with a lot of smacking and smiling. When he was done, he tossed the plate on the ground and burped louder than a bullfrog. He went over and got him a couple of the Jax out of the ice tub, used the bottle opener on them. He drank one down like it was water, sipped on the other. It was then that he looked up and seemed for the first time to see everyone there.

He went over to the table that was laid out for him, looked through the sacks and boxes at the gifts that had been brought, and said, "Load 'em up."

That meant us kids was to take all the gifts and put them in the back of the truck. None of us wanted to do that, because we knew what lay in the bed of the truck, but we had to do it. It was the way things got started, and what was in the pickup bed wasn't going to do us no harm, nor anyone else, least not yet.

We started doing that, and the dog went with us, making me nervous, on account of I figured he could rear up and grab my head in his teeth and pull it off. But all he did was get back in the truck and lay down. When we had all the gifts in the truck bed, laid out away from the thing in the middle that was covered in oilcloth, we went back to the others, and we didn't waste no time doing it.

Conjure Man finished his beer and got the clay jar, walked over to the clearing, said, "So, you all ready there, Johnny Man?" Had any colored man other than Conjure Man called him anything but Mr. Johnny, or sir, he'd have killed him. But Conjure Man had what Uncle Johnny wanted, and he was afraid of him too. Conjure Man had the darkness on his side, and he had a voice like someone who had just chewed and swallowed a mason jar, and that was something that gave you pause; you couldn't help but think that voice was coming from someplace way down deep, so deep it went all the way into the ground.

"I'm ready," Uncle Johnny said. "I ate light and drank one, so I'm ready."

That's pretty much what he always said when Conjure Man asked him if he was ready.

I stood by Mama Mooney. She put her arm around my shoulders, and it made me feel good and warm in a way didn't have nothing to do with the summer heat. It was the way I figured a child ought to feel when his mama was nearby, and that mama was worth something.

The clearing was wide and surrounded by the tables of food. In the center of the clearing the dirt was worn from the shuffling of feet, for people had been coming here for bouts for a long time, bouts between men, and then the kind of bouts that Uncle Johnny fought. Pap always said he ought not to be messing with such things 'cause it couldn't have any good kind of ending. That was of course when Pap still tried to like his brother, even though he knew he wasn't worth the powder it would take to blow his ass up.

Now, let me tell you something here, so you'll know, as an old man down at the feed store says. Souls don't go to heaven or hell. Whatever is inside of us just goes, and when it gets where it is, it's just some place neither happy or unhappy. It's just a place. Pap explained all of this to me once, 'cause Conjure Man explained it to him, way back, and how that talk between them come about I got no idea.

Pap said Conjure Man said all the souls that have ever lived and died are in this place between times and spaces, and someday our souls will be there too, just drifting and floating and mingling. It's a good enough place, Pap was told. It ain't got no strife or worry, and what you done in life is without reward or punishment.

As for them souls, well, Conjure Man could call them up with the right spells. They was kind of like ghosts, but if you had a place for them to go, a body they could slip into, they could come back. Conjure Man could control them to some extent, but they sure didn't like being here on this earth, not after being nothing for a while. 'Cause when they come back they knew then the world was just a place where people was striving for this or that, or trying to get with this man or woman, or trying to take hold of some money, or get a new hat or drive a new car, always wanting this or that, and from their new point of view wasn't none of that worth spit.

So what Conjure Man done is he made it so people that liked to box could get their chance to fight the greatest that ever lived. He'd find a dead body about the size of the boxer in question, say his stuff, and that soul would come whistling into that body with all its old skills. What had to be done then was to get the fighter in front of that dead man with the soul stuffed in him, and let them go at it. See who was the better man.

Uncle Johnny had fought them fighters in them dead bodies, and he had always won, though like I was saying about John L. Sullivan, he had his time with that one, and after the fight he was laid up for nearly six weeks. Back then I kind of thought a little more of Uncle Johnny, 'cause he wasn't bothering Mama. But it was after that fight, after her seeing him fight, that she got the fixation. The need to breed, as I heard one man say when he saw Mama crossing the street and didn't know I was listening.

The fights was private, but there was plenty knew about them, and bets were made on who would win. Lots voted for Uncle Johnny, but lots would vote tonight for the shade of Jack Johnson, who was said by many to be the best there ever was.

Out in the crowd was the general store owner, the banker, the owner of Little Beaumont's Four Star Café, housewives and farmers, a preacher or two, a teacher, and a mayor. Except for Mama Mooney and Conjure Man, everyone was white.

So Conjure Man takes that clay pot, sets it on the ground, takes off the lid, picks up a stick, pokes it inside and stirs something around. Whatever it was, it had a smell like a ripe outhouse. The stink filled the air, made it heavy as lead.

Conjure Man bent his face toward the mouth of the jar and spat a long, sticky stream of tobacco into it, and put the lid on it, plugging the stink inside. He yelled out toward his truck, "Come on over, Dead On The Bones. Come on over and into the light. Walk from the grave and out of the night. Come on over, Dead On The Bones."

Then it happened like it always did. The air turned chill and our breath puffed, and that didn't make no sense, it being dead summer, but that's how it was. I could feel Mama Mooney's arm around my shoulders shake with the cool, and she made a noise in her throat that reminded me of a scared dog under a porch.

Conjure Man's truck shook a little and then the oilcloth raised up as what was under it sat up. The cloth fell off it then, and there was the dead man. A big black man with shoulders wide as a milk truck, no shirt on.

Conjure Man called out again. "Come out of that shadow. Come out of that dead. Come out of that truck and into the light, you ole Dead On The Bones."

The dead man stood up in the bed of the truck, swung over the side of it in a way that was pretty brisk for a fella that had recently been dug up. That was how it worked when there was a fight. There was always a body, one that was fresh with no meat falling off, and no questions were asked. That made me wonder if a grave was robbed or a man was made dead with a blow to the head or a sip of a poisoned drink.

But right then I was just thinking about what I was seeing. A dead man stumbling toward our camp, walking like he had one foot in a bucket and one made of lead. The hair on the back of my neck pricked up and chill bumps crawled up and down my arms like a nest of ants.

Dead On The Bones walked between the tables and into the firelight. He wasn't wearing nothing but pants held to his waist by a rope for a belt. His bare feet kicked up dust as he came. When Dead On The Bones was in the clearing where the fights took place, Conjure Man said, "Stop them bones."

Dead On The Bones stopped, weaving a little, like a drunk trying to make the world quit spinning and find which way was up and which way was down. The firelight licked over his black skin, made it glow like a wet chocolate bar, made his flat, dead eyes seem almost alive. He was a young man, but he had lived and died rough. His face was pocked and there was a dent in his forehead.

Conjure Man cackled, took the stick he had stirred in the jar, used it to make a scratch line in the dirt in front of Dead On The Bones, then he made one where Uncle Johnny would stand.

The crowd moved. We was standing still one moment and the next we was making a circle around Dead On The Bones. Uncle Johnny stripped off his shirt and stepped up to his scratch line and took a deep breath.

"You know who I want," he said to Conjure Man.

"You want Jack Johnson. You want him in his prime. You want the man that might be the greatest boxer who ever lived. Him who beat a big white man like a circus monkey. Him that knocked out teeth and danced on his toes. Him that was quick as lies and strong as truth."

"Get on with it," Uncle Johnny said.

Conjure Man took Uncle Johnny's words like piss in the face. He turned his head slowly, glared at Uncle Johnny. I saw a flicker in Uncle Johnny's eyes. He had forgotten who he was speaking to. Conjure Man wasn't no field hand. Conjure Man didn't have any rules he had to live by, except his own. Conjure Man didn't have to say *Yes, sir*, and *Thank you kindly*, and Uncle Johnny knew that.

"I'm ready," Uncle Johnny said, and he was so polite for a moment I forgot who he was.

"All right, then," Conjure Man said. "We gonna do it on my own time, when I get to it and say when. You understand them rules that are mine?"

"That's fine," Uncle Johnny said, then tagged it with: "Appreciated."

Conjure Man relaxed. He was about his business, and I had seen his business before. Conjure Man would pick up the clay pot, take off the lid, and let that damn smell out. Then he'd lean forward and bathe his face in it. The wind would come from all its corners, come in cold and wet and through the trees, and howl like a wolf with its leg in a trap. Then Conjure Man would lean forward and call into that jar, call out the name of the one he wanted, and there would be a noise like all the world had done cracked open, and out of that jar would blow a mess of bluebottle flies, same as them that circled Conjure Man's head like he was an old cow pie. With them flies would be a thick blue cloud. Flies and cloud would jump on the dead man's head and sink right in. When Dead On The Bones lifted his chin he'd be Dead On The Bones no more, but a rotting body full of someone yanked on out from the big beyond.

I don't really remember doing it, but somehow I eased around in that crowd and got closer to Conjure Man. Closer than anybody, 'cause wasn't no one wanted to be that near him. He cocked his right eye toward me, and studied me. His eyes didn't have no whites because they was red with blood, and his black eyes had what looked to be gold streak from top to bottom, like someone had cut them down the center and found light behind them.

That eye that was watching me flicked away. Conjure Man picked up the clay pot, took off the lid, and, like he always did, stuck his face right over the jar. Oh, Lordy, that stink come out of there strong enough to lift a Buick, came out and wrapped all around Conjure Man's big old head. I felt the wind stirring. I could hear the branches creak and the leaves rustle. Then he spit the wad of tobacco he was chewing into the jar. I seen then that he was about to shout Jack Johnson's name.

I don't know I had a real idea I was going to do it before I did it, but I leaped forward, snatched the jar away from Conjure Man, stuck my face down into that stink, and yelled out my Pap's name.

Well, now, that stink punched me in the face and knocked me backward. I dropped the jar and it broke. The wind stirred up where the jar fell, and then there was more wind that came whistling cold and full from all four corners of the earth. That wind from everywhere was full of the stink in that jar and it had with it that blue cloud and those big, fat flies. The force of them winds and all that came with them dove right down onto Dead On The Bones, hit him in the top of the head with a sound like a slaughterhouse hammer smacking a big hog's head. Then there wasn't no wind and there wasn't no stink, no blue cloud and no fat flies.

All that business had gone inside him.

Dead On The Bones lifted his head and smiled.

Dead On The Bones looked at me and chuckled. I knew that chuckle. It was the kind Pap had when he caught a fish, or gave me a smile. He had done come on out of that place for souls, and he was right there in that dead man's body, one toe on the scratch line. He looked then in the other direction, saw Mama standing there, holding a beer in her hand, and when he looked at her, she knew, 'cause she dropped that bottle of beer and it busted on the ground.

Pap chuckled again, looked straight ahead at Uncle Johnny.

"That can't be you," said Uncle Johnny.

Pap opened his Dead On The Bones mouth and tried to speak, but all he had was a gurgle.

"Do something," Uncle Johnny said to Conjure Man. "Send him back. This ain't the right man."

"No, it isn't," said Conjure Man. "But he won't go back until he's good and done. So you better fight, or you better run."

"I don't run," said Uncle Johnny. "I beat him before, and I'll beat him again. Go on, let it rip."

Dead On The Bones had his foot on the scratch line, ready to go. Uncle Johnny got set, and Conjure Man yelled, "Fight."

They shuffled toward each other, gathering up dust beneath their feet.

It started out like a bout. Uncle Johnny came in like a bull, and Pap shot out a left and hit him on the nose, then hooked a right into his body. Uncle Johnny slammed his shots home, and the thing was, Pap could feel it. Dead On The Bones didn't feel nothing, but Pap, his spirit, it felt it, and it made the dead body bend a little. Then Pap was back at it. He hit again and again, with lefts and rights, uppercuts and hooks, all kinds of combinations. At first Uncle Johnny did just fine, held his own. But then on came Pap, using that dead body like it was his, smashing and hitting, and finally there wasn't no rules anymore, and it wasn't a boxing match, it was a fight to the death.

They was slamming and jamming against one another, and though Pap's borrowed body couldn't bleed, you could see it was getting tired, same as a living man. Uncle Johnny was tired too. They clinched, and Uncle Johnny had his mouth close to Pap's ear, and I could hear him say, "For me, when we did it, she sang like a bird."

I heard that just as clear as a gunshot, and I reckon everyone else out there did too. I know when he said it Mama stepped back, crunching that broken beer bottle with her flat-heeled shoes.

"Your problem," Uncle Johnny said, "is you ain't got no backbone when it comes right down to it."

Pap made a noise like a growl, butted his head into Uncle Johnny's face, pushed him back with his left palm, and swung his right in a short, sweet arc. Uncle Johnny took it right on the nose. Blood sprayed and Uncle Johnny staggered. Then came a left uppercut to Uncle Johnny's chin; it hit so hard Uncle Johnny's head flew up and there was a snapping sound, like someone had broken a green limb over their knee.

Pap grabbed Johnny's shoulders and kneed him in the potatoes. Uncle Johnny tried to clinch, but Pap wouldn't let him. He'd dance back and jab, his raw knuckles cutting Uncle Johnny's face up like he was using a razor.

On this went until Uncle Johnny got savage brave and come running at Pap. Pap stepped to the side and kicked out and hit Uncle Johnny in his left thigh with his shin. Uncle Johnny tripped and cussed and fell flat on his face.

He was trying to get up when Pap got him around the neck with that borrowed, dead man's arm, and squeezed his neck so hard that within a moment it looked like a deflated inner tube. Then there was a cracking sound like a wishbone being pulled, and then Pap got Uncle Johnny around the waist, lifted him up so his head was down, marched to the fire, and stuck Uncle Johnny's limp head right into the still-hot cooking grease. The air sizzled and there was a smell like bacon in a pan.

Pap held him like that for a while, then lifted him out of the grease and tossed him aside.

He turned then toward Mama.

She trembled. She said, "Now, Phil, you don't want to do nothing. It's you I love."

But Pap did want to do something. He come charging toward her on those dead legs. She tried to mix in with the crowd, but they weren't having that. They didn't want no part of Pap. He came and they spread, and there she was, standing lonely as the last pine in a lumberjack run. She stood there like she was nailed to the spot. And then he had her. He picked her up by the waist, raised her high.

She looked down at him, he looked up at her.

I thought for a moment he was going to put her down, but he turned his head toward the fire and smiled, and ran right at that big ole blaze of crackling logs and sputtering fire, leapt right in with his heart's desire, dropped her on her back, and lay down on top of her. The scream she let out was almost enough to make me feel sorry for her, but not quite.

They squirmed there, overturning that grease pot. The hot grease splashed onto them and over them and the fire lapped it up.

The flames spread, ash and sparks flew. That fire wasn't like any fire I've ever seen. It ate them right down to the bones in seconds, burned the bones black, turned them to a powdery ash. A blue cloud swarming with flies and blown by wind lifted out of the blaze and climbed on high, rode on up in front of the moon, weaved there like a drunk storm cloud, and then it was all gone and the air was still and the world was so quiet you could have heard a gnat clear its throat.

After a while Conjure Man said, "Well, I guess that's all for the festivities, and now it's time for me to go. Thanks for the presents. Thanks for the food. I got the bets in my pocket, and I plan to keep them. You want entertainment, you know where to find me. If you want a spell to cure up that constipation, or make some man or woman love you like they was insane, you come see me. And bring your money."

He walked on out to his truck without nobody asking for their bets back. That big black dog come out of the truck and met him, licked his hand. They climbed inside, the engine got started, the lights came on, and away they went, clattering over the pasture and onto the road, driving around a wall of trees and out of sight.

People headed out of there quick like, leaving the food, the beers, the whole kit and caboodle. In a moment's time the place was clear of everyone but me and Mama Mooney and her old car nestled up under a heavy old willow.

She said, "You ought to come home with me, sugar."

"I appreciate that," I said. "I sure ain't going back to our place. But I'm moving on, Mama Mooney. I'm moving on away from this place, going just as far as I can. I'll catch a train, I'll hitch a ride, I'll walk at night and sleep in the day, under a tree if I have to. But I'm away from the place, and away for good."

She gave me a smile and a soft pat on the shoulders, and that's how it was. Over and done.

I got hold of Uncle Johnny's shirt, 'cause I knew he had some money stuffed up in his pocket, a handful of bills. That was my seed money. I put it in my pocket with Pap's knife that I had hung on to, and then

Mama Mooney drove me to the wide gravel road, gave me a hug and a kiss, and I got out.

She drove one way, I walked the other.

It was still night, the moon was bright, and I felt good about what I had done. I walked on and pretty soon Pap was walking beside me. I could hear his feet crunching on the gravel, same as mine.

He looked like he always had, except for his head being broken open in front. He said, "I showed them, didn't I?"

"You did," I said. "You showed them good."

"You're gonna be all right, son," he said. "You gonna be fine."

"I know," I said, and then he was gone.

I walked on.

THE DEVIL WENT DOWN TO BOSTON

CAITLIN KITTREDGE

Caitlin Kittredge is the author of the Black London series, the Iron Codex trilogy, and the Nocturne City novels as well as a number of short stories and coauthored works. Her YA novel *The Iron Thorn* was a YALSA Best Book of 2012. A native of Massachusetts (Go Sox!), she conceived "The Devil Went down to Boston" as a tribute to the weird, seedy city of her childhood, which has mostly been pulled down and replaced with condos. Caitlin blogs rarely and tweets often; visit her at caitlinkittredge.com or twitter.com/caitkitt.

-1-

Ellie Keenan was twelve the first time she saw the Devil. He stood in the front room of her father's third-floor apartment, the quietest floor of a quiet block on a quiet South Boston side street. Tall and thin, the Devil cast a tall thin shadow.

Ellie wasn't supposed to be awake. It was close to midnight, and her father's bottle of Johnnie Walker would have been empty for a while. No one in the family came out of their rooms when he got like that. Sean put on his headphones and disappeared into the world on his computer. Finn waited until Dad was too sloshed to hear him and climbed down the back porch to go to his own party.

Ellie hid. She was the youngest and the smallest and curled herself up in a tight ball. She watched the shadows on her bedroom wall. The wallpaper was older, older than any of them. Cartoon cowboys and smiley-faced cacti, lassos and boots and sheriff's stars. Boy wallpaper.

Worn-out and wrong for them, just like everything else in the crappy apartment. Like everything else on the street, and the street after that, until you drove out of Southie and into a better part of the city.

But that night, Ellie heard the front door open and shut. She thought the cops might be bringing Finn back, like they did some nights. She crept down the hall, avoiding the screeching boards under the balding carpet. Peered through the pocket doors that never quite shut because they were so warped from damp.

And she saw the Devil. Saw him stand in front of the fireplace that produced no heat but plenty of drafts. Saw him lean on the dusty mantel that held a collection of grimy picture frames blocked off by rows of whiskey bottles.

As Ellie crouched, fingers digging half-moons of dry rot out of the crooked door, she felt her stomach flip. Her dad wasn't a mean drunk, not really. He yelled and sometimes he slapped her but then he'd feel bad and cry, and tell her she was his whole life.

That was a lie. The only life, the only family Declan Keenan had ever known was the one he'd found in the streets. Those hard-eyed, hard-voiced men who came in and out of the apartment at all hours, who sent Ellie's dad home with cut knuckles and wads of wrinkled, nicotine-stained cash, he'd always come when they called.

Ellie knew what her father was, what she was, her brothers too. She knew why her mother had left. It wasn't a mystery. As long as there had been Irishmen in Boston, there had been the Folk among them. They came from all over Ireland, for all kinds of reasons, spilling off the boats in Boston Harbor, at Ellis Island, leaving behind the famine and the Troubles for a place among the regular people who surrounded them, only a few lengths below Ellie's feet.

The Devil handed her father a black fountain pen. It was old, and the point was silver. It looked like a beak, Ellie thought, the beak of something hungry, something that would swoop down and carry you off in its talons.

Declan Keenan took the pen. He was sober, no fresh bottle with a slick of brown whiskey rolling in the bottom anywhere to be seen. He sat on their sofa, the same spot he'd worn a groove in. "You promise me, now," he said. His voice was rough, like it was after he'd finished crying.

She'd heard him sound that way before, though not often—the time Finn had mouthed off, and Declan had broken his nose. Forgotten the gentle slaps he reserved for his children and treated Finn like one of the losers stupid enough to try to wriggle out of a debt to Blackie Farrell, the man who'd given Declan food and shelter when he'd come to America, nurtured his power from a spark into a flame, and given him a job. The man, as Dad often reminded Ellie, to whom they owed everything. Finn had let out a half yelp, rolling on the ground, blood gushing from between his fingers, and Declan had crumpled on the carpet beside him and sobbed.

Later, after Sean had taken Finn to the emergency room, Declan pulled himself up. "I didn't mean to," he told Ellie. She hadn't wanted to say anything back, so she pretended to watch TV until he passed out.

The Devil was at no such loss for words. "I promise," he said, and he smiled. His shadow got bigger, and longer. It reached up into the water-yellowed plaster of the ceiling and tried to worm into every corner. Under the sofa, across the floor, through the wreckage of Ellie's backpack and homework, searching for something.

Ellie drew back, pressing her hand over her mouth. She saw what her father, stoop-shouldered and broken, didn't. The Devil didn't have eyes. Where they should be was darkness, sucking holes that pulled in all the light around him, that would pull you right down like a riptide on a Cape Cod beach. She wanted to scream, to warn Dad not to do anything, just to run, but she pressed herself into a corner, silent and breathless, only able to watch.

Her father signed a single sheet of paper, which the Devil took and slipped into a black case. He straightened his black tie. His shirt was white, whiter than smoke, whiter than snow. "Pleasure doing business with a Folk talent of your caliber, Declan."

Her father pressed his head into his hands. Dark hair, lank and greasy and days since washing, hung over his fingers. "I just want my kids to be safe."

"Here's a tip for your next life," said the Devil as he snapped the case shut. The latches sounded like teeth to Ellie's ears. Click-clack-snap. "If you care so much about your offspring, don't steal from a man who breaks legs for the fun of it."

Ellie's dad didn't say anything. The Devil took his hat from the table and settled it low over his brow. It disguised those horrible eyes. It made him appear as if he had no face at all.

Ellie watched the Devil, still frozen as he stepped from the front room. He took his black greatcoat from the tree where Sean's Red Sox parka and her own thirdhand wool coat hung, damp and musty from melted snow. The Devil opened the door and stepped onto the balcony, wind pushing through the broken screens that enclosed the rails. Snow fell, thick and silent as pulling a blanket over your head, but not one flake touched him.

Ellie waited until the Devil shut the door. She heard no footsteps descend the creaking stairs to the ground, so she waited until gray light replaced the gold-tinged black of the streetlamps outside the dirty, salt-crusted windows. She stood up, feeling the cramps and the needle pricks work their way up and down her legs. She slid the pocket door open and peered into the dim front room. "Dad?"

He would not answer her. The paramedics told Sean, and Ellie heard them even though they were trying to be quiet, that he'd probably been dead since late the night before. "Right around the time the snow stopped," the man said, as another pulled a sheet over Declan's face.

There were no footprints on the stairs before the ambulance came. No mark on the dusty table where the Devil's hat had lain. No one except Ellie to say he'd even been there at all.

-2-

The day of her father's funeral, it rained. Ellie sat in the front pew of the funeral home, feeling damp work its way inside her dress shoes, cheap and shiny and black, pinching at her toes, which had grown at least a size too big since the last time she'd had any reason to be dressed up. Sean sat on one side, Finn on the other. Finn fidgeted and didn't stop until they were out of the service, in the car going to the reception. He went outside in the alley with some of the Keenan cousins and kicked the soccer ball back and forth against the brick wall.

Sean stood by the buffet table and accepted the handshakes and tearful hugs from the various family members. He'd called their mother, and she was coming, but Ellie figured it wouldn't be for long. Sean was eighteen. He could take care of them, and her mother would never come back to Boston. Especially not to take care of her three Folk children, in the same neighborhood she'd fought so hard to escape.

Ellie sat in the corner on a straight-backed chair, kicking her heels against the rungs. She wasn't supposed to even be in the pub, but nobody was going to say anything. She set up three paper cups from the open bar and stuck a dirty penny she'd found on the floor under one, moving the cups around each other, skipping the penny from one to the next, sometimes with her fingers and sometimes with magic. Her dad loved the game, had run it on a street corner when he was barely older than her. The penny was a Folk twist—most kids in the tradition learned how to manipulate their talent with metal, since it was easy to grasp onto and control. They used coins and nails and other small things until they progressed to harder stuff, bindings and spells and demon summonings.

Her stomach knotted. She hadn't told anyone what she'd seen. She'd promised she never would. Even among a crew as shady as Blackie's, what had happened to her father wasn't something anyone would approve of. Whatever it was. She'd never seen a demon, never met anyone who had. They were summoned for terrible bargains, and they were bound by the bargains they struck, yes, but they were still dangerous and would still get your skull cracked if a Folk boss caught you dealing with them.

She moved the cups faster and faster, until the motion almost hypnotized her, never letting her fingers falter, until she didn't need her fingers anymore, the magic popping the penny in and out of existence, moving from cup to cup so it would never be caught. She didn't look up until a shadow fell across her.

"My girl," Blackie Farrell said. He put a hand on her shoulder. His knuckles were lumpy with scar tissue from his time as a bare-knuckle fighter, and his nose and jaw were crooked.

She knocked a cup over, penny skittering away across the bar. Ellie squirmed out from under Blackie's hand. "Hi, Mr. Farrell."

He coughed. "Sweetheart, I'm not your school principal. Call me your Uncle Blackie."

Ellie nodded. "Okay." She didn't want Blackie Farrell near her, but she didn't have a choice. You didn't turn away from his goodwill, not if you wanted to keep breathing. Sean had an after-school job, but he'd need Blackie's help if they wanted to stay in the apartment, in Boston, and not get shipped off to California whether their mother wanted them to come or not.

"You want to see a trick?" Blackie said, producing a quarter from his pocket. "I got a lot of tricks I can teach you. Your da was always on about what a clever girl you are."

He was too close, his breath too hot and stinking of whiskey and cheap cigarettes and he was staring at her with an intensity that bothered Ellie. It wasn't creepy, not like those guys Sean warned her to stay away from in the park, but it was predatory all the same. Blackie had decided what she was good for, and Ellie didn't want to find out what that was.

"Leave her alone, Patrick," someone said from behind Blackie. He flinched at the use of his proper name and straightened up, glaring at the gray-haired figure standing a few feet away.

"Mind your own, Doyle. I'm just cheering the poor girl up."

"I think she'll be a lot more cheerful when you get out of her face." Ellie looked up at Doyle. She'd seen him around her father when she was young enough to actually be impressed by magic tricks, but less and less since she'd started middle school, and her dad had started drinking every night instead of just on weekends and nights the Patriots were losing.

Blackie muttered, but he left, going to Sean and pumping his hand. Doyle followed Ellie's gaze and patted her arm. "Don't worry. That brother of yours can handle himself."

His touch wasn't oppressive, so Ellie didn't try to escape. Doyle smiled at her. "I'm not going to show you a trick. I think you can do a few of your own."

Ellie blushed. She'd always liked Doyle—he was exotic, not one of the thugs her dad usually hung around. He spoke quietly, never bragged, and always wore the same green sweater with a hole in the elbow. He'd added a black sport coat for the funeral, but nothing else had changed.

"I thought you didn't like us anymore," she said. Doyle's mouth crimped.

"Your dad was a sick man, Ellie," he said. "A good man, but a sick man. I don't want you thinking less of him, so that's all I'll say. What I will say is this: There will be a time when Blackie Farrell is going to try to use you. You're talented, by far the strongest in the tradition of any of you three kids. You tell him no, all right? No matter what he offers you. Tell him to go straight to hell. If you need anything, you come see me."

Ellie nodded, thinking that Doyle was a little crazy if he thought Blackie would ever want anything from her. She was a girl; she wasn't strong like her brothers. Folk traditions were traditions—no girls allowed, not even talented ones. If Blackie wanted her, he'd want to marry her off to one of his many grandsons, produce strong talents that would sustain the Farrell stranglehold on their little corner of the world. She wasn't meant for a life on the streets, in a crew, using magic to bend the world their way. "I guess," was all she said.

Doyle wrote a phone number on the back of a bar napkin and handed it to Ellie. "I mean it. You get desperate, you don't go to Blackie. You come to me." He sighed. "Don't be like your father if you can help it, Ellie."

He left, and Ellie went to stand beside Sean. All at once, she was cold and just wanted to be near her brother. She shoved Doyle's number deep into her pocket and forgot all about it until the next day, when Sean insisted they wash their funeral clothes. She threw it out. Doyle might want to help, but he couldn't help Ellie beat the Devil.

-3-

Ellie watched four yuppies, two men and two women, stare at the inside of the Irish Rover like they'd just landed on Mars. Ellie didn't voice her thoughts aloud—didn't they have bars on Beacon Hill? Why come all the way to Southie if you were just going to gawk, order one beer and talk loud on your cell phone, so all the townies knew that you were important, rich, and didn't really belong here?

She just went back to washing pint glasses. Nobody paid to hear her opinion. They paid her to pour real Irish beer for half the price of a bar downtown, look good in a white T-shirt, and keep her mouth shut. There weren't many places, even in Southie, that would hire you with a record, and she needed the job if she wanted to keep her asshole PO happy. And if she wanted a roof over her head, since she sure as hell wasn't going to make any money the way the Folk usually did. Cheating, stealing, and small-time scams were off the table for the next three to five years.

The tallest of the yuppies swaggered over. "Four Guinness," he said, and tossed a twenty on the bar. Ellie took the bill silently and rang it in. There was a time when a jerk-off like that, flashing his cash, wearing expensive clothes, and acting like a moron, would have ended up in the alley behind the bar lying in a puddle of his own piss and wondering where his teeth had gotten to.

But this wasn't the Southie of twenty years ago. Hell, this wasn't even the Southie of ten years ago. Slowly but surely, gentrification crept in, like a reverse blight that turned the decaying triple-deckers into studios and single-family Victorians. Then came the chain stores, and before you knew it, check-cashing joints were replaced by gourmet coffee shops, and places like the Irish Rover added craft beer to their menu and got a web site.

Ellie brought the douchebags their beer, accepted the two-odd dollars in change she was presented as a tip, and went back to her station. When she looked up again, Sean was in front of her.

"What?" she said, because Sean never came to see her if he could help it. She'd stepped out of the Folk lifestyle after it sent her to Framingham, but Sean had opted out mere months after their dad died. Ellie was still close enough to the old crew to make Sean wary.

He grimaced and leaned more weight on his cane. "Finn," was all he said.

Of course it was Finn. It was always Finn. Ellie threw down her rag. It slapped the sink with a wet, hopeless sound. "It's not like I can exactly stroll out, Sean. I've got another three hours on my shift."

"I think people can survive without your beer-pouring skills for half an hour," Sean said. He grabbed her arm, and Ellie pulled away. "Ellie," Sean said, and his voice was quiet, not the usually hard-edged tone he liked to use with her. "It's bad."

Ellie sighed. "How bad?"

"Bad enough that I'm here," Sean said. "Now come on. Car's outside."

Ellie felt her stomach knot. Every midnight call had been about Finn, since she was eighteen. Every early morning freezing her ass off on some bench at the courthouse, waiting to hear how he was going to weasel out this time, and every day off wasted at the jail bringing him soap and toilet paper.

This felt different, though. "Let me just call someone," she said. She left a message for two of the other waitresses and then got her bag. She wished she still carried. She wished she hadn't tried to grow up, be responsible, when Sean came back like he was.

Sean drove them, even though Ellie knew it hurt. His leg was full of steel pins, a steel bone to replace the one pulped by the IED. He was lucky, everyone told Ellie over and over again. Lucky to be alive, lucky he didn't lose the leg. Lucky, lucky Sean.

When they drove into Roxbury, Ellie sighed. "You didn't tell me he was using again."

"It would be obvious to anyone with eyes," Sean said.

Ellie looked up at the row house Sean parked in front of. "This isn't just about drugs," she said.

"He's in the front room," Sean said. "He's waiting for you."

Ellie tried to ignore the litter-box stink that hit her when she stepped into the den, and the combination of plaster dust, plastic syringes, and asbestos tile that crunched under her boots.

Finn sat on a stained mattress, his head in his hands. Ellie sank down next to him. "Goddammit, Finn."

He looked up at her. His face was sunken, covered in stubble, and he stank almost as bad as the air around him. "I told Sean not to call you," he muttered.

"Well, you know Sean can't resist sticking his nose into everything we do," Ellie said.

Finn's shoulders jittered. "I messed up, Ellie," he said. "I mean, really, really messed up."

A door slammed at the rear of the house and Finn jumped. Ellie tried to keep breathing. She wasn't totally defenseless without a piece. She wouldn't freeze up. Not like she had the night Dad left them.

"Just tell me what happened," she said.

"I should have bet on the Jets," Finn said, and Ellie groaned.

"Don't freaking tell me you're gambling again."

"It was the Super Bowl!" Finn shouted. "I put down more than I should have, yeah, but I was gonna make it back." He sighed. "Then I got pinched."

"Yeah, I remember that," Ellie said. "You punched a guy for no reason, you went to jail. Not exactly rocket science, Finn."

"Anyway, I got this shark breathing down my neck. Civilian, at least, not Folk or I'd be hamburger. I met this kid in lockup—Frankie Bonnaro, you remember him?"

Ellie felt the urge to bang her own head against the wall. "Please tell me you did not let that ditch-dwelling *striga* talk you into doing something stupid."

Finn's silence said it all. Ellie shut her eyes, just for a moment. "How bad?"

"He said it would be foolproof. He wouldn't even notice the money was missing for a month."

"Who?" Ellie said. In the pause, a rodent skittered across the floor above, and someone moaned from a nearby room.

"He takes the drops from the first, but he has to keep them because his guy, his cleaner only comes by every few months. He has all this cash just sitting there in the back of his club, and Frankie's cousin is a safecracker."

Ellie jumped up, kicking over an empty plastic vodka bottle. "Finn! I don't give a shit about that. Tell me what's happening now."

"I took it," Finn said, and his voice slid into a sob. "But he had a camera and he found out." He sniffled. "Blackie found out."

Ellie felt the shock drop her, faster than any gut punch. If she hadn't had so much practice staying upright even when she wanted nothing more than to pass out, she would have collapsed.

"How much?" she whispered.

Finn flopped back on the mattress. "Thirty thousand."

-4-

Ellie let Sean drive Finn home. She walked for a bit, just to think. Half hoping somebody would try to start something with her so she could expel the knot of rage and helplessness that twisted around her gut like a snake.

The same feeling had been with her, in one form or another, for almost twelve years. Ever since Dad. Ever since that soft snow-covered night.

Eventually she got a city bus over to Blackie Farrell's turf. She was the only one who could maybe, possibly do something about this. Sean wasn't one of them anymore. He was as much an outsider as a cop.

Blackie ran his operation out of a dingy little club that might have been hot once, for a weekend or two in the early 1980s. Now it was just grimy tinted windows hiding stained carpet, broken-down booths, and the smell of stale beer and staler vomit.

Dingy and threadbare though it might be, Ellie didn't kid herself. This was still a dragon's den.

A big guy in a track jacket loomed up from a chair by the door to the manager's office. "Club's closed."

"Come on, Matty," Ellie said. "I look like I'm here to dance?"

Matty's face broke apart, much like a rock wall might when hit with a wrecking ball, and he grinned. Matty and Ellie had gone to high school together. He'd dated her best friend, Beth, before she married a Japanese guy and moved to L.A. Matty was a good guy—not a smart guy, not a guy with a bright future, but he wasn't a predator like most of the types Blackie kept around him.

"I thought you was legit now," he said. "Big fancy job and all. You own the restaurant yet?"

"You friggin' kidding me?" Ellie said. "I work sixty hours a week to make what we made in a couple of hours back in the day." She sighed. "I gotta see him, Matty. It's important."

"Yeah, might not be a great time." Her friend shifted from one foot to the other. His sneakers creaked under his girth. Matty was so huge, you'd never know he was a teddy bear. Most people never took the chance of finding out. Still, Ellie worried about him. Their life wasn't built to be kind. You had to be a real asshole to survive. Like Blackie Farrell. Like her dad, right up until the end. When Declan had gone soft, he'd died.

"I've seen Mr. Farrell in a bad mood before," Ellie assured him. "I'll be fine."

Matty grunted and stepped aside. Ellie tried to shake off the nausea that cropped up. *Stop it,* she told herself. Blackie Farrell wasn't the Devil. He wasn't even close.

He looked up from his laptop as Ellie shut the door, and she didn't give him a chance to talk. "I'm here to make things right with you and my brother."

"Eleanor, my girl." Blackie Farrell's accent was pure Dublin. He sounded like a kindly leprechaun, or your fun drunk uncle. His eyes were dark as his hair and stood in stark relief in his pale, lined face. He still had his brawler's temper, too, and it had let Blackie Farrell run his radius of blocks for as long as anyone could remember. The Folk could go on for centuries. They occasionally changed names, or pretended to be their own kids, but Blackie had never bothered.

"I know what Finn did," Ellie said. "I promise he'll pay you back, with interest."

"Now that's interesting." Blackie shut his laptop. "You don't even know what my terms are yet."

He gestured Ellie to the chair across from him, but she didn't sit. He sighed. "Your brother is nothing but trouble. Your mother, bless her, was fortunate she went back to her own kind before all of this unpleasantness."

"What do you want?" Ellie held his gaze.

Blackie got up and took a bottle from a cabinet under a wire-covered window that looked into the alley. "That's a good question. You were one of mine for a long time, Ellie. You know it's not just the money. It's the principle."

"Whatever it is," Ellie said, "I'll make it right." The words fought their way past a knot in her throat. She'd never wanted to owe Blackie anything. Nobody in their right mind did. She'd gone to jail rather than speak a word against him after the cops burst in on her and Finn and the illegal card game that had been all Blackie's idea. They questioned her for sixteen hours, but she never broke, never even so much as a hairline crack. Blackie was more frightening than anything the Boston PD could throw at her.

"Back in the day," Blackie said, uncapping the bottle and taking a critical sniff, "if we found one mate or another talking to the other side, passing information to the Brits, we knew they were scared. Scared of losing their family, their freedom. Hell, black and tans would drag you into the street, shoot you like a dog without a second thought. Something to be scared of, all right."

Ellie fought to keep quiet, to not agitate him any further. Blackie could refer to the Irish Rebellion and Bloody Sunday in the same breath, and Ellie was never sure what was a lie and what he'd actually seen with his own eyes—just that he was old enough to be the meanest bastard she'd ever run across.

"Finn is scared," she agreed. "And I told him he should be. He knows he fucked up."

"We'd make an example of them," Blackie said, as if she hadn't spoken. "Much as it killed my poor soul to do so. Because an example keeps the rest in line. Might make the next one think twice before he goes sticking his nose where it don't belong." He poured a drink and tossed it down his throat, smacking the whiskey on his pale gums.

"It's not about the money," Blackie said. "It's about trust. I trusted your brother, though Lord knows a junkie and a low character like that didn't deserve it. I gave him the benefit of the doubt, and he stole from me."

He set the glass down on his desk and took a seat again. The chair spring creaked, in time with Ellie's oscillating heart.

"You pay me back the thirty plus ten and I'll leave you and our Sean out of it," Blackie said. "But Finn's gone past where I can turn a blind eye." He opened his computer again. "Or you could just stop all this pretense you're anything but one of mine and come back to work. Toward your brother's debt, of course."

"You know I'm on parole," Ellie said, "I come to work again, I'll be right back in jail."

Blackie shrugged. "That's a shame. You were by far my best earner. Much better than Finn could ever reach for. And you, I could trust. But you didn't show me respect when you came home. You spat in my face, as I recall, when I offered you money and a job, so I suppose you're right. You've nothing to offer, and it's sad your brother will pay the price."

Ellie slammed the laptop shut and missed Blackie's fingers by an inch. "I offered you my word," she said. "I may not be one of your crew, but my word is still good. You think after you let me twist in the wind for eighteen months in Framingham I'm just going to come back wagging my tail like your goddamned trained puppy?"

Blackie narrowed his eyes, tongue flicking out like the tongue of the snake he really was. "Careful, Ellie. You don't want to say something you'll regret."

"You already took my dad," Ellie said. "You can't have my brother too."

She felt a slight pop, like she was in an airplane and they'd just shifted altitude. The quiet announcement of something encroaching into the space that hadn't existed a moment before.

Her back slammed into the wall, and her throat closed, energy wrapping the muscle and tendon harder than a fist. Ellie fought, but Blackie had her dead to rights. She hadn't thought he'd actually come after her with his talents. He'd always liked her, let her get away with things he never would have allowed Finn or Sean. He'd paid for her shoes for her dance recital in the ninth grade, sat in the second row and clapped louder than anyone's actual father.

"I did tell you to be careful," Blackie said. "And I'll say it again. Don't end up like your dad, Ellie. Run back to your safe little life and forget all of this."

He rose and came to her, so close she could smell the fresh hot whiskey on his breath.

"You already lived without your da. In time, you'll learn to live without Finn," Blackie said. He hit her, one sharp jab just below her rib cage, and Ellie sank down, no air left in her. She retched on the floor until she could stand up, and then she ran past Matty and out to the alley, leaning against a wall, sheltered by a Dumpster, so no one could see her tears.

-5-

Finn still lived in the old place, had managed to hang on to it since Ellie and Sean had left.

Ellie sighed at the drift of empty beer cans and takeout wrappers piled on one side of the door, trash bag split open by rats. The wallpaper was coming off in strips, like the entire creaking house was shedding its skin.

She didn't know why she was here. Finn was with Sean; he'd be fine. Sean had guns, legal guns with permits, upstanding honorably discharged soldier that he was. And Finn wasn't without his defenses. His talents ran more to picking locks, or pockets, but not, unfortunately, picking ponies.

Blackie wanted to kill Finn, had likely been itching for an excuse ever since he'd gotten busted along with Ellie two years before. That game had cost Ellie eighteen months, but it had cost Blackie cold hard cash and, more importantly, made him look like a fool to the sharks that were always circling. Boston had changed. The Russians were here now, the tongs and the *yakuza* and all their Folk. Finn had humiliated Blackie twice over, put Blackie's blood into the water.

Ellie kicked a beer can into the far wall. Even if she paid, even if she went up for life for working for him, Blackie would still kill Finn. It was the only way to scare off the sharks.

Unless she killed Blackie first. She'd have to be insane to go against someone like Blackie Farrell. Even if he was just a man, he wouldn't be one anybody would cross on purpose.

Except her damn idiot of a brother.

Ellie sank down in the same spot she'd hidden when she'd seen her father and the man in the black suit. She knew now it wasn't the Devil, not really. There were much worse things out there. Things little-girl Ellie could have never imagined. She'd seen what people who owed Blackie would do to get out of his debt. They'd rob liquor stores, offer up their daughters, ditch it all and run in the middle of the night. Desperation made you crazy.

She got up and went into the parlor, stood where the man in the black suit had stood. The curtains had rotted away over a decade and the furniture was filthy. Finn had taken the light fixtures and the antique mantel and sold them, when he was deep in the grip of whatever he was shooting or snorting that week. He went through flush periods, where he was sober and his betting was paying off. He ran small scams on the side to bring in pocket money, pulled smash-and-grabs, hit people over the head when they owed Blackie money. Just the kind of life everyone expected him to have. That was Finn—if you expected the worst out of him, he was reliable to a fault.

Ellie sighed and kicked over a stack of bootleg DVDs next to the fireplace. She remembered sitting on this carpet after the funeral, holding Finn as he sobbed and sobbed, until she thought his ribs would break, his small hands fisting into her dress. He'd always been small, and talked big because of it. She'd felt like they were floating, untethered from their earthly existence and in a singularity made up of the tiny sliver of time between having Dad, having a family, and Dad being gone, his spot on the sofa empty, to be filled by nothing except Finn's sobs and her own ragged breath.

The sun came through the bare windows just then and caught the wall up at the ceiling, the stain that had started before Ellie was born having grown to engulf most of the plaster. Amid the pitted rot Ellie saw a mark. She got a chair and climbed up higher, shining the small light from her keychain on the spot.

The mark was faint, and she'd never have seen it if a decade of water hadn't whittled away the plaster surface, leaving dark mildew in the lines so they stood out. Scratched with something no bigger than a penny nail, it was small and simple, just three or four intersecting lines.

Ellie felt a tremor go through her, and even though it was only afternoon she felt the shadows move around her, inhaling her fear and swelling to fill the room.

She knew how her father had died now, really. And she knew how she was going to save her brother.

-6-

In Ellie's neighborhood, staying neutral didn't net you much, so she'd always admired Doyle McManus for doing just that.

Doyle wasn't like Blackie, like her father. He was Folk, but he wasn't a criminal. Not much of one, anyway. He stayed in his bookshop, watching the world go by through narrowed blue eyes buried in a face full of lines and angles.

Much like Blackie, Doyle could have been anything from old to ancient. Unlike Blackie, Doyle was one of the few people her father had trusted.

A cat stretched and yawned from atop a pile of mysteries when Ellie came through the door. Ellie waited. The cat examined her, then trotted to the back room. A few seconds later Doyle appeared.

"Never thought I'd see the day you'd come through my door of your own free will," he said. Doyle had stripped himself of his accent the moment he stepped foot on American soil. He worked at his talents, and he wasn't somebody that Ellie would voluntarily cross, even if he wasn't prone to exploding like most of the Folk she knew. The cat, a familiar, was only the start of it. Her magic was muddy and common, as was Finn's, that *striga* trash Frankie Bonnaro, the Russians and their *koldyun*. None of them came from bloodlines where magic twined with your DNA. Even Blackie had just enough power to be bigger and meaner than the next guy. Doyle was the only person Ellie had ever met to come close to the bloodlines, the sort of power that was born, not learned or stolen.

She'd always wondered if he might be from one of them, a bastard child of sorcerer nobility. They weren't unheard of—the men from the bloodlines sometimes found women from the Folk side, and sometimes there were children, usually taken in by the bloodlines and raised with a quiet agreement not to discuss their parentage. Even half-blood was better than letting one of their own slip away to the Folk.

Doyle cocked his head. "Last I recall, I visited you in jail and you told me to go straight to hell. Still standing up for Blackie?"

Ellie breathed in. She wouldn't have dreamed of confronting Doyle unless it was life or death. Unless it was Finn's life. "You've got some nerve, considering it was you that gave my dad the means to summon a demon the night he died."

Doyle didn't speak, so Ellie pressed on. "The way I see it, you helped that thing take my father from me. I'm sure he gave you a good sob story about whatever he owed Blackie, but you're smarter, Doyle. You knew what it would do to him. So now you owe me a favor in return and I'm here to collect."

The lights hanging dusty and cobweb-strung from the shop ceiling flickered and dimmed, and the hair on Ellie's neck stood on end. Doyle's cat yowled and ran off, scattering a pile of ancient *National Geographics* in its wake.

"What makes you think you get to ask anything of me? You, who thinks just because you crawl out of the gutter you leave the stink behind?" Doyle's voice wasn't loud or harsh, but it sent a cold blade through Ellie's guts and she was surprised she managed not to flinch.

"My father was no prize," Ellie said. "He was a mess ever since Mom took off. But he wouldn't have known what to do without you."

Doyle ran his finger down a stack of battered Hawthorne stories, the gold lettering almost absent from the leather spines from a century of readers' fingers. "Blackie threatened you kids. Declan never would have done it otherwise."

Ellie looked around the shop, not having an answer to that. It was exotic when she was a kid, a place where people read books for pleasure and had enough money to buy them. The dusty stacks had the promise of secrets only she'd find, because she was the only one in the family who wanted to find them badly enough. Now, in the daytime, choking on musty paper and dust mites, she saw it for the crap heap it was, the barricade that Doyle used to keep the world out.

"If you want this so badly," Doyle said, "you're desperate, and it's bad to deal with demons when you're desperate."

"You said if I *was* desperate, come to you," Ellie said. "Well, I'm desperate. And I'm not afraid."

"That should bother you the most," Doyle said. He went behind the counter and came back with a black leather bag, the kind doctors used to carry around, back when they came to your house at all.

"I'll tell you the same thing I told your father," Doyle said as he shoved the bag at her. "There's some mistakes shouldn't be undone. Not for the price you need to pay."

"It's Finn," Ellie said. Doyle had always liked her brother, let him run wild in the shop and never scolded him when he broke things or stole comic books from the battered bins under the front window.

"It'll always be something," Doyle said. Ellie picked up the case. It was surprisingly light, even though the contents didn't rattle at all.

"I'd like to just get through this time and deal with the next disaster when it comes."

She'd opened the door and jangled the bell when Doyle spoke up again, his papery voice somehow cutting through the traffic outside. "Eleanor."

Ellie stopped, because she still liked Doyle, even after he'd stopped coming around, divorced himself from the pain of his friend's death.

"It'll offer you a way out," Doyle said. "It'll give you a chance to come out on top." He coughed, a sound of gravel scraping over pavement. "Don't take it," he said. "Make a straight bargain. It won't be in your favor, but it's better than nothing."

Ellie shivered against the air rushing in from the outside, the needles of winter moisture melting on her skin. "I'm not thinking this will be an easy thing, Doyle. Don't you worry."

"Don't try to win at its game," Doyle said again. "Your father tried that, and look what happened to him."

-7-

Ellie thought about where to set up. She'd never summoned anything much beyond a few spirits, a few half-drunken words slurred over a Ouija board at parties to answer questions from beyond the beyond. *Will I get married, will Sean be all right in Iraq, will we ever get out of this godforsaken neighborhood?*

The apartment was out—that was familiar territory. That was where her father had rolled the dice and lost.

Bloodline sorcerers made deals with demons all the time. There were families out there who'd had powerful members of the demonic elite bound for centuries, symbiotic relationships granting the sorcerers power and the demon a ready source of food.

That's what she was to this thing—food. Ellie had no illusions. Folk who messed with demons ended up dead. Except sometimes they didn't. Sometimes they brokered a deal first, managed to eke out something impossible for decades of life, or a favor, or all of the power they could contain.

Demons weren't picky about what they ate, but they were always hungry.

Ellie finally picked the Blue Tone, one of Blackie's properties that he'd snapped up during the boom as a way to launder cash. There were a half dozen of these sad closed-up clubs and restaurants, strung from Salem to Revere, all of them Blackie's tax shelters.

The Blue Tone was the only one that made her sad. It was a sagging Art Deco mess, but once, a long time ago, it had been beautiful. The limestone façade glittered in the sun, made you squint so you could almost ignore the weathered plywood blocking the windows and the rusty chain on the door. Gang tags and obscenities couldn't hold a candle to the carvings above the arched, leaded windows on the second floor.

Ellie took a flashlight and a few road flares from her emergency kit in her trunk and slipped inside through the back door, the padlock there broken long ago by scavengers looking for fixtures and copper.

The kitchen was a dripping, stinky mess. A burst pipe had left a constellation of mold on the half-fallen ceiling, but when Ellie stepped through the swinging doors onto the dance floor, the setting sun sent gold bars through the upper windows, illuminating the inlaid wood and painted murals of jazz musicians, flappers, and gilded beauties faded to ghosts on the walls.

The setup wasn't hard. She drew a rough circle on the ground with a can of spray paint from her trunk, and outside it drew the same mark carved into the wall of the old apartment. She had to stop for a moment, listening to the wind creak the windows, feeling the building rumble under her as a truck passed by.

Had her father felt this gnawing desperation? He must have. Nobody would do this if they weren't desperate.

Ellie lit a few candles she found clustered in the corners of the room, memories of some long-ago break-in. She sat in the center of the circle and took out her pocketknife. She waited a long time before she cut into her hand.

It hurt less than she expected. It was cold enough that her blood flowed slow, fat droplets hitting the wood floor, hovering for a moment before they ran into the marks, crawling all around the circle as Ellie flexed her hand.

Folk tradition wasn't complicated. Blood, talent, and time was all it took. Ellie wrapped a rag around her hand and waited.

The devil she'd seen didn't approach or appear in a puff of smoke. He was simply there at the edge of the candlelight, black suit and bright white shirt, the only part of his face glimpsed the gleam of his eyes.

"I know you," he said. "I saw you once. You were smaller."

Ellie's mouth was dry with dust and fear. "I know you too."

"Are you here for revenge?" the demon said.

Ellie shook her head. "I'm here for my brother."

The demon smiled then. "Family is important to your kind. I like that. It keeps me visiting this part of the world, every winter or two. I like the winter here. The air smells like iron. Like blood."

"My brother owes a gangster thirty thousand dollars," Ellie said. Her voice, caught in her throat like a rat in a trap, sprung free in a rush. She fought against the tight fist that closed her throat and tried to keep the tremor from her words. "I don't have it. I have no way of getting it. He's going to be dead by morning unless I do something."

"The money isn't a problem," the demon said. He came closer, his black shoe touching the circle line, and with Ellie's next breath he was inside. She jumped up, backed away, knocking over one of the candles. It guttered and went out, wax pooling around her feet.

"You called me. You invited me. You can't shut me out with some paint and prayers," the demon said. "As to your brother—what will you give me? It's not a small sum, so the exchange will not be small."

Ellie waited. There was no point in pushing back just yet. She could play it cool, hear the offer, and counter. She tried to lie to herself. This was just a deal like any of the hundred back-room favors she'd bartered as a stupid kid, for clothes and shoes, for money to pay the bills, for the stuff Finn wanted so he could be like his straight friends—TV, video games, the right sneakers. Anything that fell off a truck could find its way into Ellie's hands. But not money like this.

"I'll give you a month to put your affairs in order and say good-bye," the demon said. "That's more than I gave your father. Of course, his situation was more complicated."

"I know what happened to my father," Ellie said. A month? He couldn't be serious. She'd thought a year maybe, chopped off the end of her life, when she'd be too old to care anyway. Maybe some sort of unholy favor. She'd done enough of those for Blackie. She was the most talented member of his crew, had been right up until the day she left, so all the worst jobs became hers.

"Do you?" The demon regarded her. He never blinked, not once in all the time he'd been staring at her.

"A month . . . that's like no time at all," Ellie said. Finn wouldn't last without her. Sean wouldn't take care of him the way he needed. He'd slap Finn in some rehab, Finn would run, and he'd end up dead, just as sure as he would owing Blackie the money.

And Sean . . . he was strong, but how strong? He'd have no one. No one to call when the nightmares got bad. No one to drive him when his leg acted up, no one to help him manage the snowdrifts of paperwork from the VA and his government benefits.

"Of course, there is another way," the demon purred. Ellie felt that same feeling, that same paralysis she'd felt watching him take away her father, but this time it lasted only a moment. She knew she'd say the word long before it flew free.

"Yes."

The devil was the devil she'd dreamed of, that she'd feared in that moment. The devil gestured toward the bar. "Instead of bargaining, we could simply play a game."

Ellie felt that cold draft wash over her again, the one that had crept inside and sunk its teeth into her skin a dozen years ago on the night her father died. "What game did you have in mind?"

The devil ran his fingers across the tiger maple of the bar. It was inlaid with strips of darker wood, all of it scarred and stained and covered in dust and grime. Under the devil's touch, though, the lights in the curved brass chandeliers sprang to life and a tinny song dribbled from the old cloth-covered speakers that dangled from the wall.

"There's all kinds of games we can play, Ellie. Games of skill . . ." He pointed to a crooked dartboard at the far end of the bar. "Games of chance . . ." The devil leaned over the bar and brought out a deck of cards so old most of the suits had rubbed away. "Or simply games of luck," he said, and with a flick of his wrist a pair of dice appeared in his palm. "I tend to leave that up to your kind."

Ellie tried to make herself very still, like she would when her father was angry but hadn't passed out yet on the bad nights, or when she'd screwed up and Blackie had grabbed her and shaken her, his thin fingers like wires tightening around her arms until she feared they'd draw blood.

"What game did my father play?" she asked the devil.

He drummed his fingers on the bar. "Not one he was particularly good at."

Ellie grabbed the cards, swiping them over the bar. "Best of three. I'll take a chance at each of these and if I win two of the three you do what I ask and you leave."

"And if I win?" His teeth gleamed in the low light. The song was stronger now—Billie Holiday, crooning "Solitude."

"Then I guess you get what you want." Ellie shuffled the deck and shoved them at the devil. "Cut."

He did as she asked, his eyes dancing with amusement. "Dealer's choice, I take it?"

Ellie's heart thudded through every inch of her, every vein and vessel trembling. It had been a long time since she'd tried to cheat someone, and never someone like this.

She thought of her father, the spicy smell of whiskey and aftershave, the rough pads of his fingers showing her over and over how to win even if you didn't have winning cards, because Sean wasn't interested and Finn didn't have the patience.

The devil got a two of hearts and a queen of diamonds. He huffed. "Hit me."

The four of clubs hit the bar, now gleaming and new as it had been on the day the Blue Tone opened its doors.

Ellie waited. The devil sneered. "Again."

She dropped a card. Four of spades. The devil laughed. "I like you more than your father. You at least tried."

"I still have my cards," Ellie said, and dropped them fast. Queen of spades. Jack of clubs. Ace of hearts. "I win," she said, and was glad she was leaning against the bar, so she didn't lose her balance.

The devil pursed his lips. "So you have." He spun on the heel of one polished shoe and went to the dartboard. "But you haven't beaten me yet."

Ellie followed him, rolling one of the ancient darts between her fingers. It was dusty and unbalanced.

The devil set his stance and sank three bull's-eyes, one after the other. Thud-thud-thunk, like three bullets through Ellie's heart.

He smirked at her, the devil, and stepped aside. "That's all you, my darling."

"Do you always play these games with desperate people?" Ellie asked. The devil shrugged.

"If they're willing. Some are too afraid."

Ellie tried to aim, but she wavered. Two darts hit the outer ring, piercing the gold 10 embossed on the cork panels. One didn't even hit the board, embedding itself in the grimy plaster to the left of the hook.

"What a shame," the devil said. He rolled his dice in his hand, the knucklebone rattle seeming far too loud in the high-ceilinged ballroom. "Only thing left to do now is roll the dice, Eleanor. Feeling lucky?"

Ellie breathed in, out and shook her head. "I'm not playing that game."

The devil's face twisted, and he looked less like a man for the first time, more like the elongated, distorted, shadow-coated face she'd memorized in a hundred nightmares over the years. "You're not in a position to give me any lip."

"You said it was my choice," Ellie reminded him. "I choose the game you played with my father."

He rolled his eyes. "Fine."

The devil went to the bar and got three cups. "What shall we hide under these, my dear?"

Ellie gestured at the devil's ruby tie pin. "Take it off." She tried to go out of herself, rely totally on her fingers and her talents, as she had at her father's funeral. She showed the demon the ruby pin and slipped it under the cup. She could remember watching her father's hands when she was very small. Back when he didn't drink as much and would laugh with her. She'd stand at the back of the crowd on a corner and watch him run the game, thin fingers with the dirty nails shifting red plastic cups faster than she could follow.

At home, he'd push Sean's homework aside on the dining table even though Sean whined when he did. He'd show Ellie, patiently, over and over, until she could move almost as fast as he could. He taught her how to tuck the Ping-Pong ball, or wine cork, or whatever she used up her sleeve, how to use magic to move it from sleeve to sleeve or cup to cup, and how to pop it back out and under the plastic rim again just before she tipped the cups over. He taught her that she could make it appear wherever she wanted, that luck had nothing to do with it. Not where people like them were concerned.

Ellie shut out the sharp-edged memories of her father's booze-tinged breath and the insults he screamed at all of them, the hard knuckles landing on her skull and the other nights, even worse than when he was home, when he wasn't.

Ellie thought instead of Christmas before Mom walked out, when her father would sing—very badly—"White Christmas," how he'd tell her stories using her handful of stuffed animals to act them out, and how he'd taught both her and Sean to pitch a baseball in their tiny backyard and, when Ellie came home crying with a split lip, how to throw a punch.

"You may not be the biggest, or the toughest," he told her. "But let it be known you don't take shit from nobody and I guarantee people'll leave you alone."

Ellie let her hands move almost of their own accord, relying on muscle memory. The cups rattled and she stopped, looking up at the devil. "Which one?"

He tapped the middle one. Ellie revealed the empty space under the cup, and he hissed between his teeth.

She showed him the ruby again, slipped it under a cup. When she slipped it up her sleeve that time it cut her skin, but Ellie kept her face still, only her hands moving. The record cut off and static hissed through the speakers above her head.

The devil picked again, and Ellie's stomach sank. He'd picked right. She showed him the ruby and the dull blood-colored gleam reflected in his black eyes.

"That's more like it," he purred. "I hope your brothers will pay for a nice funeral with some of that money. Like your dad's—that was a nice little Irish wake if I do say so."

"Are you interested in talking, or are you interested in playing?" Ellie snapped. The devil spread his hands.

"By all means. Let's play."

She felt blood dribble down inside her sleeve, but Ellie moved faster than she'd ever moved the cups before. She shifted the ruby with magic from her left sleeve to her right, but she was so in tune she didn't even need talent, not really. Her fingers flew, the cups rattled, and when she slipped the ruby back under the cup of her choosing, her drop was smoother than it had ever been. When the cups came to a stop, the devil studied them carefully.

"I'm afraid," he said, extending one pale finger, "that you're going to be seeing your father again very soon."

Ellie flicked the cup over. It landed on its side with a rattle, and she watched two spots of color rise in the devil's face.

The cup was empty.

"I guess I've got a few more years before I see the old man," Ellie said. "I'll take the money now."

She'd never seen such pure hatred on a creature's face before that moment. Not on Blackie Farrell, not on anyone. The devil picked up his black case, then stalked back to her.

"Do you know how many people have beaten me?"

"Don't know," Ellie said. "Don't care."

The devil sighed and then stuck out his hand. "The money will be returned to the disreputable Mr. Farrell, but I doubt your idiot brother will be spared."

Ellie took the thing's hand, surprised to find it was dry but not cool and felt startlingly human. "Probably not, but I don't need you for that. I can protect my own. You taught me to do that, when you took my father because he couldn't."

The devil started to shake her hand, then turned her arm and examined the underside. Ellie saw the dark line of blood against her shirtsleeve, and her stomach dropped.

"You cheated," the devil growled. "You cheated me. Me. You think this will end well for you?"

"You said we'd play." Ellie refused to pull away. Refused to drop his gaze. He'd made a bargain and he was bound by it. That was how demons worked, what kept them from running amok on the human race. "You said we'd play a game, but you never said we wouldn't try to cheat each other." She lifted one shoulder. "I guess I'm just better at it than you."

The devil bared his teeth, but then he dropped her hand and took a step back toward the pool of shadows at the edge of the dance floor. "This isn't the end for us, Ellie. Not even close to it. I'll see you dead for what you've done."

Ellie picked up her bag from the floor and made to leave through the kitchen. "And I'll be more than happy to pay you back for what you did to my father."

The devil didn't say anything else. The lights flickered, and when Ellie looked at the shadow again he was gone.

She left the Blue Tone and leaned against her car, feeling the cold, cutting wind of the Boston winter on her face. It smelled like greasy smoke and car exhaust, but it was the sweetest air Ellie had ever breathed.

Maybe this time, she thought, things would be different. Finn would get clean, and they'd move out to the suburbs like Sean, away from the old streets and the old neighborhood and men like Blackie Farrell. Beyond his easy reach, where he couldn't make an example of her brother. Probably not, Ellie thought, but maybe. They at least had the chance to find out. And if someone like Blackie came around again, she was going to fight. She might not be part of Blackie's family anymore, but she was still one of the Folk. She could take care of herself, her family, and she didn't need Blackie or the devil or her father anymore. She could be on her own. She'd be fine.

Ellie turned the devil's ruby tie pin between her fingers so that it caught the winter sun, and smiled.

ON THE PLAYING FIELDS OF BLOOD

BRENDAN DUBOIS

Brendan DuBois of Exeter, New Hampshire, is the award-winning author of nearly 130 short stories and sixteen novels including his latest, *Deadly Cove*, part of the Lewis Cole mystery series. His short fiction has appeared in *Playboy*, *Ellery Queen's Mystery Magazine*, *Alfred Hitchcock's Mystery Magazine*, *The Magazine of Fantasy & Science Fiction*, and numerous anthologies including *The Best American Mystery Stories of the Century*, published in 2000 by Houghton Mifflin, as well as *The Best American Noir of the Century*, published in 2010. His stories have twice won him the Shamus Award from the Private Eye Writers of America and have also earned him three Edgar® Award nominations from the Mystery Writers of America. He is also a onetime *Jeopardy!* game show champion. Visit his website at BrendanDuBois.com.

The head selectman for the town of New Salem, New Hampshire, slowly climbed down the unnamed and narrow trail that was cut through a mountain ridge in a remote area of the northern White Mountains, making his way to an apparent crime scene. It had been a long day. The hike had started in a dirt lot off an old logging road that was unmarked on most maps, and now he was about ten minutes away from getting to where he had to be. Some minutes ago he had passed an old stone wall that had been torn down more than two hundred years ago to help save the town, so he knew he was close.

His name was Grant Spencer, and he had been the head selectman for his small and isolated town for nearly twenty years. He had grown up and lived in these mountains, but now, approaching sixty, his knees and ankles were starting to ache as he descended the steep trail, a trail he hated to be on.

The trail widened and a familiar waterfall appeared, which ended in a wide pool that led off to another stream. A few more score yards down the narrow trail and he emerged to an astounding sight: a wide, grassy field, smack-dab in the middle of these high peaks. Before him were two men, wearing police uniforms for the town of New Salem: Police Chief Hollis Speare and Deputy Ezra Spencer. Ezra was also a cousin of Grant's, and Hollis was Grant's brother-in-law. They were the entire police force for New Salem.

"Hello, guys," Grant said, as he got closer, wiping his face with a handkerchief. "What's going on?"

Hollis crooked a finger, and Grant followed him to a gully near the stream, where an oak tree's roots were exposed. "A lost hiker found this yesterday. His cell phone had no coverage, of course, so we had to wait a bit before getting here after he found his way out and to the police station."

Grant looked down at where the dirt had been washed away, probably by a sudden rainstorm or squall. There were bones there, tumbled up in a pile. His chest felt tight and cold. *How many times before,* he thought, *how many times.* "This hiker. Where's he from?"

"Some place in Quebec. Had to go back home. Didn't speak English that well."

"Glad to hear that." Grant wiped at the back of his neck again and looked over at the waterfall. "Did . . . did the hiker say he saw any mist or fog when he was here?"

Hollis said, "Yeah, he did. The guy said he was scared when he saw the bones. Started running back up the trail. Turned back and then he said he couldn't see anything. Just this funny mist that rose up."

"Sweet Jesus, what a lucky guy," Grant said.

"You know it, Grant."

His knees ached even more. "Oh, crap, let's go check it out."

And as so many times before, Grant walked back out to the wide field.

Out on the wide sacred field, Long Neck trotted along with the other braves of the Abenaki, getting ready to start a daylong competition with his brothers. He had on a breechcloth, leggings, and moccasins; raven feathers and beads were in his black hair; and a long flint knife hung from a belt at his side. It was a warm day, the field was as it always was, and he carried the long maple stick with the curve at the end, the curve covered with deer sinew, to make a slight basket for the game. It had taken many days to curve the end of the stick by heating it over the smoke of a fire, but now it was in a perfect shape to play the game of the little war. He looked at his fellow braves and brothers, so very few in number, but he knew they would play the game well and for the honor of the Great Spirits, especially if the outsiders came.

He paused as the tribe's shaman approached, feathers and beads in his hair, his bare chest painted with symbols, wearing an old deer robe, knife and little skin bags hanging from his side. Long Neck held out his arms, so the shaman could scratch them with the special markings, and with a burning punk of sage, Long Neck was blessed for the game that was about to begin. The old shaman slowly worked down the line, blessing the other five braves. He took a deep breath and looked up at the holy mountains where the Great Spirits resided. The game of the little war was one he had played so many, many times before, but each one was special.

Especially if the outsiders came.

Long Neck's strong band split into two, three on either side of the field. The posts of winning were made of tree limbs, stuck into the ground, at the far ends of the field. The holy man came out to the center of the field, still praying, still chanting. In one hand was the burning sage, and in the other was the round ball, made of deer hide stitched together, with deer fur inside.

The holy man held both objects up to the sun, and then tossed the ball up into the air, and then backed away.

With a loud whoop and holler, Long Neck raced to the center of the field, the stick high in the air, oh so ready to play the game.

Heather Moore was about to lose it, but since her three hiking companions from college were far ahead, she knew it wouldn't be worth it to start raising a fuss back here by herself. They had been in the White Mountains now for three days, and they were lost. Oh, she wasn't concerned about freezing to death or being eaten by bears or anything like that, but for Christ's sake, she wished the three bozos ahead of her had just listened to her, back when they broke camp after breakfast. They were supposed to take the Rock Bridle Trail down to Route 16, where they could hitch a ride back to where they had parked the old Chevy Malibu belonging to her boyfriend, Tony Lewis. But Tony's best friend, Cal Zeller, was a history major at college and loved exploring abandoned towns and old roads, and he said that an old Appalachian Mountain Club guidebook from 1912 listed a great set of waterfalls off an old logging road in the northeast part of New Salem.

So Cal had persuaded Tony and their third bud, Steve Dolan, to explore this overgrown trail off that old logging road, and they had been descending for a while—once passing the remnants of what looked to be a tall stone wall—and she was tired, her feet hurt, and all she thought about was a Burger King Whopper and a long, long shower when she got back to her apartment.

"Hey!" she called out to the three figures descending below her. "Wait up, will you!"

But the three buds ahead of her—roommates in an apartment building just down the street from her in their college town—kept on moving down the narrow trail, walking sticks in hand, their knapsacks—red, blue, and orange—tight against their backs.

Typical guys.

Think they know everything.

She was going to yell at them again when she paused to catch her breath, and heard something.

Rushing water.

• • •

Long Neck moved along the field, hollering again, feeling the strength and joy and the righteousness of being out on the sacred field, playing the little war game, doing it all for the tribe and the glory of the Great Spirits. So far no one had scored, for they were few in number and about equal in skills, meaning the ball was passed back and forth, back and forth, with no team taking the lead.

But there had been a time before the sickness, when hundreds would play on this wide field, playing for day after day, with fires at night and feasts and songs and poems of days past. Tribes and clans would walk for days to come here, to compete, to feast, and to strengthen bonds of friendship and alliance.

Then the sickness had come, from the south, where it was said that outsiders had arrived. A coughing sickness that had swept through the tribes and clans, leaving empty lodges, cold firepits, and the occasional cry of a lonely child, abandoned by his or her dead father or mother.

Long Neck pushed that thought, those old memories, away. It was now time only for the game, and always the game. Up ahead, his cousin Cat Smile had gotten the ball and was racing toward the far scoring trees, crying in delight, and Long Neck raced very fast to catch him.

Heather stopped when she reached the waterfall. It was gorgeous. The water seemed to cascade for more than a hundred feet before falling into a nearly perfectly round pool. There were smooth, moss-covered rocks around the shore, and a burbling stream boiled its way out of the pool, descending as a stream down to a place where the trees seemed to thin out.

"Heather, isn't this cool? Huh?"

Tony climbed up to her, breathing hard, tanned face wide in a smile. His brown beard was trimmed well and his blue eyes were his best feature, bright and lively, and his knapsack hung well on his muscular shoulders. He had on a UConn T-shirt and khaki shorts, and he said, "Heather, I know this is taking time, but wait until you see what Cal found. It's amazing!"

She so wanted to turn around and go back up the trail, to the promised land of cheeseburgers and hot showers, but her boy was so full of excitement and happiness, how could she say no?

"All right," she said. "Let's see what Cal found . . . and then we'll leave, okay?"

Tony gave her a sweaty kiss and grabbed her hand. "Absolutely. You can rely on me."

Heather shifted her knapsack and followed her boyfriend down the trail, listening to the water, and when she reached an area where the narrow trail flattened out, she looked back up at the waterfall and pool.

Odd.

It looked like some sort of mist was forming.

Long Neck was racing now to his own scoring limbs, when he slowed, seeing the far side of the field, where the trees and land rose up to the holy mountains. A heavy rush of breath and another tribe member came to a stop, breathing hard. It was Deer Run. He bumped his hip into Long Neck and said, "Up there. Take a look."

There.

A mist was rising.

"The outsiders are coming. You see the sign?"

Something tight seemed to be across his chest. "I see the sign," Long Neck said.

"Are we ready?"

Deer Run nodded, one hand holding his stick, the other hand at his waist, where his long knife rested.

"Yes, brother, we are always ready."

Heather had to admit that yes, it was amazing. The field was wide and had some sort of low grass covering it, with some trees in the far distance, and other trees nearby. She had never seen such a field in the middle of the mountains.

The three young men were clustered around, looking at Cal Zeller's hundred-year-old guidebook. "Well?" Tony demanded. "Does it say anything about an open field like this?"

Cal was excited. "No, not at all. I can't believe it. Look around at how big this damn flat field is . . . and in the middle of the mountains. It shouldn't be here!"

Steve scratched at his beard. "What does the guide say about the trail after it passes the waterfall?"

"That's the thing," Cal said. "The guide says the trail ends at the waterfall and pool. It says nothing about the trail continuing down to this field. And you'd think a field this big would have been noticed."

Heather turned and looked up where they had just descended. The mist was rising up and wider. She was a journalism major at school and only took the minimal science courses to get ahead, but she knew deep in her bones that the mist didn't belong. The weather wasn't right, not with the sun up high and bright, to have a mist like that suddenly appear.

And if the mist didn't belong, neither did they.

Feeling like that didn't make sense—they were in the middle of the White Mountain National Forest, for God's sake—but none of this was making sense.

"Guys, c'mon, let's leave," she quietly said.

Cal looked up at her. "Are you nuts? We just got here."

"But Tony promised that we'd head back up after we got here. I want to go back to the main trail, get out of here before the sun starts setting."

Tony had a look on his face that Heather recognized, of the boyfriend who didn't want to appear like a wuss in front of his buds. Steve nudged Cal in his ribs and said, "Yeah, this place is cool. Let's check it out."

Tony said, "Heather, I know I said we'd head right back, but this place shouldn't be here. None of the maps or guides describe this place. I agree with Cal, we should explore some."

"What do you mean, explore? It's just a field."

Then Steve whistled. "No, it's more than just a field."

Tony said, "Huh? What do you mean?"

Steve pointed. "Look. There are people over there."

Heather felt something seize in her chest at seeing the shapes approach them. "Guys, I don't like this, I don't like this. We might be trespassing. I want to go. I want to go now."

Cal said, "We're in a national forest. How the hell can we be trespassing? C'mon, let's go."

The three young men laughed with each other and started walking away, leaving her behind. Tears suddenly came to Heather's eyes. This wasn't right. This wasn't fair. She looked back up at the mist growing bigger over by the waterfall and trail. Something tugged inside her, to turn around and quickly walk back to where the mist was, where the trail was. Even in the mist, she was sure she could find the trail, and leave this field and her companions and those men over there behind.

Tony looked back at her, a pleading look on his face. She knew what the look meant. It was asking her to be a good girl, to come along, not make waves. Tony was asking her not to embarrass him in front of his friends.

It was asking a lot.

She took one more look at the mist and the trailhead, kicked at a stone on the ground, and followed the three young men across the field.

Long Neck strode forward and then stopped, watching the outsiders approach. Deer Run stopped next to him.

"So they come."

"So they do."

"It looks like they may have a woman with them, by the way one of them walks."

"It matters not," Long Neck said.

The men had sacks on their back and wore odd, tight-fitting clothes that were quite colorful. They had facial hair and their skin was that of the outsiders, pale and flabby.

The outsiders stopped, just a few strides in front of them. The woman hung back, as was proper.

"Wait here, brothers," Long Neck said. "I will talk to the outsiders and challenge them to a game."

Another brother called out, one called Fleet Foot. "Suppose they say no?"

Long Neck laughed. "They have no choice, do they?

Heather watched in fear and fascination as the tallest of the six men stepped forward. What the hell was going on? They looked like Native

Americans but she knew that there were only a couple of reservations in New England, mostly for casinos, and there were none in New Hampshire or nearby Vermont.

The man had a long neck, his face fierce-looking, dressed up in native garb with a knife at his side. There were feathers and beads in his braided hair. There were lines of paint along his cheekbones and forehead. He carried a long stick, curved at the bottom with a small basket made of rawhide or something, and then he stood still and started talking.

He waved his free arm in a long arc, and then held up his stick and talked some more. He held up the stick, and then a ball-shaped object.

The sight of the stick with the basket at one end stirred something inside her.

And yet not a single word he said made sense.

Long Neck paused after issuing the challenge, examining each of the male outsiders looking back at him. Fleet Foot spoke up again. "It looks like they are fat and weak. I wager they have no interest, or if they do, we will defeat them without breathing hard."

Long Neck turned back and snapped at his brother. "Have you forgotten the story of Azban? Then stay quiet."

Fleet Foot shifted as the other braves laughed at him. The story of Azban the Raccoon was an old story of the tribe. Azban was a proud raccoon that challenged a waterfall to a shouting contest. When the waterfall didn't respond to Azban, the proud raccoon dove into the waterfall to outshout it. But the raccoon was swept away to his death, because of his pride.

Long Neck had never forgotten the story and its meaning.

He called out again to the outsiders. "Well?"

The three men started talking to one another, and Long Neck understood not a word.

Tony said, "What in the hell is that all about?"

Steve shifted his feet. "I think Heather is right. I think we need to get the hell out of here. I don't know who these guys are, but I don't like it."

Cal suddenly laughed. "Hey, I know what's going on."

"Then pass it on, will you?" Heather demanded, looking at the six strong Indian men, standing in a line, all staring at them with a scary intenseness. "I don't like this at all!"

"Sure," Cal said, grinning. "They're reenactors."

Tony said, "Like those guys who dress up as Civil War soldiers on the weekend?"

"Absolutely. Reenactors. And they do more than just dress up. The real hard-core types, they wear clothing that's made exactly like it was during that time, with no zippers or metal fastenings. They wear the same kind of shoes, carry the same kind of weapons, and eat the same food from back then."

Heather looked at the six men staring back at them, the tallest one seemingly the leader. "Cal . . . what were they jabbering back there?"

"Some sort of Indian language, I'm sure. Remember when I said hard-core? I've read that the real dedicated ones, they leave behind their cell phones and iPads, they sleep on the ground, they don't shower, and they stay in character. They get so hard-core that while they're reenacting, they speak like they were a Southern or Union soldier from the 1860s, and they pretend to be ignorant of anything twenty-first-century."

Heather shook her head. "I've heard of Civil War play soldiers like that. Have never heard of Native American reenactors."

"Oh, sure," Cal said. "Lots of different reenactor groups have cropped up in the past five or ten years. In Europe, there are reenactors that are involved in groups re-creating the Napoleonic Wars. Others go back to World War I or World War II. Why not Native Americans?"

Steve said, "But only six? Where's the rest of 'em?"

"Oh, I bet they have an encampment somewhere on the other side of the field," Cal said.

Heather still didn't like it. "So why are they here?"

Cal laughed. "It's obvious, can't you tell? Look at what they're carrying."

Heather slowly nodded. It was obvious, after all.

• • •

Long Neck was getting tired of the outsiders talking to each other, especially the woman. What right did she have to talk before warriors such
as he and his brothers?

He stepped closer, held out his stick. "Come now, answer me!" he
demanded. "Will you accept the challenge? Will you? Will you show us
what kind of men you are, to play the game of little war?"

Still the outsiders gaped at him, fat and sloppy, and for a moment he
thought his cousin Fleet Foot might be right. *Maybe this group of outsiders, maybe they will turn down the challenge.*

Long Neck wasn't going to let that happen.

He held out his stick to the outsiders, chose one in the center, and
threw it at him.

Heather saw the tall Native American throw a stick at Cal, who caught
it and examined it. He ran his hands up and down and turned to the
other two male hikers. "Check this out! You know what this is?"

Her man Tony stepped over, took the stick, and held it up in the air.
"Looks like a what-do-you-call-it. Stick that shepherds use to pull their
sheep around."

"Like a crook?" Steve said.

Cal shook his head and took the stick back from Tony. "No, guys,
Native Americans didn't have sheep back then. This is a lacrosse stick."
He rotated it in the air and held it up again. "Lacrosse was a Native
American field game, and this must be a stick from back then. See how
it's curved toward the end? They didn't use a big basket like they do
today. They found a good chunk of wood and held one end over a smoky
fire, so it would curve into the proper shape. Hell, back then the tribes
would have games that lasted day and night, involving hundreds of Indians, covering miles. They're reenacting a lacrosse game from hundreds
of years ago."

Heather stepped closer, and Cal said, "Hey, you used to play lacrosse
in high school, didn't you? Tony said something about that to me."

"I did, but we sure as hell didn't play with homemade gear like that."

Cal turned and smiled at the six Native Americans, stick in his hand, as he twirled it back and forth, back and forth. "I played lacrosse back in high school, too. That's what they're doing here, guys. They're challenging us to a game. With the kind of gear they had back then."

Heather stepped back. "No! I don't like this! We need to go . . . we don't have time to play a stupid game, all right? It's getting later in the day, it'll be dark in a few hours. We've been out in the woods for two days, my back hurts and my feet are tired, and . . ."

She fell silent. The Native Americans, still silent, gazed at her with contempt. Tony, Steve, and Cal looked at her as well. Cal was grinning.

"And what, princess? What else is bothering you?"

Heather saw the pleading look again from Tony, asking her, *Please, please, don't embarrass me.*

"C'mon, Heather," Cal pressed on. "What else is bothering you?"

She pointed. "Hundreds of Indians would play lacrosse back then, from different tribes. Why are there only six of them here?"

Cal shrugged. "Why not? Like I said, I bet their encampment is somewhere on the other side of the field . . . and maybe six is only the number that are free right now. I'm sure they're doing other things, like making camp, cooking, hunting. C'mon, is that what's really bothering you? The numbers?"

She kept quiet. She knew what was bothering her. It wasn't right, it didn't make sense, and all right, it scared her. Okay? Those men over there outnumbered them, were lean, muscular, and so very serious looking. Plus besides those homemade and crooked lacrosse sticks they carried, they also had knives at their sides, on what looked like rawhide belts.

She wanted to leave.

She wanted to go.

She didn't want to be here.

"Oh, go ahead, play your stupid goddamn game. But count me out."

Heather moved back and sat down on a rock.

Long Neck saw the lead man of the outsiders step forward, grinning like a fool, moving the stick back and forth, saying something in their jabbering language. He dropped his colorful back sack to the ground, and so did his two companions. Long Neck strode forward, ball in hand, and tossed it up in the air. It fell to the ground and with a series of yells, he ran forward, struck the ball, and passed it to his cousin Fleet Foot, and with a sharp jab of his hips, he slammed into one of the outsiders, pushing him to the ground.

Shouting with joy, he slapped the ball again and ran to the nearest scoring branches in the ground, glad to see the outsiders fumbling and bumbling as they raced to catch up.

Oh, it was such a delight to be faster and better than your opponents.

The game went on, with three of the Indians playing against Tony, Cal, and Steve. There were tall bits of branches or saplings that were stuck at either ends of the field to serve as goals. The other three Native Americans sat underneath a pine tree, long legs stretching out, shouting encouragement to their friends. The three guys had dumped their packs to help them run and play the game, but still, they couldn't move as fast as the Indians. Damn, those guys were good . . .

Heather shivered as she sat still on the rock. It looked like the guys were having fun, though Cal was shouting a lot, his face red, as the three Native Americans practically danced around him. Okay, maybe it would be all right. Maybe.

But she felt cold.

Why was she feeling cold?

It was a Sunday in late June. The sun was starting to sink to the western horizon, to the near range of mountains, but it was still high enough to warm everything up. And why was it so damn cold? She felt like she was about a couple of minutes away from shivering.

She took out her cell phone, checked it. No bars. No signal. Not surprising, considering how far north they were and how remote these mountain valleys were. She touched the screen, and—

It was dead.

What the hell?

The damn thing shouldn't have died just like that. She had at least a couple of more hours of battery life left, but it was like the moment she had turned it on, the power had been sucked out. Or drained. Or . . . taken away.

She put the cell phone back in her pack. Rubbed her arms.

It was so very, very cold.

A hand grabbed her shoulder and she screamed.

Long Neck turned at the scream of the outsider's woman, then laughed at she stood up and nearly fell. The shaman was standing next to her. A moment ago he hadn't been there, and now, like all shamans of power, he had suddenly appeared next to the woman. He was talking to her, holding his holy sticks and burning sage in front of him, as he explained to the woman what this game of little war was all about.

Cat Smile knocked another one of the outsiders down.

Long Neck laughed. Explaining to the woman was a waste of time, but still, the shaman persisted.

Heather jumped off the rock, turned and yelped again, and backed away. Another Indian was standing in front of her. Where in hell had he come from? He was shorter and much older than the other six Native Americans out there on the field. His hair was black and streaked with gray, pulled back in a ponytail. He had on a robe made from some sort of skin that smelled awful, and there were a knife and small bags hanging at his side. There were also tattoos on his face and arms.

In one hand he held some feathers, and in the other, he held a piece of smoldering brush or leaves that had thin trails of gray smoke going up in the air.

"Jesus, you scared the crap out of me," Heather said.

The old man started talking, in a deep, husky voice, moving his hands around. Heather stared at him. His face was wrinkled, with a long scar running from one ear, down to his chin. It was thick and ragged, as if it hadn't been stitched right. And as he talked and his mouth moved, she couldn't help but notice that his teeth were either broken, black, or brown. It looked like he had never visited a dentist in all his life.

His talking grew louder, more animated. She stepped back. The tattoos, the wrinkles, the bad teeth . . . a tiny, very young voice inside her that was suddenly quite frightened said, *This guy's for real. He's no reenactor. Heather, young lady, you better get out of here, and right now!*

She turned, waved frantically, and said, "Tony! Tony! I'm leaving! I'm heading out!"

Tony was within earshot, his shirt now off, sweating profusely, his hair matted. Steve and Cal had taken their shirts off as well. "Why? What's wrong?"

Without moving, she jerked her hand back, making a pointing motion with her thumb. "This old man here is freaking me out, Tony, and I won't stay a minute longer."

Tony wiped at his sweaty face. "What old man?"

Heather turned, started shivering.

The old man was gone.

There was at least a clear space of fifty feet in every direction, with no place to hide, but the old man was gone.

Long Neck made his third score of the day against the outsiders, and the outsiders hadn't even been within range of the far scoring tree branches. He paused, took a look around. The three outsiders had taken off their upper garments, and their bodies were flabby indeed. Only one of them had any markings at all, and it was the one with the yellow hair, who talked a lot and seemed to be their leader. He had interesting tattoos around his upper arms that looked like thorn bushes, and he wished the outsider knew Long Neck's language, for he would love to know how and where he had gotten such markings.

But there was no time today, on this playing field, to learn any language. There was just time to play the holy game, the game of righteousness, the game against the outsiders.

One of the outsiders was talking to the woman, who had a loud, screechy voice. Deer Run came up to him and shook his head. "Look at that skinny woman. Hear that voice. Do you think she belongs to all three of them?"

"If so," Long Neck said, "they are the three unluckiest men we have ever met."

Deer Run laughed and quickly tossed his stick from one strong hand to the other. "Those poor men. They certainly have no skill with the game, and they certainly have no luck."

Long Neck said, "Yet they play."

"Yes, cousin, but for how long?"

"For long enough," he said. "For long enough."

Cal came over, breathing hard, bent over at the waist. "Heather, please, will you help us out? Will you? Those guys are smoking us out there."

She said, "That's not the way I used to play lacrosse. There should be twelve people to a team, with eye gear and mouth guards. This . . . this is just made-up crap."

Her boyfriend, Tony, joined Cal, eyes once again pleading. "Heather? Please?"

"Tony . . ."

"Honey, please. A favor. Will you do me this favor? Please?"

Emotions rolled around inside her, and she saw that the lead Indian in the group was looking over at her, like he was daring her or something.

Heather didn't like the guy's look.

She got up from the rock and held out her hands. "Oh, for shit's sake, give it to me. Anything to get us out of here quicker."

She took the stick from Tony—and it was warm and moist from his play—and she trotted out to the field. The three Native Americans looked surprised and then her competitive nature kicked in, and she took advantage of their surprise and managed to quickly scoop the handmade ball away and started racing to the far goalposts.

Despite her earlier unease, she turned back and laughed, and said, "I was the best center in my high school league, guys! See if you can catch me!"

The men behind her whooped and called out in whatever language they were using, and Cal and Steve tried to keep up with her running, yelling encouragement as she raced to the two saplings at the other end of the field that marked a goal. She looked back one more time. The Native Americans were trying to catch up, but they were tired as well and there was no way they could reach her in time.

She held up the stick, made it to the saplings, tossed the ball past both branches, and turned around, jumping and holding up the stick. "How's that, suckas!" she called out. "Guess you should have spared someone for a goalkeeper against a girl!"

Cal and Steve laughed, and one of the Native Americans raced by to get the ball. Heather, laughing now at the fierce looks she was getting from the other players, started going back to the field when somebody slammed into her, throwing her to the ground.

Long Neck stood still over the woman, breathing hard, his hip aching a bit from where he had struck the arrogant woman. Deer Run came over to him, the two of them standing over the woman. Her face was red and she was crying tears, and she shouted something in her foul language, got up, and threw the stick to the ground. One of her flabby men picked up the stick.

Deer Run said, "You treated her rightfully . . . for no woman has ever played the long game."

Long Neck replied, passing his stick from one hand to another. "Perhaps."

"What do you mean, brother?"

"She played well. Better than the males who are with her."

Deer Run laughed. "You're speaking nonsense, brother. Come, we've got to get playing again."

The woman looked back at Long Neck again, yelled something, and Long Neck—despite his admiration of her play—narrowed his eyes as she walked away: the woman who had scored against them, the woman who had bested them, even for a moment.

Then the game resumed.

Heather got into her pack and took out a light blue L.L.Bean jacket. She shivered some more, her hip aching. If this had been a real game, a ref would have been all over that tall asshole like white on rice. The mist up by the trail was thicker, wider. The sun was setting some but she couldn't remember a time when she was so cold. Her cell phone was dead and she was tired, achy, and hungry. The air felt thick, strange, unmoving. Shadows from the trees seemed to be at odd angles. There were the six Native Americans out there, three playing, three resting, and the old man was nowhere around.

She rubbed at her face, her eyes. Her eyes seemed blurry.

What was that?

What was that?

Her chest was the coldest part of her body. For the briefest moment, as one of the Indians spun around and held up his homemade lacrosse stick in triumph, Heather was sure . . . Heather was certain . . .

God, I must be losing it.

God, help me, please.

For during that briefest moment, with his arms held high . . .

Heather was certain that she could see the mountain range through his arms.

Like he was transparent. Or translucent. Or something like that.

She could see right through him.

"That's it!" she called out, her voice shaky, almost squeaking in fear. "You guys can play to sundown, but I'm getting the hell out of here!"

Heather leaned forward, grabbed her knapsack, and was suddenly dizzy and nauseated.

Long Neck stopped again. They had scored four times against the outsiders, and he could tell they were getting winded, were getting tired. But the game wasn't over yet; no, it still had to be played, until they were finally defeated, and he called out to Fleet Foot, and then he turned and saw one of the outsiders go to the woman.

He seemed to be talking to her.

She was walking away.

Her companion shrugged and went over to the pile of clothes and sacks, and it looked like he was going to follow her.

Unacceptable!

• • •

Even with the cold and the dizziness and the ache in her hip, Heather smiled when Tony finally came to his senses and came over to her. He was breathing hard, sweaty, hair and beard matted. "Hey, you leaving?"

"You better believe it," she said. "I've been patient long enough. You can keep on running around like an idiot, but I'm going home. Are you coming?"

Tony looked back at Cal and Steve, trying hard to move the small ball toward the other end of the field. Cal yelled out something to Tony, and he turned back. "Shit, I don't know. Cal wants to play at least until we score, but man, I'm getting beat. Cal claims he was a star lacrosse player in high school and he said these guys are the best he's ever seen. Hate to abandon him like this."

She shouldered her pack. "I don't care. I'm going. You make up your own mind. I scored and they treated me like crap. I've had enough."

Tony took out a handkerchief and wiped his face and the back of his neck. "Hell, my legs feel like they're gonna fall off . . . all this running around and we still got a fair amount of hiking to get through before it gets dark." He picked up his shirt, his pack. "Yeah, hon, I'm coming along." He slipped his shirt on, grabbed his pack, and yelled at the others: "Hey! Guys! Me and Heather are heading out!"

Steve stopped, breathing hard, and Cal yelled out something that Heather couldn't quite understand. Neither could Tony, and he said, "Whatever, pal! I'm tired, Heather's tired, and we're going back! You should, too."

The three Native Americans clustered around Cal and Steve also yelled something, but their words still made no sense. "Christ," Tony said. "We've been playing for nearly an hour and they still haven't stopped their reenacting."

Heather waited. Waited. And she was thrilled to see Tony get dressed and pick up his gear, and she grabbed his hand. "Come on, let's get going."

"Babe . . ."

"Tony!" The sharpness of her tone surprised her. "Let's get going! Now! They can figure out later what they're doing. Okay?"

Her man seemed to hesitate for just a moment, and then she could have kissed him right there for what he said and did next. "Yeah, forget them. Sorry we dicked around so much here. Let's head out; those two can finish the game if they want."

Heather squeezed his hand, and the two of them started walking away.

Stopping when they both heard a scream of terror behind them.

Long Neck watched one of the outsiders break away from the game and go over to the woman. Even at this distance, he could tell the woman was speaking with a sharp tongue to the outsider. Were they mates? Brother and sister? Cousins?

No matter.

The game would end when he and his brothers and cousins said it would end.

No sooner.

Long Neck ran over to one of the outsiders and slammed his fist against the back of the man's neck. He yelped and fell into the short grass, and Long Neck grabbed an arm and pulled him to his feet. The outsider was sweaty, panting, and Long Neck twisted an arm behind the outsider's back, making him scream in pain.

Long Neck took his knife and placed it against the struggling outsider's throat.

"Outsiders!" he yelled out. "Listen and pay heed to me, Long Neck, the greatest little war player the Abenaki has ever seen!"

Heather stopped, mouth open in shock. One of the Native Americans had grabbed Steve and had a knife to his throat.

A knife to his throat!

"Tony, do you see that? Do you?"

"Christ, yeah," he said, voice shaky. He stepped forward a few steps, called out, "Hey! Guy! What the hell is going on? What's the problem?"

The Native American with the knife kept on yelling.

"Hey! Speak English, okay? I don't understand what you're saying!"

Heather went forward, tugging at Tony's arm. "Come on, Tony, come on."

He whirled on her. "We can't leave Steve behind! We just can't!"

"But what can we do? Look! The other Indians are coming over. We've got to go! Now!"

After Long Neck finished warning the outsider and his woman, he waited.

Waited.

His brothers and cousins were trotting over, were surrounding the other outsider.

Waited.

"Well?" he called out.

The outsider took the woman's hand and started backing away.

Long Neck waited no more.

They had been warned.

Heather backed away with Tony, holding his hand, and—

A gurgling and strangled scream, as the Native American moved his hand with one quick flash, slitting Steve's throat. Blood spurted and gushed down the front of Steve's shirt, and the Indian—blood streaming down his wrist—held up his hand in triumph, the knife pointing in the air. He shouted something and the other Indians whooped in reply.

Heather screamed and started running, and Tony ran with her, holding her hand tight. A distant voice yelled out, "Guys, don't leave me here! Christ, please, don't leave me here!"

She said, gasping, "Is that Cal? Is that Cal?"

"Don't look back! Don't look back!"

But she did look back. Cal was crying, was holding up his arms, as some of the Native Americans clustered around him, yelling, laughing, slashing at him with their knives.

Long Neck yelled out, "Leave the outsider alive! He still has to play the game!"

His brothers and cousins stopped, as the outsider cowered on his knees, his hands over his head, his bare chest and arms slashed and streaked with blood.

"Deer Run! With me! After those two."

With his brother at his side, Long Neck started running across the wide playing field, as the chubby outsider and his woman ran ahead of them.

All that existed in her world was running, running, running. She didn't want to think of Steve with the blood spurting from his throat or Cal crying as the other Indians struck at him with their knives. Tony stopped saying anything, and she looked ahead, at the grove of pines, the place where the trail had emerged, and the thick bank of mist that hovered above it.

"Drop . . . your . . . pack . . ." Tony gasped as he suddenly let go of her hand. "Do it . . . but keep running . . ."

Running with the bouncing pack on her back and trying to slip out of it was awkward as hell, but she managed to do it, the pack thumping to the ground. She managed not to break stride and she glanced back to see—

Tony, stopped, bent over, breathing hard.

The two Indians still racing out there, coming closer.

"Tony!" she screamed. "C'mon! Don't stop!"

He raised his head. Spit was running down his chin. His face was so very pale.

"I . . . can't do it . . . so tired . . . you . . . keep running . . . do it . . ."

"Tony!"

He stood up, took a deep breath. "Heather! Get your ass moving!"

Tony started tugging at something on his pack. He looked up again. "Move!"

The Indians were so close she could see their skin glisten, the color of the paint on their skin, even their damn eyelashes, as their running legs moved in a blur.

Tony's voice softened. "Heather. Should have listened to you back there. Should have. Now. Please. Go."

Crying, she turned and started running, ignoring the ache in her hip.

Up ahead were the pine trees, their trunks so wide and thick, so full of hiding places.

She spared one more glance before ducking into the trees.

Her Tony, standing there. His walking stick, which had been strapped to his knapsack, was now in his hands.

"You want a fight, assholes?" he shouted out. "Then come and get it!"

The Indians descended upon him, whooping and crying, and Tony held his walking stick with both hands and flailed at them.

Heather whirled around and made it to the trees.

Long Knife stood, breathing hard, his hands and arms sticky with the blood of the second outsider. This one had been brave, had put up a fight for his woman, but it had been a weak fight. The outsider was on the ground, his legs having collapsed underneath him after he and Deer Run had sliced at the muscles and tendons, and he was rasping and shaking.

"Deer Run," he said, deciding to give the younger one the honor. "Finish him."

His younger brother smiled with delight, blood drying on his hands and arms as well. "Thank you, brother."

A swipe of his hand and knife to the throat, coughing and gurgling and choking as the outsider put his hands to his throat, a futile attempt to stop the bleeding. Deer Run got up and kicked at the outsider's hands. Not a cruel act, but one of mercy. The quicker he bled out, the sooner he would go to his resting place. The outsider's voice rattled, wheezed, and then he was dead.

Deer Run said, "What now?"

Long Neck looked to the woods, where the woman had just disappeared into the first line of trees.

"We follow the woman."

"But the mist . . ."

"We follow the woman. She humiliated us back there, by scoring. It will not stand."

Deer Run nodded. "As you say, brother."

• • •

Heather kept running, kept moving. There! There was the damn trail! Her mouth was dry, her lungs burned, and she was certain that she was about to throw up at any second. She got on the trail, kept her pace, her mind racing, rewinding what had happened those past few moments.

The Native Americans playing their lacrosse game.

The old man scaring the shit out of her.

Tony coming over, deciding to leave . . .

The tall Indian going crazy, grabbing Steve, yelling at them.

Like no one was supposed to leave.

What the hell was going on here?

The trail rose at a gradual pace, trees and low brush on both sides, the branches whipping at her face and hands as she ran up the slope.

A sudden pain stabbed at her side, and she grabbed her ribs.

Just a stitch. That's all. Just a stitch.

She stopped, panting, breathing, bending over at her waist to try to ease the pain.

Heather looked up. The trail was still there, like a clear path, heading up to freedom.

There.

What was that?

Voices, shouting behind her.

They were close, they were on the chase, and she was the prey.

Another look at the trail.

Wide, inviting, and too goddamn obvious.

She quickly moved off the trail, into the undergrowth, and started moving as quick and as quiet as she could.

Long Neck ran up the trail, knife in hand, breathing steady but deep. The outsider woman wasn't that far ahead of them, and he was certain he and his brother Deer Run would catch her, soon enough. Bring her back to the field if possible, cut her down if not, but in any event, the game would end only when he, Long Neck, said it would end, with the other players on the ground before them.

The trail moved up at a slight slope, and it was a good feeling to hear Deer Run behind him.

Up ahead.

He held his hand out and slowed down.

Deer Run came up next to him, breathing hard but still able to speak. "What is it, brother?"

He pointed his knife to the right. A branch had been recently broken. Two flowers on the ground had been crushed and were only now slowly regaining their height.

"She's gone this way, off the trail."

Deer Run nodded. "That woman is a sly one."

"Not sly enough. We can still catch her."

Deer Run was concerned. "The mist, brother. It is nearby."

"I don't care. We can still do it. Now, follow me."

Into the dark woods he went.

Now the tears were coming as she pounded her way up the steep rise of the mountain. Why? What had happened? Reenactors? Really? They were killers, that's what they were. Killers! She wasn't sure if they were crazed locals pretending to be Indians, or real damn Indians that had managed to keep hidden all these years, but what the hell difference did it make.

At some point she would be where she could call the police, and . . . Damn.

Her cell phone and everything else was in her pack, dumped back in the field.

So what? She'd keep on running, get back to the main trail, and either run into some hikers who had a cell phone or make her way to a road.

Any way you look at it, those assholes back there wouldn't get away with it.

Up ahead, the mist was there, the odd mist that had risen after they had passed that damn waterfall.

Her chest thudded. There was a rocky trail that led to the right. If she got up there, she'd be in the mist in just a minute or two, and that'd help hide her from those maniacs chasing her.

A yell, a holler.

She turned. The two maniacs were just below her, close enough so she could throw a stone at them.

Long Neck stopped. Deer Run was beside him.

"Too close," Deer Run said.

Long Neck stared and stared at the outsider above them. She was watching them, looking down, fear and defiance in her face. The mist was just above her.

He hated to admit it.

His brother was right.

Deer Run said, "We have to go back."

He sighed and lowered his hand, the one with the knife.

"We do. We do."

Deer Run slapped him on the shoulder. "But the game will go on, it will, won't it, brother?"

Long Neck turned and started back down the mountain.

"It will go on forever," he said.

The mocking voice of the outsider woman followed them both for quite a while.

Heather couldn't believe it. They were turning! They were walking away! They weren't chasing her!

She couldn't help herself. She yelled at them, "That's right! Turn around, assholes! Go back to that damn field and get ready to get your asses arrested! I'm gonna get the cops over here damn quick, and your sorry butts are going down!"

Heather burst into tears, wiped at her face and eyes, and, as the two Indians disappeared into the woods, called out one last time: "For Cal! For Steve! For Tony! You're not going to get away with it, you miserable bastards!"

A hand on her shoulder.

She shrieked.

Turned.

The old Indian was there, staring right at her with hate and contempt and evil, and she automatically took a step back, and fell.

And fell.

And fell.

The pain was so great.

She woke up, moved, shrieked again. The back of her head throbbed and throbbed, and blood was trickling down her face. Her right leg was screaming at her and she lifted her head oh so slightly, saw it twisted in a strange way. She was on an outcropping of rocks and stone. Her left wrist dangled.

Oh God.

She closed her eyes and opened them again.

The old man was before her. He looked down at her, and what she saw scared her even more.

He was no longer looking at her with hate or anger. No. He was looking at her with a smile, with satisfaction on his wrinkled and scarred face.

Heather said, "What . . . what is it with you people?"

The old man raised his arms, started talking . . . but it sounded like something else.

Chanting? Praying?

"Please," she said, the pain running through her like flames. "It hurts so much . . ."

He kept his arms up, and Heather couldn't believe it, but he was wavering.

For a moment or two, she was sure she could see rocks and trees through the old man, like he was transparent, fading . . . but maybe it was the pain or the blood in her face. But he wasn't staying still . . . he was flickering.

Oh God.

The pain.

The old man lowered his arms, looked down at her, started talking.

Oh my.

She found it hard to believe, but she was beginning to understand him!

Not all of it, but enough to make sense.

"... *your ancestors came here so very long ago* ..."

"... *besides fire and treachery they brought diseases* ..."

"... *so many died, so many villages emptied* ..."

"... *curse upon your race and upon each generation later* ..."

"... *the spirits of our finest players and warriors live forever* ..."

"... *to play and prey upon you* ..."

"... *we of the Abenaki will live here forever* ..."

"... *and forever we will have our revenge upon you* ..."

She was so scared, she hurt so very very much.

Heather said, "Please ... so long ago ... it's not fair ... it's not fair ..."

The old man wavered so much more. He now had a knife in his hand. He bent down over her, flickered some more.

Was he going away?

Was he going to disappear?

Was he even there?

A whispery voice from the old man: "... not fair, yes, but it is right ..."

And the last thing Heather learned was that yes, he was there, and in spite of the talk of spirits and generations, his knife was real enough.

Grant Spencer, head selectman of New Salem, New Hampshire, went over again to the pile of bones, sparing a quick glance up at the rise. All clear. No mist. He returned his view to the alleged crime scene. A skull grinned up at him. He saw a rib cage, a spine, a smattering of other bones.

"Hollis," he asked his police chief. "How many this time?"

"At least three," he said.

Ezra stood next to the chief, quiet. Hollis looked down at the open cut in the soil. Grant peered in once again. "Any idea?"

Hollis sighed. "Three years ago. Four hikers from Connecticut. Went into the White Mountain National Forest and never came out."

"Oh."

The three of them stood silent. Ezra spoke up. "I bet those families back in Connecticut would find comfort knowing where the remains were."

"Yeah," the chief said.

Grant looked at the bones. "Hollis, you've got experience. Those hikers have been gone about three years. But how old do these bones look like to you?"

Hollis knelt down at the edge of the dirt. "To me? Boss, pretty damn old. Skin and tendons gone. Just a few scraps of clothing. Bones really show their age."

Grant said to Ezra, "You want to try explaining to those Connecticut families how their missing kids from three years ago now exist as old bones, maybe hundreds of years old?"

Ezra shook his head. "No, sir."

Hollis stood up, brushed his knees. "What now, Grant?"

He shrugged, remembering that dark night years ago when his father had told him the secret of their small town, and how his father's father had told him the same story, all the way back to the first settlers here, centuries ago. "What do you think? What happens on this field stays in this field, so long as they get . . . their players. And if they don't get their players, you don't want to tempt them . . . like what happened in 1810."

The other two men nodded at that. Buried deep in the safe at the town hall—among other important original New Salem documents—was a handwritten manuscript more than two hundred years old from the head selectman at the time, Hartley Speare. He wrote of the previous summer, where a young, arrogant clergyman, the Reverend Noah Powell, had persuaded his congregation to build a stone wall on the trail leading to the valley, to prevent any more unsuspecting players to go forth into what he had called "the Devil's playing field." The wall had lasted a mere season, until a mist had come down the mountains one night, and when it disappeared the next morning, four strong lads from families in New Salem had been found bloodied and killed in the town common.

"They . . . they need to stay where they belong," he added. "In the valley."

The sworn law enforcement officers of New Salem, New Hampshire, looked at Grant and nodded in agreement.

Grant said, "Rebury them. We've been reburying them for hundreds of years. We can't stop now."

A while later, Grant was hiking up the narrow, unnamed trail, his knees aching something awful. Behind him were Hollis and Ezra, keeping pace with his slow climb, none of them saying anything as they passed the broken stones from Reverend Powell's stone wall. He paused to catch his breath, and then there were loud and laughing voices from above. Grant looked back at the two police officers, and they stepped off the trail, giving space for the descending visitors.

Three men came into view, laughing and talking. All carried knapsacks, all had walking sticks in their hands. The one in front had a beard, and he stopped and said, "Hey, whoa, are we trespassing or something?"

Grant knew what they meant. Two uniformed cops were standing behind him.

"Nope, not trespassing. We're just out here on official business. Nothing to worry about. You guys out for some fun?"

"You know it. Is there a good place at the end of the trail to camp out? It's not marked on any of the maps or guides, but it looks cool."

He looked to Hollis and Ezra. Their faces were blank.

Grant turned back to the three men. "Sure. A nice open field down there, big enough to play around in. You can camp out, have lots of fun. How does that sound?"

"Awesome," he said.

"Glad to hear it," Grant said.

THE GOD'S GAMES

DANA CAMERON

Dana Cameron can't help mixing a little history into her fiction, and "The God's Games," featuring a werewolf who must prevent murder at the ancient Olympic Games, is no exception. Drawing from her expertise in archaeology, Dana's work (including several Fangborn stories) has won multiple Agatha, Anthony, and Macavity awards and earned an Edgar® Award nomination. 47North published the first of three Fangborn novels, *Seven Kinds of Hell* (2013), and "The Serpent's Tale" (Fall 2013).

When your oracle sends you on a quest, you don't drag your feet. I'd made the dangerous sea voyage from Halicarnassus on a crowded cargo ship, then risked bandits overland, to get to Olympia in a little over a week. Even traveling as fast as a mortal can go, arriving on the third day of the Games, I will admit I was reluctant walking the last miles from the boat landing. We who are born to the Fang work in secret, in the shadows. The idea of being among the thousands attending the sacred Games and holy rites at Olympia made me very uneasy.

Secrecy and peril is a fact of life for my kind. We may be gifted with extraordinary powers of longevity, strength, fast healing, and even metamorphosis, but we need those powers to fight evil and do the gods' will. So wherever an oracle sends you, there'll be adventure, danger, and glory. Which is why I'd done my duty and made love to Thyia, a girl of my village, so that if I should die, another born to the Fang would follow me. Although our women are like Amazons and fight alongside us, they must also take care to preserve our race.

Secrecy and peril; adventure, danger, and glory. Our life is never simple.

The Korax I was directed to was posing as a lowly fortune-teller at the Games. I found him easily enough in a nasty tent of dirty leather and gave him the letter from my oracle at home. After reading it, he scratched himself and threw another stick on the fire. "Okay, that jibes with what I've been seeing, my boy. Your Korax foretold a defiling of the Games on the fourth day. I saw—" He nodded at his tripod and a pile of herbs so rank they made my eyes water. "I saw a merchant named Keos plotting to kill his own brother to enrich himself."

I made a warding sign against the horrible notion; he did the same.

"Clearly, the gods have put us both on the same path: You're to prevent the murder and therefore the potential defiling of Zeus's holy Games with fratricide. Better if you can also expose the would-be murderer."

I cracked my knuckles and shifted uncomfortably on my stool, missing my hammer and my chisel. Stone working was an art, but it was straightforward. Not like human intrigue, not like the gods.

Not like oracles.

"Here," he said, handing me a small knife and a bit of wood. I hadn't seen them before they appeared in his hands. "Stop fidgeting like that."

I took them gratefully. You don't just pull out a knife in front of an oracle. And if he hadn't given me permission, it would have been disrespectful of me to carve while he spoke, as if he deserved only a fraction of my attention. "Thank you, cousin."

He grunted and poked at the fire. Without thinking, I began to carve and soon revealed the eagle trapped inside the wood. A symbol of Zeus. See? I am a straightforward man.

I said, "But if my oracle saw danger at the Games, less than a month ago, why didn't the vision go to—?"

Fatigue and hunger made me foolish enough to even frame such a question.

The Korax was in a forgiving mood, however, or was less strict than the oracle back home. "To someone nearer?" He shrugged. "I don't know, Lycos. Just give thanks someone foretold trouble, and that you're here to stop it."

Lycos isn't my name, of course, any more than *Korax* was the oracle's. It simply means that when I transform, I take the shape of a wolf. My kin who change into snakes, and are healers, are called *Ophis*. *Korax* is "raven." Ravens and crows see far ahead and lead wolves to prey.

My people, those born to the Fang, and those born to the Sight, serve the gods on Earth. As we fulfill our roles in protecting humans and eradicating evil, some of our people say we take on the aspects of the gods themselves. Some of us, like the Korax, have the Sight, or luck, to direct those who of us who fight, who track and tear at sinners. That service comes with a sacrifice, and while we must act in secret and keep apart from ordinary mortals, it is a blessed life.

"Thanks for this." He nodded to the bundle beside him, which contained the letter as well as a gift of cakes, a tradition among our people. "Go, get yourself some dinner, make your offerings, then come back."

I looked up; I was tired and hungry. Also eager to see Olympia, fabled for its temples, statues, and—

He shook his head, as if reading my mind. "We've a long day tomorrow—the fourth day of the Games. I've seen that's when the murder can be prevented. And to do it, you need to participate in—and win—the pankration. I've already had a word with the judges; you're entered."

My jaw dropped. "Me? Fight in front of all those people? I won't be able to turn into a wolf, or even a wolf-man! How can I possibly—?"

The oracle only gazed at me across the fire. This time I had stepped across the line of respect.

We who are born to the Fang never question an oracle. Never. I bowed, intimidated by the fury in his eyes. "My apologies, seer, I am fatigued. I will do as you say. And I *do* excel over all my kin in the pankration."

Which was ironic. *Pankration* means "all powers." I could fight my opponent by any bare-handed means: boxing, wrestling, kicking. No weapons, and any fighting strategy was permitted, save biting or eye-gouging. Or turning into a wolf-man.

How could I serve the gods properly without using my one unique power?

He nodded and, with a gesture, dismissed me. He turned to his tripod and flung a handful of those awful herbs onto the pan. "Hey, Lycos!"

I turned. His back had gone rigid, and he seemed to be staring at the hide walls of his messy little tent. A true vision was upon him.

"Stay away from women."

Crazy old man. Of course I wouldn't go catting about; I was on a mission from the gods. But I'd already offended him once, so I bowed to his back and thanked him.

"I'm serious. Boys, too. But I've just seen—while you're here, you need to lay off the pussy."

I bowed again and backed out.

I straightened myself, dusted twigs and herbs and spiderwebs from my shirt. There was nothing on earth holier—or crazier—than one of our oracles.

Dismissed for the moment, I was left to explore the Olympic village. When I say *village*, I don't want to mislead you—it's far more than a few houses with a well, an altar, and a market twice a week. This place was almost incomprehensible to me, and I've seen many cities. I could be accused of telling travelers' tales, but it's well known what the village is like during the Games.

The noise, the sights, from all over the world. There are fine pavilions for the merchants and better sorts, who are here to have their fortunes told, make sacrifices, make deals, and show off, too. Then there's where the rest of us live, if you can call it that: crowded, dirty (in spite of the baths), smelly (in spite of or because of the latrines), and loud, with drunken brawling and celebrating well into the night. Try to get some sleep there, in your blanket under the stars. You'd think the athletes would be focused on preparation, but most of them, as much as they crave victory, also want to drink hard and try to persuade the whores to sleep with them for free.

Despite the sanctity of the Games, there's no false modesty here: Everyone is strutting, everyone is trying to sell you something. The athletes are pretty bad, with the posing, the oiled muscles, the slagging off their opponents, all in the search for a benefactor to pay their expenses, even if it's just a meal and a night's drinking. The poets are worse, on their little platforms, with their piles of trophies and awards at their feet, bellowing out their latest works for all to hear. You'd think old men would have weaker voices, but they're looking for patrons, too, and that must give them the strength to belt out an epic or two. Or perhaps Apollo is granting them sound lungs and carrying voices, as they claim. But the philosophers are even more aggressive and will get into fistfights over their rhetoric. They might as well sign up for the boxing matches.

The prostitutes do a bang-up business, as there are no modest married women in the village, and no women at all allowed to view the Games. Oh, sure, a few sneak in dressed as men, but if you're a father of a virgin, you keep her away, or risk coming home with a debauched daughter or a hungover discus thrower for a son-in-law.

Everyone showing off, but me. I had to pretend to be *less* than I was. By choice, I would never compete against an ordinary mortal in the Games—that didn't seem fair. And yet it seemed impious *not* to use all my powers.

But when an oracle speaks, you do what he says. Denying them is tantamount to refusing the gods.

Committing murder would pollute the Games, which was like spitting on Zeus Thunderer himself. I had to prevent it from happening. It would bring the god's wrath—famine, wars, earthquakes—on all of us, not just the sinner. Not only would I have to win the pankration, without using my ability to change, but I had to stop the murder and expose Keos.

First things first. I bought a cage of pigeons—at a seriously inflated price—and made an offering at the Temple of Zeus in gratitude for my safe passage. Then I privately sacrificed to Herakles, to whom I felt most close. There were tales that Herakles was also born to the Fang, and he was certainly the first pankratiast.

Duty satisfied, I could honor my stomach. I was ravenously hungry and detected burning charcoal and grilling meats. My nose, acute even by my people's standards, led me to a most promising food seller. Lamb, fat dripping and sizzling, seasoned with wild thyme. The aroma almost drove me beyond my control, but I calmed myself and, hearing the other prices from other vendors, estimated what I'd have to pay.

"Greetings! I'll take—" I was about to say *everything*, but that would have been excessive, even for an athlete in training. "Er, three of those, please."

"Ah, you know good cooking!" The vendor grabbed a couple of grape leaves and pulled the skewers from the grill.

I sniffed approvingly. "You're from near Miletus?"

"I am!" He glanced up and down at me. "You know your food. Based on your dress, your accent, you're from around there, too?"

"Near Halicarnassus."

"Then I'll take off a quarter from the price. Always good to see someone from near home."

Miletus was about two days' travel from Halicarnassus, but we were both so far from home, it practically made us brothers. His price was fair enough—just twice regular cost, with his discount, but standard for festival rates. The aroma of the meat was heavenly. "Thank you!"

"Excellent. If you want wine, nicely watered for a good boy like you, go over there." He jerked his head to a vendor nearby. "He's a Cretan, but his wine is good, and he won't rob you too badly."

I nodded my thanks, barely able to remember to open my purse and pay the man before I wolfed down the meat. And then—

Was it Heaven itself that made me look up? My attention was drawn, like an arrow to its mark, to a curtained litter being carried down one of the makeshift roads. Past the rough-and-tumble of the temporary thoroughfare toward the gaudy colors of the pavilions, I could sense *her*, almost as if she were standing in front of me.

The thick blue silk curtain parted for just a moment, and despite her veils, the distance, the crowd, our eyes met.

Her eyes were lined with kohl; I knew she and her garments were scented with roses. Skin soft as a peach, pale as ivory . . .

A shiver went down my spine.

The curtain settled, the entourage passed by.

"Who—?" I said, scarce able to catch my breath.

"That's Phryne, the courtesan," the vendor said reverently. "One of the most famous *hetairai* in the world. She won't be at the Games, but she attends her master, Tenes, and is the centerpiece of his life. Tomorrow night, for example, her master's brother, Keos the merchant, will throw a party for the day's victor in pankration." The vendor turned the skewers of meat and sighed. "But this is as close as either one of us will ever get to her."

That was it, then: I had to win in order to attend the party to get close to Keos, and stop him from killing Tenes.

So much the better, if Phryne were there . . .

As if my wishes were coming true, I felt a soft hand sliding along my arm. "Hmmm, I like muscles. *You* wouldn't leave me wanting, would you?"

I looked down. A little prostitute had appeared out of nowhere. They'll do that.

"Leave me." I jerked away, too roughly. "Sorry, I can't—"

She spat. Short, dark, pretty, and common. Slightly buck teeth. "Yeah, right. Like you'd ever get next to *that*." She jerked her head toward the litter. "Not even with that nice fat purse."

I realized I'd left my purse gaping, the coins on view for all to see. "I . . . I have been told to avoid women, during the Games. That's all." I stashed my purse safely in my shirt. I cursed. More than most, I knew better caution than that.

"Hey, prostitutes don't count, right? Come find me, if you ever find yourself at loose ends. I'm cheap and clean, the best bargain at the Games. Ask for Cythereia."

The vendor snorted, as he made sure *his* money was safely tucked away. "Yeah, right. *You're* named for Aphrodite. Get out of here; let my customers eat in peace."

An argument ensued, and I departed. I stopped at the Cretan's and bought wine, then ate and drank absently, a rarity for me. I tried to remember a snatch of a poem I'd heard years ago, at home.

"*. . . Helen with the light robes and shining among women . . .*"

I'm better with stone than words, but that was how I felt looking at Phryne.

I tried to put her out of my mind. I dusted the crumbs off myself and a thought struck me. Perhaps I could find a way to prevent the murder without competing.

Eagerly, I began to cast about—nothing obvious; I didn't want to look as though I were tracking something by scent. Also, in a crowd like this, latrines overfilling, bodies unwashed, trash heaps made less appealing with vomit and bloody bandages, no one—especially someone with my sensitive nose—wanted to breathe too deeply. I found nothing that would help me.

I did break up a fight before it could get ugly—one look at me and my muscles, and the would-be contestants thought better of their brawl. "Save it for the Games, boys."

A little farther on, I saw a cut-purse at work. I could've snapped his wrist easily, to teach him a lesson, but I wouldn't draw attention to myself. I settled for picking *his* pocket and then redepositing the stolen purse in the rightful owner's shirt. Smooth as oil and quick as a cat.

All of this made me feel better but did nothing to help me with my goal. I headed to the pavilions of the wealthy. The stink wasn't so bad here; in fact, it was downright appetizing, what with the delicacies being prepared for the evening's celebrations, the perfumes everyone wore, and the general cleanliness of the place. The food reminded me I'd had only a very scant dinner, and could use more.

I nosed around as much as I could without raising the guards' suspicions—some of the affluent had private armies for their security, in addition to cooks, maids, grooms, and such. One guard took too much interest in me, so I backed off. I could have taken him easily, but that wasn't my job.

So intent was I in looking harmless, I stepped on something.

"Ow!" An irate female voice accompanied a hard shove to my back. "Mind yourself, oaf! These sandals cost more than you earn in a year!"

"Iris! Softly, softly, please. We're here to create pleasure, not cacophony."

"Sorry, my lady." Her contrition lasted only a moment. "But this great, ugly brute—"

A glance from her mistress silenced her.

The sight of her mistress struck me dumb.

It was Phryne, my Helen. Walking with her ladies, on her way to— It didn't matter where. It would be Elysium, while she was there.

My mouth went dry and I shook as I never did, even confronting the cruelest of villains. I'd forgotten my purpose, smitten by her beauty.

And she, a perfect Grace, *smiled*. She was used to such admiration, and yet did not mock my amazement, as she might.

I dropped my eyes and bowed. And was rewarded: A silken scarf, the color of lavender, had drifted to the ground unnoticed.

I picked it up; it floated like mist on the night air. Daring greatly, I handed it to Phryne directly, rather than to her cross maid.

Another smile sent me dizzy. A soft thrill ran through me as her elegant nails brushed my dirty, callused fingertips.

Phryne opened her mouth, perhaps to thank me, perhaps an invitation to—

Her eyes hardened slightly at something behind me, but her pleasant smile remained fixed on her face. A sickness creeping through my gut had nothing to do with the finer feelings Phryne inspired.

I glanced behind me, just in time to see a meaty fist crashing down toward me.

Though I'm taller than most, I'm very quick, even without shifting my shape. I stopped his hand before it struck, and stood with his fist trapped in mine. He was strong, though not through honest labor like mine. Nearly as tall as me, with narrow eyes and a hooked nose that gave him an unkindly look. He was one of those sleek boys who imagine they're owed something.

His carefully arranged curls and expensive clothes made me acutely aware of my broad features, my sunburned skin and unruly hair, and my rough, country garb.

I still had manners. "I beg your pardon, my lady," I said, never taking my eyes from his. "I meant no disrespect."

"Eleon! You are very quick to a lady's aid, even when there is no need." The words were gentle and commanding. "But I thank you for your assistance."

Eleon relaxed, but the outrage in his eyes never dimmed. He liked hurting people, I realized.

He nodded to Phryne. I released his hand.

She glanced at me. "And thank you, too. You rescued my favorite scarf."

Delight mingled with the continuing sick feeling. I could only nod.

"Tell me your name, that I might hear of your success in the Games."

"Nikodemos. Of Halicarnassus, my lady."

"Well, Nikodemos, you have the thanks of Phryne, and her best wishes." She gestured, and her ladies continued on their way to the pavilion. Iris with the bruised toes shot me a dirty look as she passed.

"You keep your eyes off her, dog!" Eleon said, once they were out of earshot.

"You keep your hands off her, goat!" I answered.

That time, he did not hesitate. He fell on me, with fists like hammers.

I laughed to myself; fighting was a welcome release for my sick confusion. Pummeling bullies was my specialty.

But as I fought him, I got weaker, sicker. I, who had never been bested before, who had the strength of a demigod, fell to my knees.

That was when his friends joined in.

The pain was bad, but the queasiness was worse. What was happening to me? I could throw five ordinary mortals in a fight, and enjoy the exercise. I was struggling with three now.

Finally, I stopped resisting. They dragged me away and chucked me into a sty. I landed in mud and filth, eye to beady eye with a piglet.

"If he cannot find his own way out, at least the pigs will have a good meal of him," said Eleon. His friends laughed, as they walked away.

As soon as he was gone, I started feeling better. I had never been defeated before; the humiliation stung. I'd make him pay—

My training caught up with me. I wasn't here to fight overprivileged thugs, I was here to serve the will of the gods.

I rested until I felt nearly better. One growl from me, and the piglets and their sow kept to the far side of the pen. The growing dark helped: My bruises faded, my cuts healed up, and the ache in my side, where Eleon had kicked me, finally eased. The illness faded, and at last, I could think straight.

There was no time to ponder my strange and sudden indisposition. A stench like that of our storm-tossed ship, filled with sick men and rotting meat, stopped me cold. It was far worse than the clean animal stink around me.

My people can smell evil and are compelled to seek and destroy it.

I growled again. The pigs were perfectly silent in their fear.

A glance around me—no one was there.

A prayer to Herakles, my special benefactor, and I allowed myself to change halfway between man and wolf. I could walk upright but was covered in fur and had a wolf's head, teeth, and claws. I would have nearly my full power but be less noticeable than in a wolf's shape.

That metamorphosis—what can I tell you? It is truly a gift we share with the gods, but no gift from them is a completely unmixed cup. We must undertake our duties in secret. The stories you hear, of Narcissus, Arachne, and Actaeon, changed permanently as punishment? We born to the Fang lose our ability to transform if we ever reveal our other selves. We track evil and are obliged to continue until we defeat it, unable to turn away. Our hybrid and animal forms are a sort of constant prayer to the gods: perfect service. But if we observe our laws and are faithful, the power that accompanies our transformations cannot compare to earthly joy.

I felt stronger, almost immediately, and faster. My wolfish nose picked up a trace of roses. Phryne. I shook my head, keeping to the shadow and following the awful trail, until finally, luck was with me.

That foulness followed the same path as the perfume. My half-wolf's heart did not know the same lust as a man's, but I was filled with a sense of well-being by the fragrance of roses, even as the evil reek drove me forward.

Past the better camps, to the finest; it became harder and harder to move undetected. But I was patient and was eventually aided by the drunkenness that increased as the night's parties wore on. Even a stealthy wolf-man could pass unnoticed, or unremembered.

A thousand odors assailed me, but most were of human folly. I had no time for loose women or badly behaved men, no time for those who served nothing but their own appetites. The disgusting stench compelled me to true work.

The pavilions were located on the driest ground, above the river. Some were simply large shelters; some were a series of tents, creating grand, houselike structures. My trail ended close by the largest. There were many guards here. I recognized two of the guests as Eleon's toughs.

A nervousness overtook me, similar to my earlier sickness, but I remained resolute. Fortune smiled; the wind was picking up, so three of the tent walls were down to protect the celebrants. I could spy on them unseen from behind the heavy curtains.

I saw such a display of wealth that I could scarcely believe it. Seeing this, Midas might have felt a pauper and Croesus might have hung his head in envy. The sights and smells were wonderful, and strange, and vulgar, like an overpainted whore: enticing, exotic, and repulsive all at once. Perhaps my lack of education made me think so: I had no idea what the rich might think fashionable or well done. Fortunately, in wolf form, I could note such things but not be intoxicated by them. My senses were close to overwhelmed by the excesses here, but I retained enough of a man's mind to concentrate.

The closer I got, the stronger the evil was, and my odd weakness grew. No time for illness: I'd found my prey. Three people were at the center of the activity, in the places of honor; a prosperous merchant, Keos, the would-be fratricide, was the source of the evil I sought.

And there was Eleon—damnation! He clearly was Keos's pet athlete, his muscles glistening in the torchlight, his hair bound in a circlet for the feast.

Beside the merchant Keos was a man who looked so similar, it was clear they were brothers.

When I saw Phryne seat herself near the third man, I also knew I'd found my potential victim. She attended her master, Tenes, brother of Keos.

I'd found my prey, his intended victim, and my goddess, all in the same place.

The opulence of the surroundings reminded me I could never hope to win a woman like Phryne . . .

As if that were all that stood between us. Not a sacred oath to the gods, not a warning from the oracle, not my commission . . .

I caught myself growling. Luckily, the music of the players drowned out that noise. *You're here to prevent a murder, not moon over girls. Steady on, Niko.*

Fortunately, the urge to duty was stronger than the stirrings of a mortal heart. My attention was drawn by Keos, who excused himself. Eleon followed.

I hurried after, hidden by the darkness outside the pavilion. Soon the two men were joined by another, an Egyptian, by his dress. He handed a cup to Eleon.

Eleon made a sour face.

"Come on now, it's not so bad!" the Egyptian said. "Making a face like an infant—and you some tough pankratiast! Drink it down; it will keep your humors in balance, you lunatic. If you don't take care, and take your medicine, you'll run mad again. *And* lose Keos's patronage."

Eleon was a pankratiast, too?

Eleon looked like he might slap the cup aside. Instead, he snatched it up, took three great gulps, and then flung the cup from him.

It landed with a crack of breaking pottery. One of the larger fragments bounced over to me.

I whimpered. A wave of nausea, and all thought of pursuit left me. I was so dispirited, I wished my life would end. My joints went like wet twine. The very strong felt any physical setback acutely, because they were used to strength. I knew it to be true. My people suffer little illness or lameness, usually dying violently.

The cup contained whatever was making me so ill. By drinking it, Eleon had gained a kind of power over me. Or rather, my great strength and quick healing were no good against him.

And yet I needed to get closer. Maybe if I avoided that damned cup . . .

I circled around, padding lightly. As I did, my head cleared and the strength came back to me. But I could get no nearer to Keos, not with all these people around and Eleon so close to him.

By the time I'd skirted the edge of the pavilion and dodged a party bent on some private debauchery, I realized that Keos and the Egyptian cupbearer were moving away from the torchlight.

Keos dismissed Eleon. I turned away, hoping that if Eleon saw anything in the darkness, it would be a man's form rather than my wolf's head. He stomped right past me, unseeing, muttering in a childish rage.

The Egyptian handed Keos a packet; my keen nose wrinkled. Carefully trained to identify the odor and taste of drugs and toxins, I could scent a foreign poison from my hiding spot. And they might have thought themselves out of any mortal's hearing but could not trick my sharp, pricked-up ears. Progress at last.

"Sire, if you use that tomorrow night, at the full of the moon, its powers will be at their fullest."

"And his death will seem natural?"

The Egyptian nodded. "Perhaps too much celebrating, a heart attack. No trace at all, nothing that will lead to you."

Keos clapped the Egyptian on the shoulder, and the two parted.

I now knew when and how the murder would be perpetrated. I sneaked down to the river, exchanged my wolf-man form for a man's, and ran to the Korax's tent.

"Weak in the knees, huh? Sick to your stomach?" Korax said. "What did I tell you about staying away from women?"

"It was after she'd gone, and they were beating me. Then later he drank something that made it worse!"

"No idea what it was?"

I shook my head.

"And you couldn't bring it back, eh?"

"It made me weak just to breathe it!"

The old man went to the door and whistled. A kid came running up, and the old man whispered into his ear. "Don't get caught."

About an hour and another bowl of food later, there was a bird whistle from outside the hut. The old man trotted out, and trotted back in almost as quickly, wiping his hands quickly.

He sat down, looking a century older. "It's worse than I thought. That stuff in the cup was black hellebore, which is toxic to our kind." He ran his finger along his nose in a gesture that indicated he meant our secret race. "It's one of the few things that will weaken or kill us, so keep that piece of knowledge to yourself. It's used to cure madness—and by your description of his temper, Eleon needs a lot of it. Problem is, it's not good for mortals, either. So they're probably making him worse with each dose."

He spat. "Damned Egyptian quacks and poisoners! Give me an honest physician from Kos, any day." He sighed. "The only thing you can do is keep as far away from Eleon as possible."

"But he's going to fight in the pankration tomorrow! Not only will I be fighting . . . as a man . . . but that damned black hellebore of his will make me even weaker!"

Korax nodded. "Yep. But you have to win to stop Keos and get the proof of his intentions."

A tiny grinding click of pebbles under sandals . . .

Old Korax didn't hear it over the drunken revelry outside, but I rushed out to look for eavesdroppers. I saw a page in Keos's livery shoving through the crowd.

The prostitute, Cythereia, stood right in my path, negotiating with a customer. No way to get around her; there was a juggler on one side and the food vendor packing up for the night on the other.

I jumped onto the vendor's stool and vaulted over the john's shoulders, like one of the bull-dancers of Crete. I landed with barely a stumble, but not in time. I watched as the eavesdropper broke through a hole in the crowd.

Cythereia brought me back to the here-and-now; I'd driven away her trade. "You'll jump *him* in the middle of a crowd, but you won't give me the time of day? Thanks a lot, mister!"

That brought laughs from the crowd now gathering around us. With any luck, her antics would help people forget me—I was supposed to be a pankratiast, not a gymnast. I heard some murmured discussion of the pankration bouts tomorrow, and some bets were exchanged. I'd lost my quarry, shown too much of my ability, and suffered a bad blow to my pride, all in one day.

"Listen, you! What did I say about avoiding women?"

I turned to see old Korax. "He got away. He must have spied that kid you sent nosing about and followed him back."

"Don't worry about it, Lycos. Anything he heard us discuss of our family business would only confuse him. So your cover's not blown. Get a good look at him?"

I nodded. "But I'm sure he heard us. He probably ran straight to Eleon to tell him I'm susceptible to hellebore." I'd never felt so downcast. Korax led me back to his tent.

"What if I can avoid the fight—and Eleon?" I said. "I can try to break in tonight and find proof of his master's treachery. I almost made it earlier. You know my powers."

"And you know mine. My vision says there's no sneaking in. The only way in for you is to beat his favorite at the pankration and be invited to the celebration after. That's what I saw. My gift gets clearer as we go down this path."

I'd had enough of defeat today and was anxious to avoid a fight against that hellebore-swilling Eleon. "This the same gift that tells me to stay away from women?"

He was a frail old man, but his hand hit my cheek before I could blink, and with such force it knocked me over. I heard a crack of thunder outside. I'd gone too far.

"That's for impiety and impudence. You don't have to like me, but you don't question my power. An oracle sent you here, and you crossed half the known world to obey him."

I didn't dare correct him: He knew from my letter that our oracle was a woman.

"Never challenge me again."

I prostrated myself. There was no denying that the sound of thunder had accompanied Korax's displeasure. He was no crank: Zeus was acting through him. "No, Korax. My apologies. Forgive me."

"Get up. Get out."

I nodded, picked up my blanket and bundle, and turned for the door.

"Get some rest," he said gruffly. "Down by the treasuries isn't too loud. If the gods are willing, you have a long, painful day ahead of you tomorrow."

Pankration is the most popular sport of the Games—and why not? Two well-muscled young men, naked and fighting in the mud, to the best of their ability? The idea is as beautiful as the reality is brutal. A live match is nothing as pretty as the scenes you see painted on pottery. I've heard it compared to being a kind of a dance, but that's bullshit. Pankration is a style of fighting so savage, it appealed to the god Alexander's army and to the bloody Spartans.

That was why it appealed to me, too.

The next morning, after prayers, the *skamma* was prepared: Water was added to the sandy ground where we would fight, making it muddy, unstable, and challenging. A priest passed around the urn filled with the lots. I drew, and didn't look, but prayed some more. There's always room for one more prayer, and what better place than at the Games?

Finally, the lineup was announced. I drew an alpha; I swore. Eleon drew an alternate lot. That meant he could get through all the rounds never having to fight, if he was lucky. He'd be fresh for the last opponent.

My lot meant that I'd have to go through three or four different bouts, and win them all, before I even stood a chance of facing him. The odds were stacked even higher against me now.

I almost protested, knowing what I knew about Eleon, his patron Keos, and their plans. There was too much room for cheating, and I had so long to go today. We who are born to the Fang are blessed with stamina and strength, but fighting a series of fresh opponents, under the battering heat of a summer sun in Olympia—while the crowds watched in comfort from the cool, shady hillside, mind you—was a task worthy of the demigod Herakles himself.

I saw the Korax shake his head ever so slightly. I hadn't thought he could read my mind, but then, he's an oracle and I'm no actor. I kept still.

I sized up my first opponent as we nodded to each other and the prayers were made. He was no great matter. I don't know how that bare-faced youth thought he would survive today, but it seemed a shame to subject him to a fast defeat. Perhaps he was looking for a new, well-off lover and wanted to impress some older man in the audience. I'd been in that position before myself, so why deny him a chance? I let him make the most of a blow to the chin that caught me by surprise—the inexperienced fighter is the most unpredictable, and therefore dangerous—so he had a moment to shine. Then I submitted him by sweeping him off his feet and into the mud, seizing his ankle in a lock from which he could not escape. I didn't want it thought I was toying with him.

The next was another matter altogether: short and squat and all muscle. At first I imagined he would be easy to dispatch. I had a longer reach and legs and was certain I would be the better wrestler. But he surprised me with a speed and nimbleness that literally took my breath away. Before I could blink, he'd flung himself at me and, having thrown me to the ground, was inching his way up my body, never releasing me. He was strong as Hephaestus himself, and just as ugly, with two cauliflower ears and a nose that had been flattened by years of combat. If I didn't act quickly, he would find a choke hold on me from behind.

He countered every move of mine, all the while strengthening and solidifying his own position. I tried to sneak a hand under his arm, to break his hold, but his grip was iron, in spite of the oil, sweat, and mud that covered us. Keeping my head tucked was the only reason I'd kept him from sinking that final, match-ending hold. Worse, I had to fight off the urge to transform into my powerful wolf-man form.

The trick now was to keep moving, keep him busy hanging on until I could find an escape. I drove an elbow into his gut and was rewarded with a grunt. He shifted, losing some of his advantage, so I did it a couple more times. I felt him loosen, just a moment, and twisted hard. I made it to my knees. He managed to stay on my back, though his attack was less organized than before. I braced myself and stood up.

Then I slammed us both backward.

The geometers might have had some fancy formula for describing the speed at which he'd hit the ground and the impact he made. I didn't know the equation, but anyone who moves heavy weights—say, a load of stone—understands the power of falling masses.

My breath whooshed out as my head slammed into the earth. But as bad as it was, I landed on top of *him*. I felt his hands fall away from me and his legs go limp. His breath made a whooshing noise that sounded like life leaving a body.

I staggered to my feet, the world spinning, my stomach sick. It was becoming easier and easier to maintain the pretense of human vulnerability.

A movement from the ground. I looked down. My opponent had raised his hand weakly and let it drop on my foot. I waited. His eyes were closed, his nose was bleeding—my neck and shoulder were covered in his blood—and there was a swelling in his ankle. He'd twisted it under himself when we fell to the mud. No more Games for him, at best; a lifelong limp, at worst. I could see welts rising on his gut where my elbow had found its mark, and tried not to think of the bruises welling on my body.

His hand hit my foot a second, then a third time. When he held up his finger, I knew he'd surrendered.

The priest acknowledged my victory. Cheering from the audience, and money changing hands—I'd made some men rich today and perhaps made others poor. I'd have to watch my back; people weren't above trying to save their gold by hobbling the fighters.

I shambled off the *skamma*. Korax was there and placed a cloth soaked in cool river water on the back of my neck. It was as welcome as it was a shock. "How many left?"

"One more, in about . . ." He glanced at the other part of the field. "About, say, ten minutes. One of them is very strong, one of them is smart and lucky. Don't know which I hope you get."

I nodded. "And Eleon?"

"Hasn't left his bench yet. Fresh as a lily. He might be considering a snack."

At the word *snack*, my stomach growled, despite my hurts. I was as hungry as any of my kind can be. We need a lot of food to sustain us through our exertions, even when in human form.

Korax and I watched the match that would decide my third opponent. It didn't take long; I saw a brief struggle in the mud, then a scream. One man hopped up; the other signaled submission and had to be helped away. The loser's ear had been torn off.

The victor swaggered to meet me in our match. His body was hard-muscled and showed wear from years training at the gymnasium. But I knew he was trouble because his face was unscarred; he ended his bouts quickly and decisively, before he had the chance to get marked up.

After the ritual prayer and at the signal, I ran toward him, and he toward me. I moved as if I would kick at him with my left leg, but when he moved to defend himself, I suddenly stepped forward and swung my right knee into his back. He fell forward, and I was on him, grabbing his wrists and planting my foot in the small of his back. I pulled on his arms.

He wouldn't submit, never said a word, but there was nothing he could do against me. Finally, the priest ended the bout, declaring me the winner.

I had no time to enjoy my victory. Another splash of cold water from Korax, a cupful to my lips. "Remember: The hellebore will keep weakening you until he sweats it out. But you have to hang in there, no matter what. Go get him!"

It was time to meet Eleon.

Anyone watching from the hillside could have smelled the hellebore on him, but there was no rule against that. Everyone took potions meant to make them stronger.

I felt dispirited just walking to the *skamma*. I still hurt from the last bouts, and the hellebore was slowing my usually quick healing.

The priest had barely signaled the start when Eleon was on me. No greeting, just a hard tackle to my gut.

Tired and low I may have been, but rudeness was too much. I struggled to resist the urge to transform, but my anger lent fresh strength to my limbs.

I went back several paces but then found my footing. I drove my feet into the ground like posts, and leaned into him, so that while his hands were around my waist, my entire weight rested on his neck and shoulders. I grabbed his waist. Born to the Fang or not, hellebore or not, a stone-carver has muscles and bulk. I stopped Eleon.

The problem was, the closer we were, the weaker I became. I lost my grip, his foot slipped, and we broke apart, stumbling away from each other.

The logic of fighting told me I must get in close. The logic of not poisoning myself said otherwise.

I couldn't let him decide for me. I rushed in, and when he hunkered down for another tackle, I took one last step, pivoted on my foot, and kicked him in the side. He grunted—it was a solid blow—but had the presence of mind to grab my leg.

My head swam with the hellebore; I didn't have much time. I kept my balance well enough to stay upright and beat on his head. The blows weren't accurate, or terribly hard, but they weren't love-taps, either.

With a bellow, he shoved me aside. He slammed his fist into my balls.

A shock of pain through them, and then a hopeful lull, and then a new agony, rushing in a wave through my entire body. I couldn't breathe. I fell to my knees. My eyes blurred with tears; the world swam. My body refused to obey my commands to get up, get up or face worse.

A collective, sympathetic groan from the audience. More than one man there instinctively covered his groin and flinched.

I crawled like a beast, trying to catch a breath, trying not to vomit. Distantly, dimly, I could see Eleon reeling around, blood pouring from the cuts on his head, making his face a gory mask. He wiped at it repeatedly, nearly blinded.

His weakness pleased and inspired me.

Pulling myself to my feet, every movement of my legs a chorus of agony through my belly and bruised balls, I lurched over.

A final rub on his face left a horrible smear. "Come on, donkey! Going to kick me again? Too afraid to wrestle?"

I noticed that the sickness I felt was now mostly because of his last punch, less from the hellebore, which was leaving his system as he sweated. His exertions were helping me.

He ran his hand over his face again and slicked his blood-wet hair back. "What are you waiting for?"

There was something on his right hand that hadn't been there before. He'd concealed a spiked ring in his hair. I knew in an instant, he'd kill me with it.

The crowd was getting anxious, and the priests, too, ready to call the bout on Eleon's behalf if I didn't start fighting again. That they hadn't found the weapon concealed on him during the pregame examination suggested the match was fixed. Perhaps they'd even slipped it into his hair when they were supposedly searching him.

I needed to win. The gods demanded I fight and win, or die trying.

In spite of it all—sacred duty, civic duty, and yes, human pride—I hesitated. I didn't want to die. I recognized the hellebore on the barb of the ring; Eleon knew my weakness. I knew it would stop my heart if it pierced my skin.

I thought about the oracle at home, and the Korax's orders, and yet I hesitated.

Father Zeus, aid me now. I can't rely on the animal powers you gave me, just my human ability—

A movement in the stands caught my eye; a flutter of familiar blue silk on a litter.

Phryne was among the spectators.

It was like a flag signaling the call to battle. I put my head down and charged.

My opponent, incensed by my refusal to quit, also charged.

The crowd roared approval.

I kept one eye out for that right hand and the deadly spiked ring.

His first punch landed on my temple. I fought badly, clinging to his right wrist. I flailed at his head, his body, but he was crazier than ever, made wilder by my defiance.

I twisted again, to keep him from kneeing me. I couldn't win, fighting purely on the defensive. I was going to lose . . .

It began to rain, a downpour. A crack of lightning and a low rumble across the heavens.

The rain swiftly washed away the rest of the hellebore from him. My head cleared somewhat, though every inch of me was bruised and broken . . .

I made a decision. A bad choice, but my only one. I maneuvered, still fighting poorly, giving Eleon every opportunity to do what he wanted to do.

Finally, he got an ankle behind mine and hooked it out from underneath me.

We went down into the mud, him on top of me. I held his right hand with both of mine, the spike only inches from my chin. I wrapped both legs around his waist and pulled him even closer to me.

I swung my left leg over his neck, his right hand pinned against my chest. I raised my hips and, still holding his arm, used the weight of my leg to roll him off me. Now he was on his back, my left leg over his neck, my right leg over his chest, his arm trapped in my hands.

He should have known what was coming, but he kept struggling. He'd have to be a far more sophisticated fighter to escape me now. As it was, he was tired and sore.

Insanity and rage will only take you so far.

I arched my back, pushing my legs down against his body, until I felt his elbow bending the wrong way.

He screamed, but didn't submit.

I arched more, his arm bending backward over the fulcrum of my body. He was risking a break and a dislocation now.

A low animal moan and he went limp. I couldn't tell if it was asphyxiation or pain, but he was unconscious.

I shoved his arm well away from me and rolled over onto my belly, breathing heavily. The mud squelched, and I remembered the pigs in the sty. I growled low and wolfishly in his ear. The crowd couldn't hear; their cheering drowned out even the thunder.

The priest glanced at Keos and shrugged. He stepped forward and placed the olive wreath, cut from Zeus's own grove, on my head and tied red ribbons around my arms and legs.

My heart soared. My hurts dulled and healed, and I felt like a god.

Or perhaps, with the hellebore washed away, I was merely regaining my ability to recover.

I glanced up to the litter, but it was nowhere to be seen. A thing that large, with attendants and bearers, doesn't just vanish . . .

It came to me in a moment: Of course she'd never been there. Women aren't allowed to watch the Games. Like the rain sent to wash away the hellebore, my prayer had been answered. Some god had sent a vision of Phryne to spur me on.

The crowd rushed the field. I found the Korax among them.

I should not have expected *him* to be smiling. He was shaking a finger at me.

My job was only half done.

I'd never seen anything like the celebration feast that evening at Keos's pavilion, much less been the cause of it. The Korax even bought me a new gown for the occasion. Not my taste, but fancy enough, and certainly cleaner than anything of mine.

My people tend to be conservative in their ways, downplaying our deeds, chalking them up to a day's work. Which they are, but I have to say, it was novel and pleasing to have someone celebrate my accomplishments—and as a *man*, not one born to the Fang. For something not only laudable by my people, but celebrated across the civilized world.

A heady wine, and unwatered.

After the third or fourth song, I put aside intoxicating pride and returned to business. Keos had not yet appeared at his own party, so claiming the need to relieve myself, I went to the privies. Seeing no one around, I made the transformation into a wolf-man.

The metamorphosis brought with it that godlike sense of purpose and righteousness that dwarfed the childlike adulation of mortals.

Hugging the shadows of the pavilion, I heard footsteps behind me.

"Forgive me, sir. I was sent to help you find your way—"

It must have been the wine, or my head had been turned by the fuss, or I was still weak from the day's events to have let the page get so close. I turned, snarled, and leaped on him.

The poor fellow fainted dead away with one look at me. Which was just as well.

In my new form, it was easy to pick up the trail of Keos. I followed it to a curtained-off area at the far end of the pavilion, near the line of tents used as storerooms. Two armed men watched there.

Wait—why would extra guards be needed at a storeroom, in this secure place?

I came on them quietly. One was unconscious before he spoke. The other was so amazed by the idea of a wolf-headed man that he spent too long agape in fear. Made it easy for me to incapacitate him.

No more guards, no alarms, and I opened the door to the room, certain I was about to complete my task—

Phryne looked up and saw me. She was stooped over an opened strongbox, an open lock and a small flask on the floor beside her. Keos was also on the floor, unmoving.

Her shock was momentary, confusion followed by awe. She prostrated herself before me. "Tell me the right thing to do, whatever god you are, and I will do it."

I was so startled, I slid from my transformation and was a man once again. Curiosity overwhelmed fear of discovery. "What are you doing?"

She did not look up, her voice muffled by her robes. "Only what I was bid, by my lord and master, Tenes. Sent to recover a document that would prove his brother Keos was a traitor, asking for Egyptian poisons to kill him. I beguiled Keos into bragging and I begged to see the poison."

"Is he dead?"

"No, just unconscious. He's not the only one who can use potions and poisons."

I thought quickly, made my voice as deep and . . . godlike . . . as I could. "We work to the same purpose, then. How will you convey the letter to Tenes?"

"No need, lord. I'll bring it to the edge of this encampment and deliver it to a priest. To sully the holiness of the Games . . . it will be enough to have Keos banished."

She was telling the truth, I could tell. I would watch her from a distance, make certain the exchange was effected. My goal would be achieved.

Without thinking, I stooped down and took her hand, raising her up.

As she raised her head, she gasped. "It's you!"

"Uhh—" As I've said, I'm no actor.

She drew back, as far as she could. "You had the head of a wolf! Are you a Neuri, from beyond Scythia, who can change into a wolf? Or a descendant from cursed Lycaon, who offended Zeus by feeding him a child's flesh?"

I instinctively made the sign to ward off evil. "No! You and I share the same ambition, to serve the gods and preserve the sanctity of the Games."

"Huh," she said, dryly. "I meant only to serve my master."

It suddenly occurred to me that with Keos gone, Tenes would inherit his estate and become one of the wealthiest men in the world. And Phryne would be richly rewarded.

"Tricking Keos was your idea?"

She looked down demurely. She had the craftiness of a man.

"So much cunning behind that lovely face," I said, shocked.

"And what of you?" she snapped. "Lying, sneaking about, abusing the hospitality of Keos, your host? Who knows what kind of sins you committed, to be so cursed with a vicious double nature?"

"I serve the gods!"

"And so might not I? Who knows how I was directed here, if not by the gods? I was succeeding before you arrived!"

A shout: The boy who'd fainted early had come around, no doubt. No more time to waste.

"This way." She stuffed the letter and pouch into the front of her gown and hurried out the door. She led me down through the labyrinth of pavilions. We ran into guards running toward the strong room; she neatly ducked out of my way. I threw one aside and used the other's own shield to bash him.

"Down to the river!" she said. "No one will think to look there. Hurry."

She took my hand; I followed. She knew the maze of elite lodgings well and was clever at avoiding detection. A few moments later, she stopped and waved me away into hiding. She ran to a man; when he removed his hood, I recognized him as a priest. He took the parcel and bowed to her with more respect than I expected. She said a few words, then returned to me.

"Thanks for your assistance. He will escort me safely to my master. And Keos will be taken away for questioning."

"If it hadn't been for me, you wouldn't have needed help with those guards." I realized her plan *had* been perfect, until I'd come along.

"If you hadn't come, there wouldn't have been any ruckus, and I might have been discovered missing from the party," she said impatiently. "Don't try to second-guess the Fates."

She reached up, kissed me on the cheek, and then hurried away with the priest.

I turned into a wolf. I ran, the rushing wind in my ears. It helped blot out my tumult of emotions as I made a speedy escape.

I was past the pavilions when I heard a hiss. "Hey, boy! Over here."

Korax was dressed to travel. He had my bundle with him.

"We gotta get out of here. I arranged for a horse at the edge of the village."

I shifted back to a man's form. "But everyone will know I broke in—"

"No. I chucked a gown identical to yours in the pigsty, then told a guard I'd seen Eleon dragging you back there." The old man cackled. "He'll have a hell of a time explaining—" He stopped abruptly. "Hades. She kissed you, didn't she?"

"How did you—?"

"That woebegone look. The whiff of roses. Also, I had a vision, which is why I am so prepared to run. Didn't I tell you to stay away from—?"

"But I'd completed my task! The proof of Keos's treachery is in the hands of a priest—"

Korax took my hand, his eyes rolling back in his head. "Okay, I know that one. He's no true seer, but he serves his temple honestly." He blinked, then returned to normal. "I said, no women!"

"Keos was stopped, the Games preserved!" I protested.

"Yes, yes," he said, dismissing my words. "But if you hadn't let her kiss you, you could have sneaked back to the celebration and enjoyed an entire night devoted to praising *you*. Now you're running from the greatest victory a man can know, in the middle of the night, with a crazy old man. And in every nymph you sculpt, every scrap of wood you whittle, you'll find *her* face. You'll pine for Phryne as long as you live. I'd hoped to spare you that, at least."

He was right. I'd forever hear the songs about the mighty athlete who was murdered the night of his greatest victory and have to pretend it wasn't me. I'd claim no prize money. I'd remember beautiful, clever Phryne with longing, forever.

Difficult enough, O gods, to make me a man who was also a wolf— why complicate things with oracles' riddles and a *hetaira* with the mind of Odysseus? Why give me all the powers I had, then force me to fight without them? Why also send Phryne to do the work I was sent to do? Why inspire me with a vision of her, when I could never have her?

It was as though the gods set rules for us, and then made sport of us.

It wasn't for me to question any of this, I realized, as we fled through the raucous crowds. Zeus could play us however he chose. It was his Game.

AUTHOR'S NOTE:

While descended from pankration, today's various forms of mixed martial arts have far greater restrictions regarding tactics—and the athletes are generally clothed. I relied on Neil Faulkner's *A Visitor's Guide to the Ancient Olympics* and advice from Joe Basile to create Niko's world in the early fourth century BCE.

THE CASE OF THE HAUNTED SAFEWAY

AN EXCERPT FROM HUNTER HUNTERSON'S WAR JOURNAL

SCOTT SIGLER

New York Times bestselling novelist Scott Sigler is the author of *Nocturnal*, *Ancestor*, *Infected*, *Contagious*, and *Pandemic*, hardcover thrillers from Crown Publishing, and the cofounder of Empty Set Entertainment, which publishes his Galactic Football League series (*The Rookie*, *The Starter*, *The All-Pro*, and *The MVP*).

Before he was published, Scott built a large online following by giving away his self-recorded audiobooks as free, serialized podcasts. His loyal fans, who named themselves "Junkies," have downloaded more than fifteen million individual episodes of his stories and interact daily with Scott and each other in the social media space.

Why was I in the frozen foods aisle of a Safeway store at three in the morning? Because it was haunted, of course, and my job was to make it *un*haunted.

My name is Hunter Hunterson. Technically, you can add a *junior* to that, but since Pa passed away there ain't much confusion on the name front. This here is my War Journal, where I track the exploits of Hunter Hunterson & Sons, my family business.

And what is our family business, you might ask? Monster stompin'. It runs in our blood: I'm second-generation, my kids are third.

The Case of the Haunted Safeway was a doozy, that's for sure. Stick around and I'll get into that story, but first, a little background for you.

A few months back, we chased this parole-jumping, methed-out vampire across country, following his trail of victims from our home in Slayerville, Kentucky, all the way to San Francisco. We bagged that vamp, of course—that's what we do—and turned him in to the Netherworld Protectorate for the bounty.

When we did, the local NP officials informed us that there was a job opening, on account of the local NP marshals getting eaten on the job. The supernatch were running unchecked all over San Francisco, Oakland, and the Bay Area—if I was of a mind to clean up the place, they'd make it worth my while.

I ain't much partial to this area of the country, but the money was regular, and too damn good to pass up. A man's got to provide for his family, you see, and five years from now I could have *three* kids in college at the same damn time.

So, that's how a truck-driving, gun-owning, country-music-loving Republican family came to live in the world's most liberal place. This town has already shown us some wild times: we've seen late-night diner zombies, homophobic fairies, an Oni with an attitude problem, a dead-head wizard up to no good, escaped-convict goblins, and a lady monster hunter who's way more dangerous than the monsters she's supposed to be hunting. We've been zapped, shot at, bitten, stabbed, scratched, glam-oured, punched, and pummeled.

And yet for all those turmoils and travails, it was that haunted Safeway that got to me the most. That case taught me something: there are things worse than death. If you've loved someone as deeply as I have, you'll understand when you read this.

Everything in this story is true, so I hope you enjoy this journal entry.

—Hunter

"Pa," my son said quietly, "since we're here, can we get some Twinkies?"

My son is six foot three and weighs upward of two hundred fifty pounds. He's sixteen; God knows how big he'll be when it's all said and done. All he ever thinks about is girls, basketball, monster stompin', and what goes in his belly—not necessarily in that order.

I leaned back and whispered to him: "Dammit, Bo, there's a ghost right there in front of the frozen veggies. We're here to do a job, not eat."

"We're in a grocery store," he said. "We can do a job *and* eat."

I'm happy my kids are *smart*, but I ain't too keen on it when they're *clever.*

"Bo, if I have to tell you again, I'll—"

"Sorry, Pa," he said quickly. "I'm watching the ghost."

He made a show of looking around the end cap of aisle eight to stare to his right, at the frozen food cases, in front of which floated half a semitransparent body: chest, arms, and head. Instead of legs, it seemed to balance on a cloud of blue mist; the classic case of a half-torso apparition, a default form for some ghosts.

The Safeway was a normal grocery store: ten long vertical aisles that led to a horizontal aisle along the rear. The dairy case, meat section, and a nice-looking deli section lined that rear aisle.

So far, the ghost hadn't done any damage—from what we'd been told, that would soon change.

We were there to evict or 'vaporate that ghostie, clear him out so that the Safeway night-stock crew could get back to work. We couldn't make a move yet, though, because we'd been told this haunting involved *two* ghosts—they apparently threw things, knocked over fruit displays, and basically mucked up business in general.

Bo is my oldest. He's adopted. Not that you need to be a detective to figure that out or anything, what with the fact that most rednecks like me don't have kids with pitch-black skin. He already outweighs me by fifty pounds—another little clue for you if you're keeping score.

Bo's set on taking over the family monster-hunting business. I think he's seen too many straight-to-DVD movies, which might be why he wears that floor-length leather coat. Sure, the coat has hiding places for all sorts of useful things, but I'd rather he dressed like me: steel-toed boots, jeans, flannel shirt, and a John Deere ball cap—you know, workingman's clothes.

Bo is reliable. He's also crazy strong. The way that boy swings his silver baseball bat, sometimes a zombie head will fly so far you can't see it land. When I can keep Bo's mind focused, he's the one I want at my side when the undead feces hits the magical oscillator.

Everyone in the family carries something silver. I prefer to 'vaporate the supernatch at a distance, but more often than not in the stompin' business things come down to up-close and in-person fisticuffs: for that, you need silver. My daughter, Sunshine—she's my baby, I tell ya—loves her bow and her throwing knives, while my younger son, Luke, has his prized short sword. My wife, Betty Lou, doesn't like to ding up her nails, so she carries a purse full of charmed-up costume jewelry.

Me? I've got my rhinestone-studded silver knuckles. I call 'em "Old Glory."

Betty Lou, Luke, and Sunshine were all out in the station wagon. That chapped Luke's ass. At fourteen years old, he's a skinny little fella that takes more after his ma than his pa. Sometimes he gets to face off against the undead, but only when I've already scouted the situation to ensure it's no more than a minor threat. Trouble is, Luke knows when I do that. It always makes him surly and disrespectful. I try to be patient with him, on account of he's only fourteen and I pretty much acted the same way when I was his age.

The Safeway had been haunted for years, we'd been told. Every early April, customers and staff would report weird sensations, the feeling of being watched, of not being alone. By mid-April, some customers would leave the store for good, complaining of fruit moving by itself or someone whispering in their ear: general spooky stuff that's bad for business. By the end of the month, physical manifestations would kick in: late-night damage to equipment and inventory, and—on more than one occasion— night workers were actually hurt by broken glass, unexplained burns, or falling racks. For three straight years, it had gotten so bad that late-night stock people who worked the night of April 24 promptly phoned in their resignation on the morning of April 25. The morning of the twenty-fifth, everything seemed to be fine for the next eleven months, but management still had to hire an all-new late-night shift.

Well, the store's owners had had enough; they wanted the ghosts gone.

I thumbed the button on the box attached to my belt. There was more money for us in San Francisco than we had back in Kentucky, including a nice equipment allocation. We'd used the funds to get fancy headsets that wrap around your ear and have a microphone built in. The headsets let us stay in constant contact with each other. "Luke, you there?" I said.

His puberty-cracking voice came back right away, so loud I winced. "Pa, you need me to come in? I'm ready to go!"

The headset volume was too damn high. Each word felt like a nail in my eardrum. I fumbled with the box but couldn't figure out how to turn it down.

Bo ducked back around the corner, reached out to the box, and spun a dial that I hadn't seen. The volume dropped down to normal. Kids know this electronic stuff like they know how to breathe.

"No, Luke," I said. "I don't need you to come in."

"But, Pa, you—"

"Son, right now your role is research, and if things get bad in here you're my backup. I need you and your sister out there in case things get dicey."

That was half true. We always operate with a backup element. You never know when the supernatch are going to surprise you, when one reported zombie turns out to be a horde, when a sighting of a single harpy turns out to be a bloodthirsty flock. Having backup can be the difference between living and dying. Bo and I needed backup, that part was true—the *un*true part was that our real backup wasn't Luke, it was his mother.

He answered me in that single word that every parent loves to hear from children.

"Whatever, Pa."

I needed to get Luke positive about something, make him feel useful and needed.

"Son, you looked this place up on Giggle, right? You said the Safeway used to be the site of a baseball stadium for the Giants?"

He made a sigh so heavy I would have heard it even without the headset. He always let me know how disappointed he was, but he also always does his part, and that's research. He's got a laptop that he can connect to the Internet even while out in the station wagon. I don't know how the damn thing works. Hell, he even has a little portable printer he brings with him.

"It's *Google*, Pa, not *Giggle*," he said. "Not for the Giants, for a minor league team called the San Francisco Seals. The stadium was built in 1931. The Seals moved to Phoenix in 1957, and they knocked the stadium down two years later. A department store stood here from the late sixties to the midseventies. The building was a bunch of car dealerships in the eighties. In the nineties, they converted it to a shopping center."

A lot of history at this address. The ghosts could have come from any point during that timeline, even before it, possibly. Ghosties tend to lock onto a place due to some kind of violence or tragedy. They stick close to the place where they died, oftentimes not even really being aware that they are dead at all. Vamps, demons, lycanthropes, wizards, ghouls, all of them tend to know where they are, *who* they are, and what's going on around them. Ghosts, on the other hand, are the short-bus riders of the undead.

"That's helpful," I said. "What about stories on murders and suicides at this address? You find those like I asked you?"

"You didn't ask," Luke said. "You didn't say *find those stories*, Pa, you said I should *think about* finding those stories."

The insolence in his tone. Boy wanted to play word games with me, and at a time like this? Rebellion has its time and place in a young man's heart, but that time isn't when we're facing the supernatch. He should have had that information ready for me.

"Luke, you little—"

I heard a *clonk* and a surprised cry of pain from Luke, followed by a long "Aw, mawww!"

I knew that sound all too well. When the kids got out of line, my wife was fond of a whack on the noggin. She wears a lot of heavy rings. They hurt when they hit the back of your head. I ain't too proud to say I know that pain firsthand.

"Betty Lou, you there?"

"I am, Sugar," said the love of my life. "I'll get your smart-ass son to work on those stories. And until then, he can *think* about what will happen when we get home . . ."

Her voice trailed off with the implied threat. I wouldn't want to be in Luke's shoes when this mission was over, I'll tell you that for free. She sounded mad as hell. She also sounded worried, and a little bit . . . *sad*. "Hunter, you okay in there?"

"Right as rain," I said. "We have eyes on one, ain't seen the other as of yet. You picking up any vibes?"

Among her many talents, my wife is an empath. She can feel sensations that others can't. More often than not, she picks up on the energy of an area and has visions related to both what happened and what's *about* to happen. She's not a precog, exactly, but she has a knack for figuring out what the important things are in a case even if she doesn't know why those things are important.

"Nothing specific," she said. "There's a lot of heartbreak there, Hunter. I can't put my finger on it, but something awful and tragic happened."

"How long ago?"

She paused, thinking. "Can't say for sure. There was love, then anguish so deep I can barely hold it back. I think . . . I think it's how I might feel if I lost you."

That was bad news. That could mean the ghosts came from a spat gone wrong, a love triangle, coveting another's girl or beau . . . something along those lines. That always made for a difficult situation. Just like with cops and the living, when it came to the supernatch it was the domestic violence cases that could suddenly spin out of control.

"Thanks," I said. "Sunshine okay?"

"As always," Betty Lou said. "We're here if you need us."

"Thank you, Sugar."

Sunshine is a nice girl. Maybe because she's thirteen. Betty Lou warns me that could change real soon, that my baby girl might fashion a bout of rebellion that would put Luke's to shame.

But when that happens, Betty Lou assured me she'll walk me through it. I know how to discipline boys. My baby girl? Not so much.

"Hunter," Betty Lou said, "I'm feeling . . . something to do with sports. What's the ghost wearing?"

I hadn't thought to look that closely at the ghost's fashion sense.

I pulled Bo back, then leaned out past the end cap so I could get a real eyeful of that floating half torso. It was hard to make out, but once I saw it I couldn't *un*see it.

"Well, I'll be," I said. "Tell Luke to focus his search on the history of the stadium."

The ghost was wearing an old-timey baseball jersey, complete with pinstripes.

"Luke," I said, "you find anything yet?"

Luke prefaced his answer with yet another heavy sigh.

"There was a murder-suicide in 1933," he said. "That's two years after they built the stadium, Joe DiMaggio's second year with the Seals."

Joe DiMaggio? Next to Babe Ruth, DiMaggio was probably the biggest name in baseball history.

"Joltin' Joe played for the San Francisco Seals?"

"Thirty-two to thirty-three," Luke said. "The murder-suicide story doesn't mention him, though. It happened in the locker room, between halves of a doubleheader between the Seals and the Portland Beavers. Story says that John 'The Cannon' Carlisle, a pitcher, shot and killed Francis Haupberg, a backup catcher, then turned the gun on himself."

That was certainly reason enough for a haunting. Maybe the two ghosts came back around the anniversary of their deaths and fought it out, year after year.

"Pa, looks like the Yankees wanted both DiMaggio and Carlisle," Luke said. "The Seals were asking a hundred thousand dollars each, which in today's terms"—I heard his fingers clacking away on his laptop keyboard—"would be one-point-eight million, *each*."

Over three and a half million for two minor league players. I don't know how baseball worked back then, but that's a sizable chunk of money; money has a way of making people do evil things.

"DiMaggio was worth that," I said. "That what the Yankees paid?"

"No, he got hurt," Luke said. "Blew out his knee before the deal happened. The Seals wound up getting twenty-five thousand for him, and nothing for Carlisle, obviously. The murder-suicide happened after DiMaggio's injury, but before DiMaggio went to the Yanks."

That must have been a helluva blow to the Seals organization. They wound up getting an eighth of what they'd hoped for.

"What about Haupberg, the catcher?" I said. "Was he a prospect for the majors?"

The heavy sigh again. "Pa, I told you he was a *backup*. Ain't you listening?"

I heard the sharp *smack* of a ring-clad hand hitting the back of a head, then Luke's hiss of annoyed pain.

"Sorry, Pa," Luke said in a voice that made it clear he wasn't sorry at all. "Francis Haupberg is barely mentioned in the story, other than that he was best buddies with Carlisle."

"So why did Carlisle kill him?"

"The story says Haupberg might have been having an affair with Carlisle's girlfriend."

Men had killed for far less. I mean, if someone made time with my Betty Lou? Well, I couldn't rightly hurt *her*, no matter what she did, but the man that laid hands on her? I'd be hard-pressed not to let my rage take form.

Something else about the story bothered me.

"What was the date of that game?"

"April twenty-fourth," Luke said.

The same day every year when the worst of the haunting went down—*today* was April 24.

"Interesting," I said. "It's the eightieth anniversary of that incident."

"You're a regular math whiz, Pa."

Smack.

"Aw, *Mawww*," Luke said. "Sorry, Pa."

I heard Betty Lou's voice: "Not as sorry as you'll be when we get home. Tell your father the rest."

I knew the heavy sigh was coming before Luke did it, and he didn't disappoint.

"There was another death a week after the murder-suicide," he said. "A man named Louis Lima hung himself with a rope made of gym towels, right in the same locker room where they found Carlisle and Haupberg."

If the Safeway spooks were, indeed, Carlisle and Haupberg, and their ghosts had been involved with the death of Louis Lima, it meant I could be dealing with ghosts that were willing to kill mortals. Bad news.

"Hunter," Betty Lou said, "this story fits with the emotions I'm feel-

ing from the place. Hurt, anger, betrayal . . . there's some tortured souls
in there."

Tortured souls, and a high level of paranormal activity happening
on the anniversary of a murder-suicide. Ghosts have a thing for anniver-
saries; it's like they're stuck in a tape loop that plays out on a calendar
basis. I've heard tell it's got something to do with lunar cycles and the
Earth's rotation and whatnot, but I'm a stomper, not a scientist.

"John Carlisle and Francis Haupberg," I said. "Those are our ghosts.
Now we just have to figure out how to send them on their way."

The second ghost showed up five minutes later, a legless half torso floating in a cloud of bubbling green vapor. Its pinstriped jersey matched that
of Ghost Number One, but Ghost Number Two also wore a catcher's
chest protector and a catcher's mask. Behind the mask, two glowing,
yellow dots amid a sea of deepest black.

Bo tugged at my sleeve.

"Pa, should we take 'em now?"

"Hell no," I said. "We watch for a little bit."

Ghosts are creatures of habit. Maybe *programming* is a better word
for it. They'll do the same things over and over, especially ones that
operate at a particular time of day or day of the year. Don't get in their
way and they'll probably never know you're there. Of course, getting in
their way was our job. That would come soon enough. I needed to gauge
their power before I started a tangle.

The catcher floated down the store's long, horizontal end aisle to the
rear corner and stopped in front of the frozen seafood freezer. Inside the
sliding glass doors were bags of shrimp, fish, scallops, and other goodies.
The catcher turned his back to the door and faced down the length of
the aisle. He lowered. The tile floor in front of him vibrated, shifted . . .
a glowing home plate appeared, perfectly square in the front, rear point
pointed back to the freezer.

The legless, glowing pitcher moved to the center of the end aisle,
stopping in front of the butcher's counter. Something told me he was
sixty feet, six inches away from the catcher. The pitcher wore a battered
baseball glove on his right hand, which meant he was a lefty.

A softly glowing mound rose up from the floor below him. The mist below his waist formed into legs. He settled down on the mound, leaned forward, and stared at the catcher.

The catcher's legs appeared as well. He squatted on his heels, slammed a not-there fist into a not-there glove three times, then raised the glove and opened it. His free hand slid down to his crotch, where he flashed two fingers pointing down: the signal that said the pitcher was supposed to throw a curveball.

The pitcher ghost shook his head: he didn't want to throw a curve. He wanted another kind of pitch.

"*Pa*," Bo said, as urgent as if he were the first man to discover that the world was round, "that catcher is giving the pitcher signals!"

I sighed. It's a wonder that I was able to tie my shoes all by myself before my kids came along. Back in Slayerville, Bo had been a star of his high school baseball team (and basketball team, and football team, not that I keep track of such things). Kids his age think they invented sports— I might have played an inning or two in my day.

The catcher pointed three fingers down: the standard signal to throw a slider. Again, the pitcher shook him off.

"*Pa*," Bo said, "the pitcher wants to throw the heater."

The heater: a fastball. The signal for a fastball is usually one finger pointed down.

A fastball is a pitcher's testosterone-laden equivalent of two cavemen squaring off with clubs. It's as macho as macho gets. No curves, no dips, just pure *speed*: it says, *I can throw the ball faster than you can hit it.* But, because it's a straight pitch, it's also the easiest to hit—*if* the batter can recognize it and bring the bat around fast enough to connect. If a pitcher really wants to make a batter look bad, they throw the *heater*.

The catcher pointed one finger down.

The pitcher nodded, then stood tall. He looked behind him, maybe to make sure some imaginary runner from eighty years ago stayed on second, then again faced the catcher, right shoulder pointed forward, left shoulder back, chin close to right shoulder and staring down home plate.

If the real-life pitcher had possessed even a tenth of the grace this ghost showed, he must have been something to behold. The pitcher's right knee came up to his chest as he turned away slightly and brought his glove up to his left ear. The right leg kicked out, kicked out *long*, reaching all the way to the front of the mound. His left hand cocked back. Then his shoulders torqued around and the ball shot forward with a crackle of eldritch energy.

It was a ball, true, but not a *base*ball—this was a sphere of sizzling plasma. It closed the sixty feet in a fraction of a second and smacked into the catcher's mitt with the sound of a thunderbolt striking a tree. But it also went *through* the catcher and shattered the glass of the seafood refrigerator. Bags of shrimp exploded out, trailing smoke and arcs of green slime.

The catcher threw the ball back to the pitcher. Wait a minute . . . they were playing catch? According to the newspaper article, the pitcher had murdered the catcher, then turned the gun on himself. They seemed to be getting along awfully well, considering . . . that seemed odd. *Real* odd.

The pitcher reared back again and delivered. I heard that thunderclap— more glass shattered, more frozen seafood scattered across the floor. A steaming scallop hit the tile floor and rolled toward us, flopping flat just a foot away. The ethereal energy had cooked it up real nice. It smelled delicious.

Bo licked his lips. "Pa," he said, "five-second rule—you think that scallop is still good?"

"Don't eat it," I said. "That's an order."

Bo sighed. Not the insubordinate sigh of Luke, but rather a forlorn sigh of a lost opportunity.

"Yes, Pa."

Sometimes I wonder if my boy has all his gears working proper.

The ghosts suddenly blinked out, there one second, gone the next. Was that it? The damage reports of years past had been much worse.

I stood. I listened. Then I heard the thunderclap—they were two aisles over, in the pasta section.

The ghosts looked like nice enough fellows, or had been in the past, but a job was a job. Just because they were dead didn't excuse excessive property damage, and it certainly didn't excuse them hurting people.

"Bo," I said, "we need to watch some more, but you be ready for action."

He slid his big hand into his big coat and brought out his silver base-ball bat. "I'm ready, Pa."

I reached into my pocket and came out with my fingers laced through the polished silver of Old Glory. The colored rhinestones embedded in it glimmered under the fluorescent lights. It's costume jewelry, of course, but that's the kind of stuff my wife likes to magic up with her spells. One shot from Old Glory would put a ghost down; if the silver didn't get them, my wife's spells would.

"We'll give them a chance to move along on their own," I said. "From the looks of things, though, these two can't process anything new."

I quietly headed for the pasta aisle, and my son followed.

The pitch looked high and outside. The catcher reached up and caught it, but like before, the ball hissed through his glove and smashed into the aisle, sending boxes of Raisin Bran and Cheerios flying to clatter on the tile floor.

Bo leaned close to me.

"Full count," he said quietly. "A strike here closes out the inning."

Bo thought they were playing a game, just without batters, fielders, or even a field. Every few pitches, the pitcher turned and looked behind him, as if following the arc of a flying or bouncing ball. The ghosts had been at it for several minutes. Some pitches were strikes, some were balls.

By Bo's count, we were in the bottom of the fourth. The ghosts had changed locations several times, tearing up the produce department after they'd ruined just about every box of spaghetti Safeway had to offer.

They seemed to be reliving a game. Could that have something to do with the haunting?

I thumbed the button again. "Luke, what was the score of the morning game of the doubleheader?"

I heard his fingers clattering. "Seals won five to one . . . Carlisle pitched a two-hitter with nine strikeouts."

"Did Francis Haupberg play?"

"Checking the box score . . . yeah, he did. Says the starting catcher was hurt. Haupberg went one-for-five, had a single for an RBI."

Two men, both dead from a sudden act of violence, both living out the last game they'd ever played. I had to get to the bottom of their deaths. I had to get them to understand that it was time to let go and move to the next plane. If I couldn't do that, I had to clear them out—no matter what their tragic circumstances, the dead can't be allowed to hurt the living.

"Luke," I said, "tell your mother to get in here."

Top of the sixth. I'd seen all there was to see—time to get this over with.

I turned to my right, to the hair-sprayed vision of loveliness that was the mother of my children.

"Honey Buns," I said, "you ready?"

Betty Lou nodded. "Sure am, Sugar Pie."

She adjusted her denim purse on her hip. It's more like the size of a potato sack than a purse, really; you could carry a toddler in that thing. From it, she pulled out a bracelet made of pale pink and baby blue plastic beads, and a black-and-yellow-rhinestone-encrusted bee-shaped brooch that even the most white-trash gramma would call *hideous*. The air around both of the pieces shimmered. She also wore a pair of necklaces, three sets of earrings, and the standard set of head-thwacking, fake-gold rings that my children knew oh-so-well.

I told Bo to stay back, to let his mother and me handle this. If you thought Luke was offended, that was nothing—Bo looked like someone had kicked his puppy to death. Bo is a brawler; if we'd been up against ghouls or goblins, I'd have taken him in first, but I had a feeling this situation required both power *and* subtlety. For that, I needed my wife.

I had Old Glory on my right hand. With my left, I drew a little toy that does me well in these situations. It's a modified ballistic knife. Spring-loaded, that baby can fire a razor-sharp blade out at sixty feet per second. The Russian special forces used them a few years back. Truth is they aren't that great a weapon and are accurate barely outside the range where you could just as easy reach out and stab someone, but that's if you want to *cut* something—we use it to deliver magical talismans. In this case, I'd mounted a Point of Van Kessel on the end. It's a little cross with a ruby center, made by a monk that lived back in the 1600s. We got a good deal on a half dozen of them from a monster stomper that went out of business.

The knife is a great weapon against ghosts, because nine times out of ten they simply 'vaporate if the point goes through them. The weapon doesn't do shit to something solid, like a vamper or a mummy, but against the intangibles it's plenty un-deadly.

I kept the blade flat against my left thigh. I walked into the cereal aisle. I would have stepped around the fallen boxes if there'd been room, but they covered the floor—my Red Wing boots crunched on cardboard as I walked.

"Fellas," I said loud enough to get their attention, "we gotta have us a little talk."

Ever see that movie *The Fantastic Four*? That Human Torch guy, the one who catches fire all of a sudden? That's what it's like surprising a ghost. Like I said, if you don't bug them, for the most part they keep replaying that scene that matters so much to them. But interrupt them? *Confront* them? Then they're like a spooked cat, fluffing all up to scare the bejeezus out of you. Only instead of puffed fur, they channel a healthy dose of paranormal energy.

Both ghosts flamed up, rose up, and *swole* up, swirling with vapor and roiling like storm clouds. Their eyes got all big and blazing and orange, the kind of thing that would make the uninitiated drop a brown steamer right in their drawers.

As you might have guessed, I ain't uninitiated.

"I like baseball as much as the next guy," I said, "but you boys got to go."

The catcher's head extended toward me, a floating orb stretching away from the body, supported by a horizontal column of green fire. It opened a toothy maw and roared.

Maybe I should have raised the knife and buried the Point of Van Kessel in that nightmare, but I paused—the catcher was the one that got murdered, and none of this was his fault, probably—and that cost me.

The catcher moved to his left, putting himself between me and the pitcher. Not only were they playing nicely together, but the murder victim was *protecting* his murderer?

Betty Lou took a step back. "Hunter, I think that news story was wrong."

Like a goddamn rookie, I turned to look at her, and when I did I got smacked with a supernatch fist that launched me into the Kellogg's Frosted Flakes. I hit hard and fell to the floor. I was up on my hands and knees in time to see Betty Lou throw that cheap bee brooch on the ground below the catcher—the brooch sprayed up blinding white energy that drove the ghost back.

Then I saw the pitcher: his legs were once again solid, and his knee was high up at his chest. I didn't even have time to shout out a warning before he delivered a fastball of energy that hit my beloved dead in the chest.

Betty Lou cried out and sank to her knees. I ignored my hurting body and stood, but I heard something coming from behind me. I turned in time to see twenty-foot-long snakes made of living baguettes shooting across the tile floor, kicking up boxes of Honey Bunches of Oats in their wake. Before I could turn to run, the bread-snakes wrapped around my ankles and lifted me into the air like a strung-up pig.

I still had the silver knuckles, but the knife was no longer in my hand. It lay somewhere on the floor, hidden among crumbled pictures of Tony the Tiger.

Another bread-snake slithered through the sea of cereal and looped around Betty Lou's ankles. Before she knew what was happening, she was dangling upside down right next to me.

The catcher thrummed with a hateful light. Reds and yellows pulsed deep in his monstery ghost-chest.

Betty Lou looked at me.

"Hunter, honey," she said, "I think we're in an awful lot of trouble."

The two ghosts came closer. The catcher spoke, spoke in a voice that sounded all too human.

"You found out about us," he said. "You found out . . ."

Ethereal hands reached out for us as the ghostly bodies drifted closer, two pinstriped spirits ready to do us in. If they got near enough, I'd do some damage with Old Glory. Out of the corner of my eye, I saw the plastic bracelet on Betty Lou's wrist start to glow a whitish-blue. Without speaking a word, we knew how it would go down: the catcher was mine, she'd take the pitcher.

And then a mountain of a young man stepped in front of us.

"Y'all just back off!" Bo hollered in his deep voice.

The ghosts stopped cold. They stared. But they weren't staring at Bo, they were staring at his weapon—staring at his silver baseball bat.

The pitcher smiled a hellish smile.

"A new batter," he said wistfully. "Frankie . . . eighty years . . . a *new batter*."

I felt a wave of panic. I opened my mouth to speak, but the catcher made a quick gesture with his hand and I found my mouth overfilled with cereal. Trix had never tasted so bitter.

"Bo!" Betty Lou screamed. "Don't—"

A stream of granola poured into her mouth before she could get out another syllable.

The catcher floated toward Bo.

"Hey batter-batter," the catcher said. "Let's make a bet . . . one at-bat, if you get a hit, we'll let you all go."

I chewed and spit as fast as I could, but I couldn't get through enough to make a peep.

Bo stood tall, stood brave. He stared back at the catcher.

"And if I don't get a hit?"

The catcher's Cheshire smile showed long, shimmering teeth.

"Then you get to stay here with us, batter-batter," he said. "You stay *forever*."

Bo glanced back at me. I shook my head *no*, but even as I did I saw that look in his eyes; he thought he could save the day and prove himself to me. One son is black, the other is white, but the two might as well have been goddamn Siamese twins joined at the brain.

Bo looked at the ghosties.

"I call the strikes," he said. "I won't lie. And if it's a walk, I win."

That Cheshire smile widened even wider than the ghost's head, a floating thing that could have been an evil spirit all by itself.

"Batter up," the catcher said.

If we got out of this, I'd yell at Bo. I couldn't rightly tan his hide anymore, mostly because I wasn't sure I could take him in a fair fight. The boy is just that big and strong. But yell? That I could do.

Do *later*—for now, he needed nothing but confidence from me. I didn't want my idiot child to become a goddamn ghost at the haunted Safeway.

"Come on, son," I said. "Keep your eye on the ball!"

We'd moved to the canned goods aisle, as yet unblemished by these vandalous spirits.

Bo stood at the end of the aisle closest to the front door. He had that silver bat up on his shoulder. His feet were near a glowing home plate. Around that plate, a batter's box chalked out in Lucky Charms. Squatting behind it, the ghostly form of one Francis Haupberg.

At the other end of the aisle, standing on a pitcher's mound made of Fruity Pebbles and Chex Mix, stood John "The Cannon" Carlisle.

Betty Lou and I stood a bit behind the catcher. Rather, I stood, she *hung*—the ghosts seemed to know who the real danger was to them, and they weren't about to let her walk free. They'd taken away her big ol' denim purse. They also seemed to sense that if they held her in a precarious position, I wouldn't do anything to risk her safety.

These ghosts . . . they really understood how a man in love acts when his wife's in danger . . .

I cheered my son on. Betty Lou just cried and cried. Part of that was the fear for her son, and part of it was from some overflow of emotion. She felt *bad* for the two ghosts, but she still couldn't figure out exactly why.

On the pitcher's mound, John Carlisle leaned forward. Haupberg must have flashed a signal, because Carlisle shook it off.

Bo's fingers flexed on his silver bat.

It was too late to stop this; Bo had already agreed to the terms. My son's fate now rested squarely—and literally—in his own hands.

Carlisle nodded; he'd got the signal he wanted. He stood straight, then wound up and launched a crackling phantasm fastball, a green comet that shot forward so fast I could barely see it. Bo swung hard; the bat had barely come forward before the sizzling heater smacked into the catcher's mitt with a splash of emerald fire. Bo's silver bat hit nothing but empty air.

Strike one.

Bo stepped out of the batter's box. He turned and looked back at me.

"Jesus, Pa," he said in a breath. "Did you clock that?"

Sometimes that boy asks the dumbest questions. "Sure, son . . . oh, wait, I left my paranormal radar gun in my other pants."

The catcher tossed the ball back to the pitcher.

Bo licked his lips.

"Pa, I've hit eighty-mile-an-hour fastballs. I'm pretty sure that thing was over a *hundred*."

I grabbed my John Deere ball cap and threw it down on the floor. I'm not sure if that's what you're supposed to do in those situations, but I've seen baseball managers do that move a hundred times, and, well . . . this was *kind* of like baseball.

"Y'all are cheating!" I screamed at the ghosties. "No way you threw a hundred miles an hour in real life!"

The two spirits looked at me, hollow eyes burning with orange flame. I could see through the eyes of the pitcher, see right out the hole in the back of his head where a bullet had once exited.

Francis Haupberg stood. "John threw *faster* in real life," he said.

"Is that so?" I kicked my hat for good measure. "Well, then, what speed was he clocked at?"

The catcher stared at me, then looked down the aisle to the pitcher standing on his mound of breakfast cereal. The ghost of John Carlisle shrugged.

I heard a burst of static in my headset . . . the damn thing was still working.

"They wouldn't know, Pa," Luke said. "The first use of a radar gun was in 1938, to clock pitcher Bob Feller. John Carlisle was killed in 1933. From what I can find, Carlisle was rumored to have the fastest pitch on the West Coast, majors *or* minors."

Well, wasn't that just peachy?

Haupberg squatted down behind the plate, slapped his glove three times, then held it up to John Carlisle. Bo got a mean look on his face. He adjusted his pants, then stepped back into the Lucky Charms box. He was going to get a hit. He *had* to get a hit.

Carlisle wound up and delivered. The ball came screaming in, high and inside. I could almost read Bo's thoughts in that fraction of a second when a batter has to decide to *swing* or *stand pat*—Bo stood pat, actually flinched a little on account of the ball coming straight for his face. A few feet shy of the plate, the ball suddenly arced down in a cartoonishly exaggerated path. Francis didn't even have to move his glove; the ball slammed into it, dead center over the plate.

Curveball. Strike two.

Bo stepped out of the box. Now he looked scared.

A curve like that, a heater of over a hundred miles an hour, and what appeared to be total control and accuracy? In the modern era, any team would have paid him ten million a year, easy.

The catcher held up a pair of semitransparent fingers. "That's two strikes," he said. "Three strikes, and you're out."

I swallowed. Not my boy . . . not my son . . .

Bo shouldered the bat and puffed up his big chest. "Don't worry, Pa," he said. "I got this."

He stepped into the batter's box once again. The catcher squatted down, started flashing signals down at his crotch where we couldn't see. The pitcher shook his head once, twice . . .

Then Bo stepped back, out of the box. He stood straight. He extended his arm, pointed his finger up and to the right.

I sighed—Bo was calling his shot. Sometimes, that boy's ego writes checks his ability can't cash.

The pitcher ghost smiled.

Bo thumped his chest in exaggerated bravado.

"Fastball," he said. "I dare you. You ain't getting that cheese by me, meat."

I shook my head. My son watched too many damned movies.

John Carlisle held his glove to his chest, gathered himself. Bo squatted down, oversized body moving with spooky athleticism for a man of his dimensions.

The pitcher raised his right knee high, wound up, and then his arm whipped forward so fast I could see the bones inside. Bo started his swing before the ball left the pitcher's hand. The pitch started out high and slightly outside: a home run ball. Bo went after it. I thought he was going to knock it out of the park (so to speak) but as his bat came around, the ball suddenly broke down and in, dropping from six feet above the ground to just an inch above it when it smacked into the catcher's mitt in another splash of green fire, well under Bo's powerful swing.

A slider.

John Carlisle had been a lefty with a nasty curve, a hundred-plus fastball, *and* a slider? He wouldn't have been worth ten million a year . . . he would have been worth *twenty* million.

All of that was beside the point, of course, on account of my oldest son had just gambled away his immortal soul.

Baguette-snakes shot across the floor, tangled around Bo's ankles, and lifted him high. Next thing I knew, I was again hanging upside down, not that far from my wife, who was in the same state.

When I think of all the things my family and I have faced down over the years, well, I'm not exaggerating when I say it seemed damn hard to believe our end would come not from a demon, not from a vampire, not from a werewolf or even from a rabid unicorn—we were going to die at the hands of a pair of baseball-playing ghosts.

The catcher stood in front of Bo. The ghost looked toward the haunted Safeway's front door, and then he pointed, pointed at the green Coinstar machine.

The ghost was calling *his* shot.

"Uh-oh," Bo said.

The bread-snake tossed him as if he weighed fifty pounds instead of two hundred fifty. His big body slammed into the Coinstar machine, smashing plastic and bending metal. Bo fell to the floor, motionless.

The ghost of Francis Haupberg floated upward. His legs evaporated, turning into a stormy swirl of blue and green vapor.

Haupberg stared down at me.

"The batter is *out*," he said. "Now, you die."

I reached out a hand to my wife, and she reached hers out to me.

She looked at me in a strange way. Her upside-down eyes narrowed, like she was on the edge of figuring out a puzzle. Then her eyes widened with realization. She turned to the ghost of Francis Haupberg.

"All this rage and betrayal and hate and anguish, it wasn't because of some *woman*," she said. "You two weren't just teammates . . . you were *lovers*."

. . .

Betty Lou's words stopped the ghosts cold. They shimmered. Shimmered and *shrank*. The terrifying visages seemed to vanish, replaced by two men wearing loose pinstripe uniforms with the word *SEALS* in a curve across the chest, black old-time baseball hats with a white S on top of a white F.

Lovers? But . . . they were baseball players. That couldn't be right . . . could it?

Betty's lower lip quivered. Tears ran up her forehead, into hair that didn't move a lick thanks to the aforementioned hair spray.

"Tell me," Betty Lou said to them. "I can feel the hurt, the pain. Tell me, I need to know what you went through."

The ghost of John Carlisle spoke.

"They wanted me to go to New York," he said. "But they wouldn't take Francis."

Francis spit a glob of glowing green onto the tile floor. The glob dissolved into nothing.

"I tried to get John to go by himself," he said. "It was the Yankees, you know? But John . . . he wouldn't do the right thing."

John Carlisle shook his head, a simple expression with a simple, clear meaning: *The right thing was to stay with you.*

I still couldn't get over it. *Gay?*

"Not sure I get it," I said. "I mean . . . you two . . . *together?*"

Betty Lou's head snapped to face me.

"Hunter Jake Hunterson! Don't tell me my husband is a closet homophobe!"

Me? A *homophobe?*

"Come on now, Betty Lou. You know me better than that."

"Do I? You're surprised two people could love each other so much they'd stay stuck to the mortal coil just to be near each other? Or are you just surprised that two *men* could love each other that much?"

I didn't have an answer for that, because she was right: I was surprised. The effeminate fellas I'd seen around San Francisco, holding hands and whatnot, well, I had no problem with that . . . but these were *men*, these were professional athletes.

I wanted to get the focus off me and back on the task at hand.

"What kept you in San Francisco?" I asked Francis. "Why didn't you go to New York with John?"

Both ghosts looked away. I'd struck a nerve. I immediately understood: at a time when baseball was king, the New York Yankees courted John Carlisle. They had *not* courted Francis Haupberg. Francis couldn't even break into the starting lineup of the minor league San Francisco Seals, let alone sign on with the Yanks. *Pride:* it was pride that kept Francis from following John to New York.

Maybe he was gay, but he was still a man; gay or straight, a man's pride can destroy all sorts of wonderful things.

"I should have gone," Francis said quietly. "Maybe it would have been okay if DiMaggio hadn't got hurt. Then the Seals owners would have got a hundred thousand dollars for him, would have made their money, but with DiMaggio hurt the Yanks only offered twenty-five grand for him—that meant my John was the team's big payday. When John wouldn't go to the Yankees, because of *me*, well, a silent partner in the Seals started to sniff around."

Francis was already dead, but this admission was killing him, tearing apart what soul might remain.

Betty Lou cried silently. She could feel their pain. Me? I could see it, plain as day. My own tears weren't that far behind.

"Louis Lima," I said. "He was the silent partner?"

Francis started punching a fist into his glove, over and over.

Carlisle answered the question.

"Yeah, Lima," he said. Carlisle looked so real, so *human*. He was just a kid, or had been, twenty-five years old with the world opening up to give him a dream life. That dream had vanished in an afternoon between the halves of a doubleheader.

"The team owners had borrowed a lot of money to build the stadium," he said. "Some from the banks, and some from the mob. Lima was supposed to get half of what the Yankees paid for me and DiMaggio. Joe got hurt, so Lima lost money there. Then when I wouldn't leave without Francis, Lima got mad."

Francis kept punching his fist into his catcher's mitt. "They watched us. They found out about us. Once they did, well . . . they acted like I was worthless. An animal. I was this . . . this *thing* that kept them from making their money off John."

He finally looked up, looked me in the eyes. The pain there, the anguish: it wasn't his fault, but that didn't matter—he knew his stubborn pride had cost him everything, cost them *both* everything.

"I was *disposable*," Francis said. "Lima's boys roughed me up, told me to leave. I wouldn't. Then . . . then it got worse."

John Carlisle looked deflated. It was hard to believe that moments earlier he'd been a cauldron of whirling supernatural energy.

"They shot Francis," he said. "I was supposed to meet Francis at the stadium between games. Usually the place cleaned out between games. The stadium . . . it was *our* place. We knew people were watching our apartments. We thought at the stadium . . ."

He didn't need to finish. Two people in love, wanting to be intimate, in a place that encompassed their whole lives together. That was their crime? Nobody deserved to have that taken away. Nobody.

"Francis got there first," John said, his voice quiet. "Lima shot him, left the body for me to find. It was supposed to be a message—go to New York, or else. But when I saw Francis there . . . I couldn't imagine life without him. I picked up the gun and I . . . I . . ."

John looked down. All of his energy had fled. He was just a young man, destroyed by heartbreak. Eighty years after pulling that trigger, he still couldn't quite say the words of what he'd done.

Green light flickered around Francis. He was getting angry.

"I got that bastard Lima," he said. "He found out the hard way that I wasn't going to move on; not even *death* could make me move on. I didn't know what had happened, just that I couldn't leave the stadium, and that I could *do* things. I strangled him with dirty gym towels. He found out about us, and I got him."

Found out about us. That was the same line he'd used when he'd seemed ready to do away with Betty Lou and me. It wasn't that we'd found out about them being ghosts, it was a key phrase from the violence that had ended their lives: *You found out we were gay.*

More green energy. Francis seemed caught between desolate pain and pure rage.

"We just wanted to play baseball," he said. His eyes starting bubbling with black fire. "That, and be together, but we couldn't do both. It wasn't . . . men don't do that. Not ballplayers, anyway."

I felt a wash of guilt. It was almost as if he'd read my mind.

It suddenly saddened me to realize that while so much had changed in the last eighty years, some things stayed the same. I couldn't think of one openly gay pro baseball player. Or football player, or hockey player. Considering that the people with the smarts think one out of ten guys bat for the other team (forgive me, I had to work that analogy in here *somewhere*), professional sports seems to be an oddly hetero-male-only fraternity. That, of course, doesn't add up; there have to be gay pro athletes, but even in these modern times they don't feel comfortable coming out. Eight decades later, and maybe there were pros suffering the same potential judgment that wound up costing John and Francis their lives.

"I'm awful sorry for you both," I said. "What happened to y'all, it ain't right."

Francis Haupberg's face shifted into something other than human.

"We just wanted to be together," he said. "Now we're stuck here, *forever*. And you . . . you found out about us."

That was it, and we knew it. Betty Lou squeezed my hand.

"At least Luke and Sunshine will be okay," she said. There was fear in her voice, sure, but she'd mastered it. She knew we were going to die, but she'd face it like the warrior that she was.

That was my Betty Lou, my Valkyrie. I didn't want to die, but the two of us going together . . . maybe that was for the best, because I'm not sure one could live without the other.

Carlisle's legs turned to blue smoke. He floated up. His pinstripes morphed into waving, biting worms. His eyes glowed with the heat of a volcano. A geyser of steam sprayed out of a hole in the back of his head.

The two ghosts approached.

I squeezed Betty Lou's hand.

"Love ya," I said.

She nodded. "I love you too, Hunter. You're my one true thing. If there is another side, I know I'll see you there."

Damn that woman, always had to one-up me in the eloquence department.

The ghosts came closer, burning with hate, living storm clouds thrumming with held-back lightning. I smelled the dirt and fresh-cut grass of the ball field where they'd spent their happiest days.

Betty Lou closed her eyes. I kept mine open—always wondered what my last minutes would look like, and I wasn't going to miss them.

I heard the store's front doors slide open. Betty Lou's eyes snapped open as we both looked to the entrance, a matched feeling of dread in our souls that far outweighed the fear of death.

Luke walked in. My skinny boy, my fourteen-year-old son, strode right into the store.

The two ghosts instantly moved toward him.

Luke should have turned and run, but instead he walked right up to them.

"I can help you," he said to the ghosts. "You both need to listen to me."

The two spirits swelled and pulsed. They flashed with red, yellow, and orange light, spinning with visible rage and fury over the lives that had been stolen from them. Maybe they were good men once upon a time, but now they were uncontrollable and violent, ready to strike out at anything or anyone.

I shouted at my son: "Luke, get your ass out of here! Your mother and I have this!"

Luke rolled his eyes. "That why you're hanging upside down, Pa?"

The ghosts closed in on Luke. The Safeway's lights dimmed and flickered as they drew more energy from the air around them—they were going to tear my son apart.

Then Luke held up a piece of printer paper, waved it like it mattered.

"I heard your story over my Pa's radio," Luke said. "If you mean what you said about each other, I can perform a wedding ceremony, right now. You can't get your lives back, but you'd be together. *Really* together."

The two ghosts stopped cold, just inches from Luke. As usual, Francis Haupberg did the talking.

"Bullshit," he said. "You can't marry us . . . it's not legal."

Luke smiled. In the face of that horror, he actually *smiled*.

"You're wrong, sir," he said. "Prop Eight was overturned in the Supreme Court."

The ghosts turned their glowing heads to look at each other, then back to Luke.

"Prop Eight?" Francis said. "What is that?"

"The law that *blocked* same-sex marriage," Luke said. "It happened after y'all died."

Can ghosts look confused? Well, those two did.

"Blocked it," Francis said. "But it wasn't legal to start with."

"Same-sex marriage became legal in June 2008," Luke said.

Carlisle's ghostly hand scratched at his ghostly head.

"And that was Prop Eight. It made gay marriage legal?"

"No, Prop Eight made it *illegal* again," Luke said. "Five months later."

Carlisle started to pulse purple. "So it *wasn't* legal, then it *was*, then it wasn't?"

Luke nodded as if it all made perfect sense. "And now it is. Do you guys want to jibber-jabber all damn night or do you want to get married?"

The ghosts again flashed angry colors. I tried to move my feet, but I couldn't; paranormal-charged baguette ankle cuffs are a lot tougher than you'd think.

Any normal kid would have been pissing in his pants at the sight of two oversized, infuriated ghosts, but Luke was no normal kid. He'd been around the family business since the day he was born. He'd joined in missions at the tender age of ten, 'vaporated his first supernatch at just eleven when a family of wereboars raided our house in Slayerville. He'd been there and done that: Luke stared down those ghosts like a schoolkid who knows how to box stares down a puffed-up bully.

And then, I saw *why* Luke was so calm. Near the store entrance, by the ruined green Coinstar machine, my thirteen-year-old baby daughter, Sunshine Hunterson, stood over Bo's big, unconscious body. She had a bow in her hand, drawstring back at her ear, a Point of Van Kessel–tipped shaft pointed right at the ghost of Francis Haupberg.

Francis Haupberg didn't notice her. Neither did John Carlisle. Haupberg floated closer to Luke.

"We'd need a priest," Francis said. "You're too young to be a priest."

Luke waggled the piece of paper. "I'm newly ordained by the Universal Life Church Monastery."

Betty Lou shook her head. "Luke! Don't lie to them, you'll only make it worse."

I wasn't sure how much worse things could get, but I kept my trap shut.

Luke sighed and rolled his eyes. "I'm not lying, Ma. I'm ordained. I just did it in the car five minutes ago, on the Internet."

"The *Internet*," Francis said. "What's that, a place on Fisherman's Wharf?"

Luke started laughing. I wanted to throttle that boy, throttle him out of pure fear—he had no idea what he was facing. Maybe he wasn't as *brave* as I thought, but rather far more *stupid* than I'd guessed. If these ghosts took him, I'd lose him forever.

"The Internet is a new thing," he said. His normal, smart-ass expression faded; for once my boy looked serious. He looked . . . empathetic. He looked like his mother looks when she's listening to someone vent about their troubles.

"You guys got a bad deal," Luke said. "The world is a different place now. There's still a lot of hate, sure, but you'll get no hate from me, no hate from my family. It's been eight decades—you can finally be together the way you always wanted to be."

The two ghosts pulsed and flashed. One moment their faces looked normal, the next they looked like blazing skulls, the next twisted masks of pain and fury, but through it all I could see their eyes. Even for the supernatch, the windows are the eyes to the soul.

And those souls wanted to believe.

John Carlisle's flame faded away. He floated down. Once again, he looked like a normal man dressed in a ball cap and a soft, pinstriped uniform.

"Francis," he said, "let's do it."

The Francis ghost flamed brighter, flamed *higher*, and in that moment I was sure I'd lost my child.

"He's *lying*," Francis said. "It's a trick, John! He's going to trick us and make us move on, and I *won't move on without you*!"

John stepped between the ghost of his lover and my son. He reached up into the green flames, put his hand on the flaming arm.

"Francis, please stop," John said. *"Please."*

Francis stared down for a few moments. Then he nodded, and his flames faded out. He floated to the ground. He reached up to the hand on his arm, interlocked fingers. Holding hands, the two ballplayers turned to face Luke.

"Okay," Francis said. "Let's do it."

Luke smiled. "Awesomesauce," he said. He smiled at Betty Lou.

"Hey, Ma? If you're done hanging upside down like that, can you help me plan a wedding?"

John wanted to walk down an aisle. We didn't have a church at our disposal, so he got aisle six: Chips, Salsa, and Ethnic Foods. You might be surprised to hear it, but I didn't know much about gay marriage etiquette. Francis didn't want to walk down an aisle, John did, and that was that.

Bo got his Twinkies after all. The store was trashed; I didn't think the Safeway owners would mind if I left some money and took a box for the boy. He munched away, as happy as he could be considering how dinged up he was from his dance with the Coinstar machine. Other than a big bump on the back of his head, he hadn't suffered any serious damage—if you didn't count his pride, of course.

He also got his scallops, but he wasn't eating those. They were still in the bag, still frozen. Sunshine held the bag to the back of Bo's big head. She patted her brother's shoulder as they waited. Bo and Sunshine stood off to the left, as friends of the *grooms*—note the plural, thank you very much.

The former pitching prospect of the New York Yankees was out of our line of vision, in the next aisle over getting ready. Betty Lou was helping him.

Francis and I stood at the end of the aisle, waiting. Luke stood behind us. Bo had made him a little podium out of blue milk crates. For once, Luke was the tallest person in the room.

Somehow, I'd wound up being the best man at a gay ghost wedding. Luke said that me being the best man was *important* and *necessary*, but I had a hunch he thought it was funny, on account of my initial reaction to John and Francis being a couple.

My son is pretty much a smart-ass.

Well, Luke had saved the day, and for that he got to call the shots. Best man I was.

Francis cleared his throat. He was obviously nervous, but other than that he looked damn near normal, like an extra in that old Kevin Costner baseball movie.

I wasn't sure what to call him. He was probably sixty years older than me, but he had the face of a twenty-four-year-old—the age he'd been when some homophobe had put a bullet in his back.

Still, I recognized that look on his face, recognized it from experience. I had to make sure he was ready for this.

"Uh, Mr. Haupberg?"

His eyes snapped toward me; just a touch of that green fire burned up. I leaned back. "Take it easy," I said. "I'm here to help, remember?"

The flame faded out. He looked away. "So you tell me," he said, but he clearly knew I was speaking the truth. Now he looked nervous *and* embarrassed.

All of a sudden, I had flashbacks to high school, when my buddy Bobby Jake Carvin got married to Bessie Ann Dermot. I remember wearing that ridiculous tuxedo (teal, with lime ruffles—maybe I don't know fashion, but I know ugly when I see it). I remember Bobby Jake sweating like a sinner in church (to be fair, that's exactly what he was), looking so nervous I thought he might collapse. I remember what I said to him then. As bizarre as it seems, I used that same line in the haunted Safeway.

"Francis," I said, "if you don't want to go through with it, now's the time to bail."

His eyes snapped to me again, this time, thankfully, free of that spooky flame.

"But . . . I . . . I've been waiting for this for eighty years."

I nodded. "That don't change the fact that marriage is a big deal."

He licked his lips, rubbed at his eyes. Sure, he was a century old, but maturity-wise he was just a kid who played baseball for a living. Hell, he wasn't that much older than my Bo.

"Listen to me," I said. "If you're not *sure*, then you don't have to do anything. We'll figure something else out."

"Like *what*?" he said. "Not get married, so my spirit can rise every April and I trash whatever building happens to be here at the time?"

I put my hand on his shoulder. It felt solid, real.

"I've got contacts in the Netherworld Protectorate," I said. "Son, if you don't want to get married, we'll figure out what to do. Betty Lou and I will help you."

Francis looked at me much the way Bobby Jake had, like I was the only rock he could lash himself to during a Grade-A tornado.

My face turned red again as I realized something—maybe Luke hadn't made me be the best man on a lark . . . maybe he'd known Francis might need an older man to help him, to play the role that older men have played for younger men since time began. I glanced back at my son, still standing on his podium of milk crates. He smiled at me. A *knowing* smile.

How can a fourteen-year-old be that wise?

After this was done, I needed to have a talk with Luke. A *long* talk. There was much for me to learn about that youngster.

Francis swallowed hard, leaned closer to me.

"You're married," he said. "Was it the right thing to do?"

Betty Lou walked into sight at the aisle's far end. That meant John couldn't be much longer. I thought about Francis's question as I looked at my wife. She was more beautiful than the day I'd first laid eyes on her, and at that time she was already the most beautiful thing that God had ever created.

"Yes, it was the right thing to do," I said. "The single best thing I ever did in my life was to get hitched to my high school sweetheart."

Francis nodded, slowly. "And you . . . you never strayed?"

I laughed lightly. "Many men do, but not me. If you're one of the lucky few who finds the right woman . . . er, sorry, the right *partner* . . . then that won't be a problem."

I didn't even know if ghosts *could* stray, at least in the biblical sense. Like I said, they often don't really understand that they're dead. Or, maybe I had it wrong; for all I know, ghosts can get it on just as much as the living.

"You'll be fine," I said. "This moment right here? This ceremony? This is the hardest part."

Francis looked down. The nervousness seemed to fade a little bit.

"Thanks," he said. "That helps."

I saw Betty Lou smile, that look she gets on her face when the kids dress up nice. Then John Carlisle came into view. He wore a pinstriped black suit, something straight out of a gangster movie. He looked like a million bucks.

And damn, if he didn't look like the happiest man on the planet. Or the happiest ghost on the planet. Probably both.

I glanced at Francis. He was smiling, too, his eyes wide, perhaps in disbelief that this was really happening.

I leaned in close. "You had your doubts—sure you want to do this?"

He nodded without looking away from John. "Yeah," he said. "Even more than I wanted to play in the big leagues. More than I ever wanted anything."

Betty Lou and John walked down the aisle. I'd done my part, keeping Francis in place long enough for him to realize what his heart had been telling him all along. Just like I'd done for Bobby Jake, just like my daddy had done for me.

John and Betty Lou reached us. She stepped to the right. John stepped forward. He and Francis stared at each other. They both smiled that wide, easy smile that true lovers share.

Luke held up his hands. "Let us begin," he said, and then he did.

Ghosts are complicated things. They're all looking for resolution, something that will let their souls finally rest. Most of the time, you can't give that to them. In the Case of the Haunted Safeway, though, turned out we could.

Luke performed the ceremony. I ain't never been so proud of that boy, I'll tell you that for free. He saved the day. More than that, he ran with an idea, put himself at risk, and gave those two poor souls what they deserved—*peace*.

When he finished the ceremony, the two ghosts glowed a soft blue, like a lit-up summer cloud. They looked beautiful (and I don't often think of men as *beautiful*, mind you). Then, they kissed, and when they did, their noncorporeal bodies merged together, became one.

They faded away like wisps of dissipating fog. We don't know what became of them. Unless they come back next April, we never will.

I finished up the case knowing that I had underestimated the mettle of my smallest son, and overestimated the common sense of my biggest. Bo's size made me forget he's still just a kid, and he still needs my guidance. I love them both just the same, though, ain't nothing ever going to change that.

I also learned a little bit about myself, some things I ain't proud of. I didn't have anything against the gays, but, truth be told, I guess I didn't really believe two men—or two women, for that matter—could love each other as intensely as I love my Betty Lou. Well, I learned better. Those boys had given up everything for each other. Most male/female couples I know will never come close to that level of commitment and sacrifice.

Once upon a time, I was a racist asshole, and now I have a black son.

And, once upon a time, I didn't think of homosexuals as being capable of real love, and I wound up the best man at a gay wedding.

As my daddy once told me, all you can ask for in life is to keep learning.

Thanks for reading my War Journal. I hope you enjoyed it, and if you want to read more, well, there ain't no end to the stories I can tell.

Stay away from rabid unicorns,
—Hunter

PRISE DE FER

ELLEN KUSHNER

Ellen Kushner's award-winning novels include the Fantasy of Manners *Swordspoint*, *The Privilege of the Sword*, and *Thomas the Rhymer*. Kushner's own audiobook recordings of her three Riverside novels, with herself as narrator, were released by Neil Gaiman Presents. With Holly Black, she coedited *Welcome to Bordertown*, a recent revival of Terri Windling's original urban fantasy series. The longtime host of public radio's *Sound & Spirit*, she lives in New York City and travels a lot. Ellen says: "When Toni and Charlaine asked me for a sports story for this anthology, there was a long pause, during which I must confess I was thinking: 'Just what about *me* says *sports* to you?' Then I realized that I am best known for novels in which people stick each other with long pointy bits of metal, and that in some cultures that evolved into a sport . . . if, sometimes, a dangerous one."

"You're not deceiving anyone, you know. It is perfectly obvious that you are a woman."

I nearly dropped my foil, but did not. It's not just that unescorted men aren't allowed in the halls of Saint-Hilaire. Even if someone's visiting brother had escaped the eagle eye of Madame la Directrice and wandered into the fencing salon for some reason, surely he would be wearing something a bit less . . . showy? And not be presenting himself in a tight jacket of wine-red brocade, with white lace and ruffled sleeves, like an ambassador from a London Carnaby Street boutique?

"Monsieur," I said, standing at rest. "Your grasp of the obvious is astonishing."

He made a little bow—just enough to acknowledge the touch. His hair was even longer than that of the boys I'd seen in Paris, who had so scandalized my grandmother. It was tied at the nape of his neck with a ribbon.

We were speaking French, that being the language of the school, and of the country it was in. The Academie Saint-Hilaire des Jeunes Filles is situated in an old chateau snuggled between the fields and orchards of Basse-Normandie, just far enough from Paris to make it next to impossible for its students to get there and back in one day (or night) to indulge in the sort of behavior that got them sent there for the summer in the first place.

"And you, *mademoiselle*, you do not fear discovery as you are?"

He had a point. He was not the only one who might want to know what I was doing alone in the Saint-Hilaire *salle d'armes* after hours, when I should have been in my room in the south tower, snoring across from pretty little Madeleine de Mailly—or possibly studying. Not that I had a Bac to pass. I was returning to New York for my senior year at Norton at the end of the summer. But there was no point in failing, where I could pass.

When attacked, you have two basic choices: retreat or parry.

"Sir," I said, "since I am already discovered, what need to fear? Unless, of course, you propose to raise the alarm. But might that not also raise questions of discovery for you yourself?"

He raised a slender hand to the lace at his throat: a formal, theatrical gesture. For a moment, I felt that we were in a play, actors on a stage late, late at night in the salon of the old chateau of Saint-Hilaire, back when it had been the chateau's reception room, its long mirrors reflecting candlelight for the elegantly clad, and not the questionable forms of young women struggling with their parries and ripostes.

"Having offered no insult to your so-charming self, but only a single astonishingly obvious, useless observation, what need have I to fear discovery here?"

Oh, dear. A flirt as well as a dandy. Dangerous combination. He was attractive, and he knew it. I would not engage. I didn't trust him. I raised my foil. "That is not my concern. If you will excuse me, I have serious work to do."

He bowed again, a little deeper, and took a step back, yielding the floor to me. So there was nothing I could do but go back to my drill: attacking myself in the mirror in Quarte, in Sixte . . . Disengage and double-disengage, over and over to strengthen my wrist and teach my body to unlearn that bad habit I have of leaning into my attack instead of just fully extending my arm before the lunge.

I did not like having him behind me, but at least I could see him in the mirror—so when he made a gesture of annoyance, I stopped at once.

"Your grip," he said, "is entirely too tight. And if you do not stop leaning into your attack too soon, you will get yourself entirely killed, should you attempt this movement anywhere but on the comic stage."

I gaped.

No bow, this time; just that little gesture of hand to throat, and from his forefinger the flash of a ring red as blood.

"I bid you good day, *mademoiselle*."

He turned and placed his hand on the mirror behind him. It had a door handle I'd never noticed before. His long hand turned the handle down; the mirror swung back into the darkness, and he disappeared into it.

I heard the chapel bell chime midnight. Later than I thought. I put my foil back in the rack and headed through the *salle*'s main door to the hallway. The huge windows of the old chateau were awash with moonlight, and so I found my way up the stairs to my room.

"Coffee, not chocolate," Madeleine murmured in her sleep when I closed the door behind me. She must have thought she was at home, with a maid coming in to serve breakfast. I undressed as quietly as I could.

Although I was raised in New York and known at Saint-Hilaire (rather rudely, behind my back) as *l'Americaine*, my mother was French— or so I'm told; I never met her. She divorced my father as soon as I was born and took off for Monaco with an Argentinian polo player. They were killed in one of those celebrity road accidents on those notoriously treacherous coastal roads that seem to exist only to separate the wealthy from their sports cars.

But every summer, once I was housetrained enough to sit at the dinner table with a linen napkin that stayed on my lap, I visited my *grandmère* in Saint-Tropez. You do not know what boredom is until you have spent weeks in the company of slender, bronzed people with slender gold chains around their necks and wrists, diamonds in their ears, wearing only the bottom halves of very expensive swimsuits, lying around trying to perfect an even deeper bronze. Sometimes they were joined by girls my age, who competed with them for boredom with inane conversation about movie stars, clubs, clothing designers, and why it is critical not to shave your legs, but to have them waxed, my dear, always waxed, because otherwise it grows back twice as thick!

But at least I learned fluent French. And when *Grand-mère* offered me the opportunity to study at Saint-Hilaire—so that I could "improve my reading and writing, while getting to know the Right Sort of People"— I seized it.

Never mind that my fellow students were distinguished principally by their laziness and ignorance of anything beyond their small world of privilege, fashion, and money. Which is why, instead of summering in Nice or on a yacht, they were spending the summer cramming for their Terminale, the final year of Lycée that includes the university entrance exams, before their parents had to admit they were stupider than dirt and would never pass the Bac.

But the Saint-Hilaire summer program was where Simone Gaillac had chosen to teach fencing that summer. I would have gone to the seventh circle of Hell, and roomed with girls far more terrible than these, to study with her.

I think she knew that was why I was there; at least, she spoke warmly of her American colleagues, women she'd fenced with at the London Olympic games in '48, where she had won glory for a war-torn France.

"I respect them, of course," Mme Gaillac told me on our first day, "but it is good that you come to France to study. France is where fencing began." She addressed the class, lined up in our white fencing jackets and knickers: "The art of fencing was created here originally to help our ancestors train to fight serious duels. Duels of honor. Duels to the death."

We all nodded, as though we heard this sort of thing every day; no one wanted to appear shocked or thrilled in front of the others. "Their fighting was not precisely like ours; it evolved over the years. Theirs involved more blade-to-blade contact, and the target was the whole body, naturally. And their steel was *sharp*! The foil we use today"—she lifted hers—"is based on the eighteenth-century smallsword, whose goal was to kill. But with their sharp weapons safely blunted, fencers could work on the speed and elegance of their thrust"—and she executed one flawlessly—"and the precision of their intention, without risking their lives! Medicine in those days meant that even a simple wound could kill. One must know where the other's blade is at all times. And once you know that . . ."

She turned again to me. "*En garde*, please, *mademoiselle*." I raised my blade for her demonstration. "Let us say I execute a *prise de fer*—you know what that means, in French?"

"It means 'to take the blade,'" I said. "But we use the French term in American fencing, too: *Prise de fer*. It's when you force your opponent's weapon into a new line, away from their original intention."

"Very good. And what are some of the ways that I might do that to you?"

"Ah, a beat?"

"Yes. Now, extend." As I pointed my weapon at her chest, she rapped hard on my foil. I felt the shock down my arm; my blade moved aside. "What else?"

"A bind?"

"Yes. Make an attack." I lunged, trying to be aggressive even though I knew what was coming, aiming my point for her torso. Her foil's forte neatly swiveled along mine, almost too fast to see, though again I felt it, and my point found itself diagonal to where I'd been aiming, well away from the target—while her point moved in to touch my chest.

"Thank you." She nodded, and I stepped back. "You see also how I held my opponent's blade where I wanted it, so I could make my attack? Good. Before the summer is over, you will all be expert at the *prise de fer*, like my little *Americaine*, here."

My roommate raised her hand. "If someone takes your blade like that, can you still recover?"

The *maitresse* nodded. "I will show you that, too. It has all been thought of, by the original swordmasters, and those who came after. In the end, it is a question of who controls the bout. Who controls the conversation of the steel?"

She looked around at all of us. "Of course, today our lives do not depend on our proficiency. But just as we study now in a school that was once a chateau, enjoying its beauty and history while we appreciate its modern function, so we respect the origins of our sport: the strategy, the aggression, the precision, and, yes, the *honor* of the duel, the foundation of the art of fencing."

A tall blonde classmate declared, "Americans fight all their duels with guns!" and demonstrated with a cocked finger: *"Pom! Pom-pom-pom!! Take zhat, you rahht!"*

The other girls were laughing, poking at each other and imitating her.

"Silence!" Madame was stern. "What is your name?"

The blonde's color was high, but she kept her chin up and looked our instructor full in the face. "Céleste de Puysange, *madame*."

"When I speak of honor, Mlle de Puysange, I speak also of the way we comport ourselves as we study the sword. Respect for one's opponent is the foundation of fencing. We do not interrupt one another, or mock, ever, another student. Is that clear?"

"Pom!" Céleste muttered at me, on the way out. *"Pom-pom-pom!"*

Of course, the lit teacher asked if I was German.

I stood up to address her, as students do in French schools. "No, *madame*. My father's family came to America in the last century."

"Amé-ri-caine," Mme Gabin said, rolling the word in her mouth as though she were trying to decide whether it was a vintage she liked. "Splendid. We all admire so much your President Kennedy. A gallant man. Your father fought, perhaps, in France?" It was so obvious that she was trying to place me. Of course, she was thinking of the gum-chewing GIs, not of the French officers many of my classmates were descended from.

"No, *madame*." Maybe she meant well, but I wasn't going to let her patronize me. "My family is of the Blumberg department store in New York. We are not a military family."

My response forced her into a new line of inquiry, but she wasn't willing to be direct and ask, Was I a Jew? How did I gain entry to Saint-Hilaire? Flustered, she fell back on, "You speak French very well."

"Thank you, *madame*." I finally gave her what she wanted, by way of explanation: "My mother's father was de Boieldieu."

Mme Gabin said something nice about the distinguished military record of the de Boieldieu family. But I knew I'd made a huge tactical error. In France, you never, ever brag on your ancestry or your money— not overtly—and here I'd done it twice, just to assert control because my back was up. Mistake.

The girls let me know it. They didn't titter; they coughed, which was a way of expressing opinion in class without being called on it by the teacher.

After class, they clustered around me in the hall. "So, this Blumberg store, it is like La Samaritaine in Paris? or Printemps? or Bon Marché?" Apparently, the French had invented not only fencing, but the department store as well.

"Or Galeries Lafayette?" Madeleine made sure her favorite was included in the list.

"A bit," I replied. "It's bigger."

"No wonder your clothes are so chic!" Céleste said. A low blow, and inaccurate: *Grand-mère* had made sure all my clothes were bought in Paris, at just the sort of Right Bank establishments all their mothers favored.

Never mind. Not having a social life meant that I could devote myself to fencing—not just classes, but taking the time to drill seriously every day. The summer would not be a dead loss. I'd only discovered fencing a few years ago at my summer camp in the Berkshires, which was full of idiots of a different kind: sports-crazy East Coast girls who only cared how well you could hit some ball or other. Volleyball, softball, tennis . . . If I tried to stay in my bunk reading a book, the counselors would drag me out and lecture me about team spirit. The only sport offered there that did not involve a ball was fencing, and you were your own team of one. My spirit improved greatly from then on.

Back at the Norton School, I became a varsity fencer, but that means just what you'd think: no competition there. My dad was a nut about grades, especially math. He anxiously watched me for signs of frivolity, lest I take after my mother. So he wouldn't let me study in a real fencing academy after school, though I did take lessons on those Saturdays when we weren't out at the house on Long Island.

A year from now, though, I'd be headed to college—one of the Seven

Sisters, if Dad had his way, and why not? Some of them have splendid fencing teams. I wanted—no, I *needed* to qualify. Four years of college would give me four years of serious competition. After that—Well, that was enough to aim for, for now.

And so every spare hour found me in the *salle d'armes*.

"Your faith in your ability to improve yourself is most inspiring."

I heard the voice before I saw him behind me in the mirror.

"Don't turn around," he said. "Maintain your focus."

"I'm not a performing monkey."

"And yet you dress like one, in your little white breeches."

He was one to talk about my fencing breeches! Today, his brocade suit was blue, and a rather girlish blue at that, with silver buttons down his coat that were clearly meant for show.

I said, "What are you doing here, anyway?"

He looked directly into my eyes in the mirror. His were strong blue, too, a striking contrast to his dark hair. He raised his hand to the ruffles at his neck, again displaying the ruby ring. "I trust I may come and go as I wish, in this house."

I wanted to turn around so badly. But I refused to yield my stance. "I suppose you may, if no one stops you."

"Let me see your attack," he said. "I am concerned for your distance." I hesitated—not, of course, from fear, but because to follow his command would be to give ground to the arrogant stranger. "Do you doubt," he said, "that I know what I am talking about?"

I remembered his assessment of my weakness the other night. *Good Lord,* I suddenly thought; *what if he's a colleague of Mme Gaillac's?* Maybe I was getting coaching from an up-and-coming young Olympic athlete? That would explain why he had the run of the place.

All right, then; I'd show him what I could do. I backed away from the mirror, keeping an eye on my reflection-self, and lunged in Sixte—but a little short, in order to deceive my opponent as to my distance. I thought it was very elegantly done. But as I leaned in to make my perfect touch:

"Non, et non, et non!" So he was an idiot, after all. Damn. "You cannot risk these tricks, if your opponent has the longer reach!"

"I have right of way," I said stiffly, holding my pose. It wouldn't hurt to work on my stamina any. "Unless she—"

"Ohhhh, so you are in the right," he interrupted, with sarcasm so brutal that, if he had been armed, I would have turned on him. "And that is all that matters. Yes, yes, we know that little game. But I tell you, *mademoiselle*, this is not the Middle Ages. God is not always on the side of the man who is in the right." He laughed bitterly. "Which is, for some of us, a very good thing indeed."

"You speak in riddles, sir." (In French, that doesn't sound nearly so much like a paperback romance.)

"As one must, *mademoiselle*, if one is not to be easily understood by fools."

I lowered my weapon, but my back stiffened. "Do you call me a fool, sir?"

"Did you take my meaning thus?" He cocked his head, not denying it. "Alas! You are offended! Perhaps you wish to extend a challenge?"

"As you say, sir, this is not the Middle Ages." I shrugged, more disappointed than hurt, but still annoyed enough. "I had thought you a swordmaster, but you are nothing but a riddling clown."

"Is that so?" He seemed surprised, off-balance; but he quickly regained his hauteur. "If you will permit this riddling clown one small suggestion, then?" I waited. "When you make your mincing little attacks, aim for the head. The head, or the legs. It is harder to pierce the heart than you suppose."

If he was flirting, he'd chosen a more appealing metaphor than most. But it wouldn't do to let him know that.

"I seek to pierce no one's heart," I said.

"Then you are indeed the rarest of women." He bowed and left the room.

Half the girls at Saint-Hilaire had brought their own horses, and spent time they could have been studying down at the chateau's stables, taking extra dressage courses, or just riding around the countryside. A few of them had chosen fencing as well and joined Mme Gaillac's students for our classes. The best and most athletic of them was the unpleasant Céleste de Puysange, a tall blonde with a terrific reach. Her best friend, Nicole Fleurie, a curvy one with wide hips, would clearly rather have stuck with the horses, but where Céleste led, Nicole followed.

"*Mesdemoiselles*," Mme de Gaillac said today after warm-up, "please face the mirror for footwork."

We advanced and retreated back and forth, a chorus line of clunky white nymphs in our canvas fencing costumes, hair pulled back in high ponytails, distinguished from one another only by hair color and height. My hair is thick and curly. *Grand-mère* had had it cut in Paris to an atrocious length that a single clip would hold only if I'd bother to set it with curlers to straighten it out at night. Which I hadn't. It kept escaping and getting in my face; I had to stop to put it all back into place.

"Oh, la," Céleste muttered across the line; "poor little *Americaine*, tired out already?" Nicole made a pitying noise. "You should climb the steps of all those big skyscrapers back home, to give you more stamina."

"Oh," I retorted, "but in New York, all our big buildings have elevators."

"No talking, ladies," Mme Gaillac said. "And now, get your masks, please, and partner up for work on the parry-riposte. Defense is not enough; you must know how to follow up your advantage to score a touch."

Céleste and I looked at each other briefly, automatically. Of the room, we were the two serious fencers; at least, she'd had decent training. Partnered with anyone else, we each had to slow down.

Ostentatiously, Céleste turned from me and chose my roommate, pretty little Madeleine de Mailly. Nicole quickly tapped another girl, and no one chose me.

Which meant I got to practice parry-ripostes with La Gaillac. So there, Céleste!

The final minutes of each class were actual fencing bouts, with opponents assigned by our teacher.

"Mlles Fleurie and de Puysange to fence, and for judges, Blumberg and de Mailly."

I'd once seen a beginner simply drop her foil and duck when Céleste lunged at her along the *piste*. It's true that attitude can go a long way toward helping you dominate a match. A tilt to the head, a glare through the mask, can go farther than you'd think to establishing who controls the action. I stood to the side, diagonal to Céleste, to observe any touches Nicole might make on her front. Which weren't likely. On the *piste*, as in the dormitory, Nicole was a natural follower. But her quick responses to Céleste's lead stood her in surprisingly good stead here. The moment Céleste lunged at her, Nicole's body, alert to her friend's every move, automatically parried as it should, deflecting the attacking blade.

They both looked a bit startled. But Céleste recovered enough to continue her attack as if nothing had happened, while Nicole made the riposte she should have done first, the one we'd been drilling.

The two friends touched each other almost simultaneously. Nicole gave a little squeak of surprised delight at scoring a touch, then jumped back guiltily.

"Halt!" cried Madeleine. I nodded agreement.

"The blades are in conversation," our instructor said formally. "The judges read the phrase. So, Mlle de Mailly first: What did you see?"

"Simultaneous touch?" Madeleine said nervously.

"Indeed?" Mme Gaillac asked. It sounded like a challenge. "Who had the right of way?"

"Céleste!" Madeleine was utterly flustered. Fencing wasn't really her sport. She looked back and forth, from me to Céleste. I saw Céleste's grip tighten on her hilt. Mlle de Puysange did not like to lose. "Céleste lunged first, and she hit Nicole, right on target!"

"Mlle Blumberg? What conversation did you read?"

"Attack from the right," I said, which was Céleste. "Parry from the left, breaking the phrase. So the continued attack from the right was invalid, because she'd lost the right-of-way." Céleste hissed behind her mask. "Riposte from the left," I went on, "and touch to the left."

"Mlle de Mailly, do you want to reconsider your call?"

Poor Madeleine was actually trembling. "I—I'm not sure—"

"It was an accident!" Nicole said.

"You did have right-of-way," our teacher said cheerfully, as the bell rang for the end of class, "though you must work on a quicker riposte. Bout to Mlle Fleurie!" Under her eye, the opponents unmasked and shook hands. "Until Tuesday, ladies. Have a good weekend."

Céleste walked past me, fluffing her hair with her fingers, her shoulder turned to me. But I distinctly heard it: "Go home to America."

When the room had emptied, I went back to work on that effective little disengage-riposte. But I was not entirely surprised when I heard his voice behind me:

"Very nice. But why do you restrict your movement so?"

I did not stop. "What do you mean?"

"Your parry in Sixte is always too low, and to the exact same spot. If you do it thus—" And he executed a swift movement, like a dance, ending with his sword arm cocked up with the elbow near his ear, the tip of his imaginary blade pointed directly at his imaginary opponent's eye. *So?* I thought. *What's the point of threatening someone's mask?* "If you desire a low blow, here's one your teacher may not have taught you." Another beautiful move, bending his body like a comma sideways, an arabesque ending with a wrist tilt that would have set the point neatly through an opponent's knee.

"Wow," I said. He was completely off-target—but what a move!

Today, he wore no jacket; his white shirtsleeves were full, and ended at the cuff with a bit of a ruffle. He shook the ruffle back from his wrist and extended his beringed hand to me: an invitation to try it myself.

And so I did. Clumsily, at first, but with his coaching I finally got it to his satisfaction.

"*Brava!*" he cried.

"My teacher would never approve," I added, just to be clear.

"Teachers can be jealous. They guard their secrets carefully. But I can assure you, yours will be impressed." His smile was very charming. Disarming, one might say. "I like you, *mademoiselle*. You have guts." (Well, in French it's *du coeur*: You have *heart*. Like the baseball team in *Damn Yankees*.) He leaned against the wall, his arms folded over his long embroidered waistcoat. "Tell me: What makes you so devoted to the sword?"

I considered the question. Not that I haven't been asked it before. I have a different answer for everyone, though, and I wasn't sure which one was right for him.

"Is it the desire to show off your fine legs?" he mused salaciously.

"No; I think you are not vain. Do you seek to set yourself apart from other ladies, with this delicious quirk? No; you are too serious." He pushed a strand of hair back from his face. "Can it be that you wish to be able to defend yourself, and maintain your own honor thus?"

Somehow he was right behind me, practically breathing down my neck, though I could not feel his breath. He was the same height as I. I felt a little giddy.

"Don't be afraid," he murmured. "You have the weapon. I am unarmed."

"I think," I said, "that you are not unarmed, sir. Not at all."

The door to the salon opened with its usual racket of ancient latch and hinges.

"Yes, it is tiresome, Nicole, but I must practice some."

It was the voice of Céleste de Puysange in the open doorway, speaking to someone in the hall. "Oh, I know. But it's only a matter of time before La Gaillac pairs me with *l'Americaine. She* practices, you know. How would it look if I let her defeat me?"

She turned into the room, closing the door behind her.

The man jumped back. *"Peste!"* he swore. Céleste looked rather splendid in her fencing gear, slim, blonde, leggy, and athletic; I took a certain pleasure in the fact that he was acting as if he'd seen a bug with too many legs. "What is *he* doing here?"

"Calm down," I told him. "It's not a boy, it's only Céleste."

She noticed me for the first time, and saluted me wryly. "And good day to you, too, Isabelle."

"See?" I went on for his benefit. "She can be polite when she wishes."

"Yes," Céleste said briskly, "unlike some. But then, I was raised to it. Are you quite all right, Isabelle? Or are you practicing your conditional case where no one can hear your mistakes in grammar?"

It was almost a relief to have someone from the outside witnessing her utter bitchiness. I turned to look at him—

And he was gone.

"Well, Mlle Blumberg? What are you staring at?"

Distraction in a bout is dangerous. I'd think about him later. I pulled my attention back to Céleste and the fight at hand: "Did you drop something in here?" I asked her. I meant to imply that there was no other reason for her to be in the room, even in her gear. But she replied, "Not at all. I merely wish to practice." She took a foil from the rack. "I trust I am not disturbing you?"

For a moment, I thought about inviting Céleste to fence a round with me. It was true that Mme Gaillac had not paired us yet in any bout. She said it was better for both of us, to work with beginners; it would slow us down and sharpen our basic skills. How sweet it would be to fence with someone decent! But Céleste might not see it that way.

I beat a retreat.

I had time for a long shower before changing for lunch. I spent it thinking about how the man could have vanished without Céleste seeing him. A trick of the mirrors, perhaps? Or a simple diversion of attention, coupled with a swordsman's skill, to slip through the hidden door?

I decided to stop thinking about it until after lunch; then, I could go back and investigate. You did not want to miss Saturday lunch at Saint-Hilaire. In France, good food is considered as much a human right as fresh air and sunshine. Even the most simple meal at Saint-Hilaire was a feast. The only annoying thing was that we had to come to the table dressed in skirt and blouse, nylons and decent pumps—no loafers or tie shoes, let alone slacks!

We sat at the long tables of the great hall, already set with tall glass bottles of mineral water, along with the usual baskets of cut-up baguettes, and fresh farm butter. Today's meal began with a very promising *paté de campagne*, gorgeously laid out on a platter decorated with radishes and slices of *cornichons*, miniature pickles that cut the buttery unctuousness of the *paté* with little explosions of vinegary sharpness. I waited as patiently as I could while the platter proceeded down the table toward me.

But as it neared, Céleste put her hand on Nicole's wrist, lightly, like a fan tap, saying reprovingly, "Do not pass Mlle Blumberg the *paté*."

"Whyever not? Is there something wrong with it?"

Céleste said, "It might disagree with her. Rich food is very bad for those with nervous dispositions."

I wanted that *paté*. "I assure you, Mlle de Puysange, it takes more than a little *entrée* to scare me."

"Really? I was so concerned to find you all alone in the *salle d'armes*, talking to yourself."

I had walked right into it. I reached for my glass of mineral water, to wet my dry mouth and buy a moment's thinking time.

The other girls leaned forward. Céleste, all pretense of civility gone now that she had me where she wanted me, crowed to them all, "There she was, and when I came in, she jumped a mile, and said, *'Calm yourself! It's only Céleste!'* "

The table exploded into giggles.

"Perhaps you should see a psychoanalyst, Isabelle. I hear they are very popular in America."

Before I could answer, silly little Madeleine de Mailly said brightly, "Doesn't Jean-Paul Belmondo see a psychoanalyst? My mother says they are very chic in film circles right now."

"Belmondo is a tortured soul," Marie-Hélène said solemnly. "Have you seen his latest film?"

"My sister has seen it three times already," Madeleine replied, nibbling on a *cornichon*. "*And* she talks to his photo when she thinks no one is around. Perhaps *she* should see one."

From the faces of some of the girls, it seemed that perhaps several of them should seek help immediately. They all got into a debate about whether they'd sleep with Belmondo if he insisted.

I did get some *paté*; nobody noticed or cared what I ate. It didn't even matter if what Céleste had claimed was true or not. As long as I was humbled and silenced, an object of ridicule, they could ignore me. For now.

The moment coffee was served and napkins folded and the *demoiselles* dismissed from table, I rushed back to the *salle d'armes*, without even changing out of my skirt.

I was pretty sure I remembered which mirror had the door handle he always used. But none of them did. Not a single one. The closest I could find was a piece of lumpy woodwork, set in the molding at the right height. It was a spot that clearly had been filled in, sanded over, and repainted. I traced the outline of the entire panel. You could convince yourself that it had opened, once upon a time.

"So. You are a young woman, after all."

He was simply there, gazing frankly at me in the mirror. Standing behind me, as always.

"I can't say I think much of the outfit, but at least you are not dressed for combat. Don't tell me you've given it up?"

"You mean the odious Céleste?" I wondered if he'd seen the way I had yielded the *salle* to her, and very much hoped that he had not. But who knew what he did and did not see? "Not at all," I said, borrowing the hauteur of *Grand-mère* (or so I hoped). "There is an old African proverb: 'Don't shoot your arrows at the monkeys; save them for the lion.'"

He grinned wolfishly. "An excellent sentiment. It is a lion, then, this other blade?"

"No: monkey. A fool and a scoundrel."

"And refuses your challenge?"

"I haven't challenged her."

"You should." I did not answer. "You would most surely defeat that one."

"I don't know that."

"I do."

I had to ask. "Did you watch her practice?"

He looked down at his hands, avoiding my eyes. "I know what that one is made of. You can do it easily."

"With the little tricks that you have taught me?"

"They are not the only ones I know," he said softly. "As often as you return, I will show you more and more."

I stood very still. He did not press me. He just stood watching me for a flicker of movement, a sign of intent.

Maybe I tightened my jaw a fraction, or even clenched a fist, thinking about Céleste. Thinking about defeating her with moves only I knew.

Whatever it was, it seemed to satisfy him. He nodded and bowed. "So," he said, "perhaps I will see you again soon. When you are ready for combat. And more 'little tricks.' I bid you good night, *mademoiselle*."

And, again, he turned the handle of the door that wasn't there, opened it, and disappeared into the darkness . . . leaving me standing alone in the sunlit room.

It was that that unnerved me—and confirmed in my heart what my brain already knew. What was on the other side of that door? A dark corridor, lined with tapestries, or pictures of ancestors, or . . . ?

I looked out one of the tall windows. Nothing, that's what. A wing that had been taken down. There was nothing on the other side of that wall but air.

Outside, a golden afternoon was being wasted in the French countryside. I raced up to my room, changed into pedal pushers and sneakers. There were school bicycles in the old stables; I pedaled off down the road to a dairy farm that welcomed local schoolgirls.

Unlike my classmates, M. and Mme DuBois loved me for being American. Every time the old farmer saw me, his eyes would tear up as he told me how, not twenty years ago, the American troops had come marching down the road with candy for the children, having chased the Bosch like vermin from the fields of Normandie. He would take my hand in his work-hardened one, and grasp it hard. M. DuBois's breath smelled of tobacco, his blue work smock was patched and faded, and his eyes were bright and blue, until they blurred with emotion. He always gave me extra of whatever I bought from the farm, and refused any more payment.

So I took my bag of cherries, and went back to the chateau, and lay on the roof, working on my tan and rereading *Gone with the Wind* until the dinner bell rang.

Madeleine was already in our room, changing out of her riding clothes for supper. "Glorious day," she said breathlessly. "*Le Magnifique* and I rode all the way to St Martin and back." Had she really named her horse after the magic steed in Cocteau's *Beauty and the Beast*? Or was she just being affected? Yes, I'm sure her horse was truly magnificent.

"If you wanted," she said, "you could borrow a hack and ride out with me tomorrow."

"I can't imagine," I said, zipping up my skirt, "that a *hack* could keep up with *Le Magnifique*."

She turned a little red. "Oh—sorry—I didn't realize—"

I hate when people don't finish their sentences. "What?"

"Can't you—Ah, that is, you don't ride."

"Of course I can ride. I learned in Central Park. We do have stables in New York. Like the Bois de Boulogne. We even have ducks in a pond. It's very civilized."

"I've never been there."

"I don't think you'd like it," I said. I helped her with her dress zipper, because those things up your back are pure hell, and one must be civil, even to one's opponents. But we didn't make conversation as we went down to supper together. The last thing I wanted was for her to start asking me if I really had problems talking to myself.

I did not return to the salon that night. I had already practiced that day, after all, and taken a class as well. Of course, the mysterious man might not even be there. Perhaps I had offended him, and he was gone for good. But if he did wait for me, he could wait a little more. On Sunday, I had homework to complete. Monday, my class schedule was very heavy.

Tuesday morning came, and I fenced badly in class. It was very strange being in the salon with all these other people, when I was used to having it alone with him. "Attention, Mlle Blumberg!" Mme Gaillac called out. "This is not the cinema! Please do not target the knee of your foe."

The other girls sniggered.

"You are amused, ladies? None of you is exactly impressive this morning. Maybe this will wake you up. Speed drills." She took out a large stopwatch. "Put on your masks, please. Then line up in two lines opposite one another, well apart. When I say *Begin*, fence with your opposite. Do not stop, and do not count a touch, just keep going until I cry *Halt*, which will be at the end of three minutes for each bout. And then, move on to the next person."

It was glorious. I regained my focus, and my joy. Each new opponent was a puzzle to be solved, quickly and efficiently. Having watched them all in class, I had a pretty good sense of each girl's strengths and weaknesses. If you came straight at her with a direct lunge (and a solid glare), Marie-Hélène jumped back, utterly neglecting to defend herself. Françoise could be tricked with a simple feint into an ineffective parry every time. Madeleine had no defense against a disengage. True, we weren't counting touches, but I knew as the drill went on that I left behind me a line of vanquished opponents.

Then, there stood Céleste.

"Begin!"

Céleste attacked strong and hard, her usual pattern to assert control of a match from the start; but I retreated strategically, making her follow me. With her fabulous reach, she managed to make a touch. *Noted and filed,* I thought, and feinted an attack in Sixte that she parried brilliantly, only I wasn't there, I was under her guard and straight in where I wanted to be, a clean touch to her front. This pleased me so much I tried it again in Octave, but she was a quick study and didn't take the bait—indeed, and I hate to say it, she went right past my feint, not only touching me but parrying on the way back. Boy, she was fast. I counterparried, riposted, and hit her anyway, because it wasn't a real bout. But we both knew.

After that, we each backed off, and stood *en garde*, gently stepping back and forth while each tried to suss the other out. Fencing is a bit like a big game of Rock, Paper, Scissors, with your whole body and long, pointy weapons. We exchanged a little simple bladework, just to see if the other could be faked into an unconsidered move. I could see Céleste's eyes through the mask, a blue as clear as my strange master's, perfectly focused on me. And then—

"Halt!"

All around us, girls were removing masks and shaking out their hair, laughing and exclaiming over how much fun it had been.

Céleste raised her foil in salute. "Until the next time," she said.

On my way out of class, Mme Gaillac drew me aside. My heart thrilled; she had noticed, then, my strong work with Céleste. I tried not to smirk as she began, "That little bout was something to behold, my girl. You have the aggression, speed, and strategy. But you are too proud." I felt the blood drain from my face, as though she had actually pierced me with her words. "You are fighting with passion and anger—in short, you are *fighting*, not fencing. Leave your feelings at the door to the *salon.* It is the sword that matters, not yourself."

I was biting the inside of my cheek to hold back tears. How could she be so *unfair*?

I sat by myself at dinner and excused myself early, so I could go and practice in the long, golden light of a French summer evening.

"Welcome, *mademoiselle.*"

There was courtesy in his voice. *He* didn't think I was a disaster. Whoever and whatever he was, I was glad to see him.

"Are you prepared for your lesson?"

Silently, I nodded. And we began.

It was all wrong, of course. What he showed me involved ways to hold your shoulders or bend your knees so as to disguise your actual reach, which would work only if you were hurling your weight from back to front on a vicious throw. And hits that were far off target: ways of slicing the forehead to blind your opponent with blood; ways of pinking their kneecaps, stabbing their shins, and piercing their arms.

I loved it all. It was like having spent years sketching, and suddenly being allowed to paint with oils.

"And the throat," I said eagerly; "surely that's a good one?" Of course, ours are protected by the collar of the jacket and the bib of the mask. And it is not a valid target. But even a button-tipped foil, at sufficient force, can do real harm in that soft, vulnerable spot.

He raised his hand to his own throat again. I had thought it an affectation—but now, it looked oddly protective.

"You are insatiable," he said with a weak smile.

The sun was still at that beautiful point before it set. The room was painted in levels of gold, soft and diffuse; the ancient gilding of the molding's highlights glowed along with the rays along the floor, all reflected at different angles in the mirrors.

"So you will show me . . . ?"

He hesitated. "I think not. I am tired." He had never been tired before. "That is enough for one day. It grows late."

I wondered if, for once, he was seeing the same sun that I was—if, somehow, we were drawing closer together.

"Must we stop? There is still plenty of light." I waved my arm at the window, half-turning to do so.

"Do not turn around," he said sharply. "The mirror is your best teacher."

"I thought *you* were my best teacher."

"Cheeky girl." He smiled.

"Who taught *you*?" I asked.

"My father hired me good masters here at the chateau. But then I went to Paris, to study with that Italian for a while. That thing I showed you—with the *flanconnade*—that was his." He sighed. "Perhaps I should never have come back here." His back was to me, looking out the window. I wondered what he saw. "I grow tired of waiting." He turned fiercely back to the mirrors, back to me: "You will remember, yes? You will remember everything? Do you swear it?"

"Yes, I will. I'll try."

"In a real fight, there is no second chance. Each move must be definite, with a definite goal."

"Yes."

"It is very strange," he said, touching his hand to his throat in what I was coming to know was a gesture of unease. His eyes seemed dark, his face pale, not lit by the golden light at all. "I seem to wait alone."

"Not alone," I breathed. I reached out my hand to the mirror, as if I could touch him there, somehow.

"Yes. I have you, do I not?"

"Yes," I breathed. I leaned forward, that old habit of mine.

"And you will always return to me?"

In any match, the outcome depends on who controls the action.

I drew back my hand. "What is your name?" I asked boldly.

"Honoré." He shrugged. "Of course, after what happened, it should be *Des*honoré—But I have not yet been defeated. My honor remains intact."

"Ah, yes?" I didn't look at him.

He didn't like that. "My cousin, you understand."

"Really?" I did a little bladework, tried to sound bored.

"He has excellent taste in women. And no manners"—he lashed the air with an invisible blade—"whatsoever."

I nodded. "One must, of course, teach such people a lesson. He is a swordsman, your cousin?"

He shrugged. "Not much of one. It does not concern me, if . . ."

I held my breath. But he would notice that, so I made sure to breathe steadily, quietly, regularly.

The last rays of the sun slashed across the floor.

" '*If,*' sir?" I prompted. But there was no one there.

Madeleine was reading under the covers with a flashlight, after lights out. I knew perfectly well she was rereading her dog-eared copy of

Angelique et le Roy. I'd had a peek at what lay beneath the cover of the bosomy blonde being leered at by the Sun King, Louis XIV. Shocking stuff: ambitious women hopping in and out of bed with whatever noble-man would do them the most good—leaving their poor husbands to challenge lovers to the death for their nonexistent honor . . . the exploits of the French adventuress made Scarlett O'Hara look like *Little Women.*

Her light flickered and died. Good, I thought; I was only waiting for her to go to sleep so I could sneak back to the *salon* to find Honoré. He needed me. And I had promised to return.

She said, "Isabelle? Have you any batteries?"

"No," I lied. I needed my flashlight for the dark school corridors. "Go to sleep."

I got up, pulling my bathrobe on over the fencing clothes I already wore, and stuck my flashlight in my pocket.

"Where are you going?" she said sleepily.

"Where do you think? Just down the hall. I'll be right back. Go to sleep."

I flipped on the salon's elderly, flickering wall sconces. Half the fake candle-bulbs were out, but with the mirrors' reflection, it was enough to practice by. And enough to see him, when he appeared.

"Cannot you sleep, either?"

He was wearing a long, heavy brocade dressing gown, over a white nightshirt that looked a lot like one of his daytime ruffled ones.

"I cannot rest," he said. "I am tired of waiting. But it is not my fault, you understand?" He was pacing the room, back and forth before the mirrors, which caught him and threw him from one to the next as he passed between them. "I did what any man would do. The woman tempted me, and I did eat." In a moment, his hair was going to come loose from its ribbon. "I cannot find my sword. I have been looking everywhere, and I cannot find it."

Automatically, I held out my foil.

"I don't want your toy," he said. "Your dancing master's toy. This is a serious business. I must defend my honor—and hers, of course." He laughed an ugly laugh. "See? I told you: God does not always favor he who is in the right, or my cousin would surely defeat me. The challenge has been issued. I must fight him, and I must win. Or it is all over for me."

I turned off the electric lights. With the moon, and the outside gatehouse lamp, it wasn't too dark to see. I sat slowly down on the floor and laid my weapon aside, so that I was defenseless and lower than him. People will tell you things, then.

"What are you waiting for?"

"An end to all this waiting, child. And then, perhaps I can rest, and not be plagued by dreams." He shook his head. "I dream it, as if it's already happened. Over and over. I lunge, he parries me with a bind, I kick him away, he is on the ground . . . Feint, parry, it goes on and on . . . But then he springs at me, and pierces me, *here*—" He touched the soft spot at the base of his throat, and the ruby on his finger glinted there. "And then—and then it all begins again." His hair fell loose around his shoulders, a fine brown cascade.

Again I reached out my hand, as if I could stop the pacing, or push back the hair from his face. But those things I could not do.

"How can I help?" I asked.

"I grow mad with waiting. Let the fight begin!"

I looked around the room. All the foils in the rack were just like mine, the buttoned practice weapon in my hand. Nevertheless, I went to the rack, my hands hovering over the pommels as if I could divine one that would have the power that he needed. . . .

The old floors creak like crazy. I could hear the footsteps in the hall outside. I hushed at once, and listened to the latch being slowly turned, the door creaking open, the muffled whispers and stifled giggles.

"Is she here?"

"No, it's dark."

"Good."

Their flashlights threw reflections like arrows all over the room.

"Have you got it?"

"I don't want to touch it—Here, you take it!"

"Don't be such a baby."

Five girls; three flashlights. None of them Madeleine's.

"Right, then; which one's hers?"

They were looking for my fencing mask in the cabinet where all our equipment was stored. My glove, too, probably, but I had that on.

I stepped from the shadows.

"Good evening," I said, feeling a bit like Honoré. Nicole screamed. Something clattered to the floor—a tin of black pepper. "May I ask what you're doing here? And don't say you've come to practice fencing; I'm too young to die laughing."

"We were looking for you," Céleste said arrogantly.

"Well, you've found me. Now, *scram*."

"You don't tell me what to do in this house." Céleste raised her hand to her throat, where a gold chain hung. "I come and go as I like here."

"Unlike the rest of us?"

"Didn't you know?" Her fingers twisted the chain, and I saw a flash of red, a jewel hung on it. They closed around it as if it gave her authority. "My great-great-grandfather was Seigneur of Saint-Hilaire."

"What happened? Did he gamble the place away?"

"Oh that's right," she sneered, "you were sent here to improve your knowledge of French, weren't you? So maybe you never heard of the Revolution?"

I flushed, but parried, "Lucky for you someone kept the old place up, then, so his descendants could come back to remedy their essential stupidity."

"Do you really think I'm worried about my Bac?" Céleste's hand rose to the necklace at her throat again. "In Paris, I'm top of my class at Lycée Henri IV. I'm here for the same thing you are: to study fencing with Mme Gaillac."

She brushed a lock of perfect hair back from her sculpted face. "You look very comic when you're surprised. You think you know everything, don't you?"

"Maybe," I said. "But at least I don't go sneaking around trying to ruin other people's property."

"Awww," she crooned, "*pauvr' Americaine!* That's all that concerns you, isn't it? Your property? All the fast cars and big houses your big skyscraper department store buys. Of course, you Americans think you can do everything, now, with your money—with your Jew money."

"Céleste!" Marie-Hélène exclaimed, shocked.

"Well, it's true! Everyone knows it."

I reached for my mask. "Arm yourself," I said.

Céleste lifted her head, like a hound scenting game. But she said dismissively, "Are you mad?"

"What do *you* think?" I busied myself with my equipment. "Come on, Mlle de Puysange. For the honor of Saint-Hilaire. Unless you'd rather wait until class, so that La Gaillac can make sure we do it properly, according to the rules?"

"Hold this." She handed a can of hair spray to Nicole. Oh, lovely; that's what they'd been planning to do to the inside of my mask, that and the pepper, so that wearing it would be unbearable. Céleste pulled a spare jacket from the rack, found her own mask and glove, and tested a couple of foils from the rack before choosing one.

Someone turned on the sconce lights. We took our places on the *piste*, with the other four girls in the judges' positions.

In the mirror, I saw Honoré, quite clearly. He saluted me, and I saluted Céleste, and the bout began.

"Halt!" cried Nicole, the first time I touched my opponent. But we ignored her. It felt too good, too right, to be dueling at full force, jabbing at each other with long, pointed things; backing off and evaluating, advancing and feinting and returning each other's blows. Hers hurt when they landed, even through the jacket; I was going to be black and blue tomorrow, but I didn't care. We were well matched, and we'd been watching each other for weeks. It was as if the entire summer had been one long training for this moment.

She beat on my blade, throwing my next attack out of line with sheer force: a *prise de fer*. The sound of the steel was exciting, and threatening, too. I felt the shock of the contact snapping on my own blade, running down my foil and up my arm. In a normal bout my counterattack would have been worth nothing, since I'd lost right-of-way—but I had been trained by Honoré, and that didn't matter to me now. She made a lovely *coupé* to get back in line—but I slammed my foot on the floor in *balestra* and flew directly at her, straight for her throat. And, over her shoulder, saw my master smile.

These things can happen by accident. We've all heard the story of the fencer's foil that went up his opponent's arm inside his sleeve, piercing a lung. Nobody's fault.

I realized that I was going to hit Céleste up and under the mask bib, just at the soft point of her throat. I could sense it already there, as though there were a line from the tip of my foil extending through the air to where the gold chain rested with the ruby on it, crushing or even piercing her windpipe. In the flash of time remaining before my body carried me there, I did the only thing I could do: I opened my hand.

My sword clattered on the floor as I skidded forward, toppling awkwardly without any balance, to land at Céleste's feet. I lay there panting, and I heard her gasps for breath above me. She took off her mask and bent down.

"You're crazy, you know that?"

"Yeah," I said; "I know."

Céleste's friends surrounded her, cooing and petting her, helping her off with her jacket and glove, drying her off and putting her equipment away.

I just lay where I was. Breathing. Letting the air go in and out of me.

They turned off the lights when they left the room.

I waited for him in the mirror. And heard his voice behind me.

"I cannot breathe! Oh God, I cannot breathe, I'm drowning—"

I turned from the mirror, and saw him.

A young man, white-faced and sweating, clutching at his throat while the blood and the life went from him. The choking, the pallor, the gushes of red on the white shirt—it went on and on, longer than humanly possible . . .

"Honoré." I reached out my hand to him. His eyes were staring, shouting for help while his mouth had no breath to speak.

I turned back the mirror. "Honoré!"

He was whole, but trembling, there in the glass. "You failed me," he said, hugging his chest tight, his blue eyes burning bright above the bunched lace at his throat. "You said that you would help me! How can I rest, while he still lives?"

"He doesn't live," I said, as evenly as I could.

"You killed him, then?" he sneered. "Strange, that is not what I saw. I saw you cast away your blade at the moment of triumph, and spare him to be my torment again and again—"

"I did not fight your cousin."

"It was someone else, then? Someone else who wears my family's ring around his neck like a victor's prize?"

How had I not seen? Not just the ring, but the gesture she made with it, the color of her eyes—

"That bastard always wanted Saint-Hilaire. He set me up with that whore of a wife of his—I never fancied her, not really, but she got under my guard, you know how women are—my cousin set me up, just to give himself just cause to fight me."

"And then," I said steadily, clear in my understanding, needing to hear it aloud, "he killed you."

"I am twice the swordsman he is. He could never kill me. I live, and I will defeat him—"

"He died long ago, and you died before him."

He hissed. "That's a lie."

"Is that a challenge, sir?" I had to speak in words that he could understand. "Shall we duel to prove who lies, and who sees clearly?"

"I will punish your insolence!"

"Kiss me, then," I said, fighting not to cry. "Or kill me. I don't care."

In the mirror, his image shuddered. He must have been trying. A spot of red appeared at the base of his throat, and spread, gently, through his shirt.

But it was not much of a risk. I was speaking, after all, aloud to an empty room, to nothing but a memory that refused to die.

"You are my sword," he gasped. "Next time, you will not fail me. I know you hate him as much as I do. I've seen it, in your face."

"I am not going to kill his descendant—or possibly yours—no matter how awful she is."

His image hardened again. He was wearing black, white lace, and diamonds. "I wait, then."

"You'll wait a long time. Without rest. Please—" I knelt before the mirror. It was all I could think of to do. "Please, believe me. These dreams of yours are real; they are the truth. Believe me, and go in peace. Go away, Honoré."

In French the words for *mirror* and *ice* are the same.

"I'll wait," the ghost said. "As long as it takes, I'll wait."

What else could he say, true to his nature as he was? The dead do not change.

I leaned my head against the glass and closed my eyes, blotting out the sight of him, the sight of the dark, mirrored room.

I thought about the duel, and about the weeks of summer still to come, before I would be free to go home. I thought about New York, about my final year of high school, about applying to Smith and Vassar and Bryn Mawr and Wellesley, about leaving home with a suitcase monogrammed with my initials, for a place that was neither my father's house nor *Grand-mère*'s.

I thought about fencing, and intention, and being thrown into a new line by someone else's blade. And how to form a new intention and keep on.

When I opened my eyes, he was gone.

There was a gentle rap on the door. Madeleine stood there, wrapped in a dressing gown and carrying a candle. Her brown eyes were worried, but she held the candle steadily.

"It's late," she said. "Would you like some cocoa?"

"Yes," I said. "I think I would."

AUTHOR'S NOTE:

For their generous help with the niceties of swordplay and French culture, the author thanks Anne Guéro, J. Allen Suddeth, Kat Howard, Maud Perez-Simon, Ken Burnside . . . and a mysterious French fencer named Clément.

DREAMER

BRANDON SANDERSON

Brandon Sanderson has published eight solo novels with Tor—*Elantris*, the Mistborn books, *Warbreaker*, *The Way of Kings*, and the young adult fantasy *The Rithmatist*—as well as four books in the middle-grade Alcatraz versus the Evil Librarians series from Scholastic. He was chosen to complete Robert Jordan's Wheel of Time series; the final book, *A Memory of Light*, was released in 2013. His most recent YA novel, *Steelheart*, was released by Delacorte in September 2013. Currently living in Utah with his wife and children, Brandon teaches creative writing at Brigham Young University.

"Dreamer" is a blend of what Brandon normally writes—big epic fantasies with interesting styles of magic—with something a bit more weird.

"I've got him!" I yelled into the phone as I scrambled down the street. "Forty-ninth and Broadway!" I shoved my way through an Asian family on the way home from the market. Their bags went flying, oranges spilling onto the street and bouncing in front of honking cabs.

Accented curses chased me as I lowered the phone and sprinted after my prey, a youth in a green sports jacket and cap. A bright yellow glow surrounded him, my indication of his true identity.

I wore the body of a businessman, late thirties, lean and trim. Fortunately for me, this guy hit the gym. I dashed around a corner at speed, my quarry curving and dodging between the theater district's early-evening crowds. Buildings towered around us, blazing with the lights of fervent advertising.

Phi glanced over his shoulder at me. I thought I caught a look of surprise on his lean face. He'd know me from my glow, of course—the one visible only to others like us.

I jumped over a metal construction barrier, landing in the street, where I dashed out around the crowds. A chorus of honks and yells accompanied me as I gained, step by step, on Phi. It's hard to lose a man in Manhattan. There aren't alleyways to duck into, and the crowds don't help hide us from one another.

Phi ducked right, shoving his way through a glass door and into a diner.

What the hell? I thought, chasing after, throwing my shoulder against the door and pushing into the restaurant. Was he going to try to get out another way? That—

Phi stood just inside, arm leveled toward me, a handgun pointed at my head. I pulled to a stop, gaping for a moment, before he shot me point-blank in the head.

Disorientation.

I thrashed about, losing sense of location, purpose, even *self* as I was ejected from the dying body. For a few primal moments, I couldn't think. I was a rat in the darkness, desperately seeking light.

Glows all around. The warmth of souls. One rose from the body I'd left, the soul of the man to whom it had really belonged. That was brilliant yellow, and now untouchable. Unsavory, also. I needed *warmth*.

I charged for a body, no purpose behind my choice beyond pure instinct. I latched on, a lion on the gazelle, ripping and battering against the consciousness there, forcing it down. It didn't want to let me in, but I *needed* that warmth.

I won. In this primal state, I usually do. Few souls are practiced at fighting off an invasion. Consciousness returned like water seeping underneath a door. Panic, horror—the lingering emotions of the soul who had held this body before me, like the scent of a woman's perfume after she leaves the room.

As I gained full control, vision returned. I was sitting in one of the diner's seats looking down at the corpse of the body I'd been wearing—the body Phi had killed.

Damn, I thought, chewing the last bite of food the woman had been eating as I asserted control. It left a faint taste of honey and pastry in the mouth. *Phi had a gun.* That meant the body he'd taken had happened to have one. Lucky bastard.

A group of old women in cardigans and headscarves squawked in the seats around me, speaking a language I didn't know. Other people shouted and screamed, backing away from the body. Phi was gone, of course. He'd known the best way to lose me was to kill my body.

Blood seeped out of the corpse and onto the chipped tile floor. Damn. It had been a good body—I'd gotten lucky with that one. I shook my head, lifting the purse beside me—I assumed it belonged to the woman whose body I'd taken—and began to dig inside. I was an old lady, like the others at the table. I could see that much in the window's reflection.

Come on, I thought, standing up and continuing to search in the purse. *Come on . . . There!* I pulled out a mobile phone.

I was in luck. It was an old flip kind, not a smartphone, which meant it wasn't locked or passcoded. Ignoring the yells of the old lady's dining companions, I walked around the corpse on the floor, stepping out onto the street.

My exit started a flood, like I was the cork popped from shaken champagne. People left the diner in a run, many white-faced, a few clutching children.

I dialed Longshot's number. She was the one Phi was hunting, but she wanted to be useful. We often left one of our number back in a situation like this anyway, using him or her to coordinate. With the rest of us jumping bodies and finding new mobile phones, the best way to stay in touch was to have one person keep a set number and phone, taking calls from the other four and relaying messages.

The phone picked up after one ring.

"It's Dreamer," I said.

"Dreamer?" Longshot wore a body with a smooth, feminine voice. "You sound like an old lady."

"That's because I am one. Now." My voice bore a faint accent from the soul that had held this body. Things like that stayed. Muscle memory, accents, anything not entirely conscious. Not languages, unfortunately, but some skills. I'd once stayed in the body of a fine pianist for a couple of weeks playing music alone as the ability slowly seeped away from me.

"What happened?" Longshot demanded.

"His body had a gun. He ducked into a restaurant and popped me in the head when I followed. I don't know which way he went after that."

"Damn. Just a sec. I need to warn the others that he's armed."

"This could be a good thing," I said, glancing to the side as a couple of cops pushed through the growing crowd. "The mortal police will be after him now."

"Unless he Bolts from his body."

"He's on his third body already," I said. "He doesn't have many to spare. Besides, Bolting would risk losing the gun. I think he'll stick to the same body. He's brash."

"You sure?"

"I know him better than anyone, Longshot."

"Yeah, okay," she said, but I could hear the implication in her voice. *He knows you too, Dreamer, and he got you. Again.*

I lowered the phone as Longshot hung up and began calling the other three. I itched to be off, chasing Phi down again, but I had to be smarter than that. We knew where he was going—his goal would be Longshot, who hid atop a building nearby, unable to move. What we needed to do was make it tough for him to get to her.

Phi wouldn't escape me this time. No more failures. No more excuses.

"Excuse me?" I said, hobbling over to one of the police officers trying to manage the crowd. Damn, but this body was weak. "Officer? I saw the man who did this."

The officer turned toward me. It's still surreal to me how people's responses to me change depending on the body I'm wearing. This man puffed himself up, trying to look as if he was in control. "Ma'am?" he asked.

"I saw him," I repeated. "Short wiry fellow. Tan skin, maybe Indian, with a green jacket and cap. Lean face, high cheekbones, short hair. Perhaps five foot five."

The cop stared at me dumbly for a moment. "Uh, I'd better write this down."

It took a good five minutes for them to get down my description. Five minutes, with Phi running who knows where. Longshot didn't call me, though, so I didn't have anywhere to go. I'd know soon after one of the others spotted him. Two of the others would be out like I was, hunting

Phi on the streets. One last man, TheGannon, guarded the approach to Longshot's position.

A team of five to deal with one man, but Phi was slippery. *Damn it.* I couldn't believe he'd gotten the drop on me again.

I was finishing my description of his body for the sixth time when Longshot finally called me. I stepped away from the officers as they got corroborating information from other diner patrons and called in the description. An ambulance had arrived, for all the good it would do.

"Yeah?" I said into the phone.

"Icer decided to get a vantage atop a building on Broadway. She caught sight of our man moving down the street, almost at Forty-seventh. Moving slowly, like he's trying to not draw attention. You were right, he's in the same body as before."

"Awesome," I said.

"Icer is on her way down to hunt him. You're not going to let your past issues with Phi get in the way, are you, Dreamer? Phi—"

"I put the cops on his trail," I said. "I'm Bolting, but I'll keep this phone."

"Dreamer! You'll be on your last body. Don't—"

I closed the phone, turning back to the policemen. I chose a muscular man with dark skin. He wore a white shirt instead of blue, and the others had called him Lieutenant.

"Officer," I said, hobbling up, trying to get his attention without alerting the other police.

"Yes, ma'am," he said distractedly.

I faked a stumble, and he reached down. I grabbed his wrist.

And attacked.

It's harder when you're already in a body. The soul immediately gets attached to the body, and forcing out and into something else can be tough. Besides, when you're out of a body, the primal self takes hold, and it helps you—nearly mindless though you are—*claw* your way through another soul's defenses.

Some people say you can control the primal, body-less self. Learn to think while in that mode. I'd never been able to do it. Anyway, I had a body already, and part of my energy had to be dedicated to holding down the soul inside, that of the old lady. At the same time, I had to attack the police officer and force his soul aside.

The man gasped, eyes opening wide. Damn. His soul was *tough*. I strained, like a man straddling between two distant footholds, and shoved. It was like trying to push down a brick wall.

I will get him, this time! I thought, straining, then finally toppled that wall and slipped into the new body.

The disorientation was over more quickly this time. The officer stumbled as he lost control of his limbs, but I had the body before he dropped. I caught myself on a planter, going down on one knee, but didn't collapse fully.

"Lorenzo?" one of the others called. "You okay?" They'd covered the corpse with a white blanket. It lay just inside the door to the diner. Fleeing people had tracked blood out in a mess of footprints, but some diner occupants and employees still huddled inside the restaurant, shocked by the horror of the death. I could remember that fear, vaguely, from when I'd been alive. The fear of death, the fear of the unknown.

They had no idea.

I nodded to the other officers, standing back up, and when they weren't looking I slid the phone out of the hand of the old lady. She stood frozen and slack-jawed. Her soul would reassert itself over the next hour or so, but she wouldn't remember anything from our time together.

I pocketed the phone and began to jog away.

"Lieutenant?" one of the officers called.

"I have a lead," I said. "Keep going here."

"But—"

I left them at a run. The police thought the killing to be a gang-related hit, and so far, they hadn't shut down the streets or anything. Maybe they would, but it was better for me if they didn't. That would mean more bodies for my team to use, if they needed to.

The cop's body felt strong and energetic. I was left with the faint impression of a melody the cop had been singing in his head before I stole it. That and . . . a face. Wife? Girlfriend? No, it was gone. A fleeting image lost to the ether.

I jogged around the corner, keeping an eye out for the glow of a body that was possessed. This area was close to Longshot's building. If Phi got to her . . .

She wouldn't have a chance against him. I slowed my pace as I reached the place where Icer had spotted Phi. There was no sign of either one.

I wove through the crowds of lively, chattering people. The cop was tall, giving me a good vantage. It was strange how unaware people were. Two streets over, people stood in chaos, horror, or disbelief. Here, everyone was laughing and anticipating a night at a show. Street vendors cheerfully took tourist money, and dull-eyed people earning minimum wage handed out pamphlets nobody wanted to read.

Phi would be close. Longshot's building was just down the street, with her atop it. He would case the area, planning how to attack.

I waited, anxious, tense. I waited until the earbud I wore—tapped into the official police channels—spouted a specific phrase. "Marks here. I think I see him. Broadway and Forty-seventh, by the information center."

I started running.

"Don't engage him," the voices crackled on the line. "Wait for backup."

"Lieutenant Lorenzo here," I shouted into the microphone. "Ignore that order, Marks. He's more dangerous than we thought. Take him down, if you can!"

Others on the line started arguing with me, talking about "protocol," but I ignored them. I unholstered this body's gun and checked to make sure it was loaded. *Now we're both armed, Phi,* I thought. I charged around a corner, people flinging themselves out of my way once they saw the uniform and the gun raised beside my head. The shouts that chased me this time were of a different type—less outraged, more shocked.

Gunfire ahead. For a moment, I hoped Marks the cop had done as I told him, but then I saw a glowing yellow figure drop to the ground. It wasn't Phi.

Icer, I thought with annoyance. Indeed, Phi—still wearing the body with the green jacket—scrambled down the street after dropping Icer. I didn't have a very clear shot, but I took it anyway, pulling to a halt, raising the gun, and firing the entire clip.

This body had practiced with a gun. I was far more accurate than I had any right to be, bullets spraying the walls—and, unfortunately, crowd—right near Phi. I didn't hit him. I got *so close*, but I didn't hit.

"Damn it!" I said, charging after him. The crowds nearby were screaming, throwing themselves to the ground or running in stooped postures. Phi was heading straight toward Longshot's building.

Another gunshot popped in the air. I moved to dodge by reflex, but then saw Phi drop in a spray of blood.

What?

A cop stood up from beside a planter, looking white in the face. That would be Marks, the one who had called in the sighting. The cop raised his head in horror, looking around at the mess. People groaning from gunfire gone wild, the dead body Icer had been using, and now the fallen Phi.

The cop walked toward Phi's body.

"No!" I yelled. I scrambled for my microphone, running forward. "Someone tell Marks to stay back! Marks!"

He stiffened, then dropped. I cursed, trying to reach him, but there were so many people about, huddling, looking for cover, getting in my way. I drew closer, fighting through them, in time to see the body of Marks—a young, redheaded man with a spindly figure—stand up again and turn in my direction. Phi was on his fourth body. He lowered Marks's gun toward me.

Not again, you bastard, I thought, throwing myself to the side as four shots fired into the crowd. Only four—the gun had been partially empty.

I came up from my roll, thankful that Lorenzo was so athletic. My body knew what to do better than I did. Phi was already off and barreling toward Longshot. No subterfuge now, no casing the place. He knew that shots fired into a crowd would make this place go dangerous very, very quickly.

I ran after him, yelling into my microphone, "Marks has been working with the target. I repeat, Marks has been working with the target. In pursuit."

Well, that might just sow more chaos. I wasn't certain. I pulled my earbud out as I gave pursuit. The mobile phone from the old lady was ringing. I put it to my head as I ran.

"Icer is down," Longshot said. "It was her third."

Damn. I was out of breath.

"I think he got Rabies too," she told me. "He was only on his second body, but I can't reach him. He must not have a phone yet. It's you, Dreamer."

"TheGannon?"

"Gone," Longshot said softly.

"What the hell do you mean, gone?" I demanded, puffing.

"You don't want to know."

Damn, damn, damn! TheGannon was our door guard. "Phi is still armed," I told Longshot. "If he gets to you, try your best."

"Okay."

I pocketed the phone, holstered my gun, and gave the run everything I had. The street had gone to chaos quickly. With the wounded lying about, the people dropping papers and possessions as they ran and screamed, the cars stopping and people hiding inside, you'd have thought it was a war zone. I guess it kind of was.

I slid across the hood of a car, keeping pace with Phi—even gaining on him a tad—as he reached the target building. He didn't go inside, however. Instead, he pushed into the building *next* to it, a low office building with reflective glass windows.

He doesn't know that TheGannon is gone, I realized, charging after. *He's trying to keep himself from being pinned.* The office building and the target were similar in height. He could easily jump from one roof to the next.

He still had a lead on me, and it was a good minute or so before I hit the door, shoving my way in. This time I watched for an ambush. I didn't find one; instead, I saw a door on the other side of the entryway swinging shut.

"What's going on here!" a security guard demanded, standing beside his desk near the door.

"Police business," I yelled. "That doorway? It's a stairwell to the roof?"

"Yeah. I gave your buddy the key."

Damn. He could reach the roof, lock me out, and then jump over and take out Longshot. Phi was a clever one, I had to give him that much credit. *Why doesn't he go to 'Longshot?*

I entered the stairwell. I couldn't worry about gunfire. I had to charge up those steps as fast as I could. If he shot me, he shot me. There was a chance that would happen, but if he got to the roof, I lost. And I would *not* let him get away again!

I heard puffing and footfalls above me as I took the steps. My body was in better shape than his, but I'd been running longer than he had. Still, talking to the guard must have slowed him down, and I seemed to be gaining on him.

I rounded another corner in the white-painted stairwell, passing graffiti and concrete corners that hadn't seen a mop in ages. I *was* gaining on him. In fact, when I neared the top floor, I heard rattling as he worked on the door.

No! I forced my way up the last flight of stairs, reaching the top right as Phi pushed it closed on the other side. I slammed into it, exploding out onto the rooftop before Phi could lock it.

He stumbled away, red hair plastered to his head with sweat, shoulders slumping from fatigue. He tried to get out his gun, fiddling with an extra clip, but I tackled him.

"You're mine, this time," I growled, holding him to the rooftop. "No slipping away. Not again."

He spat in my eye.

Admittedly, I wasn't expecting that. I pulled back in revulsion, and he kicked me in the leg, shoving me off and throwing me to the side.

I cursed, wiping my eye, scrambling after him as he ran across the roof. The target building was next door, maybe five feet below this one, no gap between. My body's muscles were straining after that climb. I could still hear shouts from the chaos below, sirens wailing in the distance.

Phi jumped onto the rooftop. I followed. Longshot was there, wearing a young woman's body, backed up against the far corner of the building. Phi ran for her.

I screamed and threw myself forward, plowing into him just before he reached her.

And that tossed both of us off the building.

It was the only thing I could have done. If I'd gone slower, he'd have reached her. At this speed, I couldn't control my momentum. We fell in a heartbeat and crashed to the ground.

Disorientation.

Primal forces, driving me toward heat and warmth.

No. *That was my last.*

The thought bubbled up from deep within. Some say it's possible to control the primal self, the freed self.

I lashed out this direction, then that, but somehow held control. I could see Phi's spirit moving turgidly toward a body, and I somehow forced myself to follow. Two glowing fields, like translucent mold, seeping along the ground unseen to mortal eyes. Still a chase. A chase I would *win*.

I reached him just before he got to the warmth, and I latched on. I held tightly, clinging to him, and like an unwieldy weight, stopped him from getting into the body. He battered at me, clawed at me, but I just held on. I'd lost knowledge of why I did what I did, but I *held on*. For a time, at least. An eternity I could not count.

Finally, he slipped away, as he always does.

I found another warmth, then opened my eyes to a smiling face. "Longshot?" I said, disoriented. I was lying on the ground in a new body, a construction worker, it appeared. The contest was over; I'd be allowed this body now.

"You did it," she said, glowing. "You held him down long enough for Rabies to get here! Once Phi got control of his last body, Rabies already had it in custody! You won, Dreamer."

"He cheated."

I sat up. Phi sat there in the body of another construction worker; the two men had been taking cover here, it appeared, near the base of the building. I could tell it was him. My brother always has this self-satisfied leer on his face, and I could recognize him in any body.

"What? That's nonsense." The businesswoman would be Icer, from that tone in her voice. She sat on the edge of a planter nearby. "We got you, Phi."

"He shot into the crowd!" Phi said.

"So did you!" I said, climbing to my feet with Longshot's help. After spending so long . . . too long . . . outside a body, the warmth felt good. It had probably been only a few minutes, but that was an eternity without a body.

"You were playing detective, Dave," Phi said, pointing at me. "*I* was criminal. I can shoot innocents. You can't."

"By whose rules?" Icer demanded.

"Everyone's rules!" Phi said, throwing up his hands. "You've got five, I'm only one. The criminal has to have a few advantages. That's why I can kill, and you can't."

"It's five on one," I said, "because *you* bragged you could take us all on your own, Phi."

"You cheated," he said, leaning back. "Flat-out."

"Man," Rabies said, wearing the body of a thick-armed black man. He stood a little off from us, looking at the chaos of Broadway, with police, ambulances. "We kind of caused a mess, didn't we?"

"We need to ban guns," Longshot said.

"You *always* say that," Phi replied.

"Look," Longshot said. "We won't be able to use Manhattan for months."

"Eh," Phi said. "I'm doing a race with TheGannon across the country next. What do I care?"

"What happened to TheGannon, anyway?" Icer asked.

Longshot grimaced. "We had an argument. He left."

"He bugged out in the middle of a game?" Icer said. "Damn that kid. We should never have invited him."

"They're coming over here," Rabies said. "To check on the bodies of the two cops. We should split."

"Meet up in Jersey?" Longshot asked.

We all nodded, and the glowing individuals went their separate ways. They'd probably dump these bodies soon, working their way out of the city by hopping from person to person in whatever way suited them.

I ended up going with Phi. Side by side, walking away from the dead cops, hoping nobody would stop us. I was tired, and Bolting to another body didn't sound pleasant.

"I *did* get you," I told him.

"You tried hard, I'll give you that."

"I won, Phi. Can't you just admit that?"

He just grinned. "I'll tell you what. Footrace to Jersey. No limit on bodies. And just for you, no guns. Loser admits defeat." With that, he took off.

I sighed, shaking my head, watching my older brother go. A footrace? That meant no cars, no subways. We'd have to run the entire way, jumping into new bodies every few minutes as the ones we were using grew exhausted—like a poltergeist version of a relay race.

Phi never knew when to stop. I didn't remember a lot about when we'd been alive, back when our capture the flag games had been limited to controllers and a flatscreen—but I did know he'd been like this then, too.

Well, I could beat him in a footrace. He wasn't nearly as good at those as he was at capture the flag.

I'd win this time, and then he'd see.

FALSE KNIGHT ON THE ROAD

A SERRATED EDGE STORY

MERCEDES LACKEY

Mercedes Lackey was born in Chicago, Illinois, on June 24, 1950. The very next day, the Korean War was declared. It is hoped that there is no connection between the two events.

She was raised mostly in the northwestern corner of Indiana, attending grade school and high school in Highland, Indiana. She graduated from Purdue University in 1972 with a bachelor of science degree in biology. This, she soon learned, along with a paper hat and a name tag, will qualify you to ask, "Would you like fries with that?" at a variety of fast-food locations.

In 1985 her first book was published. In 1990 she met artist Larry Dixon at a small science fiction convention in Meridian, Mississippi, on a television interview organized by the convention. They began working together from that time on and were married in Las Vegas at the Excalibur chapel by Merlin the Magician (aka the Reverend Duckworth) in 1992.

They moved to their current home, the "second weirdest house in Oklahoma," also in 1992. She has many pet parrots and "the house is never quiet." She is approaching one hundred books in print, with five being published in 2012 alone, and some of her foreign editions can be found in Russian, German, Czech, Polish, French, Italian, Turkish, and Japanese. She is the author, alone or in collaboration, of the Heralds of Valdemar, Elemental Masters, Secret World Chronicles, Five Hundred Kingdoms, Diana Tregarde, Heirs of Alexandria, Obsidian Mountain, Dragon Jousters, Bedlam Bards, Shadow Grail, Dragon Prophecy, Half-blood Chronicles, Bardic Voices, SERRAted Edge, Doubled Edge (prequel to SERRAted Edge), and other series and stand-alone books.

Billy Ray Johnson listened attentively past the thunder of the three-carb, supercharged V8 under the hood of his Ford Fairlane. He knew every grumble and roar of his machine; what he was listening for was something that *wasn't* it. The rumble he was listening for would be a Chevy, which would be the cops, more than likely, and that would mean he'd need to lie off the road a piece until they cleared out. All the 'shiners hereabouts ran Fords or Hudson Hornets. Sometimes he regretted not getting a Hudson; they gripped the curves like a cat about to be tossed into the river. But the Ford was faster. Fastest car in the county, probably the fastest car in this part of the state.

It was a perfect night for 'shine running. Which was not to say that it was a beautiful, clear night with a full moon. Outsiders might consider that a perfect night, but a clear, bright night meant the cops could see you running up the mountain a mile away. Tonight was a quarter moon, and you couldn't see it for the overcast and the fog. Not enough fog to slick up the road, and it wasn't an even blanket, but it was enough to make driving a challenge if you didn't know the roads the way Billy Ray did.

Right now he was on a piece of section line that just had patches of fog on it, not enough to turn the clay under the gravel greasy. Thanks to the fog, the thick woods to either side of the gravel road were like walls, just a hint of individual trees in the sidewash of his headlights as he sped by. He was laden down, trunk full of cartons of tightly packed mason jars full of 'shine cradled in newspaper so they wouldn't bang together and break, tank built into the backseat full and sealed, and some extra-special bottles tucked in flour sacks under the front seat. He was early, by his reckoning. He'd made good time. He'd make better time when he got to the hardtop road. Seventy-five miles to Shelby, where he'd turn over his load, collect his money, and head back home again.

Moonshine had bought and paid for this car. Moonshine bought and paid for everything his ma and pa couldn't grow or hunt for themselves and the kids. Life was rough on the mountain; hardscrabble farming, plowing the few bits of land that weren't vertical without any mechanical help, just with plow blade and a mule. In theory it was possible to live completely off the land, but in practice, unless you didn't mind dressing yourself and the kids in leather and furs like a bunch of Indians, and you didn't mind doing without things like bread, it wasn't. What Billy brought in running 'shine paid for the flour and the stuff for clothing, all the things that made life a little easier.

Ma worried, but Billy even knew what he'd do if he got caught; he'd be a first-time offender and the judge in this county had a reputation for offering people like him the prison farm or the army. He'd take the army, and send his pay home. It wouldn't be as much as he got for 'shine running—a hundred dollars a month instead of a night—but it'd be better than nothing.

But he didn't plan on getting cau—

The hell! he thought, as his headlights cut through a patch of fog and hit the side of a car parked right across the road at a crossroads *he* didn't remember being there, and he stood on the brakes to avoid piling into it.

Which he did, just barely, and only by hauling on the hand brake and sending the Fairlane slewing sideways in a shower of gravel.

The first thing in his mind was—*revenuers!*—and his heart, already racing, went into a panicked gallop, as his brain went into overdrive calculating how to sling the Fairlane all the way around and gun her back up the road he'd just come down.

But in the next moment he realized—no, that was never a cop car, or a revenuer car, nor the FBI. There were no markings, no lights—and no cop car, not even FBI or Treasury agent, had *ever* looked like this one.

It set his mind into a tailspin then, all thoughts of escape vanishing—because he could not identify it. At all. And he knew every make and model of every car ever built, at least in the U.S. of A. It *had* to be foreign. One of those cars he'd read about the few times he'd gotten his hands on a racing magazine, with names he couldn't even begin to figure out how to pronounce. What the hell was it doing out here? Was the driver lost, or stuck? In either case, *what the hell was it doing out here?*

It was low, and lean, and sleek. Solid black without a hint of chrome anywhere. It matched no make or model he had *ever* seen, not even in pictures. Some rich man's made-just-for-him racing car? There had been one magazine, with photos of cars with outlandish bodies competing in some Frenchified race . . . *Grand Prix*, they called it. But what in the name of God was something like that doing out in these mountains?

And what in *hell* was it doing parked in the middle of a crossroads he would have sworn hadn't been there the last time he'd made this run?

He'd pulled the Fairlane to a stop mere feet away from the mystery car, and now the driver's side opened, and the driver stepped out. Calm. Cool. If the positions had been reversed, Billy Ray would have been out of that car before the Fairlane stopped moving and heading for the brush—and when the crash didn't happen, he'd have been heading *out* of the brush with a fat stick in his hand to administer a whuppin'.

Like the car, the driver was all in black from head to toe. Black pants, black jacket zipped up against the damp chill in the air, black gloves. He wore a black hat—a Stetson—pulled down low on his head, so you couldn't really see his face. He strolled around the front of his beauty of a car, walked over to Billy's window, and tapped on it.

Too astounded by all of this to think at all at this point, Billy automatically rolled it down. Little cold, damp wisps of fog drifted in through the window, along with a faint scent of leather and a hint of something expensive and spicy.

"Billy Ray Johnson?" The stranger's voice was low, smooth, *rich* sounding.

"That there'd be me," Billy admitted, the words coming out of his mouth before he thought.

The stranger leaned back against his car and crossed his arms over his chest. "I heard," he said, making no attempt to disguise his high-class accent, words coming out of his mouth that sounded more like what you'd hear on a radio show one late night, tuned in by accident from some place far, far away, than anything these mountains had ever echoed. "I heard that your Ford is a fast car."

Now there were finally thoughts running through Billy's head. That he was in the middle of a run. That this was no time to be palaverin' with a stranger in the middle of the road. That the *smartest* thing he could do would be to throw the Fairlane into reverse, hightail it back down the way he'd just come, and take another section-line road to the hardtop.

But Billy's mouth wasn't nearly as smart as his brain. "It's fast," he heard himself say smugly.

"I *heard*," the stranger continued, "that you're the fastest driver in the county."

Billy's mouth was really, really stupid tonight. "I am," he heard himself say even as he considered punching himself in the face to get himself to stop. "Ain't nobody faster."

The stranger nodded, as if all this were exactly what he expected to hear. "Well, then. Are you prepared to prove how fast you and that piece of American iron are? Because last I saw, me and my girl were the fastest in three states, and I intend to make it four."

Now that made Billy Ray angry, and when he was angry, as his ma had pointed out to him time and time again, his temper burned up every bit of brains he had. "Now look here, mister, you might be *fast* on black-top an' straight roads, but you and that car ain't really *fast* less'n y'all're fast on roads like you ain't likely ever seen afore—"

"Sounds to me as if you're inviting me to a race," the stranger said, smoothly, with just a hint of . . . challenge.

And Billy Ray was not the man to let a challenge pass unanswered. "Reckon I am," he replied, his chin stuck out belligerently.

"That was what I was hoping to hear," the stranger said with deep satisfaction. "Let's make it interesting. Here to the county line. If you win, you get this"—and he patted the fender of his machine.

Now, Billy Ray was no stranger to avarice. He'd lusted after the Fairlane ever since the model came out, and it had taken him a lot of runs to pay for her and her modifications, even after getting the "special price" from the dealer that all his boss's runners got. But just the *curves* of the stranger's beauty of a machine made that desire seem like a grade school crush. Whereas this was the lust of a man for a red-hot woman. He wanted that car, as he had never wanted anything in his life. Already in his mind he was boring her cylinders, mounting a supercharger. . . .

But there was one tiny little bit of reason left in his brain, just enough to choke out, "And what if I lose?"

"We'll talk about that at the end of the race," the stranger laughed.

"Don't worry. It won't be anything you can't afford. In fact, you probably won't even miss it."

Well, the stranger must have been insane, but then, foreigners generally were. A lot of the men of the mountains had come home from the Big War with stories about those crazy French, Italians, and English—

So long as he wasn't betting the Fairlane, he didn't care in the state he was in—half angry at the condescending tone of the stranger, half on fire at the challenge. He backed up the Fairlane to the tree line and slowly got her pointed in the right direction. The stranger's maneuvering was more graceful, a smooth curve of a backward turn that came within a hair of the Fairlane's bumper without ever touching it, and put him door-to-door to Billy Ray.

The driver revved his engine. It had a throat like nothing Billy Ray had ever heard before; a deep, throbbing rumble, deeper than the Fairlane. Not a growl, not a howl, but still something primal. A roar. A jungle roar.

It put the hair up on the back of his neck, and for the first time, he felt a sense of warning. . . .

But it was too late to do anything about it now.

"You count it off!" the stranger shouted through his open window to Billy Ray.

That was an invitation to cheat, to jump the gun. The stranger was taking the measure of him.

Well, Billy Ray was going to measure up as a man. He might be doing something he could go to jail for in order to make a living, but he never had cheated in his life, and he never would.

"*On your mark!*" he shouted, one foot on the gas and the other on the brake. "*Get set! GO!*"

There was not a second's worth of difference between them as the two cars leapt forward into the night.

Now . . . racing like this was taking a calculated risk. Whether or not someone tried to arrest them both depended largely on who was prowling the night tonight. If it was Treasury, revenuers—they'd see two fast cars out neck and neck and figure no way either of them was carrying 'shine. The extra weight of all those gallons of liquid alone was going to handicap a vehicle and if there was a crash, the very last thing you wanted was a car soaked in alcohol about to catch fire. If it was state troopers—now they might take an interest in stopping the race and arresting them both for speeding. If it was local cops—they knew Billy Ray's Fairlane, and while they surely knew he was a runner, they'd never actually *caught* him, and in a case like this one, seeing him pitted against a furriner and a strange car . . . it would be a case of letting Billy Ray uphold the honor of the county and show that outsider just who ruled the roads hereabouts. Why, they might even use their new radios to make sure the road stayed clear, once they figured out the route.

And tonight was a damp, cold, foggy night. Hard to see. Hard to navigate if you didn't know the roads like someone born and raised in one of these hollers. He'd bet that if there was anyone out looking for 'shine runners, it would be the local boys.

They were "running by the tree line," as one of the other 'shine runners said. If you asked someone, they'd say this was a two-lane road, but that only meant there was enough room for two cars to get out of the way of each other and not end up hung up in the brush. The right side of the Fairlane was getting beat to death with twigs, but that wouldn't be as bad as it was for the stranger, who'd be getting his driver's side whupped. There wasn't more than five inches between them, and they were door handle to door handle, two sets of headlights lighting up the whole road as they bounced over the uneven surface.

At least it wasn't washboard here. And at least it was as straight as an arrow.

Billy Ray was planning ahead, far ahead. He knew where this road came out onto the two-lane blacktop, and of all things, he wanted to be ahead and *stay* ahead on the blacktop as far as Cherokee Mountain. It didn't matter if he was only a few inches ahead; he needed to be on the inside of the road when it hit the mountainside. Because there were no guardrails on Cherokee Mountain, and not a lot of verge, and the inside lane was the only safe place to be.

If he could hold on to his lead up to the mountain, he'd keep it when the road started climbing.

Unless the stranger was crazy . . . or crazy-good.

Or completely without fear, which it was looking very like he *was*.

Any sound was drowned out by the song of the two engines, the howl of the Fairlane and the guttural roar of the stranger's machine. He glanced over at the car that was pacing him as if the two vehicles were Siamese twins, and barely made out the stranger in the headlight wash, Stetson still pulled low down on his forehead, hands on the top of the wheel, staring intently ahead.

Billy Ray didn't dare do more than glance, just enough to get a fleeting impression. Even though the road was straight, there were plenty of hazards. Any one of the bumps could throw the Fairlane into the stranger's car, or vice versa. Deer could jump out onto the road. Hell, at the speeds they were going, a rabbit could make one of them skid into the other.

And the blacktop was coming up—

He sensed it, then oh-so-briefly recognized it, the darkness that meant the trees were gone, and he swung the wheel more on instinct and knowing the road in his gut than by anything he actually saw. The Fairlane's tubeless tires shrieked as they hit the surface and skidded before digging in and Billy was thrown to the side by the force of the turn, holding on to control by his nails and teeth. The tires bit into the asphalt, and the Fairlane howled away, and—

And that *damned* black machine was right there with him, as if it were glued to him! She was a little behind him, her headlights just about even with where he sat, but a moment later she was back, side by side, the two of them racing down the two-lane blacktop as if they owned it.

The blacktop road wasn't straight; it swerved and jinked around the bottom of the valley, following the contours of Higgins Crick. Billy Ray had never powered down this road, this fast, at night. This was white-knuckle driving, and there was one thing of paramount importance. He absolutely had to be in the lead by at least a little at the point where the stranger realized they were going up the face of the mountain. He had to have the inside lane on the mountain. Taking the outside at this speed—

Well, there were stories about that, and they generally ended in a pile of twisted metal.

He had both windows down, and the air was thick with the scent of cold, fresh water and green river weeds. He glanced out the side of his eye at the other car. They were so close he could have reached out and yanked on the stranger's door handle. The stranger was nothing but a dark silhouette against the headlight wash of the blur that was the forest on his side of the road.

He was waiting for something only he, or someone who knew this road as well as he did, would know. And there it came—the scent of pine. There was going to be a dip and a rise, and anyone who wasn't ready for it would automatically pull back on the gas.

He hit the dip and jammed the pedal to the floor, the Fairlane actually taking to the air over the rise. The stranger dropped back almost a full car length; Billy kept his foot down.

But the stranger wasn't surrendering; not with plenty of miles between here and the county line. Slowly the stranger's car crept up, somehow gaining what he'd lost an inch at a time. At the point where Billy Ray felt the road starting to rise, climbing away from the crick and starting the climb up the side of the mountain, the stranger's hood was even with his door again. But that was enough.

He found a little more pedal, and a little more acceleration. As he began to pull ahead again, he glanced back.

And the hair on the back of his neck stood straight up.

Glaring at him through the windshield where the driver would be was a pair of hell-hot, glowing green orbs.

And that was when he finally came to his senses; when he recognized what he should have figured out a good long time ago. Like, back at the crossroads, when the stranger talked about wagers, and offered to bet his car, a car of a sort Billy Ray had never laid eyes on even in pictures.

The stranger wasn't . . . human.

Billy Ray was racing with the Devil.

As his body wrenched and hauled on the steering wheel, sending his car thundering up the mountain road, his mind was moving almost as fast in a panic. The stranger had dropped back, seeing the wisdom of not taking the outside lane when there was nowhere to go if you encountered another car in the outside lane, and the danger of skidding off if you lost even a little control or hitting a patch of the stones that were always coming down off the rock face. But when Billy Ray looked up to his rearview, he could see them, faintly, through the headlight glare. Those eyes, those inhuman eyes, green and glowing.

Billy Ray's granny'd had a great store of tales about the Devil;

granted, there were other critters this driver could be, according to those stories, but they were *all* unholy. She'd had tales, and songs too. Little Billy had listened avidly, and a good thing he had, too, because somewhere in all those stories and songs was the key to getting him out of this mess. Or so he was praying.

Not that praying was going to do him any good right now. Billy's granny had been very clear on something in her tales. God wasn't going to be hornswaggled by a last-minute repentance and pleas for mercy. God was like Granny. *"You made that there bed, you're a-gonna lie in it."* It was one thing for a good man to be tricked by the Devil; God would take pity on such, and send him help. But a bad man would have to get his own self out of the mess. And Billy Ray knew he was a bad man.

Not so much because of the 'shine running. That might be against man's law, but it was a plain, bad law that had no reason to exist except to enrich some men at the expense of common folks. There hadn't even been such a law until Prohibition, but then after, the revenuers had figured out there was a lot of money to be made for the government by keeping the likker-making in the hands of a few and taxing the hell out of it. That was greed, and sin, in and of itself, to deny a man the ability to take his own corn from his own land and do what he wanted with it.

No, it was because Billy had done more than his fair share of sinning, for all that he was a young'un. Cussin' and lyin', getting drunk and not just having a drink or two, fornicatin' . . . and he'd had lust for the stranger's car, which was right against the commandments, lusting after what your neighbor had. No, he was a bad man, and God was going to be no help to him.

So what he needed was cleverness.

Some of Granny's stories had been new, or at least came from this side of the ocean, but a lot had been old, going all the way back to the family roots in English soil. And the one he could remember now was the one that he'd acted out to the amusement of his ma and pa, singing out the lines for the clever lad, while Granny sang the ones for Old Scratch. *"Never nohow call him by his name,"* she'd warned. *"Or he'll come, soon or late, he'll come!"* Well, Billy had called out that name often enough . . . and here was proof that Granny was right.

He was driving this road on pure instinct, relying on the memory of a couple hundred such runs to tell him *where* to hit the brakes and crank the wheel over a fraction of a second before the next hairpin turn came into view. And the stranger was still right on his tail, headlights burning furiously through the rear glass, green eyes glaring through the light-haze.

"The False Knight on the Road" . . .

In the song, like now, the Devil had appeared in disguise, in the guise of a man of wealth and status. He'd confronted a little boy—probably a very naughty little boy, since God hadn't sent an angel with a flaming sword to drive Old Scratch away—but a clever little boy. Billy hauled the wheel around another turn and searched the song for a way out of his predicament.

"Oh where are ye going?" said the False Knight on the road.
"I'm goin' to my school," said the wee boy and still he stood.
"And what is on yer back?" said the False Knight on the road.
"Me bundles and me books," said the wee boy and still he
    stood.

All right, what did that tell him? What had Granny said? The wee boy showed courage: standing right up to the Devil. But not lying. Lying would have given the Devil leave to snatch him up on the instant. And he wasn't insolent; insolence wouldn't have let the Devil *take* him, but you didn't anger the Devil, for he might well kill you. God would have your soul, but that wasn't a great consolation if you were dead.

"What sheep and cattle's them?" said the False Knight on the
    road.
"They're mine and me father's," said the wee boy and still he
    stood.
"How many of 'em's mine?" said the False Knight on the road.
"As many's got blue tails," said the wee boy and still he stood.

He was sweating with fear and his heart was pounding along with the throbbing engine. Granny had explained that one. If the boy had said "none," that would have given the Devil a pretext to find one or more sheep that "could" belong to him—a ram with curled horns, maybe, or a black sheep. That would prove the boy a liar and forfeit his soul. But by setting a condition, the boy had bested him. And that made him angry, and *that* kicked off the dangerous part of the song, where the boy had to counter every curse the Devil threw at him, and throw it back.

> "I wish you were in yonder tree!" said the False Knight on the
>   road.
> "A ladder under me," said the wee boy and still he stood.
> "The ladder it would break!" said the False Knight on the
>   road.
> "And you would surely fall!" said the wee boy and still he
>   stood.
> "I wish you were in yonder sea!" said the False Knight on the
>   road.
> "A good boat under me!" said the wee boy and still he stood.
> "The boat would surely sink!" said the False Knight on the
>   road.
> "And you would surely drown!" said the wee boy and still he
>   stood.
> "Has your mother more than you?" said the False Knight on
>   the road.
> "They're none of 'em for you," said the wee boy and still he
>   stood.

And there the clever boy even diverted the harm from his siblings.

> "I think I hear a bell!" said the False Knight on the road.

That would be the death knell—the Devil had lost patience, and if he could not have the boy's soul, then he would have his life!
But the boy knew the answer to that—

"Aye, it's ringin' ye to hell!" said the wee boy and still he
    stood.

Turning it from a death knell to a church bell. And that—that was
it! No demon, nor fairy, nor the Devil hisself could stand against a church
bell, and it was, by the feel of the air and the finely tuned time sense Billy
had honed over many, many trips, close to midnight. If he lost the race—
if he lost the race—if he could just keep the Devil talking until the church
bells from Holy Grace Baptist rang up from the valley, he'd be saved.

Now, if he could get up this mountain and win the race, he had
nothing to fear. And that was his best chance.

And he was close, close to the top, for the road had started to narrow
still further, to the point where cars approaching each other at this part
of the road would stop and inch forward, door handles actually scraping,
to get past each other. Surely not even the Devil would chance trying to
pass here, at the speeds they were going. His heart started pounding, and
not with fear, but with triumph. He was going to win! He was going to win!

And then he heard it.

Behind him, a new note rose in the throat of the great black beast
that the Devil was driving. The howl rose to a scream, and with a scant
five hundred yards to the top and a thousand to the county line, the sleek
machine accelerated like nothing Billy Ray had ever seen before, *tore*
past him on a lane that could not have been more than three fourths of
a proper lane wide, and shoved itself in front of him so quickly he had
to brake to avoid ramming it—

And then, to add insult to injury and shame to it all, the red taillights
ran off up the road and out of sight so fast you would have thought the
beast was powered by rockets and not by an engine at all.

Of course it's not powered by an engine, Billy thought with his
stomach in knots and his mind in a whirl. *Or at least, it ain't an engine
that any man's hand was in the building of.*

For one brief moment, as he made the last turn and headed for the
county line, he hoped that the Devil had got so far in front of him that
he might could make a run for it.

But no.

There he was, the bastard, his sleek car parked square across the road, blocking it, right on the other side of the county border. And him leaning up against it, hat still pulled down over his face.

Billy rolled up slowly and turned off his engine. Just as slowly, and racked with terror, he got out of the car. From the Fairlane came the tick-tick-tick of cooling metal. From the stranger's car . . . nothing.

How far was it to midnight?

"Well," said the Devil. "There's the little matter of the bet."

"Aight," Billy agreed, sweating. *How to turn that against him?* There was nothing there to use! *How to keep him talking?*

But the Devil was already talking. "I'll have what's under the front seat of your Ford Fairlane, Billy Ray," he said, with a hint of laughter in his voice. "And don't you trouble to tell me there ain't nothing there. There's six old-style bottles there, all wrapped in flour-sack towels and corked with their tops waxed, all full of *proper* corn whiskey, made from 'shine from a clean, clean still, all good copper and no lead solder about it, and aged in charred oak barrels, and I'll be having them all."

Billy almost fainted with relief. The Devil wanted *whiskey*? That was *all*? He'd have given the Devil his whole cargo and thrown in the Fairlane—

He hardly knew how he managed to get the passenger door open. His hands shook so much getting out the "special" bottles that it was a wonder he didn't drop them. He didn't even stammer thanks when the stranger gave him six flour-sack towels full of broken glass to stick back under there, and give him the excuse for why those special bottles of real whiskey weren't there no more.

All that he could really do, when the stranger had pulled the car far enough off the road that he could get by, was put the pedal to the floor and speed away. . . .

"Great Harry's Ghost, did you see his *face*?" howled Dylan ap Dai, throwing the Stetson onto the head of what had been a sleek automobile and was now a stunning black horse and exposing his pointed ears as the wind at the top of the mountain blew back his hair. The elvensteed snorted and shook her head so the Stetson settled into place, looking quite at home there.

"Aye, that I did, ye daft bugger," said his cousin Caradoc, coming out of the woods at the side of the road, followed by his own mount, a silver stallion. "Poor lad, he thought you were the Devil! Shame on you, for putting such a fright into the boy!"

"Well the shame's on him for carrying such a delectable cargo I couldn't resist the challenge!" Dylan retorted, and twirled his finger around the top of the one of the bottles that hadn't made it into his elvensteed's saddlebags. The wax obligingly peeled off and the cork extracted itself and Dylan took a pull of the bottle. "Oh, aye . . ." he sighed. "There's the sweet dew of the mountain . . . here, taste that and see if it was worth a challenge."

He handed the bottle to his cousin, who took it, exposing the badge of Elfhame Fairegrove on his chest as his cloak lifted a little. Caradoc took a considering sip, his eyebrow rose, and he took as deep a draught as Dylan had. "Why is't yon mortals can make such delectables and we cannot?"

Dylan shrugged. "And what d'ye think of yon challenge-race?" he demanded, taking the bottle back and having another mouthful. "*I* think we've found us a new sport."

"Safer than a challenge-joust, for certain sure." Caradoc claimed the bottle, and pondered over his second drink. "I reck me Lord Keighvin Silverhair will find it as tasty as he finds this drink."

"Then we've two prizes to carry home, sweet cuz!" Dylan laughed, and slapped his fellow elf on the shoulder. "So, let's hie us hence, and give him the winnings and the word!"

A moment later, two sleek sportscars, one silver, one black, sped away along a road that, until a moment before, had not been there. Then the trees swallowed them up, and they were gone.

JAMMED

SEANAN MCGUIRE

Seanan McGuire was born and raised in Northern California, explaining her love of redwoods and fear of weather. She writes urban fantasy under her own name and science fiction thrillers under the name Mira Grant. When not writing, she watches a lot of horror movies and television and attends a lot of Roller Derby, as well as attending conventions and arguing endlessly about the X-Men. She lives in a crumbling farmhouse with too many books and three abnormally large blue cats. Seanan is exactly as much of a geek as this bio makes her seem.

> Nobody ever got eaten because they ran too fast.
> Maybe a few people went over cliffs they didn't
> see coming, but that's probably a better way
> to die.
>
> —ALICE HEALY

A NONDESCRIPT WAREHOUSE IN NORTHEAST PORTLAND, OREGON
NOW

I sank deeper into my crouch, waiting for the whistle to free me from the starting line. Princess Leya-you-out crouched next to me, the white star on her red helmet cover marking her as the current jammer for the Concussion Stand. We were halfway through the first bout of the season, and this was the first jam Leya and I were skating against each other. Every other round, it had been my team captain, Elmira Street, versus Leya, while I skated against the newer, slower, Holly Go Lightspeed.

The blockers were a solid mass ahead of us, obscuring the open track. That didn't matter. I'd seen it before.

Then the whistle blew, releasing the swarm. Leya and I lunged onto our tiptoes, dancing and shoving through the pack. Meggie Itwasthewind—one of my best friends on our mutual team, the Slasher Chicks—managed to knock two of the opposing blockers out of the way, and I was loose, picking up speed as I began my nonscoring pass around the track. As long as I could make a full circuit before Leya broke out, I was home free.

I love Roller Derby.

I skated that jam and the next two like my pleated camouflage miniskirt was on fire, shooting around curves as if they had personally offended me. We were up by thirty points by the time Elmira tagged me out, and I was feeling the pleasant burn of a bout well-skated in my thighs and lower back. Roller Derby is an awesome workout, especially if you like your cardio with a decent dose of blunt-force trauma. I collapsed into my chair, taking a swig from my water bottle, and watched the skaters circle the track.

Sometimes it can be hard to tell who's skating for which team. Not so when it was the Slasher Chicks vs. the Concussion Stand. The Concussion Stand uniforms were styled after the classic theater cigarette girl, pairing red and white striped shirts with red booty shorts, fishnets, and lots of eyeliner. My team wore white tank tops spattered with fake blood, knee socks, and the aforementioned camo miniskirts. We looked like we'd been attacked by a serial killer in the woods behind some summer camp, which was exactly what we'd been going for.

The captain of the Concussion Stand, the lovely Pushy Galore, performed a flawless block on Elmira Street. While my captain struggled to break free, Princess Leya launched herself into a power jam, circling the track multiple times before Elmira could get back into the action. I shook my head and leaned forward to check my laces. Roller Derby is not a forgiving sport. A few bad jams can change everything.

"Final Girl! You're in!"

I raised my hand just in time to catch the piece of fabric that marked me as the official jammer. Elmira Street skated past to a chair, looking disgruntled. "I got this," I said, pulling the star-blazoned cloth over my helmet as I rolled toward the track. The opposing jammer, Holly, offered me a polite nod. I nodded back and hunkered down, waiting for the whistle to blow.

The whistle blew. We launched ourselves forward.

The first challenge any jammer faces is the pack: four blockers from each team, all dedicated to keeping the opposing team's jammer from breaking free. Once we shove, scramble, and squirm through that human barrier, the jammer faces a new, more serious challenge—the other jammer. In order to control the jam, you have to be the first one to lap the track, becoming lead jammer and top bitch until the whistle blows again. (No, I don't know why the word *jam* has so many meanings in Roller Derby. It's like *fuck*. It's a noun, it's a verb, it's a sentence! It's the honey badger of conversation! Just assume that whatever part of speech the word is playing right now, it's accurate.)

I shouldered my way through the blockers and took off, building speed with practiced precision. I didn't know whether Holly had managed to break out of the pack yet: I just knew she wasn't in front of me, and for the moment, that was good enough.

The track curved and the blockers came back into view, Holly still stuck in their midst like a bug in amber. Swell. On the one hand, this meant I was about to become lead jammer. On the other hand, it meant another pass through the bodies of my peers, which was always annoying.

Meggie saw me coming and shifted over, creating a narrow channel down the inside of the track. I could take it, if I was brave enough, and confident enough in my ability not to get knocked out of bounds.

Roller Derby is not a sport for cowards. I sucked in my breath, making myself as thin as possible—not the easiest thing in the world, since the Boob Fairy started visiting when I was twelve, and only stopped last year—and turned sideways, hitting the gap at full speed. The blockers from the Concussion Stand barely had time to register my presence before I was past them, with clear track ahead of me and points beginning to pile up for my team. I allowed myself a split-second grin, put my head down, and kept skating.

Holly eventually broke out of the pack, but I'd circled the track four times by then, aided by luck, timing, and a fantastic group of blockers who saw victory in their grasp if they could keep me moving. The whistle blew on a final score of Slasher Chicks 174, Concussion Stand 171. The rest of my team sprang to their feet, swarming the track as we became a swirling vortex of laughing, hugging, bleeding girls.

"Let's drink some beer!" we shouted.

Our fans in the stands roared, shouting back, *"Let's smoke some pot!"*

We turned to face the stands, some of us with our arms around each other's shoulders, some of us standing alone. I had Meggie with her arms wrapped around my waist and Elmira with her shoulder pressed against mine, and it was moments like this that I lived for: moments where I got to feel like I was really a part of this world, and not just an eternal tourist, always passing through.

As a team, we shouted the last part of the Slasher Chicks credo to the room: *"Let's have premarital sex! I love premarital sex!"*

The match was over. We took our victory lap, and applauded the Concussion Stand as they took their final lap around the track. Then the whistle blew for intermission, and we scattered.

My name is Antimony Price, and I'm a social worker for monsters.

Full introductions take longer than I like, so here's the Price family history, Wikipedia version: Once upon a time, we were bad people who killed monsters because we thought God wanted us to. Apparently, we also thought God was an asshole. A whole lot of other people helped us kill monsters, because we belonged to the Covenant of St. George, which is basically a big bucket of assholes. One day, we realized we were in danger of becoming assholes on a permanent basis, and that some monsters were actually pretty cool. So we quit and started helping the monsters—who prefer to be called "cryptids"—instead of going all *I Am Legend* on them in dark alleyways.

The Covenant didn't like us quitting, we didn't like the Covenant telling us what to do, and things got bloody for a while, culminating in the Covenant of St. George "wiping out" my family line. They didn't, obviously, but as long as they think they did, everybody gets to be happy.

We help North America's cryptid population avoid assholes who want to kill them, the Covenant of St. George gets to be smug about slaughtering us in our beds, and nobody gets hurt. Most people don't know we exist. Most people don't know that cryptids exist, either.

We do have to fly under the radar, to avoid someone from the Covenant figuring out that we're still alive and kicking. That means code names and aliases and finding creative new ways of learning essential skills like kicking ass, maintaining cover, and eating track at thirty miles per hour without losing any teeth. You can probably see where Roller Derby was the perfect solution. Derby girls go by false names anyway, so I didn't feel as bad about telling them my name was Annie Thompson, not Antimony Price. Skating with a derby team will sure as shit teach you teamwork, and skating with broken toes or bruised-up shins will teach you pain tolerance.

It's a good life, if you can handle it, and if you don't mind women on roller skates slamming into you at high speeds while you circle a flat track in pursuit of transitory glory. I enjoy it. But then again, I'm a little weird.

The match was being held in the warehouse where we normally staged our practices and had been broken into two bouts: the Slasher Chicks vs. the Concussion Stand, which was over, thanks to my spectacular jamming skills (and okay, maybe the rest of the team helped too), followed by the Rose Petals vs. the Stunt Troubles. Intermission came between the bouts, to allow the second group of skaters time to warm up, and to give the spectators time to drink more beer.

Half the skaters from the Slasher Chicks and Concussion Stand were still on the track, circling as one big, happy family. I looked at them longingly. It would have been nice to join the free skate, but my cousin Elsie was waiting for me in the stands, and if there's one thing Elsie hates, it's waiting. I grabbed my water bottle and made my way to the old storage closet that we were using as a temporary dressing room.

Carlotta—better known as "Pushy Galore" when she was skating—was there when we arrived. She was Elsie's on-again, off-again girlfriend.

At the moment, I was pretty sure they were on, which gave us reason to be friendly. "Good skating out there today, Thompson," she said.

"Thanks," I said, moving to retrieve my duffel bag from the pile in the corner. I unzipped it, pulling out a clean black tank top with the league logo on the front. "You guys were pretty awesome, too."

Carlotta snorted. "We need to work on our blocking. Next time, we won't go so easy on you."

"Looking forward to it." I had time to pull my shirt over my head before a hand touched my elbow. Years of combat training told me to grab the hand and break the associated wrist before it introduced a knife to my ribs. I may be the only person on the planet whose reflexes have been *calmed* by Roller Derby. I finished removing my shirt and turned to meet the wide blue eyes of my teammate, Meggie. No, I corrected myself; she was out of uniform. Her name was Fern. "What's up?"

"Are you going to sit with Elsie?" she asked, in her piping baby-doll voice. It matched the rest of her. Fern was a spun-sugar confection of a girl, with pale blonde hair and the kind of quirkily pretty features that would have gotten her scouted for *America's Next Top Model* if she hadn't preferred roller skates to high heels. She also wasn't human. Fern was a sylph, a type of cryptid therianthrope whose shapeshifting was limited to increasing and decreasing her personal density. Breaking the laws of physics was all in a day's work for her.

"For a little bit," I said. "Do you want to come?"

"Are you sure she won't mind?"

"She'll have Carlotta to distract her, so even if she minds, she won't notice," I said, pulling on a pair of jeans over my bloodstained knee socks. "Isn't that right, Carlotta?"

"Fuck you," said Carlotta genially.

"There's that classic Concussion Stand charm." I slung my skates and duffel bag over my shoulder, leaving my hair in its messy braids. "Come on, Fern. Let's go get good seats for the heavy petting."

Fern giggled and followed me to the door, pausing only to wave to Elmira Street—now just Elmira, since she was out of uniform and on her phone, furiously texting her legion of boyfriends. They never came for the matches, but if tonight was like every other night, one of them would be showing up with Indian takeout by the end of halftime. Elmira did not look up to acknowledge our departure.

We emerged from the storage closet and into the cavernous warehouse, where the rattle of skates against polished wood seemed much louder now that I wasn't wearing my helmet. Bleachers formed a shallow shell around the track, adding an air of class to the event; many Roller Derby bouts are skated without anything resembling seats for the audience. It's easier to drink when you don't have to do it standing up, though, and one of the concessions was run by a local brewpub, which had helped to hook us up with a set of barely used bleachers from a defunct local dodgeball league.

(Yes, that's weird, and no, none of us pushed the issue. Portland is a city that thrives on being a little bit to the left of normal. I had no trouble with the idea that we once possessed a competitive dodgeball team. I had a slightly larger problem with the idea that it had somehow *failed*.)

Elsie had, as usual, claimed a prime spot in the front row of the bleachers, spreading herself and her possessions out until she had space reserved for four. She waved when she saw us, and smirked until we were close enough for her to say, "I figured you'd bring Fern with you. Hi, Fern."

"Hi, Elsie," said Fern shyly. She liked my half-succubus, nonskating cousin, probably because when the three of us hung out together—or even with Carlotta—there was no such thing as "abnormal." We were all different in our own ways. Carlotta and I were human, but I was a skinny, busty Caucasian girl who still lived at home with her parents, while Carlotta was a solid, curvy Latina who had her own adult life, complete with mortgage and finance-related day job. Elsie was half-human, on her mother's side, and had been happily unemployed since finishing her five-year journey through community college.

At the moment, Elsie was rocking a Concussion Stand logo shirt, denim cutoffs just this side of street legal, and wedge-heeled shoes that would have led to serious injury five minutes after I strapped them onto my feet if I'd tried to wear them. The bottom inch of her sleek blonde hair was dyed electric purple, matching the capped sleeves on her black T-shirt. She looked perfect, as always.

I plopped down next to her. "Gimme," I said.

To Elsie's credit, she didn't toy with me or try to pretend she didn't know what I was talking about. She just pulled a foil-wrapped packet out of her purse, handing it over. I unwrapped it and beamed.

"Snickerdoodles. You are my favorite cousin."

"Only because I brought you cookies," said Elsie mildly.

"I'm cheap," I said, and handed Fern a cookie.

Elsie looked like she was going to say something, but stopped, sitting up a little straighter. I followed her gaze to find Carlotta emerging from the storage closet. I grinned.

"You have got it bad for that skater girl," I said.

"I wouldn't say I've got it bad . . ." protested Elsie. "I just enjoy her company."

"Uh-huh. And pigs can fly."

"If your slingshot is big enough, sure," said Fern.

We turned to look at her, but were saved from the need to reply by the sound of screams coming from behind the bleachers. Elsie and I exchanged a glance, and she stayed where she was while I jumped to my feet and ran toward the sound of danger like a character in a bad science fiction story.

What can I say? My parents didn't do a very good job of instilling me with a sense of self-preservation.

Most populations are split when it comes to the sound of screams: half the people will run toward them, hoping they can help, while the other half runs away from them, remembering what happens to first responders in horror movies. The ratios get a little skewed when you're talking about a warehouse full of derby girls and drunk Roller Derby fans. I was fast, but I wasn't close enough to be the first person on the scene. I wasn't even the fifteenth. A crowd had gathered behind the bleachers by the time I finally tracked the screaming to its source.

What was interesting was that the screamer kept changing. Someone would scream and run out of the crowd, only to be replaced by someone else doing the exact same thing. I elbowed my way into the mob, not being all that careful about the people around me, until I broke through the interior edge and stumbled into the open space at the center.

In retrospect, I should have realized it would take something like a severed, fishnet-clad human leg—still wearing a roller skate—to cause that much of a ruckus at the Roller Derby. At the time, I just froze, taking in the leg and everything that it implied.

Something in the warehouse had killed a derby girl. A member of the Concussion Stand, if the laces on her roller skate were anything to go by. And since the Concussion Stand had been on the track up until a few minutes ago, whatever it was, it was probably still in the warehouse.

"Well, shit," I muttered, and turned to push my way back through the crowd.

If anyone noticed that I didn't seem particularly upset, they didn't say anything. Most of them were too busy jockeying for a closer look they would regret the next time they tried to go to sleep. The modern world doesn't exactly go around preparing people for the sight of severed human limbs. Call it a failing in the basic survival curriculum of the universe. More people were running in from all directions, and I could hear little screams and exclamations of surprise coming from the other side of the bleachers as the news began to spread.

Fern was standing a few feet away from the mob. I met her eyes as I said, "We've got a girl down. I need you to get the NSOs and tell them there's been an accident. I'm going to go notify Carlotta."

"Why Carlotta?" asked Fern.

"Because the girl who's down was a member of the Concussion Stand."

Fern paled as she caught the past tense in my statement. "Okay, Annie," she said, and ran back the way we'd come. Sylphs can move faster than almost anything else on two legs, as long as they're not running against the wind. She'd find the NSOs—nonskating officials—before I would have figured out where to start looking. Better yet, she looked inherently innocent in a way I stopped being able to manage before I hit puberty. The NSOs would have asked me a lot more questions than they would ask her.

I didn't run back to Elsie and Carlotta, but I walked fast, trying to keep my expression blank and scan the crowd for signs of danger at the same time. It wasn't an easy combination, and I announced my return by tripping over my own duffel bag and crashing into the bleachers, nearly landing on Carlotta.

"Not my type, Thompson," said Carlotta, shoving me off. Then she paused, seeing how pale I was. "Annie? Did you find out what all the commotion is about?"

"Carlotta, there's . . . there's been an accident." I swallowed. Somehow, this was harder than I'd expected. I've been a cryptozoologist for my entire life, but most of the time, my job doesn't include looking humans in the eye and telling them their friends are dead. "One of the members of the Concussion Stand . . ."

Carlotta lurched to her feet, demanding, "Who?"

"I don't know, I—"

"Dammit, Thompson!" She grabbed me in a way that would have meant a personal foul on the track, her fingers digging into my shoulders. "I know you're not a people person, but you can't even tell me who's hurt?"

"I can't tell you because there wasn't a head!" I spoke more loudly than I'd intended to. Carlotta went white, letting go of my shoulders. Heads turned in our direction. I swallowed and said, "There's no body. Just a leg. But it's wearing a skate and fishnets, and the skate has black and purple laces."

"Oh, God." Carlotta pushed past me, running for the edge of the bleachers.

I turned to find Elsie staring at me, eyes wide and disapproving within their rings of glittery eye shadow and too-black kohl.

"That's your idea of sensitivity?" she said. " 'Oh, it's just a leg'?"

"I didn't mean—"

"You're sick." She stomped after her girlfriend. I stayed where I was, resisting the urge to strap my skates back on and head for the hills while I still could. I wouldn't do it. I *couldn't* do it. Whatever had killed that skater did it quickly, cleanly, and without being seen. Nothing human could have done it that well. And if our killer wasn't human, that made it my problem.

The panic was still isolated in patches throughout the warehouse, probably because a little screaming was par for the course at a big Roller Derby match, and most people still didn't know what was going on. I scanned the crowd until I found the women I wanted—and thank the god or gods of your choosing, they were standing together. I bolted toward them, ignoring the muffled shouts of protest in my wake. What's pissing a few folks off if it means saving a lot of lives?

"Thompson?" said Elmira, blinking.

"Hey, Final Girl," said her companion. Cylia—better known on the track as Triskaidekaphilia—was the captain of the Rose Petals, one of the teams that was about to skate. She was a lithe blonde with blue streaks in her hair and cat hair liberally dusted across her pink and black uniform.

"Hi, Elmira, hi, Cylia," I said. "I need to talk to both of you before somebody pulls the fire alarm. Can we go somewhere?"

Cylia frowned. "What's going on?"

The crowd around us was noisy and enthusiastic and paying no attention to us. I took a breath and said, "One of the members of the Concussion Stand is dead. I don't know who, except that it isn't Carlotta, because she was with Elsie when I found the remains. The blood was too fresh for this to be some sort of *Criminal Minds* body-dump shit, and the cuts I saw looked more like claw marks than knife wounds. Fern's gone to alert the NSOs, at which point I'm assuming the warehouse will be evacuated—"

As if on cue, the fire alarm blared through the warehouse, drawing exclamations of surprise and dismay from the people around us.

"There we go," I said. "Look, if this goes normally, the police are going to show up, they'll search the place, declare it a crime scene, and close it for a few days while they try to find the rest of the missing girl. And maybe they will, I don't know. Human killers are sort of outside my bailiwick."

"Are you saying you think this was an *inhuman* killer?" demanded Elmira.

I gave Cylia a sidelong look, fighting the urge to roll my eyes. Elmira knew about the cryptids in our league—she called them "girls with diffabilities," which was a cute little portmanteau way of saying "monsters I like"—but that didn't mean she understood them. "Pretty sure, yeah," I said. "I'm going to need you to keep the rest of the Slasher Chicks away from here, except for me and Fern. Cylia, can I get your phone number?"

Elmira put a hand over her face. All around us, people were streaming toward the doors, still clutching their beers and bags. Pulling a fire alarm was a great way to empty the building, but I wasn't worried about losing our killer. Anything with claws big enough to have made the marks on the dead girl's leg would have ears to match, and was probably cowering in a closet or crawlspace by now, waiting for the noise to stop.

"Thompson, are you planning to sneak back in here and bait a monster that's already killed one person, rather than doing the sane, sensible thing and leaving this to the authorities?"

"Sorry, but yeah," I said, baring my teeth in an admittedly feral grin. "It's just that in a situation like this one, I sort of *am* the authorities. But don't worry. I promise we'll try not to damage the track."

Elmira groaned.

More than half the league quietly melted into the shadows after the fire alarm rang. No one had smelled smoke inside, and the grapevine is strong within the derby community; within five minutes of the evacuation, everyone who hadn't actually seen the leg behind the bleachers knew about it. Even those who wanted to stay and show their support were just as likely to excuse themselves. Princess Leya put it best when she slung her skates over her shoulder, shook her head, and said:

"The Portland PD tries hard, but sometimes, you just gotta get the fuck out of Dodge before somebody asks to see your papers."

"I get that," I said. I was lurking at the edge of the crowd, where I could do a quick fade into the trees if it looked like someone wanted to question me. Speak softly and keep your face out of the news reports, that's the Price family way. "Can I call you when we're going back in? I could use you."

Leya, who was a chupacabra in addition to being a damn fine jammer, nodded. "You've got my number. I want to find whatever did this to my girl and make it sorry it ever fucked with us."

"I'll call soon," I said.

"Okay," said Leya, and walked toward her car. I turned back to the crowd.

The dead girl turned out to be Tanya Durham, better known as Holly Go Lightspeed, the newest Concussion Stand jammer. They'd identified her by the tattoo on her ankle. Knowing her name put her death into upsetting focus. Carlotta had been borderline hysterical when the identification was made, and was still more upset than I'd ever seen her. She was sitting in the smoking area, sobbing, with her team clustered around her like they could make it better through sheer proximity. I cringed when one of those girls broke from the pack, turning and stalking toward me.

Elsie at least waited until she was close enough that she didn't need to shout before demanding, "Well?"

"Keep your voice down," I said, glancing at the police. They were still occupied with interviewing our NSOs. I'd managed to keep myself from being identified as "the girl who found the leg"—which I technically wasn't, I was just the first girl who'd been thinking clearly enough to alert the authorities—and I wanted it keep it that way.

"Why, because the police might somehow psychically realize you could be fixing this shit, and instead you're hanging out under these stupid, scabby trees, waiting for the noise to stop bothering your precious ears?" Elsie scowled. I had never seen her this angry, and not for the first time, I was glad her pheromones were weaker than her brother's. The last thing I needed right now was to be manipulated into charging into danger. "Don't you care that a girl is *dead*?"

That stung. "I care as much as you do, Elsie, but what do you want me to do? Attracting attention won't bring her back, and we made so much noise getting out of there that whatever killed her is either gone or hiding. I need to give it a chance to calm down and come back."

"And then what?"

"And then I go in with Fern, and Cylia, and Leya, and we find whatever the fuck is in there, and we deal with it."

Elsie nodded. "Carlotta and I will be expecting your call."

"What?" I stared at her. "You can't be serious. Elsie, Carlotta's human, she can't—"

"You're human too, and you don't see me telling you that you can't hunt whatever killed Tanya," Elsie countered. "Carlotta's not stupid. She's not going to rat anybody out."

"I can't blow anyone's cover, Elsie. It wouldn't be right."

"Here's the thing. I got a sort of modified version of the family code, since I'm, you know, an abomination of nature and everything? And the version I got says I can tell my girlfriend when she's surrounded by people who can help her when she's hurting. This is the worst thing she's ever experienced. I have to help. *You* have to help." Elsie shook her head. "You can argue all you want, but if I find out you came back here without us, we're done. I'm not going to stand by you if you won't stand by me, and I thought derby was about teamwork and building a community. You're not playing with the team right now, Annie. You're playing like a Price. I expected better from you."

She turned and stalked back toward the smoking area. She didn't look back at me. She didn't look back at me once.

I got a ride home from Cylia; Elsie was staying at Carlotta's, and neither of them wanted to talk to me. Since I wasn't one of Holly's teammates, and I hadn't been seen speaking to her right before she disappeared, my name hadn't come up for questioning. Thank God for that. I hadn't been looking forward to running from the police.

Cylia pulled off by the side of the road in the woods surrounding my family's home. "Are you sure I can't take you all the way?" she asked. "I'm not comfortable dropping you off in the middle of nowhere."

"I'm good," I said, grabbing my duffel bag as I undid my seat belt and slid out of the car. "My parents aren't big on unannounced company. I'd rather not cap the worst night ever by having a huge fight the minute I walk in the door, you know?"

"I get that," said Cylia. She cocked her head, eyeing me. "Still, you have to admit this is weird. Almost as weird as you being a human who hangs out with a succubus and doesn't bat an eye at me being a jink. What's your deal, Annie Thompson?"

"My name says it all," I said. "I'm the Final Girl." I shut the car door before she could ask me any more questions. To my relief, she didn't roll down the window. She just waved and pulled away from the shoulder. I stayed where I was and watched her taillights dwindle down the dark, wooded road.

Cylia was going to press until her questions were answered: I knew that, just like I knew that since she was a cryptid, I could tell her who I was without fear of Covenant reprisal. Still, I couldn't help but feel like this was the beginning of the end of my Roller Derby career. I'd been able to skate for as long as I had because when I was on the track I was Annie Thompson, and not Antimony Price.

As I stepped into the woods to begin the hike to my house, I felt like I finally understood my big sister's attachment to her dance alias. Sure, it was frivolous, and had gone on long past the point where it could be considered reasonable, but it was nice to be part of a community that didn't expect anything from me. As long as Annie Thompson showed up for practice, everyone was happy with her, and no one was waiting for her to save the world. Antimony Price had *rules*. Antimony Price had *expectations*. Annie Thompson . . . all she had to do was skate.

I took a break after I'd gone about a quarter mile, listening for indications that I was being followed. Silence greeted me, broken only by the distant hoot of one of the local owls. I started walking again, pulling my phone out of my pocket.

Elsie isn't my only cousin. She has a brother, Arthur, better known as "Artie." Like Elsie, he's a crossbreed, half human, half incubus. Unlike Elsie, he doesn't leave the house very often. It was almost midnight. He still picked up on the second ring. "Annie? What gives?"

"You didn't know it was me," I scolded. "I could have been a Covenant operative who'd taken this phone off Antimony's broken body."

"True enough," said Artie. "Since you're not, what gives?"

"One of the girls on the Concussion Stand was killed tonight."

Silence.

"She skated in the match against the Slasher Chicks. Something killed her after she left the track."

"Uh, Annie?" Artie's tone was hesitant, like he already knew he wouldn't like my answer. "Why did you say some*thing*, and not some*one*?"

"Because whatever killed her did it in a warehouse full of spectators without being seen, and got away with most of her body in a matter of seconds. If it hadn't dropped a leg, we probably wouldn't know she was gone."

"Okay, that's disgusting. So what are we looking for?"

"I don't know. What could do something like this? You're the one with the mad research skills, and I'm the one walking alone through the dark, creepy woods."

"Not to sound pessimistic, but 'fast, stealthy, and capable of either eating or toting away most of a person' doesn't narrow down the list at all. If you said 'it was invisible,' that would be something. Is there any chance it was invisible?"

"It could have been," I said. "It could have just been really fast. We found the leg behind the bleachers, which were filled with people at the time."

"Then I've got nothing, because I've got too much to have anything. Find me more information and I can tell you what it might be." Artie sounded frustrated. I couldn't blame him, since I *felt* pretty frustrated. "When are you planning to go back to the warehouse?"

"How do you know I'm planning to go back?"

"I've met you."

I laughed a little. "The police are currently searching the place. I'll watch the news to see if any of the officers mysteriously disappear, and if not, I figure they'll clear out soon. I've already notified most of the cryptid girls in the league that I'm going to need them to help."

"That's good."

"I was wondering—"

"No, Annie." He sounded sorry, but firm; there was no wiggle room in his refusal. "I know you need help, and I know you think I should get out more, but I'm just not in a good place for leaving home."

"Artie—"

"I will do everything I can to help from where I am. I'll do research, I'll tell you what kinds of weapon to use and what kinds of weapon will be laughed at, and I'll be a shoulder for you to cry on, but I'm not going to leave the house. I'm sorry."

I sighed. "I know, Artie. I know." Artie had never been a social butterfly, but we used to be able to get him out of his room for things like conventions and trips to the comic book store. It helped that he'd been stupid in love with our adopted cousin, Sarah, since he was old enough to know girls were something he was allowed to be interested in. Sarah felt the same way about him, not that I could persuade either of them to believe it. She'd gone to New York with my sister Verity, supposedly to audit college math courses, but really to keep my brainless big sis out of trouble.

She failed, and she got seriously hurt. She'd been staying with my grandmother since then, putting herself back together one piece at a time. Artie hadn't spoken to her since the accident. He hadn't left the house since then either. It was like he thought going outside would be giving up on her somehow, and the universe would know. It was a silly, superstitious way of thinking . . . but I couldn't blame him. If staying inside made him feel like he'd get his Sarah back someday, I wouldn't drag him out.

"It's okay," he said. "I'll pull out the field guides and scan the local Bigfoot hunter forums to see if anyone's spotted anything strange in your neck of the woods."

"Thanks. Call any time if you find something—and I mean that. Sleep isn't going to be a priority tonight."

"Are you going to ask your folks to join you?"

That made me pause. Mom and Dad were cryptozoologists and hunters in their own right. Inviting them on the hunt would be the smart thing to do. It would also erase any chance I had of maintaining my cover. Sure, "Annie Thompson" got involved in more weird shit than she had any right to, but she did it mostly by accident, and with all the best of intentions. Antimony Price would bring a lot of baggage to the table, and she wouldn't really make anything better. Being a Price girl never did.

"Only if I have to," I said. "I'd rather take care of this on my own."

"I get that," said Artie. "Just please, if you're going to do that, can you take care of it without dying? I'd miss you if you were gone."

"Who would you talk to about the X-Men?"

"Exactly," said Artie.

I smiled. "So speaking of the X-Men . . ."

We talked about comics for the rest of my trip home. By the time I reached the front gates, I felt almost human again. That was a good thing, because I had a lot of research to do, and not much time to do it in.

The sound of my phone ringing six inches from my head woke me at the crack of—I peeled my face off the keyboard and peered at the computer clock. The crack of eleven o'clock in the morning. It was late enough that I couldn't bring myself to yell at whoever was on the other end of the phone as I flipped it open and managed an exhausted, "Why shouldn't I murder you?"

"Because it's either a manticore or a chimera."

Artie's words were like a bucket of cold water on my addled senses. "Are you sure?" I asked, sitting up straight.

"I got a friend in the Portland morgue to send me pictures of the dead girl's leg, and the claw pattern could be either, but it's not going to be anything smaller. Factor in the climate, the time of year, and some weird 'I think I saw a lion' posts on the Bigfoot boards, and those are your options."

I dug my knuckles into the side of my leg, hoping it would help me wake up. It didn't. "Shit."

"My thoughts exactly."

Manticore are intelligent enough that they can make moral judgments, and they can be trained not to eat humans, although they don't like having their diets restricted. Chimera aren't so forgiving. They'll eat whatever they can kill, and no one's ever successfully domesticated one. There was a third option . . . "Any chance it's a feral Sphinx?"

"Body count's too low."

". . . right. How do I kill a chimera?"

"Bullets. Lots and lots and lots of bullets."

"That's simple, at least." I sagged in my seat. "Please tell me you have some good news."

"I also checked with one of the guys I know on your local Police Beat, and the police aren't currently monitoring the warehouse. You're good to go back whenever you need to."

"Then we're going back tonight."

Artie sighed. "I sort of figured you would be. Don't die. Please?"

"I'll try," I said, and hung up, turning my attention back to my laptop. The browser was open to a page on lindworms. I'd been reading about their dietary habits—not good—and how much destruction they could do—even worse—when I'd finally passed out. "Right," I said, and stood. I needed breakfast before I went back to reading about things that were guaranteed to ruin my appetite.

Time to leave for the warehouse came sooner than I had wanted it to. Time is funny like that. Cylia and Leya had both been home when I called. Fern hadn't answered her phone. I left a message, counting on her desire not to see me turned into human confetti to make her show up. I was about to make the most awkward call on my list when my phone rang. I blinked at the display and raised the phone to my ear.

"Elsie?"

"Carlotta and I are about twenty minutes out," she said, without preamble. "If you don't want me coming to your front door—and I *know* you don't want me coming to your front door—you need to be on the frontage road when we get there. Otherwise, I'm driving straight to the house."

"Don't do that," I said automatically. I paused. "Wait, you're coming to get me?"

"Did you think I was going to make you skate here? You'd arrive after we'd all been shredded. Be on the road or I'll see you in the driveway." She hung up.

". . . right." I shoved my phone into my pocket, shouting, "Mom! I'm going to go fight a monster I haven't identified yet!"

"Don't get decapitated, dear," she called back.

I shook my head. "Parental oversight," I muttered, stepping outside. Sometimes it's hard to forget that I'm the youngest child in the family—I came after the heir *and* the spare, and my parents are happy if I make it through the day without setting anything on fire or dropping anyone who doesn't deserve it down a pit trap. Great for doing whatever I want without worrying about rules getting in my way, lousy if what I want is for my mother to realize that I'm running off to get myself killed and at least offer me an extra knife or something.

The frontage road where Elsie was going to pick me up was located about a quarter mile from the house, and the easiest way to get there was by taking another stroll through the woods. At least the sun was up this time. I walked quickly, trying to relax and focus. Whatever was waiting in the warehouse wouldn't get easier to subdue—or to kill—if I tied myself in knots over it before I knew what I was up against.

Elsie was parked on the shoulder of the road when I emerged from the trees. I stopped where I was, blinking, before I broke into a jog, quickly covering the space between us. She scowled through her open window. "You're late," she accused, once I was close enough to hear her.

"You're early," I countered. "Hi, Carlotta."

Carlotta, who was sitting in the passenger seat, smiled wanly. She didn't look like she'd slept. "Hello, Annie. I hope you had a better night than I did."

"Probably, yeah," I said, opening the back door and tossing my duffel bag onto the seat. It landed with a clanking noise that made Carlotta's eyes widen. I slid in after it. "I'm really sorry about Holly."

"Just shut the door so we can go, okay?" Elsie turned the engine back on. "We can all get in touch with our feelings after you kill the fucking thing."

I shut the door. Elsie pulled away from the shoulder, slamming her foot down on the gas hard enough to send us hurtling along the road. I scrambled to get my seat belt on. Elsie was a fairly safe driver under most circumstances, but it only takes one argument with physics to ruin everyone's day.

"Is it true?" Carlotta sounded uncharacteristically meek. I turned toward her, finally taking in all the small, frazzled details of her appearance as I realized how shaken she really was. She looked like a woman whose world had shifted 180 degrees while she wasn't paying attention, leaving her unsure which way was up.

"Is what true?"

"That you . . . do you kill monsters? Is that what you are? A monster hunter?"

I directed a glare at the back of Elsie's head. "That's an oversimplification."

"But you'll kill *this* monster. It killed Tanya—Holly—and now you're going to kill it, right?"

"I . . ." I took a deep breath. "We'll see, okay? I have to do everything I can to figure out what happened before I know what to do in response."

"It killed my friend," said Carlotta without inflection.

I winced. "Look, I'm sorry, but I don't know what it is yet. Maybe it had a reason for what it did. Maybe it didn't understand."

"Not helping," said Elsie grimly.

I closed my eyes. "I'll do the best I can," I said.

I didn't say anything else during the drive. Neither did Elsie or Carlotta. I think we all agreed that it was safer that way.

Leya, Cylia, and Fern stood in front of the warehouse, trying to look like they weren't loitering at a crime scene. The warehouse door was standing slightly ajar. They were all wearing their practice clothes, and I was relieved to see that everybody had their skates.

"Hey, guys," I said, walking up. "You ready?"

"You know what's in there?" asked Cylia.

"We've got two options, neither of them good. It's either a manticore or a chimera. Either way, it's big, it's ugly, and it's hungry."

"Eh," said Leya. She shrugged, the motion of her shoulders suggesting joints that didn't follow the rules of human anatomy. "I've seen ugly before. We can kick its ass."

"Good," said Carlotta, stepping up behind me. "I assume you won't mind a little help."

Leya blanched at the sight of her human team captain. "I—"

I held up a hand. "Carlotta won't tell anyone anything," I said. "She just wants payback."

"We understand," said Cylia. "If I'd lost one of my girls, I'd burn the world down before I let someone tell me I didn't get to avenge her."

"Since we agree that no one is leaving, can we get down to the important business of risking our necks?" I asked. "Elsie, you're standing guard. If it looks like the police are coming to check things out, dissuade them by whatever means necessary."

"Why am I standing guard?" my cousin asked, sounding affronted.

"Because you don't skate, and we need to be fast. Whatever killed

Holly was fast." She was also the one with preternatural powers of per-
suasion, but I didn't want to say that in front of her girlfriend. I pulled
my skates out of my bag and turned to the other girls. "Everyone but
Leya, full protective gear; this is like any other game, except for the part
where something in that building is going to try to kill you."

"So it's *exactly* like every other game," said Leya, earning nervous
laughter from Cylia and Fern.

"Fern, once you're geared up, I want you to go inside and do a lap
around the place, top speed," I said. "If you see *anything*, get out of
there, but try to get a good look as you retreat. We need to know what
we're up against."

"Okay," said Fern, and produced her skates.

"Hang on," said Carlotta. "Are you sure it's safe to send her in
alone?"

"Trust me," I said. "Nothing can catch Fern when she pulls out the
stops." As if to prove me right, Fern got her skates on and took off toward
the warehouse, moving so fast that she became a pale blonde blur before
she disappeared through the open door. I turned back to Carlotta. She
was gaping, openmouthed. "See?"

"I think she just violated a law of physics," said Carlotta. "Maybe two."

"Three, actually, but who's counting?" I sat down on the pavement,
reaching for my own skates and pulling them on. "She'll be back in a
minute. Everyone, gear up, and remember, this is not a drill, but that
doesn't make it a Three Stooges routine. If you're not sure you can take
a shot, don't take it. If you think you're in danger, get out. I don't know
what's in there, I don't know if we can kill it, but I know we're going to
give it a really good try. Everybody follow?"

"Today, you're the team captain," said Carlotta. "I follow."

"Good. How far are you willing to go?" I looked toward Leya, who
pressed her lips into a thin line before pulling her shirt off over her head.
I nodded, satisfied, and resumed tying my skates.

"Why is my jammer topless?" demanded Carlotta.

"I'll be bottomless in a second," said Leya.

"You wanted to be part of this," I said, and climbed back to my feet.
"Helmets on, those of you who need helmets. It's time to party."

• • •

Fern's circuit of the warehouse had turned up no monsters. She *had* spotted several new gouges in the concrete floor, which confirmed Artie's candidates for the monster in the warehouse: only the manticore and chimera had claws that could cut stone.

It was dark inside the warehouse, lit only by the thin sunlight filtering in through the skylights. "Fern, lights," I murmured. "Leya, you're up."

"On it," said Fern, and darted into the shadows, once again moving almost too fast for the eye to follow.

Leya didn't say anything. She just nodded and ran for the track. She shed the remainder of her clothes as she moved, and was naked by the time she cleared the bleachers. *"Hoy! Monster!"* she shouted, and proceeded to turn inside out. Not literally, but that's what it looked like, as her skin was suddenly pulled inside her body and replaced by a naked, glistening hide patched with black and orange scales and pierced irregularly by vicious-looking spines.

Carlotta made a choking sound.

"Chupacabra," I said.

The lights came on. Something in the rafters screamed. I smiled grimly. I couldn't help myself. It's hard not to smile when a plan starts coming together.

My smile died an instant later, when the thing from the rafters hit the track in front of the transformed Leya. "Oh, *fuck*," I said, and drew the gun from my duffel bag.

The creature advancing on Leya was clearly a chimera. It had all the hallmarks: a lion's head, a goat's body, a serpent's tail, and vast, leathery wings just barely in proportion with the rest of it. It was the size of a full-grown bull, and since Leya was about the size of a large coyote, this wasn't going to be a fair fight. Roller-skating across concrete didn't put me in the best position to aim, but I wasn't going for a kill shot, just a distraction. Once I was close enough to be sure I wouldn't hit Leya, I fired.

The chimera roared, leonine head swinging around to face me. I fired again for good measure before turning and skating in the opposite direction, heading as fast as I could back toward the other girls. Cylia was already down in a jam position. Carlotta was still standing frozen, staring at the chimera.

"Move!" I howled. "You're here to be a distraction, so for the sweet love of fuck, *move!*"

All of them scattered, even Carlotta. Fern flashed by, a blur on a mission. I glanced back and saw her slam into the chimera, which was actually knocked sideways by the impact. Her wheels dug gouges into the track before she rebounded and skated away. She must have modified her density at the last second, trading insubstantiality and speed for as much weight as she could summon.

The chimera bellowed, and bellowed again as Leya leapt out of nowhere and locked her teeth on its left wing. It tried to shake her off and she bit down harder, holding her ground. Cylia skated by, and the chimera struck at her, demonstrating the raw speed it must have used when it killed Holly. Its aim was off, not by much, but just enough that she was able to duck out of the way. That would be her natural luck-eating abilities saving her ass. None of the rest of us could count on anything like that. We'd have to count on what we *did* have.

Our incredible skating prowess. I hunkered down, ignoring all known gun safety rules, and skated as fast as I could toward the thing with my pistol out and ready in my hand. Its strike radius couldn't be greater than the length of its limbs plus the flexibility of its neck. With Leya providing a distraction, the math turned more complex, but in my favor. I was readying myself to fire again when Carlotta skated between me and the chimera, a length of two-by-four in her hand.

"Where the hell did she get that?" I demanded.

No one answered me. Carlotta slammed her makeshift weapon into the side of the chimera's head, shouting, *"This is for Tanya!"*

The chimera didn't even bellow. It casually swatted her aside with one paw, sending her crashing into the bleachers, then shook Leya off its wing as it turned. The chupacabra hit the ground hard, yelping as she slid across the track. Luckily for her, the chimera ignored her in favor of stalking toward the fallen Carlotta.

Fern was still skating circles around the warehouse, looking for another opening. She was moving at a speed that could have been fatal to anyone as solid as a human. And that gave me an idea.

"Fern! Cylia!" I shouted. "Whip!"

The whip is probably the most universally recognized move in derby, thanks to a certain movie starring Drew Barrymore. Your jammer is trying to make it around the track, so you form a living whip of derby girls and lend her some extra speed to put her past any obstacles. It's effective when it works, and stupid as hell when it doesn't, and in this case, doing it wrong might get me killed. No pressure.

Fern slowed enough to grab Cylia by the wrist and tow her around the track to me. Cylia grabbed my hand, flinging me at the chimera as hard as their combined momentum would allow. I stayed low, trying not to lose speed as I hurtled toward the beast. Then, when I was close enough, I unloaded my gun into the back of its head.

The chimera stopped stalking. The chimera wobbled. And then, with a final-sounding *thump*, the chimera fell. Which would be when I lost awareness of the events in the warehouse since—thanks to momentum and the blood on the track making it difficult to stop—that was when the chimera fell on me.

I woke up to find Elsie shaking me by the shoulder, a concerned look on her face. I pushed myself up onto my elbows. Nothing felt broken. That could have been the shock talking, but I'd take it. "Anyone dead?" I demanded.

"No," she said. "I think Carlotta has a broken collarbone."

"The chimera?"

"That *is* dead." Elsie shook her head. "You shot the shit out of that thing."

"Overkill can be fun." I decided to risk sitting up all the way, and looked around. Cylia was near the bleachers chatting with Leya, who was in human form and had put her clothes back on. Fern was skating around the body of the chimera, moving at a more reasonable speed now that the danger was past. Carlotta was sitting by herself. I nodded toward Carlotta. "Is she all right?"

Elsie sighed. "I don't know."

"Did you tell her . . . ?"

"That I'm not human? No. We're not at that stage in our relationship." Elsie cast another glance toward her girlfriend. "After tonight, we may have to get there pretty soon."

"Yeah." I held out my hands. "Help me up."

Elsie tugged me to my feet, and stayed where she was as I skated slowly over to where Carlotta was sitting. She looked up as I approached.

"This is why you chose the name Final Girl, isn't it?" she asked. "Because the world's full of monsters."

"They're not all monsters," I said, sitting on the bleachers beside her. "Leya's not a monster. She's just a girl who sometimes runs around on all fours for funsies."

"Yeah," said Carlotta. She didn't sound like she believed me.

I sighed. "I'm sorry you had to see this."

"Holly deserved to have me here." Carlotta looked up. "Holly deserved to *be* here."

There are no pretty words in this world that will bring back the dead, and so I didn't even try. I just sat with her, giving her the time she needed to absorb the way her world had changed. I'd call my parents soon, and let them know we had a dead chimera to dispose of. We'd go home, and we'd meet on this track after the blood had been washed away and the gouges had been repaired. That would all happen later. In the moment, I froze, sitting in the mostly empty warehouse, looking at the body of a beautiful monster, and listening to Carlotta cry.

Fern skated up and sat down on my other side. "We won," she said. "Yay us."

"Yay us," I agreed. I looked toward the others, motioning for them to come and join us. They did. Without hesitation, they did, settling around us until we formed the bloodiest derby tableau ever. "Teamwork, huh?"

Carlotta actually laughed through her tears. It was a beautiful sound. "Don't think this means we're going easy on you next game."

"I wouldn't dream of it," I said.

We were derby girls, and that made us a team that was bigger than labels or league divisions. Nothing—not death, not secrets, not the dead chimera in the middle of the track—was going to change that. And that was pretty cool.

"Who wants pizza?" asked Cylia.

I closed my eyes and smiled.

HIDE AND SHRIEK

ADAM-TROY CASTRO

Adam-Troy Castro has historically brought the suck to any sport he has ever been coaxed into playing, but he has a little bit more luck as a writer. His short stories have been nominated for eight Nebulas, three Stokers, and two Hugos. He has won the Seiun for his collaborative novella *The Astronaut from Wyoming* (written with Jerry Oltion) and the Philip K. Dick Award for his novel *Emissaries from the Dead*. Adam's current project is a series of middle-grade novels about a very strange but very heroic boy named Gustav Gloom. Of "Hide and Shriek," he writes, "Lovecraft, or Lovecraft-influenced fiction, has figured in a number of things I've written recently, including the Gustav Gloom novels and this little exercise in silliness; you'll note that, unlike Howard Phillips, I don't take it at all seriously. My experience with hide-and-seek includes a couple of cases as a child and as an adult playing with child relatives where I found some absolutely brilliant location to secrete myself in and stayed there, only to wait for ungodly periods of time as the other participants drifted to some other pastime and completely forgot that I was involved at all. The experience was, in a word, squamous."

They were Elder Gods.

Almost no vocabulary known to human beings applies to anything having to do with their earthly existence, which began at some point before the first pathetic hominid stared slack-jawed at motes of light in the sky and is likely to continue after the careless ways of Man sends the last of our great edifices crumbling into dust.

They lived by rules beyond our comprehension, according to dictates alien to our imagining. If they hadn't wanted to come forth and eat us occasionally, there would have been about as much point in trying to understand them than as in arranging a diplomatic summit between a Nobel laureate and a paramecium.

They were also, by inclination as well as circumstances of birth, right bastards. But look hard enough, and far enough, and you will find some points of congruence, some motivations easy to fit within our puny minds that are not too alien to be discerned within theirs . . . and one of those was boredom.

After all, eternity lasts a truly *goddamned* long time.

To wit: You think you're in hell, just stuck at home waiting hours for the cable guy? Imagine that your life span can be measured not in years but in eons, and that you have agendas that require the occasional colloquy with another being like yourself who (like you) was there when the Milky Way was still under construction.

Imagine that your associate has not shown up precisely on schedule and that you've floated in the aether watching the stars shift colors according to the precise physics of their own billions of years of life, and imagine that for you time is not sped up to match your proportional life expectancy, a blessing that would make the births and deaths of those stars look like a trillion strobe lights.

Imagine that for you the hours pass at precisely the same rate they do for us, that you feel every second and every minute, that you get exasperated at the same rate and sigh exactly as openly as a commuter waiting on a street corner for a missing bus, and that the centuries continue to pass as you perform the equivalent of standing on one foot and then the other, feeling the remaining time left in the universe gradually count down toward zero.

That is what an Elder God goes through, living out the eons of its existence.

It's nobody's definition of fun.

Hence the game.

There were three participants, brothers of a kind; unholy spawn of the same obscene process that you would have to be blind, deaf, and demented to classify as sex. (It did involve fornication of a kind, and eggs, and other things, but astrological alignment and various horrific rituals also played a part, and, frankly, you don't want us to even start to get into it, because if we did your mind would shatter from the sheer awfulness long before we even started describing the foreplay. About all we can convey is that if you were capable of understanding the process that spawned them, and the vaguely disreputable taint the circumstances carried even among their own kind, you would not have much to add to our earlier estimate: bastards.)

Time was the least and most malleable of the things they had to kill, and they happened to be together, squatting like foul multi-tentacled toads on the blackened bones of a mortal race it had taken them no time at all to terrorize into extinction, when it occurred to all of them that in destroying this latest batch of toys they had left themselves with nothing of any entertainment value to do.

This perturbed them.

Neck wattles throbbed, tentacles writhed, slitted eyes fell slack, and three soulless souls contemplated the long, interminable agony of years spent waiting for another race of Man to invite their interest.

Their direct words would leave any one of us blackened cinders, so we are forced to paraphrase freely. The sense of it, or at least as close as we can come to the sense of it without spontaneous combustion, follows.

N'loghthl, Lord of Phlaaarg, looked glum. "Man. This sucks."

The Septic Breath Of All Existing Foulness replied, "You said it, brother. This really stinks on ice. Why is there never anything to *do*?"

"It's gonna be even worse when we topple the pillars of heaven, dismantle all the laws that give the universe shape, and reduce all of creation to eternal suffering and chaos. There really *won't* be anything left to do, then. That's going to be positively *squamous*."

"*I'm* not looking forward to it," admitted The Septic Breath Of All Existing Foulness, "but come on, guys, by the time that happens we'll be too old for fun anyway. I'm talking about *now*. All our toys are broken and it's going to take forever to grow some new ones. I'm bored."

The third and smartest of the brothers, who had no name as we understand the term but was associated by the others with The Sound Made By A Billion Damned Souls, Writhing In Eternal Despair—for sanity's sake, we'll call him {Eternal Despair}, for short—said, "Perhaps we could make a game of it."

"What kind of game?" inquired The Septic Breath Of All Existing Foulness.

"Well, we're well past time to indulge in our eons of slumber, right?"

The periodic need for eons of slumber was a nuisance, but it was built into Elder God metabolism the same way regular hibernation was built into the life cycle of grizzly bears. Sometimes it was referred to as "Eons of *Unholy* Slumber," which amounted to gilding the lily.

N'loghthl snarled. "And?"

"So let's do this. Let's all find places to hide, on worlds where cute little civilizations have started to form. Only this time we'll spread around some clues and portents to alert the apes that we're around, somewhere."

"That's stupid."

"So are they," said {Eternal Despair}. "Don't you see? That's what makes it a game. We're betting on their stupidity, and who among us manipulates it best."

N'loghthl and The Septic Breath Of All Existing Foulness laid their thousands of cold, pitiless eyes upon one another, trading gazes of infinite darkness and infinite malice, which had nevertheless brightened just the slightest bit with an interest that neither one of them had felt until now.

They had to admit it. For all their immortal lives, {Eternal Despair} always had come up with the best games, games involving prophecies and cataclysms and torrents of gleaming ichor that always ended with entire populations of little things being laid to ruin in the most entertaining manner possible . . . and this one, even in its earliest planning stages, already promised the kind of resonant, despoiling joys that were always best appreciated by unapologetic stinkers such as themselves.

It fell on The Septic Breath Of All Existing Foulness to prod the smartest of the three brothers with an eager, "Go on."

"Well," said the smartest brother, "the point would be to lay it on as thick as possible. Be obvious. Make certain they know that if they ever do awaken us, it'll be The End Of All Things as far as they're concerned . . . and give them reason to leave us to our rest. But also, just for shits and giggles, leave vague promises that whoever *does* betray his kind by setting off the alarm clock, earns power and treasure and everything his little numbskull mind desires. It's a given: it might take a few million years, but sooner or later, each and every one will be discovered and released by some gullible cretin with no conscience and an underdeveloped sense of consequences."

"So how is that any fun?" N'loghthl inquired.

"It's a challenge, my dear brothers: a competition among us for the title of most nefarious. The winner would be the one who made the warnings most dire, and the rumored rewards of trespass most tempting, while nevertheless managing to remain undisturbed by stupid mortals for the longest period of time. The losers forfeit to him all the worlds and souls they've managed to accrue so far. What say you?"

N'loghthl and The Septic Breath Of All Existing Foulness hesitated, for they knew how cunning their brother was, compared to them. They knew that there had to be some trick, some gimmick, some disgusting inherent corruption, some squamous element, that would stack the deck in his favor. But they were also Elder Gods, and they were bored. So they each pricked a warty, leprous finger with a needle of pure angel bone and contributed to the kitty that would hold the sum total of all their wagers. And then they each departed, in the span of a single vile thought, to construct their respective places of concealment.

N'Loghthl erected his crypt at the bottom of a black chasm a thousand miles into an inhospitable desert, a place a week's march from the nearest oasis, which didn't contain pure water but instead a powerful hallucinogen designed to inflict visions that could reduce the noblest man's soul to a gibbering shell, screaming forever in the depths of his own personal hell.

That oasis was itself six months' journey from the nearest civilized outpost, which was only civilized if you count upright buildings as civilized and was only even that if you counted a twenty-degree slant on most walls as officially upright. The outpost was inhabited entirely by outcasts and perverts and inbred defectives, people who had been thrown out of every decent town inhabited by Man and had, by a process similar to sediment dropping to the bottom of a cup of dirty drinking water, wound up in this town best imagined as a kind of lint trap for humanity. We need not devote much concern to the affairs of that town, except to stress again that in order to reach N'loghthl's hiding place a traveler first had to reach that foul oasis, and to reach the foul oasis one first had to trudge six months through a desert of fire, and to reach that desert of fire one first had to pass through the town . . . which was in and of itself the kind of place nobody ventured unless they'd been chased there.

Altogether, it wasn't the kind of journey anybody completed unless they were already mad.

Even so, many were the treasure seekers, parched and ragged after a long ride from the vile flesh pits of the terrible cities that were the closest this entire continent came to civilization, who got as far as the oasis, espied the glittering turquoise waters of the lagoon framed by verdant ferns and gently swaying sunflowers, and thought themselves delivered from a horrible death by thirst; they'd say things like, "I dare say, Carstairs! I thought I was done for, but as soon as I take a sip of this fine bubbling elixir, all of my troubles will be—Aiiiiieee! Aiiiiieeee!"

The *Aiiiiieee, Aiiiiieee* would of course be the sound the speaker made after he ripped off all his clothes and a great deal of his skin and fled back into the burning sands, shouting nonsensical syllables that translated to complaints that none of his right angles were in any way still perpendicular.

At the bottom of that spring, N'loghthl had planted a chest with a lock that fired razor-sharp darts at the forehead of any explorer foolish enough to pop the lid. Inside the chest sat a book reeking of evil—literally, as in not just smelling bad but smelling malicious as well—containing secrets that amounted to even more direct routes to Aiiiiieee-land.

Any adventurer foolish or desperate enough to hike that far away from civilization, damned enough to reach the oasis and yet prudent enough to test the water without drinking it, while still managing to get to the chest with his sanity intact and to somehow devise a way to open it with his forehead intact, then had to figure out that the only page that could be read safely was one secreted in the binding, with the treasure map to N'loghthl's tomb and strict words to the effect that waking the sleeping Elder God would lead to a life of infinite wealth and power for he who accomplished it, followed by utter ruin and damnation for the rest of humanity.

Most people who got that far were sane enough to consider this a rather bum deal, shudder, toss the chest back into the water, and head back to civilized climes.

Most of those who remained paused to consider the trustworthiness of a note slipped into a book that drove people crazy at the bottom of waters that drove people crazy, that was itself locked inside a chest that could fire a dart at their heads, a thousand miles from the nearest outpost of civilization. They said, "You know what? This really isn't worth the tsuris." Then *they* tossed the chest back into the water. Their mothers hadn't raised any idiots.

Of those that remained, only a few survived the subsequent trek to N'loghthl's tomb, and of those who reached the tomb on hands and knees, only a few solved the intricate and deadly puzzle of the quadruple locks, and of those that got past the quadruple locks, only three were able to descend through fifty floors of increasingly horrific death traps to reach the door guarded by all the rotting skulls.

And of those three, only one was stupid enough to open the damned thing expecting fabulous riches.

His name was not in any language you've heard of, but given how far he'd needed to flee from humanity in order to get that far, and how evil he needed to be in order to even want fabulous riches in a world where he thought everybody else would be enslaved forever, you would not be surprised to discover that it translated as Jerkface.

Jerkface had given up everything to get this far. He had spent his youth, his reputation, his family, and his soul tracking down the rumors of a hidden tomb occupied by a sleeping god who could grant him everything, and he now stood before the door, emaciated and bleeding and covered with scars and naked but for the one fuzzy slipper the various death traps and pitfalls on the way in had not succeeded in ripping from his body. He wore the expression of a man who could not possibly believe that what lay ahead of him could be in any way worse than the hurdles he'd left behind, which was another reason his fellow human beings called him Jerkface: his utter and complete failure to learn from past experience that there was always another step down, even after rock bottom.

He stood before the oval of perfect darkness as the black smoke came pouring out, and as the smoke resolved into a sulfurous face with a thousand eyes, and as a thousand eyelids blinked over a thousand slitted pupils. In a voice older than time, N'loghthl croaked, "Mortal! Thou hast freed me! I ask but one question before I bestow your reward! How long have I slept?"

Jerkface had learned the precise period of imprisonment from some hieroglyphics he'd needed to decode on the way down. "A year and a half, O Great One."

The pause that followed was downright comic.

"Excuse me," rumbled N'loghthl. "Did you say a year and a half?"

"One year, five months, two weeks, and three days. The inscriptions are quite clear on this point; you were installed here the very same day as the coronation of King Ghilistaq the Seventh, the day the great Comet Phlaaarg passed through the Constellation of Ignirifahs; and yes, that was one year, five months, two weeks, and three days ago, give or take a few hours depending on which calendar system you subscribe to. Just under a year and a half."

N'loghthl realized then just how inadequate his own contribution to the great game had been, and just how tremendous his humiliation would be when his brothers found out. His rage was for him no more than a snit and still, by all human standards, infinite. His glare made Jerkface's brain matter liquefy and pour in pink streams from his nostrils. As the corpse hit the dusty tomb floor, the irritated Elder God coiled his ten thousand tails around his barbed ribs and curled into a ball to weep, knowing that he would not be able to get back to sleep at any point during this millennium, and caring only that, with luck, one of his brothers would wind up as badly humiliated as he had been, so he would not be forever alone in his ignominy.

In this way another thousand years passed.

In choosing his own hiding place, The Septic Breath Of All Existing Foulness incorporated an epiphany about the nature of Man that his clueless brother N'loghthl had completely missed.

This was not necessarily an indication that he was smarter or more perceptive than N'loghthl, though that happened to be true on both counts. It had more to do with the nature of his particular awful presence, as distinguished from his brother's. N'loghthl was, after all, a physical being, with physical attributes, including fangs, heads, claws, tentacles, and several limbs of varying shape designed to shatter the mind of any mortal who ever beheld them. He was a veritable cornucopia of obscene body attributes that looked like a flaming explosion in an anatomy lab and were very well suited to a creature whose immediate response to a mortal interloper was to bite his head off and whose immediate way of dealing with an encroaching civilization was to stomp on it while roaring.

These were all perfectly acceptable approaches to a problem. But early in his own development as an Elder God, at that point in relative infancy when creatures like himself got to decide in just what ways they'd offend the very pillars of creation, The Septic Breath Of All Existing Foulness decided that it was better to embody Evil the Concept as opposed to Evil the Monstrous Thing; he decided that he would be the unseen, intangible thing that lurked in corners and made shadows so chilly. He wanted to be the creature who inspired fear by absence rather than presence, the creature who by having once briefly been to a place rendered it horrific forevermore, rather than the creature who had to actually hang around in his lair and twiddle his thumbs, waiting for prey.

And so he had become what he was, the vague whiff of corruption that on first sniff smelled like a raccoon had died somewhere behind the walls, that on second sniff led those who perceived him to think that the unfortunate corpse must have been something bigger than a raccoon, on third sniff produced nausea, and on fourth sniff overwhelming cosmic horror.

Okay, so it was a more conceptual thing, which didn't really work for everybody, but he had it down *cold*.

The bottom line is that he was used to subtlety, and well acquainted with hiding. He knew that in any game of hide-and-seek, actual locations placed too little trust in the seeking spirit of humanity. Man's very business was spreading its foul taint from one pole to another. Given a surprisingly short head start, the abominable ape had sought out and colonized the most inhospitable regions on the face of any given planet. He had defied all common sense and built cities on swamps, cities in earthquake zones, cities in places where there was no water and no food.

He had walked across frozen wastelands, barely escaped, and returned with peg legs to replace limbs lost to hypothermia. (Then gone back.) There was no point in building a bloody tomb, as N'loghthl had done. No matter how obscure the clues, Man would get there within a generation.

So The Septic Breath Of All Existing Foulness hid himself in obscure innuendo.

In a play written by a madman, and only performed twice for kings who immediately slaughtered the actors for their effrontery, he was the foul expression that suddenly passed over the features of a lovely ingenue, which for one heartbeat made her look less than human.

In a deadly plague that ravaged the brothels of a merchant city known as Kar-En-Nur, he was a random string of senseless adjectives that appeared well into the delirium of all sufferers, seconds before they expired.

Following a baffling fit of madness that overcame a much-beloved priest known for his infinite kindness, he was the precise pattern of blood spatter on the walls behind the mound of worshippers who had arrived, first thing Sunday morning, to seek that kindly figure's blessings for the upcoming harvest.

He was the vinegary taste of cheap wine.

He was every horrid circumstance that had ever taken a perfect day and caused it to turn black and brittle on the edges; the thunderstorm that rained down on picnics; the sudden gastric upset that prevented consummation on wedding nights; the way noses wrinkled when an awful stench rolled in from the sea and nobody could explain why.

He played fair. He absolutely did. All of these clues, and uncounted thousands of others, could if placed together in the proper order and considered with the correct degree of madness while the stars gathered in precise alignment, all come together to suggest a certain fatal suggestion in the mind of a human being. That suggestion would be enough to establish the premise of a certain malignant intelligence behind it all, and that premise would be awe-inspiring enough to imply that the intelligence might be contacted and petitioned, and that implication would be sufficiently irksome to linger, and the nightmares that resulted would be traumatic enough to rip a portal in the barrier between *what cannot be* and *what unfortunately is*, and that portal would disgorge a book, and that book once translated would provide an incantation, and . . . well. You get the rest.

This was, of course, a rather serpentine way to go about it, but that was the very point of the game, after all.

So The Septic Breath Of All Existing Foulness curled up in his lair, and burbled, and spewed, and farted, and generally made the air around himself noxious, which was as unpleasant to him as it would be to any of us, but that was the nature he had chosen, which has a lot to say about thinking through all the ramifications of one's life choices before one makes them.

He waited. He slept. He played solitaire. He lost track of time. Then he heard the incantation spoken, muffled by the dimensional barriers but still fully clear to his ears, and he manifested on our plane.

Dripping acidic saliva, he said, "Hello."

The philosopher who had accidentally summoned him looked up, paled, and said, "Shit."

The two brothers whose hiding places had proven inferior drowned their sorrows in a place that would make no sense to us, but which we might as well imagine to be a sleazy dive with watered-down drinks and waitresses in dire need of mustache waxing.

It wasn't precisely that, of course. Again, we can only perceive these phenomena safely by recasting them in the terms our minds can process without shattering. Suffice it to say that it served the same function such an establishment fulfills on our plane of existence, in that it catered to beings who needed a place sufficiently squalid and disreputable to indulge their worst paroxysms of self-loathing; and considering that given how profane and vile their activities managed to be even when things were going well for them, it must have been a despicable dive indeed. You might want to imagine a corner booth with roaches skittering across the sticky table, even if N'loghthl and The Septic Breath Of All Existing Foulness might have found that particular ambience downright pleasant. In any event, this was not a good place. It was considerably worse than Trenton.

N'Loghthl threw back his drink, too morose to take pleasure in the way the rightful owner of that beverage blackened and boiled in the process. "He's gonna be *intolerable*."

"He's intolerable already," pointed out The Septic Breath Of All Existing Foulness. "Being intolerable is what we *do*."

"True. But you know what I mean. The longer he remains hidden, and thus proves he designed his hiding place more cleverly than ourselves, the more arrogant and superior he will prove to be when he slithers forth and discovers just how badly he defeated us. As much as I treasure the thought of millennia free of his infernal snottiness, we have to sabotage him. The sooner we lead some mortal fool to his lair, the less ammunition we leave him with, to trumpet his greatness when he finally does rise again."

The Septic Breath Of All Existing Foulness drew himself back, like an affronted pony. "You're suggesting we cheat."

"Why, yes."

The Septic Breath Of All Existing Foulness gave that all due consideration, which means in practice that he saw the sense of it right away. "Very well. But we shall honor the spirit of the game, in that it must still be a mortal worm who resurrects him. It shall only be our pleasure to . . . shall we say, goose the odds, to lead the fool to where {Eternal Despair} hides."

"Agreed," said N'loghthl.

They shook obscene appendages, and plans were made.

Not long afterward, on yet another Earth congenial to Man, Professor Artis De Glough stood at a lectern in front of a packed lecture hall, peering at a student body that was there, largely, to laugh at him.

De Glough was one of those odd specimens who accrue around certain universities, not out of any great level of academic achievement, but more in the manner that cat hair or lint accumulates in the corner of rooms.

He had been accepted as an undergraduate because of a college essay that was passed from one member of the faculty to another in awe, because it blew entire zeppelins' worth of smoke at the question of his own qualifications and ultimately collapsed upon itself in a heap of nonsensical sesquipedalian verbiage. The deciding vote had been cast by the dean of students himself, who fervently declared, "We *have* to enroll this guy." Saner heads never prevailed. De Glough then had proceeded directly from a very odd and demented time as a student (acquiring passing grades in large part only because his theses were so impenetrable and insane that the faculty frequently passed him only out of curiosity over what he was going to do next) to a very long and notorious time as professor (where he somehow achieved tenure in large part because nobody in the administration wanted to be responsible for how spectacularly unprepared he would be for nonuniversity employment).

He was, in a very real sense, the institution's pet, and though his duties were largely limited to laboring in his dim basement office on the three thick volumes on Elder Gods he produced yearly, he was by contract required to give a single three-hour lecture annually, and attending at least one of his incoherent presentations was considered such a rite of passage for undergraduates that they always packed the university's largest hall, jockeying for seats from which they could observe him with the proper degree of dismay and incredulity.

He wiped the beaded sweat from a brow like parchment, and wrapped up this year's contribution.

". . . beings," he emphasized, pointing an index finger, "incalculable in power, malevolent in intent, gazing upon all the poor achievements of our civilization with pitiless orbs capable of piercing the gossamer veils that reduce the abyss between our world and theirs to the translucent planes layered in a manner that resembled the phenomenon of pentimento on oil paintings."

As he paused for effect, not a single rustle could be heard among the hundreds in attendance. He peered up from his prepared text, and a few of the more nearby members of his audience imagined that they could see the dust of his subterranean office space puff from between his withered lips like clouds.

"Thank you."

Some of the attendees had to elbow others who had fallen asleep, but once everybody was roused De Glough received the usual standing ovation.

There were, as usual, no questions, which was a good thing, as questions might have provided impetus for another three-hour lecture. De Glough was left standing at the base of the stadium-shaped lecture hall, trying to align his yellowing lecture notes for better insertion into his briefcase, the only briefcase he had ever used, which had a broken brass lock and was held together by bungee cords. The dust on his spectacles was so thick that his magnified eyes looked like tiny fish trembling at the bottom of twin pools of pus.

"Excuse me? Professor Dee Gluff?"

De Glough looked up and saw something that he had almost never encountered at any of his lectures: sincere unfeigned fascination, shorn of obvious irony and spawned from no force other than actual intellectual appreciation. It had been years since he had seen such a thing, and he would have been stunned by it even had it not come from two young ladies of alabaster skin and spectacular pulchritude, each more beautiful than the other.

This was, of course, an impossible formulation. The phrase "each more beautiful than the other" was one he'd heard before in reference to other groupings of young ladies, and had indeed appreciated as hyperbolic poetry, but he'd dismissed it as a mathematical impossibility since no constant, X, here defined as the measurable degree of one's beauty, could be both greater than and less than Y, here defined as the measurable degree of the other's beauty, simultaneously. In no rational algebra is X *both* > and < Y. It's a logical impossibility. But once he allowed his gaze to not only flicker from one bright face to the other, but also return for a fresh measurement, he saw that their mutual gloriousness functioned as a feedback loop, wherein X added the value of Y to itself and Y then did the same, ad infinitum. He was witnessing an aesthetic asymptotic curve, increasing slope as it accelerated toward the immeasurable ultimate.

Despite a suddenly dry throat, he managed, "Not Dee Gluff. De Glough."

Icon of Pulchritude Number One blinked prettily. "Excuse me?"

"Not Dee but Day. Not Gluff but Glow. De Glough."

Her limpid eyes widened. "Your name is pronounced 'Day-Glo'?"

"Correct."

"I'm so sorry."

Having lived with it since grade school, Professor De Glough was even sorrier. "I deeply appreciate that. How may I help you?"

The two visions of loveliness glanced sideways at one another, then peered back at him, each instant a perfect heartbreak on a scale De Glough had not experienced since acquiring a stepsister in adolescence.

This much you need to know about Art De Glough: he was by most of the standards of academia as well as everyday life an absolute lunatic. Driven by obscure ancient texts reeking of bygone crackpottery and redolent of more mouse piss than actual wisdom, he clung to theories about silly things like incomprehensible Elder Gods slumbering into dark places while awaiting their opportunity to slither forth and topple civilization. Every single book on his home shelf was bound with brass hinges and could only be opened with the proper key. He used the word *squamous* in everyday conversation, which is one good reason why he rarely had any. But he was also a romantic at heart, vulnerable to the infinite charms of a dazzling smile beneath a pair of radiant eyes.

Nor was this mere lust, the familiar hunger many pedants in tweed feel for the needier maidens among the student body, who have earned a historical reputation at such institutions for their shared misapprehension that the profound and deeply wise figure at the base of the lecture hall is oft-times a good place to find instruction in matters more intimate and life-changing than anything to be found in the course syllabus. Though not exactly a man of this world, as all of his practical knowledge was limited to the forgotten lore of other spheres entirely, De Glough had always been aware of such activities among his fellow faculty members, and had always prudishly disapproved. No, he had always yearned for true love. He had always dreamed of his Juliet. But the skills required to meet her (let alone win her) were as far beyond him as the operating specs of the Large Hadron Collider were beyond a naked mole rat.

He was a romantic, a knight in dust and tweed. There was absolutely no chance of either of these two young ladies requesting a favor that he would not have granted, out of sheer misplaced gallantry.

He was, however, totally gobsmacked when the one on the right said, "We believe *we* can help *you*."

• • •

The conversation changed venues to a small but comfortable off-campus apartment that boggled the Professor not just because of its capacity to retain sunlight on every surface even as a torrential electrical storm raged just outside its bay windows, but also by accoutrements that, despite his lifelong inexperience, struck De Glough as quintessentially, indeed almost ludicrously, female: among them shelves lined with candles of every conceivable shade and aroma, a silk-shrouded four-high-poster bed piled to Himalayan altitudes with tasseled pillows, and a small menagerie of stuffed animals, some of which bore valentine-shaped hearts. It was in gestalt a virtual tsunami of estrogen, piling high in the shallows and rising to terrifying heights before crashing down to plow through any recalcitrant testosterone on land.

Somewhere along the way formal introductions had been completed, and the two ladies had provided their names. The one with hair like scarlet fire was named Tammi N'loghthl, a sobriquet she thrice had to repeat for his disbelieving ears before she lowered her splendid lids demurely and explained that she was one-twentieth Cherokee and that it was an ancestral word meaning She Who Dances Among The Crystal Waters.

De Glough found this unlikely but was not inclined to question it.

The one whose raven locks set off a brilliantly white smile—and who had just the faintest taste of bad breath, a possible testament to a tobacco habit not yet in direct evidence—had introduced herself as Septima Fowl. He found that just as unlikely but was unwilling to question it either.

The ladies, who had both slipped into sheer silk camisoles and now knelt side by side on the bed licking their lips and finding obscure reasons to arch their backs and thrust their secondary sexual characteristics forward, told him that they'd just shared a vacation in Guatemala where Tammi had found a medallion they now wanted the good Professor to examine.

He managed to hide any disappointment he might have felt over this being all about a dusty old artifact, and removed the magnifying spectacles from his jacket pocket.

One short examination later, he said, "Interesting."

"How so?" asked Tammi N'loghthl.

"These markings around the rim? I know these runes. They come from a very ancient language native to a trans-Lemurian civilization predating what is normally considered recorded history. Indeed, there's strong disagreement over whether that civilization or even the alphabet ever really existed, as most authorities take the position that the cave markings providing us what little we know of its alphabet was just the claw gouges left by a dying rodent as it suffered its final convulsions from food poisoning. I have argued that since the markings comprise hundreds of figures repeated in predictable combinations, this hypothesis only makes sense if it also makes sense to posit a small army of dying rodents, perishing in unison and with identical convulsions in what amounts to a kind of mortality conga line. The archaeological establishment, naturally, took this as a delightful and wholly logical explanation, rejecting my intended sarcasm and with it my insistence that an actual alphabet is involved."

Septima Fowl shuddered, not out of fear. "What's it say?"

"The language itself has never been translated, unfortunately, but we can divine some clues to the medallion's significance from the bas-relief carving on this side, in which some kind of tentacled monster is depicted showering a priest with gold coins while flames as high as the sky leap from the city shown in the backdrop. The obverse, which looks like a network of rivers feeding together toward an ocean coastline, is clearly a primitive map, and this skull symbol at the place where those rivers converge is clearly a destination. I would presume that the medallion is in a sense an advertisement, offering a vivid come-on of the offered rewards as inducement toward following the directions in the small print."

He shuddered and placed the medallion aside, like a plate of food he couldn't finish. "It's an interesting find, but I'm afraid I can't provide much more help than that. I have no intention of buying what this medallion is selling."

The twin pouts directed at Professor De Glough functioned as illustrations in the fine art of transforming rich lower lips into jutting shelves, upon which the ladies implied the myriad disappointments of an unfair world. "Why not?"

"Because I believe it," De Glough said. "I think this artifact is genuine and that the apocalypse it promises in exchange for fleeting material gain is not worth any price. I would urge you ladies to take a nice cruise, somewhere out where the waters run deep, and toss this little obscenity overboard so it can never pass through the hands of Man again."

This was precisely the kind of moment that cried out for the speechmaker to grab his hat and place it jauntily on his head before nodding and walking out. De Glough actually looked around for a hat before remembering that he didn't own one. He made it up with that nod, which was firm and wise and served the purpose of the missing headgear in that it put the cap on the conversation.

But when he walked out, Tammi N'loghthl and Septima Fowl ran after him, catching up on the stairs and bouncing alongside him with an enthusiasm that brought a swoon from the male neighbor ascending those same stairs with a basket of laundry. "But Professor! Your reputation!"

"Is excrement, and I'm so well accustomed to being inundated by entire fathoms of scorn that being summoned to the surface for public vindication might well rupture all my tissues with a case of the bends."

"The importance of this find!"

". . . is akin to the importance of a venomous snake that has slithered into a backyard tool shed I never use, in that I appreciate knowing it's there and understand that it can change everything should I be foolish enough to go to the trouble of discovering it, but I am wise enough to know I can also sleep quite well and continue to happily draw breath without ever giving that discovery my seal of approval."

This much is true: even Elder Gods walking among mortals in human form are vulnerable to the dizzying effect of tortured metaphors. Tammi N'loghthl and Septima Fowl paused in midstep, their beautiful masks slipping just a tad as the ancient beings behind them caught up with the conflicting imagery. Had De Glough been looking at them at the moment this occurred, he would have seen Tammi N'loghthl's perfect lips part, a crack spread across both her cheeks like a crevasse ripping open in a glacier, and a mass of writhing cilia within gorge with infuriated blood. He would have noticed Septima Fowl's doll-like perfection shimmer and fade, becoming a ravaged flaming skull that was, for some reason, still wearing lip gloss despite the absence of lips.

But De Glough did not turn around and as a result did not see either of these things.

By the time the two faux ladies had seized control of their temporarily ravaged appearances and succeeded in wresting their attractiveness ratings back into the realm of positive numbers, the Professor had made his escape.

"Shit," said Tammi N'loghthl.

By now you should know that the word emerging from that mouth was not actually *shit*, but some oath of infinitely greater blasphemousness that would have caused the skin of any human eavesdropper to bubble and run like hot wax.

"He should be frayed for his impudence," said Septima Foul.

Tammi N'loghthl inquired, "Don't you mean 'flayed'?"

"I may be wearing this ridiculous body, my brother, but I know exactly what I said. Mere flaying is too merciful a fate for him. Instead, the little worm should be frayed, one loose thread at a time."

Tammi N'Loghthl considered that and found it pleasing. "Later. I will provide the"—and here, the being inside the comely flesh referenced an implement of torment never imagined by Man, that would have made the most treasured toys of Torquemada look like a pair of toenail clippers purchased at Walgreens. "But until then, he is still our most likely prospect, and he still needs to be lured . . ."

Plan B, as the brother gods would have called it had they utilized any alphabet we know, went down one midnight two weeks later, at the precise moment when the Professor was crossing a busy intersection midway between the dank basement where he kept office hours (and had indeed gone more than a decade without ever being consulted by a single student) and his home (which was just as dank though not, strictly speaking, a basement). The Professor staggered a little, as the weekend was coming up and he was bringing home his latest opus, the seventh volume of a work in progress classifying the various flavors of ichor. He also had a paper clip in his shoe, which kept jabbing into his big toe and which he would have stopped to remove were it not also in the innermost of three layers of sock. The Professor's firm policy of always wearing a green sock inside a red sock inside a black sock was the least of his many eccentricities and would require a significant digression to explain, though we can say that it was a habit driven by his many years of scholarship and was prompted by a warning in the memoirs of an apothecary from a civilization that had crumbled some ten centuries before Atlantis; to wit, it always pays to wear protection. The apothecary had been referring to prophylactics, of course, but the Professor was fuzzy about such things, one reason he was always so scrupulous about keeping his toenails filed.

As he limped north toward that intersection, it was impossible for him to avoid noting the two strange girls from the prior lecture, strolling toward him on the opposite side of the street.

It was equally difficult for him to avoid observing the black van that whipped around the corner to cut them off.

The girls clutched each other and shrieked prettily as a pair of thugs burst from the passenger doors.

At this point, the word *thug* is probably leading you to imagine a pair of gun-wielding American hit men, but no, they were thugs, as in *thuggees*, as in members of the Kali death cult from nineteenth-century India. They were two half-naked guys in diapers, shouting angry declarations that only a human sacrifice could possibly punish the nonbelievers for their effrontery.

The world of academia being what it is, this was the fourth time the Professor had seen something like this happen on campus.

The girls made no visible attempt to escape, but rather continued to just clutch each other and shriek, inviting rescue as the two little guys in diapers advanced upon them. The speed of their villainous advance was no greater than the speed of a tourist in Hawaiian shirt standing in line for the roller coaster at a theme park; it was in fact a speed designed to allow the Professor to heroically dash across the street and, with a few wild swings, send the cultists flying and rescue the girls from a fate worse than death.

The Professor rendered this plan unworkable by not dashing across the street to rescue the girls from a fate worse than death.

Nor did he stir as the two guys in diapers each seized one of the girls by an upper arm and tugged her toward the van, still at the speed of a mobility scooter straining to navigate a curb.

It wasn't that the Professor possessed no streak of heroism. He very well might have. But skilled as they traditionally are at lying, Elder Gods are crap when it comes to acting, and even worse when it comes to choreographing action scenes. The Professor's failure to manifest as hero only made this worse. The scene they had choreographed slowed to a near stop, begging for interruption, until the girls and their supposed kidnappers were all forced to shuffle along like people with thirty-pound weights strapped to their ankles. The pathetic cries for help became less oh-God-oh-God-won't-somebody-save-us, and more the complaint of actors aware that a scene has completely gone south but wholly unsure why the unseen director hadn't yelled *Cut* yet.

Eventually, when the girls and their thugs had put off their actual departure for as long as they reasonably could, the van doors slammed and the vehicle remained idling at the spot long enough to establish that the key concern of whoever sat beyond the wheel was not a frenzied escape but the concoction of another strategy that might induce the Professor to get involved.

After a moment the van carefully pulled away from the curb, proceeded to cross the intersection, and, in a wholly laughable attempt at simulating a skid, deliberately steered itself toward a light pole. The result was less a crash than a gentle whump, but it was enough for Tammi and Septima to burst from its doors in tops now ripped to accentuate their cleavage and, running like people who had no idea what to do with their arms, flee toward the Professor in the theory that proximity might accomplish what spoon-fed opportunity would not.

"Omigaaaaaaahd Professor De Glough thank Gaaaaaaad you're here, you've got to help us they know we have the medallion they want to sacrifice us help help help you've got to HELP—"

The girls huddled behind the still nonplussed Professor, treating him like a tank capable of repelling assaults from vastly superior numbers even though he was older, smaller, and not nearly the paragon of health and vitality they clearly seemed to be. Three thugs emerged from the van, which had not suffered so much as a dent from its gentle impact.

All three looked spectacularly confused and indecisive over what the script was now. One muttered something to the other, who responded with a shrug so clearly what-the-fuck in its philosophy that it might have been visible from orbit. What the fuck, right?

They began waving their daggers and crying, "Blasphemers, blasphemers."

Halfway across the street it began to occur to them that the Professor was neither advancing nor retreating, and their dagger waves grew halfhearted and almost embarrassed, their cries of "Blasphemer!" as without heart as the sales pitch of a teenage kid who's been talked into becoming a door-to-door Fuller Brush salesperson for the summer. That kid thinks, *Yes, I know this is bullshit, but at least say so before I get through too much of this, and I'll be out of your hair and on to the next house.* These allegedly menacing thugs wore the same expression and conveyed the same attitude.

The Professor rolled his eyes and delivered his expected line with an equal lack of conviction. "Stop where you are," comma not exclamation point, "these girls are under my protection," comma not exclamation point, "to get them you'll have to go through me," period and full stop, with not one syllable uttered at any register more frenetic than the deeply bored.

This completely unmanned the thugs, who on cue shouted *"Aiiieee"* and *"Flee, my brothers"* and the rest of that rot before piling back into the van and, judging from the noticeable delay before they pulled away, scrupulously fastening their seat belts.

Tammi N'loghthl threw her arms around the Professor and smothered him with kisses, proceeding with the pretense that he had just pulled off the bravest thing she'd ever seen. "Oh! Professor! You saved our lives! But what will we do if they come back?"

He gently disentangled himself. "Young lady, I have spent the past two weeks fantasizing about the two of you, but please don't think I'm as big an idiot as you're treating me. That display was downright pathetic."

"B-but look!" Septima wailed. "Our clothes are ripped and everything!"

"Yes, I see that. I also see how artfully they're ripped. I'm insulted when people who seek to con me don't put on a better show than that. I gather that I'm now supposed to buy that the two of you have become the targets of some vile international death cult because you toyed with forces beyond your ken, and immediately drop everything I'm doing to follow you to Ecuador, or wherever you claim to have found that medallion."

"We said Nicaragua," said Tammi N'loghthl.

"No," said the Professor, mildly but with the finality of a slamming door, "actually, you said Guatemala. Feel free to see me during office hours."

Tammi N'loghthl and Septima Fowl gaped as he stormed off, having resisted their blandishments not just once, but twice.

"He should be filleted," said Septima Fowl. "Not flayed or frayed, but—"

"Oh, shut up," said Tammi N'loghthl.

They returned to their lair to gnaw on a frat boy's leg as they discussed their remaining options.

The final and most apocalyptic act in this clash of wills took place a week later, during the Professor's scheduled office hours, in what was until that point reliably the very quietest and most uneventful room on campus.

The girls didn't show up and offer him their undying gratitude. They didn't appeal to his sense of male gallantry. In fact, they didn't even show up as girls. Mostly. Instead, they manifested, not quite as large as life but certainly larger than they had manifested so far, their eyes burning embers and their lips dripping cocktails of pus and maggots. Perdition's flames rose from their shoulders. Their otherwise still-perfect breasts, bared for the occasion, now displayed the faces of past damned souls, gibbering in madness, where other ladies have areolas. This was a rather off-putting feature.

Professor De Glough, who had been sitting behind his desk poring through many a volume of forgotten lore, slammed the latest on the stack with a force that sent clouds of dust billowing from its antique pages. "Ah. Here we go."

"SEDUCTION FAILED. APPEALS TO YOUR INTELLECTUAL
CURIOSITY FAILED. APPEALS TO YOUR SENSE OF CHIVALRY
FAILED. NOW WE SHALL APPEAL TO YOUR SENSE OF FEAR.
YOU SHALL HELP US FREE OUR SLEEPING BROTHER AND END
OUR GAME, OR YOU WILL KNOW TORMENTS LASTING TEN
THOUSAND LIFETIMES."

"Aha," said Professor De Glough. "That is what this is all about? A
game?"

"THE RULES OF THE GAME WE HAVE PLAYED WITH OUR
BROTHER REQUIRED HIM TO BE FOUND, WITHOUT ASSIS-
TANCE, BY AN UNWITTING MORTAL. WE HAVE ALREADY
BROKEN THOSE RULES BY PLYING YOU WITH BLANDISHMENT
AFTER BLANDISHMENT. WE INTENDED TO PRESERVE THE
GAME, IN SPIRIT, BY LURING YOU TO THE TOMB IN
NICARAGUA—"

"Guatemala," the Professor said.

A firestorm of sheer coruscating hatred blasted all four walls with a
blast of hellfire sufficient to blacken the walls and reduce all of the Professor's office furnishings, save for his desk, to ash. "WHATEVER."

"My word. It certainly looks bad for me."

"IT LOOKED BAD FOR YOU FROM THE VERY MOMENT WE
TURNED OUR OMNISCIENT EYES IN YOUR DIRECTION. HOW-
EVER, YOU HAVE TRIED OUR PATIENCE AND EXHAUSTED
OUR ENTHUSIASM, SO WE WISELY FORGO THE INFINITE
SERIES OF FRUSTRATIONS THAT WOULD NO DOUBT ACCOM-
PANY ANY ATTEMPT TO SHEPHERD YOU TOWARD THE ORIG-
INAL INTENDED SITE OF YOUR DESTRUCTION. OUR DEAREST
WISH NOW IS ONLY FOR THIS STUPID WAGER TO BE OVER. SO
WE HAVE LOOTED THE TOMB, EXTRACTED THE ACCURSED
CHEST OURSELVES, AND NOW PLACE IT BEFORE YOU. YOUR
SOLE RESPONSIBILITY IS TO OPEN IT. OUR BROTHER WILL
KNOW THAT WE CHEATED, BUT THAT IS A SMALL PRICE TO
PAY, JUST TO BE DONE WITH THIS BULLSHIT."

The Professor tented his fingertips and rested his chin upon them, as
he inspected the small stone box that had just materialized on his desk
blotter, like a bowel movement abandoned there by some stray dog. It

was a most unlovely chest indeed, with carvings that resembled steaming viscera and jewels of unfamiliar origin that might have been the gall-stones torn from some species of great antiquity. It was so redolent of evil power that he did not have to open it to know that the creature inside was terrible in a fashion that rendered even the terrible creatures before him insignificant by comparison.

"And that 'bullshit,'" he inquired, "that you seek to be done with, and that you would in fact make sure you were done with once your brother was released, would include my life, my civilization, my world, my species, everything we have ever striven for, or sought to build?"

"CORRECT."

"Then no."

The two entities before him combined into a single vision so blasphemous that any true heaven, beholding it, would have turned all of creation into a single container of bleach. "FOOLISH MORTAL—"

"Mortal, yes. Foolish, perhaps. Stupid, no. I may be a crackpot, but I am also a very intelligent man. And it strikes me that what I hear from you is the true source of bullshit in this room."

"YOU DARE—"

"Please. The game cannot be about drawing some random mortal man to some buried tomb where your sleeping brother awaits, because there are easier ways for two seductive women to get gullible males to follow them to the ends of the Earth. Nor can it be about opening this pathetic box, which is such a simple artifact that any human being other than myself could have pried it open at any time. No; in either case, were that all this was about, you could have reacted to my prior refusals by shrugging your then-pretty heads and finding some more tractable target for your wiles. But you haven't, and so it strikes me that you must then need me, and only me, as your ally, for some reason central to your purpose. From there it is just a short logical leap to the realization that the most secure hiding place is not some little casket of stone, but the power of sheer human obstinacy. Your brother does not lie secure beneath earth or stone or any lock that can be opened by a key. He would have been found long ago if that were so. He lies behind my own initially instinctive, and now wholly reasoned, refusal to help you. It is the greatest of all possible hiding places, and I tell you now, it shall remain secure . . . for I now believe I was built by him to refuse you, and refuse you I always shall."

N'loghthl and The Septic Breath Of All Existing Foulness raged, their fury growing far too great to be bounded by such a mortal space. The building above caught fire and was reduced to an ashen skeleton. The campus became a blackened crater, miles across, forever toxic to any who would ever dare to cross its outer rim.

The Professor's tweed suit vaporized, and he remained where he sat, just as tweedy when naked, blinking at the fury of two spoiled gods, while remaining untouched by their tantrum. "Are you quite done?"

"YOU ARE AN INSIGNIFICANT HUMAN GNAT!"

"Significance," he said, "can be measured by the ability to affect powers greater than yourself. A microscopic blood clot is hardly insignificant when it induces a fatal stroke in an emperor. I am far below you in aggregate power but clearly above you in influence, and therefore hardly insignificant by any standard. It seems, in fact, that in playing my role as your brother's surrogate in this matter, and doing it well, I have defeated you. Your game is over. All that remains is for you to concede defeat."

This resulted in even more fulmination, lasting a day and a night and day and a night, and incorporating more cataclysmic events, which outside the Professor's little bubble of safety and the perimeter of absolute destruction that surrounded him, induced civilization's pundits to invoke the phrase "biblical proportions" more than anybody had since that one time in 1997 when a porn magnate released a film set in the harem of King Solomon.

Inside the bubble, however, there was just the Professor and his implacability, the two Elder Gods and their fury . . . which, once profligately spent, arrived at the only place it could, with N'loghthl and The Septic Breath Of All Existing Foulness spent as well, staring daggers at the speck of a creature whose defiance had brought them to this eventuality.

"Do you concede defeat?" the Professor inquired.

They did.

"That is eminently reasonable of you. I, however, am aware that once I accept your concession, my usefulness as your brother's jailer, and therefore as the one force that keeps the two of you at bay as well, is ended . . . and I harbor too much affection for the world to let that happen. I therefore designate one bribe that I am willing to accept in exchange for my agreement to open the box. It is a highly unlikely bribe, one that you will be able to predict by sheer logic. I am willing to sit here for all eternity if I must, to refuse all other inducements. In this way, I save humanity."

The tantrum that followed was even worse than the prior ones, in that it had the extra added obscenity of whining.

It was an impasse, and if we take anything from it, it is our perception of Professor De Glough as an uncomplicated, one of a kind, world-saving hero; a man who when all of existence depended on him stood between all of us and Armageddon.

It should be noted here, because what follows renders it irrelevant, that the bribe the Professor had in mind was the simple word *Please*. He had quite rightly bet all our futures that neither N'loghthl nor The Septic Breath Of All Existing Foulness would ever come up with that word on their own, even if provided a thousand times a thousand eons to mull the problem over; it was, he divined, wholly beyond their character, and he was so right in this assumption that, were they and their sleeping brother the whole entities that mattered here, humanity would have been able to survive and flourish and thrive and rise and achieve a destiny beyond the whims of any of their kind.

Really, he deserved a medal, or at least a great big hand.

Alas, we find we must report that he had failed to consider one thing beyond even his capacity to predict, something he might be forgiven for missing, given the power and the scale of the creatures he was dealing with.

For him, it manifested as a sight that made his eyes boil in their sockets, and his brain dribble out of his ears; a shape of infinite complexity and infinite awfulness, congealing in the air behind the two Elder Gods he had stymied; a creature who was to them what a whale is to the tiniest minnow. He was shattered and gibbering before his mind could put together what he had learned from them—that they were siblings and that they were playing a game—and point out, with cold and pitiless logic, that among men as well as Elder Gods, there is a certain class of creature known for getting bored, and making up games, a class of creature looked over by another who can be trusted to come running, whenever a game gets out of hand.

So we're sorry to have to tell you this. We really are.

But the last thing Professor De Glough saw before his heart burst, and darkness was loosed upon the Earth, was Mommy coming to make sure everybody was playing nicely.

ICE

LAURA LIPPMAN

Laura Lippman grew up in Baltimore, in a neighborhood very much like the one described here. Okay, it was the exact same neighborhood, and the two stories joined here, about two girls, were inspired by real-life events. Historical note: Baltimore, which was hard-hit by rioting after Martin Luther King Jr.'s assassination, began observing King's birthday in the 1970s, long before the federal holiday was created. A *New York Times* bestselling author, Lippman has published eighteen novels, a novella, and a book of short stories. Her nineteenth novel, *After I'm Gone*, was published in February 2014. She lives in Baltimore and New Orleans. She ice-skates whenever possible.

Atheena could run. Boy, could she run.

She ran down the hill at full speed. Because she could, because the hill was there and when you are ten years old, running down a hill at full speed makes as much sense as anything else you might do. You can roll down a hill, too, but that is a game for lazier, gentler grassy slopes, with plenty of land to catch you at the bottom. This hill was studded with trees, which snapped and slapped unless you were fleet and nimble, short and skinny. Atheena was all those things. Her brother lumbered along, slowed down by his size, crying out when he felt the stinging, winter-bare branches on his face. Those branches never touched Atheena.

Atheena flew down the hill, her lungs bursting with happiness. It was such a beautiful day, more beautiful than any January day had a right to be, more like March. They were off from school for Martin Luther King Jr.'s birthday for the first time ever, a holiday just for schools, nobody else. Her mama didn't have off, but Atheena and her brother did.

It was funny, though, how boring a day off from school could become before it was over, how easy it was to use up all the fun. The day had started fine—Mama's kiss on the top of her head as Atheena burrowed under her covers, enjoying an extra hour of sleep. Cartoons and Nesquik and Pop-Tarts, *Dialing for Dollars*. Then outside, a walk to the corner store with the dollar Mama had left for her. One for her and one for her brother. Then they had sort of run out of things to do until Bobby thought to go exploring in the woods behind Hillside Road.

And now here they were, running, running, running down the hill. There was a pond at the foot of the hill. It had never occurred to Atheena, whose school bus crossed that pond on a bridge every day, that she could reach it on foot, yet here it was. The pond, still all ice after last week's hard freeze, looked like a shiny white diamond winking at her. If she ran fast enough, she could probably glide across it, like those skaters did. The Winter Olympics would be starting soon and she liked to watch the skaters and the skiers, although her Uncle Rodney always said those were sports for rich folks and white folks. Atheena had puzzled over that because she was pretty sure that all rich folks were white, except for maybe Miss Diana Ross and the Jackson Five. Not even the people on Hillside Road were truly rich, big as their houses were compared to the one where she lived with Robert and Mama.

They were racing and she was winning. Robert was two years older, but she was faster and, oh, how it irked him, losing to his baby sister. *Can't catch me, I'm the gingerbread man!* Of course, when she got to the bottom, he could catch her. Wouldn't it be funny if she said exactly those words and didn't stop, just flew across the ice to the other side? Mrs. Burke had been reading them this story, *Uncle Tom's Cabin*, about slavery and such, said it was important to know certain things if they were going to celebrate the birthday of Dr. Martin Luther King Jr. here in Baltimore; they needed to know how far they had come, how it used to be that the stories of black people were only listened to when told by a white woman, and while this woman was a good white woman, Dr. King had showed the world that they had words, too, they didn't need white people to tell their stories.

Atheena ran down that hill like Eliza running from Simon Legree, like Moses escaping Egypt. Go down, Moses. Go down, Atheena. It would be hard to run on the ice. She had taken many a fall on ice in her time. Maybe she should try to walk across the spine of the rickety old dam, the one that created the little pond out of a stream that usually just tumbled and churned across rocks. But no, that dam was so full of splinters and stuff. She would just get up a lot of speed, then glide across the ice. It would be like surfing, not that she had ever done that, either. She ran straight at the frozen pond and launched herself across it, arms out, gliding, gliding, gliding. It was the closest a person could come to flying and have her feet on the ground, Atheena thought.

She was almost to the opposite side when she felt the ice shudder. Could ice get cold? Or did ice shiver when it got warm? It shuddered once, twice, then gave way the third time, collapsed beneath her. If gliding had felt like flying, then this was like falling from the sky.

Atheena couldn't swim. Neither could Robert. Swimming, too, was for rich people and white people. Her brother stood on the bank screaming for her, but Atheena never surfaced. The water was barely over her head in the spot where she fell. But that was enough, that was all it took. The stream's murky waters, which looked so lazy and still on the surface, were strong enough to press her against the old dam and hold her there. She was cold, then surprisingly warm, so warm—

"And they never found her body, not even when they had to rebuild the dam after Hurricane Agnes that summer," Gwen told Mickey, a flashlight beneath her chin.

They were sitting in Gwen's bedroom, under a makeshift tent made from Gwen's bedspread.

"That doesn't make any sense," Mickey said. "It's not very deep there, even when the stream is at its highest. She was either there or she was washed over. And if she was washed over, they'd have found her right away, her head all busted and stuff on the rocks."

"It's a *mystery*," Gwen said. "That's the point of the story. She just ran down the hill and tried to cross the ice, fell through and was never seen again."

"The only mystery I can see," Mickey said, "is how it could have happened on Martin Luther King's birthday before Agnes. We didn't

even have that holiday five years ago." Agnes had been a big deal and
Mickey remembered it, the water rushing down Purnell Drive, carrying
cars away. But she didn't remember the holiday, much less a little girl
dying on it.

"I think we did," Gwen said. "I'm pretty sure we did."

"How would you know? You didn't live here then."

"My father told me. He heard about it down at the hospital. They
were talking about how we had a school holiday next week and someone
said that it was so sad, how a little black girl died on Martin Luther King
Day the first or second time we had it. Just ran down a hill, right into
the water. And her named for the goddess of wisdom, too. That's irony,
my dad says. Do you know what irony is?"

"Of course," Mickey said.

She didn't. And even though Mickey understood Gwen was asking
only because she liked to explain things, not because she thought less of
Mickey for not knowing them, she wasn't going to admit her ignorance
this time. Gwen knew lots of things and she liked to share them. If she
had her way, they would play school in the afternoons, but the last thing
Mickey wanted to do was play school after being there every day.

She was so tired of Gwen explaining things to her.

Gwen was her friend, her best friend. "Your only friend," Mickey's
mom said, meanly. It wasn't her fault that there weren't any other eleven-
year-old girls around here. And Gwen was a very satisfactory friend most
of the time, with a cool house and a cool mom and amazing treats in a
big drawer in the kitchen that you were allowed to have whenever you
wanted up until thirty minutes before dinner. Gwen's mother went to
the grocery store every Saturday morning and the rule was that all the
kids in the house—Gwen, her older sister, Fee, her brother Miller before
he left for college last fall—could pick anything they wanted, and as
much as they wanted, then eat it as fast or slowly as they wanted. Gwen
always picked out one or two treats for Mickey and when Mickey looked
into the treat drawer and saw the package of circus peanuts—not real
peanuts, but the orange-y marshmallow ones—she felt like someone in
a pirate movie, staring into a chest that made your face glow gold.

Lately, though, Mickey was getting tired of Gwen's stories. Gwen
liked to talk. Mickey liked to *do* things. Not sports so much—she wasn't

good at sports. But she yearned to spend the afternoons outside, roaming the wild, overgrown park that surrounded Gwen's house. Gwen could sit inside for hours, even on a beautiful day, moving her stuffed animals and dolls around in service of a story, playing tea party and school and hospital and drugstore. She really did tell wonderful stories, although Mickey was beginning to suspect she stole them from books. The only details Mickey contributed were usually taken from *One Life to Live*.

But now it was January, a cold, snowless January. The promises of Christmas—promises that had failed to be kept, in Mickey's case—had come and gone, and the year stretched ahead, with so little to look forward to. There would be Valentine's Day—cupcakes, cards. The teacher said everyone had to give a card to everyone, which was torture for Mickey, as it meant getting money from her mom, or trying to go around her mom and wheedle it from her sort-of stepdad, Rick, who always gave her what she wanted—unless her mother decided to stop him. "On principle," she said, but the only principle Mickey could see was that her mother didn't want her to have things she wanted. That was how Christmas had gone down, her wish list ignored because her mother decided she should get "better" stuff, more expensive things. Stupid clothes and a little handheld hair dryer, which her mother used most mornings. Besides—the one-valentine-for-everyone rule? It was so unfair. It was made for girls like Gwen, who was plump and too smart, so no boys liked her. Boys liked Mickey and she didn't even try to make them. She would have gotten a Valentine's Day card from every boy in the class *without* a rule. It seemed to Mickey sometimes that all the rules were made for people like Gwen by people like Gwen—teachers and such. Like, one day, a million years ago, some teacher didn't get a Valentine's Day card from a single boy, so she made a rule that everyone had to give a card to everyone. But that was unfair to people who couldn't buy the best cards. Mickey's mom would want her to get that awful pack of silly cards, the babyish ones without envelopes, with skunks and bears and puppies saying stupid stuff.

No, if Mickey couldn't get Rick to take her to G.C. Murphy's for the good cards, she'd rather not buy any cards at all. Maybe she should convince Gwen that it was a cool thing to do—

The overhead light snapped on, making them jump.

"Why are you inside, sitting in the dark?" Gwen's mother, Tally, the kind of mother who said, "Call me Tally," had sneaked up on them. She was generally cool, Gwen's mother, but she moved about the house like a cat, surprising them.

Gwen hid the flashlight beneath her skirt before pulling the bedspread from their heads. Mickey wasn't sure why it mattered if she had the flashlight. But Gwen's family was funny that way. There were things that Mickey would never touch in a million years—fragile things, valuable things—that Gwen was allowed to handle. But then Gwen's parents would get upset because she used a flashlight. They were nicer than Mickey's mom, no doubt, but at least Mickey knew where she stood with her mom. Tally was sweet most of the time, and then she went on these tears. Mickey could see one forming now, as she moved around Gwen's room, pulling up the blinds so they snapped, grabbing and folding the quilt they had used for their game.

"Mary mecco," she said to the quilt. "Do you know what this cost?"

"We were just playing," Gwen said. Mickey was staring at the quilt. Why was it called Mary?

"The sun's out. You should be outside."

"It's cold," Gwen said. It was, really cold, and had been for a week, the kind of cold that made the inside of your nose freeze so it felt like the ceiling at Luray Caverns, all stalactites and things.

"The pond has frozen over. I saw everyone skating when I drove up to the store. You should go skating."

It sounded like a suggestion, but Mickey knew it wasn't.

"I don't have skates," Mickey said. She really didn't.

"There's probably an old pair around that would fit you. Maybe even mine, although we'd have to roll up a pair of socks and put them in the toes."

Now was the time to say that she didn't know how to skate. So why didn't she? It was hard for Mickey to say she didn't know how to do things. It was so much easier to pretend that things weren't worth doing. Like arithmetic, for example. Or making a diorama for Maryland Day. So much easier to take the zero than to try to explain that her mom didn't have an empty shoebox, much less the time to sit with her and help her make little replicas of ships, the Ark and the Dove. Gwen had gotten an

A on her diorama, but—Tally had ended up doing most of it, even making a Father Andrew out of the kind of plastic doll you found on wedding cakes.

"That's okay. I'll just go home," Mickey said.

"Don't be silly," Tally said. "I already called your mother and said you were having dinner with us."

"Will you skate with us, Mom?" Gwen's voice was hopeful. Tally was very pretty and, although not particularly young, she looked very young, with her long hair and slender figure. She looked younger than Mickey's mom, in some ways, and Mickey's mom was always one of the youngest moms. But her mom was prettier, Mickey decided with a sudden, fierce loyalty. She never loved her own mom more than when she was around Tally Robison in one of her moods.

"No, I'm busy," Tally said. Doing what, Mickey wondered. Her mom worked, but Gwen's mom just sort of—floated. Gwen said she was writing a book, but that was the kind of lie that Gwen would tell. Oh, Tally did peck away at a typewriter some afternoons, but real people, people you knew, didn't write books and it was silly to pretend they did. Mickey wasn't sure who, exactly, wrote books, but it wasn't normal people. People on television shows, maybe, or the president.

Tally's old skates actually fit Mickey without a pair of socks in them, although there was a little extra room in the toe. "It's the fit at the ankle that matters," Tally said, tying the skates tight while Mickey and Gwen sat on a broken concrete ledge that everyone apparently used for this purpose. Gwen was ready first and she skated backward away from the ledge. Show-off.

"I worked at a rink when I was growing up in Boston and no one could lace a skate as tight as I could. I was also the only girl who ever drove the Zamboni."

"What's a Zamboni?"

"A machine that cleans the ice."

"Is it hard to drive?"

"Not particularly."

"Then why didn't they let girls drive it?"

"Sexism," Tally said. "Mickey—don't you want to skate?"

"Oh, sure."

"Then why don't you?"

"Oh, I'm just—just warming up," she said. Gwen had already launched herself across the ice. Gwen wasn't athletic, but she had learned to skate somehow and she made her way into the middle of the pond without falling. And it was okay to fall, apparently. People were falling all over the place, not just little kids. Up toward the far end of the pond, near the bridge that led to Mickey's house, boys were playing hockey.

Tally gave Mickey a hard look. "It's okay if you're not good at it. Falling is part of learning."

And everyone should get a valentine from everyone.

But Mickey said only: "It's just been a long time."

Mickey knew that Tally would help her—but only if Mickey admitted she didn't know how to skate. And then Tally might summon Gwen back, order her to teach Mickey, which would be worse somehow. She would rather sit here a thousand years than admit that there was something else Gwen could do that she couldn't. Wasn't it enough that Gwen made A's and won the school poster contest and wrote poems that could get put up on the bulletin board even though they didn't rhyme? She wasn't supposed to be good at outdoor things, too.

"I had a treat just a little bit ago," she said.

"So?"

"My mom says ice-skating is like swimming. You can get cramps."

"Oh, Mickey—"

Fiercely: "My mom *says*."

So Tally left Mickey sitting on the concrete ledge, saying only: "Don't bang the blades against the concrete. It will dull them. Walk back when the sun goes down. It's not safe to stay here after dark."

It was cold, sitting still, especially if she couldn't swing her legs. Mickey could change back into her shoes and boots, walk home. Tally Robison wasn't the boss of her. But Tally would have called Mickey's mother by now, told her about dinner, and her mom would be mad at Mickey for leaving the pond without a grown-up's permission. At least, she would say she was mad about that. Mickey knew she would really be mad about having to make Mickey's dinner when she thought she was off the hook.

Could it really be that hard, skating? Mickey managed to stand, only to have her ankles collapse until her feet felt like two L's standing back to back. Stupid Tally, who had laced her skates, announcing all along how good she was at lacing skates. Mickey edged back to the concrete ledge, retied them. Better. But she still couldn't figure out how to move in them. Gwen seemed to skate without picking her feet up at all. How did that work? Mickey tried to walk toward her, picking her feet up and down—and fell immediately.

"Damn it," she said, and a nearby mom looked at her with horror. Mickey ignored her. She knew worse curses.

She retreated again, removed the skates. Why couldn't she just wear her shoes and boots on the ice? Yes, she knew it would be slippery, but it wasn't like she had never walked down an icy sidewalk. She removed the skates and put on her boots. It was amazing how loose and free her ankles felt after being inside the skates. She stood, walked onto the ice, and caught herself before she fell. Okay, this was going to be hard. But she soon found that if she rose on her tiptoes and ran, she could then slide for great distances. A few adults called after her, said things like, "You're going to hurt yourself," or "You really should have on skates," but Mickey never had a problem ignoring adults. Besides, she wasn't falling, not that much, no more than Gwen, with her fancy white skates. People began watching her, Mickey, the girl in boots. She even joined in a game of Crack the Whip, taking the last position and letting the skaters pull her along, then laughing hysterically when they released her, flying so far up the pond that she almost ended up in the hockey game, where the Halloran boys, who were sometimes called the Hooligan boys, yelled at her and shook their sticks. Who cared? It was like flying. She had invented a new sport, shoe-skating. It was so much fun that Gwen had to remind Mickey that they were to leave at dusk, that dinner was waiting.

The cold snap hung on for the rest of the week and Mickey went back to the pond every afternoon, refining her new sport. Gwen came, too, but she seemed to be mad at Mickey. She was just jealous, Mickey decided. Anyone could ice-skate, but only Mickey could shoe-skate. By the third or fourth day, she almost never fell at all. "She must have a lower center of gravity than other people," she heard one mother say to another. "Or she's just graceful, like a dancer," the other said. "It's almost as if her feet aren't touching the ice at all." That was how it felt to Mickey—as if her feet barely touched at all.

The pond was still frozen the next Thursday, when they had off for Martin Luther King Jr.'s birthday. Mickey had permission to spend the entire day at Gwen's house, and she wanted to go straight back to the pond. The weather was beginning to warm, so the pond wouldn't be frozen much longer. But Gwen dawdled, allowing the hours to slip by, and suddenly it was lunchtime and Tally was in one of her moods, which meant they had to sit down and have tomato soup and grilled cheese sandwiches, neither of them normal. The soup was spicy, the cheese smelled funny, and even the bread was weird. But, finally, Gwen and Mickey were at the pond. Gwen sat on the concrete ledge while Mickey practiced her "figures," tracing numbers and letters, not that anyone could see them. But she could. On a weekday, in the early afternoon, the pond was almost empty; only the Halloran boys there, no grown-ups. Only the kids got off for King's birthday.

Gwen continued to sit, refusing to put on her skates.

"I'm tired of doing this," she said. "It's boring."

"Try doing it like I do," Mickey said, knowing Gwen couldn't, enjoying her chance to be superior. She put her arms out, rose up on tiptoe, took her tiny little steps, then lowered her heels so she was flat-footed. She could cross almost the entire breadth of the frozen pond. She looked back to see if Gwen was admiring her but saw that she had turned her back on the pond. In fact, she had her face pressed into her hands. Stupid Gwen. She was probably crying, baby that she was. If the Halloran boys noticed, they would tease her, then start in on Mickey. Plus, why was Gwen crying? She had her ice skates; she could come out if she wanted. She just hated for Mickey to be good at anything. And when Mickey was good at something—shoe-skating, getting Valentine's Day cards, knowing the names of plants and bugs—Gwen said it didn't count. Gwen was so unfair. Gwen was a bad friend. Mickey was going to go over there and tell her so. She rose up on her toes, got her usual running start, and—

She had not noticed how thin the ice was getting here, near the shore, above the dam. It seemed to wobble beneath her, sort of like hard Jell-O. Then, just like that, it broke beneath her and she plunged into the water.

• • •

She was drowning.

That was her conscious thought, her only thought: *I am drowning.*

She looked up: There was sky above her, or at least a patch of promising brightness. She had gone straight down, so the hole was still above her head. The danger, she knew, was that she would be sucked toward the dam and under the ice and she would not be able to break through. She had to fight her way back to that brightness. Mickey could swim, she was a decent swimmer, but her clothes were so heavy now as they took on water, and when her toe found the mushy bottom and pushed off, she felt heavier than she had on the surface, quite the opposite of what she usually felt in the water, where she flipped and turned like an astronaut in zero gravity. She rose slowly, slowly, slowly, but her head finally broke the surface and she was able to heave her body out of the water back onto the ice, where she stayed low, afraid to move. Gwen was screaming, but doing nothing. The hockey-playing boys didn't even seem to know what was going on. At any rate, they didn't stop their game.

Mickey flattened herself on the ice as much as possible. Maybe if she moved upstream, toward the bridge, the ice wouldn't be as weak. She probably should retreat toward the middle of the pond, where the ice would be thicker, less affected by the thaw. But the shore was so tantalizingly close. Mickey edged toward it on a diagonal line, hugging the ice. That should work. She crawled like an inchworm, humping her butt in and down in the air. Flattening, humping, flattening, humping. Oh, she hoped the Halloran boys didn't look now. They would never let her live it down.

She was only three feet from shore when the ice gave way again. The second fall was worse, in part because she belly-flopped in, so her face and body took the shock, but also because she knew now how hard it would be to get out. She heard Gwen screaming, screaming, screaming and then it was quiet, the way it always was in movies when things happened underwater. Her feet found the bottom again. She was over her head, only barely. She should be able to push to the surface, but the water was stronger than she was and it was taking her now, moving her, bullying her, forcing her up against the dam, away from the light.

She heard her own voice: *I'm going to die.*

No, you're not, a voice in another part of her head insisted. *Push.*

I can't. I tried. I'll just hit the ice.

Then break it.

What?

Push. With your hand. It'll give way. But you gotta hit it hard.

This was not her voice. How was a voice in her head not her voice?

Show me, Mickey pleaded. But was she asking herself or someone else?

Can't. But you can do it.

She raised her arms above her head. How could this lazy stream of water have so much strength below the surface? She pushed off, tapped the ice, but nothing happened.

Harder.

I can't. I can't.

Yes, you can. You have to. It's the only way out. You can't swim back now. You gotta break the ice.

I can't.

You wanna live, you better. I can tell you this much—you don't want to stay here.

Mickey looked straight ahead and saw a pair of green eyes almost glowing in the murky water. They could be—what? The eyes of a catfish or whatever else might live here in the long-polluted stream. But she knew these were not a catfish's eyes and they scared her so much that she found the strength to push toward the surface again, the voice calling after her, insistently in her ear, almost as if someone were riding piggyback.

Make fists. Hit that ice like it's somebody you want to hurt. You ever want to hurt anyone?

Yes. Yes, I've wanted to hurt people.

Me, too, the voice said. *Me, too.*

And with that, Mickey cracked the ice above her head, broke the surface, then let the water pin her into the corner formed by the dam and the concrete ledge. There, clinging to the rough side, she caught her breath and let Gwen help her out. She probably could have gotten out on her own, but it felt good to see Gwen's arms reaching for her.

"Don't tell my mom," Gwen said.

"Of course." Again, this was one of the things that Gwen's parents would get upset about, while Mickey's mother wouldn't mind, given that she was alive.

"We'll go in the house through the basement, wash your clothes and put them through the dryer. You can sit down there in a towel until they're ready."

"Sure," Mickey said. "Gwen, when I was under the ice—"

"You had a tetanus last year, right?"

"Yeah, and I didn't get cut, I just swallowed a lot of water. I'll be okay. Gwen—that story, about that girl. The one who ran into the water. Did it really happen?"

"I told you it did. My father told me about it. You're lucky you're not her."

"Why was she running like that? Across the ice?"

"Just playing some stupid game with her brother. Tag or something. I don't know. She tried to run across the ice and she fell in. You really shouldn't wear shoes on the ice."

Not shoes, Mickey thought. It wasn't about the shoes. Something else happened to that girl. Atheena. How did she know her name. She just did. There was a girl, named Atheena, who had tried to run across the pond and fallen in. Why had Atheena been running?

But Atheena, who had ridden Mickey's back up and out of that filthy water, she hadn't waited around to tell her all she wanted to know. There wasn't time to tell the white girl about how Atheena's brother had brought a boy to the house, a boy he was specifically forbidden to bring around. Marvin. Ugly, thuggish Marvin. Bobby wasn't supposed to bring anybody to the house when Mama wasn't there, and Marvin wasn't welcome even when Mama was there. Atheena didn't want to be in the house with them, so she went outside and sat on the back steps, hands thrust into her pockets because she had forgotten her gloves. It was only one in the afternoon. Mama wouldn't be home until five o'clock.

The boys came banging out the back door. There was a small, sad tree in the yard, naked and cold. Marvin broke a branch from it. Mama would be mad. She loved that tree, a dogwood, bloomed pink every spring. "Let's play a game," Marvin said. "Like hockey. And your sister will be the puck."

Atheena turned to go back in the house, but Bobby blocked the way. There was nothing to do but run past Marvin and through the back gate, then into the woods beyond Hillside Road. The boys were slower, in part because Bobby had to grab his own branch, and carrying the sticks slowed them down, but she could hear them behind her.

She ran down the hill, almost blind in her panic, while they shouted at her, saying terrible things about what they would do. She was smaller than they were and able to duck the branches that snapped and whipped around them, but what good was being faster when she ended up trapped between the pond and the boys? She could run along the shore, but she wasn't so fast that she could get back to the road before they caught up with her. She would have to go across the ice. That was the only way. There were houses on the other side, and houses meant people. They couldn't do whatever they meant to do to her if people were around. It seemed safer to walk along the dam line, where Atheena would have something to grab if she slipped. She inched her way across, her brother and Marvin standing on the shore, shouting horrible things at her but scared to follow. She was almost to the other side when the ice seemed to hesitate beneath her, just like the girl in her class who never knew the answer to anything. "And what is the name of Dr. King's most famous speech, Quintana?" *Ummmmmmmm*. "We are working on our seven times today. What is seven times seven, Quintana?" *Ummmmmmmmm*. And then Mrs. Burke's pointer would slap across her desk. "Pay attention, Quintana, or I am going to have to send a note to your mother."

So the ice said *Ummmmmmmmmmm* and then cracked beneath Atheena's feet, the sound as sharp as Mrs. Burke's pointer slapping across a desk. Atheena plunged into water colder than anything she had ever known. An igloo could not be this cold. The cold seemed to make the water thick, too, even where it was not ice. And although the surface was only six inches from her head, it might as well have been a hundred miles. She didn't know how to swim, didn't have the first idea what to do. Her legs, so fleet on the ground, pedaled as if on an imaginary bike; her arms waved as if she were trying to signal a school bus that was pulling away from the curb, leaving her behind. The water pushed her, lazy but determined. No matter how she battled it, the water came back, nudging and pushing, telling her where to go until she could go no farther. The dam's rickety boards caught on her clothes and hair, held her there.

And there she stayed, the little girl who ran into the pond. Because she was silly, because she didn't know better, because she couldn't swim. She could hear it all, the stories told over and over again. Did you hear about the girl who just ran into the pond? That was Robert's story, not hers. She heard her brother's lying words, heard her mother's tears. She watched the light change above her, signaling the change of seasons, calculated when the dogwood bloomed—and when its flowers dropped. One year, two years. She saw the light grow dim when the ice closed over her again, saw children's feet, agonizingly close, moving above her. Winter, spring, summer, fall. Her mother's tears were not as loud or frequent; people spoke of her less. Three years, four years. The story stopped being told.

Did the girl know, the one who had fallen, that Atheena had grabbed onto her back and ridden her to the surface, then just kept rising? Had she felt Atheena's fingers digging into her coat and hair, her breath in her ear? They had broken the surface together, but where the other girl reached for her friend, Atheena kept rising. The last thing she saw, as she looked down at the pond that had held her so long, was that soggy white girl clinging to her friend—chest heaving, hair streaming water. Did that girl even know how lucky she was to be alive? Probably not. But she would say she did and that was all that mattered. Would she remember Atheena? Probably forever. There would be a new story now, about a different girl, a new warning. There would always be cautions and stories, stories told just to scare other children. Atheena understood that now. The girl who played with matches. The boy who didn't look both ways. The girls who talked to strangers. The boys who walked home in the storm. Atheena had been held in place not by the water or the splintery boards, but by her own story. Now that there was another story to replace hers, Atheena was free. Atheena was gone.

Atheena could run.

BELL, BOOK, AND CANDLEPIN

TONI L. P. KELNER

Though Toni L. P. Kelner is not a native New Englander, she has grown fond of candlepin bowling since moving to Massachusetts. Not that she's any better at the game than she is at ten-pin bowling—she's no good at any sport—but at least she isn't as likely to drop the ball on her foot. *Games Creatures Play* is the sixth anthology she's coedited with Charlaine Harris, and this story is her second about the Allaway Kith of Salem, Massachusetts. Kelner won the Agatha Award for Best Short Story, and other stories have been nominated for the Anthony, the Macavity, and the Derringer. Under her own name, she's the author of the "Where Are They Now?" Mysteries and the Laura Fleming series, and as Leigh Perry, she writes the Family Skeleton Mysteries.

I should have noticed the curse as soon as I walked into the Candlepin Castle, but it's not like I've got a lot of experience with evil spells. Or with any spells. I'm Elspeth Allaway, and we witches of the Allaway Kith don't wave wands or spout magic words. We have Affinities. Sure, all of us can sense magic and smell lies, but the big action is in Affinities, and each one is different, as if we were a magical Legion of Superheroes. My mother can weave emotions into rugs and blankets, and my cousin Maura's thing is absorbing energy via phones. Another cousin is the Pied Piper of plants—I've seen vines reach for her when she walks by. My own Affinity was what was responsible for my being so eager to get to work that I didn't notice the curse.

Well, that and being pissed at my mother. She'd called just as I was heading out the door and had ripped me a new one. Oh, she hadn't yelled or screamed—I'd have preferred it if she had. Instead she used that calm, even tone of hers to tell me how disappointed she was that I'd used my Affinity in a non-life-affirming way the previous weekend. It hadn't been that big a deal, just a little prank, but she'd found out somehow—I was guessing my perfect cousin Ennis was behind it. Anyway, Mom decided I needed a refresher course in the Law of Return, as if she hadn't started brainwashing me the second after the midwife slapped me on the butt, and she ended up lecturing me for fifteen solid minutes. After that I was jonesing for some serious decibels.

See, my Affinity is for sound. I can block it in like a set of noise-canceling headphones or go the other way and amplify better than any woofer or tweeter ever made. I also collect sounds—from voices to squeaky doors to musical notes to sound effects—and then replay those sounds at any volume from subliminal to ear-shattering. This lets me play great jokes or perform immature stunts, depending on whether you laugh at fart noises.

I like being around noise any time, but when I'm upset, nothing soothes me like a little cacophony. Hence my pleasure at arriving for my shift at the Candlepin Castle, West Sommers's premier candlepin bowling alley. In fact, it's West Sommers's only candlepin bowling alley, but that's no reason to abandon a semi-decent slogan. The pay is lousy and the hours are worse, and I don't even particularly like bowling, but you can't beat the noise. Balls crashing into the pins, bowlers cheering for their strikes or yelling at those last two pins to fall over even though it never works, the ball return smacking the balls together, and people talking over everything else. On weekends, you get loud music on top of that, and we host an awful lot of kids' birthday parties. That makes it heaven to those who prefer the noise-seeking lifestyle.

Somebody who'd never played might think the candlepin style of bowling New Englanders prefer would be quieter than ten-pin, but it's a trade-off. The balls are smaller, only about four and a half inches in diameter, but since they don't have finger holes, you get that satisfying thunk of solid balls. The pins are smaller, too, but the machines don't clear them away between the balls, so that gives an extra dollop of sound. Best of all, each bowler gets three balls in a box, which means more collisions for me to savor.

Since I'd had exams all week, I hadn't worked since the previous

Saturday, so I paused just inside the door to soak in some of the glory. Though it was early in the evening and there wasn't much business, the Castle is a barn of a building, with creaking floors and echoes and clanking ball returns. I'd figured being a few more minutes late wouldn't matter, but my manager Amar really gave me the stink-eye as I clocked in.

I took a look at the schedule posted by the time clock and was glad to see that I'd be working the counter with Jake while Rayleigh and Belle had the snack bar. Rayleigh and Belle are fine, but they've been BFFs since kindergarten and when I work with either of them, they always seem vaguely disappointed that I don't know all their in-jokes. Jake and I, on the other hand, have our own in-jokes.

With Amar on duty, that was more people than we usually needed for a Thursday night, but we had a league championship scheduled.

With one thing and another, it was probably fifteen minutes after five when I joined Jake at the front counter, where he was spraying disinfectant into rental shoes.

"Hey. What's up?"

"You're late," he said.

I looked around the Castle. There was one lone family foursome on lane one, and maybe half a dozen pair of shoes still needed to be sprayed. "Dude, you could handle this in a coma."

"That's not the point, Elspeth!"

"Okay, I'm sorry." With anybody else, I'd have snapped back, but I'm usually willing to give Jake the benefit of the doubt. Werewolves get touchy at that time of the month. "Full moon coming?"

"Stupid much? It's just past the new moon. I'd think a witch would pay attention."

"Dude!" He and I were the only arcane types working at the Castle, and as far as we knew, the only ones at Cassidy College. We'd sniffed each other out during freshman orientation—literally, in Jake's case—and had been buds ever since. Normally that friendship included not mentioning each other's unusual abilities, but Jake seemed to have forgotten. Fortunately no other employees were close enough to hear, and the members of the foursome were squabbling too enthusiastically to hear anybody else. "If the moon isn't calling, why are you being such a butt?"

When he turned away from the shoes to glare at me, I felt his magic rising and could see his outlines start to blur, as if he were about to change into a wolf right in front of me. Then he took a deep breath and settled back into his usual lanky, gray-eyed, messy-haired self.

"Sorry," he said. "It's been a lousy couple of days. Hell, it's been a lousy week!"

"What's been going on?"

"All manner of crap. Amar got mad at Theresa Monday night and fired her in the middle of her shift. He said she was skimming from the cash register."

"Was she?"

"Maybe, but it wasn't cool to fire her in public like that. Then some douchebag accused us of rigging the scoring system. The man can't bowl for beans, and he blames us."

"Typical."

"On Tuesday, two guys in the Seniors League got into a fight over interference, and we had to call the cops."

"Seriously?"

"Neither guy would back down, even when the cops handcuffed them, but once they got outside and realized they were on their way to jail, they calmed down. Nobody pressed charges or anything."

"That's good. The last thing the Castle needs is players getting arrested."

"It gets worse. Last night there were two more fights—one started while the cops were on the way to deal with the first one. By the time it was all settled, the cops were making noises about shutting us down."

"Can they do that?"

"If they can't, the lawsuit might."

"What lawsuit?"

"A kid got his finger smashed in the ball return, and his mother is threatening to sue."

"That's insane."

"Then this afternoon, there were two birthday parties booked, and both birthday kids wanted the unicorn party room. Not only were the kids screaming, but I thought their fathers were going to throw down in front of them. So yeah, everybody is in a pissy mood. If it were up to me, I'd cancel tonight's championship, but you know Amar doesn't care about my opinion." His voice started to rise again. "Nobody listens to me!"

"Jeez, Jake!" I said. What was he sniping at me for? I hadn't even been there, so none of it was my fault. And why was everybody acting like it was such a big deal for me to be a couple of minutes late? Maybe I should just walk out and let Jake work the counter by himself. Wouldn't it be funny if he lost it, went furry, and clawed up everybody in the place?

That's when I stopped myself. Not even in my most warped vengeful daydreams did I think it would be a hoot for a werewolf to attack innocent people, let alone what being found out would do to Jake and the rest of his Pack.

At last my magic-sensing kicked in, and I realized that something was seriously wrong. Not trusting myself to speak, I walked out from behind the counter and went through the front door and into the parking lot. Everything was normal, a little too quiet for my tastes, but good for most people.

I stepped back inside and felt myself growing agitated and angry. Out again. Calm. Inside. Bitchy.

That settled it.

I went back behind the counter, where Jake was spraying the last pair of shoes. Nobody was within range, but I used my Affinity to block anybody from hearing us—Jake calls it creating a cone of silence from some movie he saw. "We've got a problem. We've been cursed."

"Yeah, cursed by idiots," he snarled.

"No, I mean the Castle is under a curse."

"For real? Is that why we've had all these disasters?"

"And why you've been such a jerkface."

"I have not been—"

"Would you mind aiming the spray somewhere else?"

He looked at his hand as if he'd forgotten he was still holding the can of disinfectant, and carefully put it onto a shelf. "I guess I have been kind of an asshole. So is this curse like a spell? You told me you guys don't do spells?"

"We don't, but other witches can."

"Can you do a counterspell?"

"No spells, remember? And I don't think any of us Allaways have an anti-curse Affinity, even if there were any nearby." My family lived in Salem, Massachusetts—which is both funny and appropriate—but I go to college in West Sommers, which is a three-hour drive in good traffic. "Do you know anything about cursing?"

"According to my Pack, more than I should."

I resisted the urge to snipe at him for being a smart-ass, figuring my irritation was probably the curse affecting me. "I've never run into one before—"

"Then how do you know it's a curse?"

"Go outside for a minute."

He looked skeptical, but he did it. Then he did it again before coming back to the counter. "Man, curses suck. So what do we do?"

"No idea."

He continued to look at me expectantly.

I sighed. "I guess I can call my aunt Hester after work. She knows a lot of things." She was the logical one to consult, but I was hoping I'd come up with a different plan before end of shift.

On lane one, the foursome's quarrel came to a head. The parents started screaming at each other as the smaller boy tackled the larger one and started pummeling him.

"On second thought," I said, "why don't I call Aunt Hester right now while you take care of that?"

Castle employees aren't supposed to make personal calls on the clock, and I didn't want to try to explain to Amar how talking to my aunt was actually work-related, so I took my cell phone into the staff bathroom. It's more private than the customer facilities and usually cleaner.

"Aunt Hester? This is Elspeth."

"Hello, dear. I've been waiting for you to call."

Aunt Hester is actually my great-great-aunt, and she creeps me out. Her Affinity is to see the future and she tends to rub it in. I've always wondered if she ever exaggerates how much she sees. I mean, how would I know if she was really expecting my call?

As if to stomp out my doubts, she said, "So you've got a curse. Nasty things, aren't they?"

I told her what was going on, and she told me as much as she was willing to. The thing about Aunt Hester is that she never tells everything she knows, which drives me nuts. It's a game of I've Got a Secret that never ends.

When I'd gotten all I was going to get, I said, "Thanks for the info. I'll call later to let you know how things turn out."

"I already know, dear. You better go now. Your friend is quite upset."

That was when Rayleigh from the snack bar burst into the bathroom, bawling like crazy.

I should have checked to see what her deal was, but crying is one noise I can do without. Besides, I figured that whatever she was crying about, it was likely another example of the curse at work, so it would be better to get back to Jake to make sure he was holding on to both his temper and his human form.

The fighting foursome had left, I was glad to see, so I didn't bother with the cone of silence. Jake was growling about some shoes that had been placed in the wrong slots, though not much more than usual. I exerted just a bit of my Affinity to conjure a creeper hiss from the game Minecraft right behind him, which usually gets a snicker. Today, he just looked impatient.

"Well?" he demanded.

"Aunt Hester said that it sounds like a Perturbatio curse, which messes with our emotions. It doesn't create meanness, but it does intensify any bit of nastiness you've already got. So instead of being a little irritated when somebody is late, you get uber huffy."

"Come on, Elspeth! I'm under a curse. You can't hold what I do under a curse against me."

"You're right. The curse is just making me bitchy." He looked suspicious, so I kept going. "At least we don't have to worry about the roof falling in or the ball return throwing balls at our customers."

"What about the kid who got his finger caught?"

"Kids do that all the time. Maybe the curse intensified his tendency to stick his finger where it doesn't belong, or his mother's being sick of watching him every second. Besides, from what you said, it wasn't the finger that was the problem. It was the reaction that was way out of whack."

"You got that right. The woman was so mad I thought she was going to have a stroke. So how do we stop a curse?"

"If we're lucky, there's a cursed item hidden somewhere in the Castle."

"You've got a strange idea of lucky."

"If it's an amulet or something, all we have to do is find it and either destroy it or put it someplace where it won't bother anybody until the magic wears off." Aunt Hester had used that as an excuse for the day's second lecture on the Law of Return. As if I'd been seriously planning to put a cursed item under the bed of an ex-roommate who'd regularly eaten all my Cheerios and borrowed my clothes without asking.

"What if we're not lucky?" Jake asked.

"She said, and I quote, 'Oh, I can't break a curse, dear. If it were me, I'd just wait it out.'"

"That's it?"

"Pretty much." Okay, she had said some other stuff, but nothing that Jake needed to know. Still, I was glad it was witches who could smell lies and not werewolves, so he wouldn't notice that I'd left a detail or two out.

"Then let's hope we're lucky. How do we find the amulet or whatever it is?"

"That's where you come in, bloodhound boy." Even in human form, other than when lies were involved, Jake's sense of smell had mine beat by a mile.

"Man, I spend half my time trying not to inhale in this place. You have no idea how rank those rental shoes smell to me, and the nachos in the snack bar aren't much better."

"Sorry. I can't try to sense it because the whole building is affected. I could wander around and see where I'm most pissed off, but—"

"Never mind. What does it smell like?"

"Corruption and evil."

He gave me a look.

"That's what Aunt Hester said! Just see if you can smell anything more disgusting than the shoes."

Under the pretense of emptying trash cans, Jake spent the next half an hour wandering around the Castle, but he was shaking his head when he came back.

"Nada."

"Did you check everywhere? The party rooms? The bathrooms? The trophy case?"

"I even sniffed our balls."

"Don't all werewolves do that?" I really shouldn't have said that to a guy under a curse, especially when I'd forgotten to put the cone of silence back up, but it just came out.

Fortunately, he laughed and unlike crying, laughter is a sound I like. I thought I felt the curse lift a little, just for a second, but it sprang back like a mystical rubber band.

That's probably why the other Castle employees looked at us as if we were crazy before going back to their curse-caused crankiness.

Jake said, "That means the building itself is cursed, right?"

"Which means we get to wait for it to wear off."

"How long will that take?"

"Aunt Hester says it depends on the experience of the practitioner, the strength of the motive for the curse, the phase of the moon . . ."

"She doesn't know?"

If she did, she wasn't telling, but I didn't tell Jake that. Nor did I tell him that he'd wasted half an hour sniffing when Aunt Hester must have known there was no cursed item. Getting him mad would only give the curse more ammunition to work with. "She did say that curses start out weak, grow stronger until they reach a peak, and then fade at that same rate." Extra casually, I said, "Didn't you say that things started to go bad on Monday?"

"I think so. I worked a half shift on Sunday, and it seemed normal."

"Are things better today, or worse?"

A pan or something clattered onto the floor in the snack bar, and this time it was Belle who ran for the bathroom crying.

"Worse," Jake said, which I'd already figured out.

"Then we don't know if it's at its peak yet."

"So it could get worse?"

I nodded.

"Know what? I think I feel a bad bout of the flu coming on." He reached over and put his hand on my forehead. "If I'm not mistaken, you've got a fever, too."

I pushed his hand away. "Stop that. I'm not leaving."

"Elspeth, you said you can't get rid of the curse. What's the point of sticking around?"

"I don't know," I admitted, "but at least I can keep an eye on people and make sure they don't get hurt."

"Let Amar do it. That's why he gets the big bucks."

"He's as affected by the curse as anybody, Jake."

"And it's not getting to you?"

"It's making me a little crazy, but at least I know what's happening. The thing is, I feel kind of responsible. Being a witch and all." That wasn't the whole truth, and the smell of my lie wafted across the counter, at least for me. "Besides, I don't want the cops to shut the place down. It's the noisiest job in town." The only place close was the movie house, but the new manager liked showing deep, meaningful films without a single explosion or shootout. "But it's different for you, having to deal with all this as a werewolf. I don't blame you for wanting to get the hell out of Dodge."

"Are you saying you don't think I can control my wolf?" he said ominously, and stepped way inside my personal bubble. "Like I'm some kind of animal?" He stepped even closer, and I backed up against the counter as far as I could go. "Like I'm a monster?"

"No, no, you're good, you're cool, you're—"

"Psych!" He grinned as toothily as any wolf.

"You son of a bitch!" I said, shoving him back.

"Damn straight. And if you can take it, I can take it."

"Okay, then. We've got this covered."

We traded fist bumps, but he wasn't fooling me any more than I was fooling him. The league championship started in less than an hour, which meant that eight four-bowler teams would be arriving any minute, along with their families and friends. So we were about to have seventy to a hundred people in the Castle, all of whose emotions were going to be mangled and magnified by the curse.

It would have been nice if we could have relied on Amar, since he was the boss, but apparently the curse had intensified his laziness. Jake said he'd barely left his office all day. As for Rayleigh and Belle, they'd spent most of the week's shifts in tears, so we weren't expecting much support there, either.

"At least it's the Thursday night league," I said. Thursday's teams played for fun—they didn't take the game or themselves seriously. "They won't be too bad." If Aunt Hester had foreseen me saying that, she must have laughed her ass off.

Trouble started right after the teams and their supporters started showing up. First off, the Bowling Banshees and the Good Vibrations nearly came to blows over which team was going to bowl on lane one, even though it was no better than lane two or any other lane. We used a coin toss to decide that one, but only after each team inspected my quarter to make sure it wasn't double-headed.

Then the Sonic Boomers started screaming because their best bowler hadn't shown up, so our clock had to be wrong, even though every cell phone in the Castle showed the same time. When the guy finally arrived two minutes after the official start time, the other team captains wanted him disqualified. I got Amar out of his office long enough to wave around a copy of the league's rules that stated a player could be up to fifteen minutes late without penalty. That quieted everybody down for a few minutes.

The spectators were just as contentious. One woman tried to butt in line at the snack bar and ended up with soda "accidentally" spilled on her brand-new shoes. She couldn't decide who to hit up for a replacement pair—the woman who'd poured the soda or the Castle for not having tighter lids on our drinks. By that time the curse was getting to me enough that I had to resist the impulse to tell her that she should count herself lucky to have an excuse to throw the ugly things away.

Finally the serious bowling began, only fifteen minutes later than planned, which Jake and I considered a triumph under the circumstances. The format was simple. Each team would play three strings, and the team with the highest combined score won. All eight teams would start Game One at the same time, but as each team finished, it could move on to Game Two, and then Game Three. Each team had a judge to keep an eye out for foot faults, lob line penalties, deliberate fouls, and so on. Since the league wasn't usually that competitive—the prize was a six-pack of beer per player—they hadn't hired pro judges. Instead, they were using volunteers from another league, which was supposed to keep them objective. The system would have worked great any other night. As it was, fights with the judges began almost immediately.

Not only did the players argue with their own judges every time they were called out, but they tried to rat out the other teams for supposedly witnessed rule breaking ranging from delivering the ball before the pinsetter had completed its cycle to violating right-of-way. Of course the judges were just as messed up by the curse as the players were—one of them insisted he had authority to ban a player from candlepin bowling for life.

It was a nightmare, and several times Jake and I were on the verge of pulling the fire alarm and clearing the place out. Only the knowledge that we'd lose our jobs kept us from it. Instead we kept fighting emotional fires as they ignited.

After a while we fell into a routine. I stayed at the counter and used my Affinity to listen for trouble. It was pretty slow there anyway, since most league players had their own shoes. The only problem was the one woman who kept asking for shoes that were smaller than her actual feet, and then complained that all our shoes were mismarked. Even without the smell of her lie, I could see that she wore at least an 8. But she swore her feet were tiny, and tried every pair of 6s we had before starting in on the 7s.

Once she'd squeezed into a 7½, I could concentrate listening in on everything happening in the building. Not everywhere at once, of course—that would have driven me insane. Instead I focused on one corner of the room at a time, or the snack bar, or the bathrooms, and so forth. It's hard to describe to anybody who doesn't have my Affinity—which is anybody else in the world—and the closest I could get when explaining it to Jake is that I was running a virtual cursor all over, and clicking on spots to listen in.

Jake stayed out on the floor, and whenever I heard something looming, I used my Affinity to tell him, making it sound as if I were right next to him but so that nobody else heard me. He said it was weird as hell to hear my voice coming out of nowhere, but it worked.

Once Jake knew where to go, he'd do his best to defuse the situation using his supernatural strength or that air of menace werewolves are so good at projecting. Once I think he growled.

I took care of any problems I could from a distance. When I saw a kid about to push another kid down, I pulled a sound snippet out of my memory to scare him—my old math teacher's voice saying, "Sit down immediately!" It worked on them just as well as it had on me back in the day.

I don't think we'd have survived if every crisis had needed intervention. Several of the upsets I overheard were pretty bad, but weren't likely to turn violent. One guy broke up with his girlfriend over the phone—if she'd been in the building, he'd have been in danger, but she was in Connecticut. An older man was convinced that somebody was out to steal his brand-new set of Epco bowling balls, but he didn't threaten anybody. He just kept his balls zipped up securely in his bag, watched the bag like a hawk, and used the Castle's balls, which probably didn't help his game any. One girl had a boyfriend with commitment issues, and apparently the curse was reinforcing her fear that she was doing something wrong. She spent the whole night asking her friends for advice, and from the things those women told her, either they were being extra bitchy because of the curse or they were the worst friends ever.

By nine, all but the last two teams had finished bowling—the Wilhelm Screamers and Jan's Grapenuts had had so many arguments with the judges and each other that they were just finishing their second strings. Though I was starting to think we'd make it through the night relatively unscathed, I hadn't given up my arcane eavesdropping, and I let my focus float toward the back of the house while Jake played guard dog up front.

The party rooms were locked tight, Amar was holed up in his office with a six-pack he thought we didn't know about, and for the first time in a while, nobody was crying in the ladies' room. I switched my attention to the men's room in time to hear a conversation already in progress.

"That bastard Foley cheated! That was a clear foot foul in the third box of the first string and everybody knows it!"

"She doesn't love me anymore—I can tell something is wrong. I spent months saving for this ring, and another month waiting for the engraving, but there's no reason to give it to her now."

Okay, it wasn't really a conversation. More like dual monologues, one from a sore loser and one from a total loser.

Griper: "He knew just what he'd done, too. Did you see him laughing?"

Whiner: "If I propose and she turns me down, I don't know what I'll do. I've never loved anybody the way I love her."

Griper: "I wanted to wipe that smirk right off of his face, but I can wait. He'll be the last bowler tonight, and I've got it all planned."

Whiner: "How can I live without her?"

Griper: "I know damned well Foley rigged the game—there's no way some kid who just started bowling last year could be that good. You can bet that his last box will be a strike. That's all right. As soon as he makes that strike, it's payback time. With everybody looking at him, nobody's going to notice the gun. One shot and he's history."

There was a kind of gasp, and I guess Whiner finally realized what the other guy was talking about. "You're kidding, right? I mean, you wouldn't really shoot him, would you?"

Griper laughed. "Of course I'm kidding. I don't even have a gun."

A horrid stench crept across the counter. Griper had been lying. Both times. He hadn't been kidding, and he damned well did have a gun. And I didn't recognize the voice.

I rushed out from behind the counter, ignoring the woman who wanted to complain about having the wrong size shoes again, but before I could get to the bathroom, Amar grabbed me by the arm.

"How many times do I have to tell you kids that there are no personal phone calls allowed on the job?"

"What?" Was my mother calling with a fresh lecture, or had it taken him that long to find out about the call I'd made hours before?

"Your crazy aunt has called me six times, and said she wouldn't let up until I gave you this message. Do I look like a secretary?" He shoved a scribbled note at me. "One more call from her, and I'll fire your ass. You hear me? Now get back to the counter and do your job!" He stomped back to his office and the waiting beer.

Without stopping to read the message, I ran to the hall outside the men's room, hoping to get a look at the guy with the gun. But nobody came out, and when I listened in, I realized nobody was inside. The murderer-to-be was mixing with the other people in the Castle, and I had no way to track him.

Jake showed up at my elbow. "What's wrong?"

"Come back to the counter." Once we were there, I conjured a cone of silence to tell him what I'd heard.

"That's it," he said. "We've got to get these people out of here now. I'm pulling the fire alarm." He headed toward the nearest wall box.

At that moment, I finally looked at the piece of paper in my hand. All it said was, "Check your texts." I pulled my phone out of my pocket and a second later, screamed "STOP!" for Jake alone. He shook his head as if his ears were ringing, which they probably were, and trotted back.

"What is wrong with you?"

"Aunt Hester sent this." I showed him the message on my phone.

Don't pull the alarm. Fire alarm + Perturbatio = riot. Cops = same effect.

"You've got to be kidding me! Now what do we do?"

"I don't know." I just knew we had to do something fast. The Screamers and the Grapenuts were starting their final strings. "Look, we know Foley is the target. All we have to do is keep an eye on him. If we see anybody aim a gun at him, we get between them."

"Screw that. I'm not letting you jump in front of a bullet. I am taking you out of here right now!"

He took my hand and started pulling me toward the front door. I yanked back as hard as I could, but I was no match for a determined werewolf.

"Stop it, Jake! I have to fix this."

"Let 'em fix it themselves."

"No, I can't let this happen! It's my fault!"

He stopped pulling me, though he didn't let go of my hand. "What are you talking about?"

"You said things started to go wrong on Monday, right?"

"Yeah."

"That's because Sunday night I did something I shouldn't have. A bunch of guys were having a party at my dorm, and they were so loud even I couldn't study with all the commotion, let alone sleep. And I had an exam first thing next morning. So I conjured up some sounds from a cop movie. Banging on the door, 'Open up, this is the police!' even a barking police dog."

"That's awesome. I bet you scared the crap out of them."

"Not awesome. One of them was on academic probation or something, and he was afraid he'd get expelled, so he climbed out of the window and fell."

"Was he hurt?"

"He sprained his ankle, but it could have been worse." In her lecture, my mother had told me in detail how much worse it could have been. "So the curse is my fault."

"How do you figure that? There's no way that guy could have known who did it. And why would he curse the Castle instead of going after you?"

"You don't understand. I know the guy didn't curse us—he's got no magic. It was the Law of Return."

He looked blank. Apparently werewolves live by different principles.

I said, "The Law of Return says we should only send good energy into the world so that only good energy will return to us. It's like the Golden Rule on steroids. Instead of just 'Do unto others . . .' it's 'Whatever you do unto others will turn around and bite you on the ass.' When I played that prank, I let bad energy into the world, and the curse is bad energy coming back at me. In a karmic sense."

"I'm no witch, but according to my philosophy class last year, karma doesn't usually run on such a tight schedule."

"I know it sounds crazy—"

"Because it is."

"—but when I realized the curse started Monday, I asked Aunt Hester if the Law of Return had anything to do with what was going on, and she said, 'Of course it does.' That means it's my fault, and if I don't stop that guy, that murder will be on me, too. Now let go of me before I call for help. Really loudly."

"If I do, you're going to try to protect that guy Foley, aren't you?"

I nodded.

He made a face, but he released me. "Okay, let's do this."

"Jake, you're the best."

Though we'd never been anything but buds, I hugged him and gave him a kiss. It was just a quick one, but I could tell from his reaction that he'd have been happy to let it last a little longer. Come to think of it, so would I, had it been a better time.

Jan's Grapenuts and the Wilhelm Screamers were playing on lanes nine and ten, so everybody in the Castle was clustered around them. Half of them could have had weapons drawn and I wouldn't have known it. Will Foley, a tall man who was normally completely laid back, was pacing back and forth while waiting for his turn to deliver.

"Any ideas other than throwing myself on top of Will Foley?" I said.

"Maybe I could smell the gun oil or bullets or something," Jake said.

"Do you know what a gun smells like?"

"Not really. For some reason the Pack doesn't like guns. Keeping them within reach of a bunch of people who lose it every month seems like a bad idea."

"We're not big on having them around either." A couple of generations back there'd been a member of the Kith with an Affinity for guns. It hadn't ended well.

Unless any of the bowlers started more arguments with the judges or themselves, we had maybe half an hour to figure out who the bastard was and stop him from shooting Foley.

Jake and I separated to make our way through the crowd, sniffing and listening respectively. Every few minutes I'd send him a message asking if he had anything, and each time he growled a negative. With people crammed so close together, and the game reaching its end, emotions were running high and the curse was at its most powerful. We had to stop twice to head off minor violence, which meant we had that much less time to spot the killer.

The Grapenuts had finished their last string, and they were in the lead, but the Screamers could still take it if they bowled well. And assuming Foley didn't get shot and default on the game.

Jake and I were getting desperate, and for the first time since my Affinity had made itself known, I wished I had a different one, something that would help me find the shooter. There were so many people, and any one of them could have had a hidden gun, expect maybe the one gal in a minidress—she didn't have room to hide a Kleenex.

Then time ran out. As Griper had predicted, Foley was the last bowler of the night, and the Castle was nearly silent as he lined up his shot. He was known as a great bowler and I didn't need Aunt Hester to tell me he was expecting to make a strike—it was in his every movement. He bent over to make his delivery and . . .

And I conjured the loudest, juiciest fart I'd ever produced, making it seemingly come from Foley's butt.

At first there was only shocked silence as the sound echoed through the building, so I added a giggle from the middle of a clump of people and a chuckle from some people in the back. While I was trying to decide which snicker to use, somebody laughed for real. An instant later, so did somebody else, and an avalanche of hilarity began. It was as if all the tension of the night had been released at once.

For a second I hoped the curse had been dissipated or dissolved or whatever verb applied to reversing a curse, but I felt the magic spiraling up and then down, no longer spread all over but instead targeting one person: Will Foley. His face was deep red, he was holding a two-pound-plus purple pearl Starline ball in both hands, and unless I missed my guess, he was about to lob it at somebody.

Everybody likes laughing—nobody likes being laughed at.

I walked toward him, hoping he wouldn't decide I'd make a good target. "High five, dude!" I said, raising my hand, and amplifying my voice just enough to cut through the continued chortles. "That was awesome! I don't know how you managed to set it up, but people are going to be talking about that for years."

"I didn't—" he started to say.

"And fixing it so you'd be the last bowler? Pure genius!"

I could see Foley's shoulders loosen, and he transferred the ball to his left hand so he could slap the hand I still had up in front of him.

"It was pretty funny, wasn't it?" he said tentatively.

"I just wish I'd videoed it for YouTube. It would have gone viral. Warn me next time, okay?"

"This was probably a onetime thing."

I nodded as if understanding his self-restraint, then stepped back. "Let me get out of the way so you can finish the string. Good luck!"

"Thanks." He got into the spirit enough to turn and bow to the crowd, getting a round of applause in return.

As soon as I could, I looked for Jake, and sent my voice to him. "Did you spot him?"

"No. You?"

"No, damn it." I sat down in an empty chair, closed my eyes, and really let my Affinity loose. There were so many conversations that it actually hurt to listen to them all, but I eliminated as fast I could, blocking people talking about funny farts, the games, ice cream after the game, an extramarital quickie in the parking lot—eww.

Finally I heard a voice I recognized from the bathroom. Not Griper, but the lovestruck Whiner. He was bleating to somebody about how much he loved his girlfriend and that his life would be over if she didn't love him back. I opened my eyes to look at the guy, and realized I knew him. Klip, Klips, Klipt . . . That was it, Rob Klipsch. He bowled regularly at the Castle but was one of the worst bowlers I'd ever seen. I squeezed my way to him, tapped him on the shoulder, and conjured a cone of silence around us.

"Mr. Klipsch?"

"Yes?"

"When you were in the men's room earlier, did you drop a hundred-dollar bill?"

"What? I mean, yeah, that was me."

I didn't need to smell that—he lied as well as he bowled. "Seriously, it must have been somebody in there with you. Who was it?"

"Paul Harmon? I don't think he dropped any money either."

"I'll go check with him." I left him mourning the lost C-note along with his girlfriend.

"Jake," I asked, "do you know a guy named Paul Harmon?"

"Yeah, he was last year's high scorer for the league. He's on Foley's team."

I'd assumed the killer had to be from one of the other teams. Killing one of your own teammates was just wrong. "He's the one with the gun!"

"Shit, he's right behind Foley. I'm on it! Stall!"

But it was too late. Though I tried to throw a bee buzzing right behind Foley's ear, it didn't distract him from delivering the ball, and as I watched, he made the most perfect strike I'd ever seen. The Castle erupted in cheers and Harmon started to pull his hand out of his pocket, but Jake had managed to get in front of him.

"You're blocking me," Harmon was saying, but Jake said, "Give it up, man."

"Get out of my way!"

Almost instinctively, I threw a cone of silence up around the two of them.

Meanwhile, having made a strike, Foley got an extra shot. Another strike. The cheers were even louder that time, and I was petrified Harmon was going to use the opportunity to take his shot, but Jake was still keeping him occupied.

Foley had one last ball, and everybody was watching him. He delivered, the ball rolled, and . . . Another strike!

The cheers were loud enough for me to get drunk on, but my attention was on Jake and Harmon. It looked as if they were arguing, but I couldn't penetrate my own cone of silence without everybody else hearing what was going on. Then an impressively tall, wide guy got in my way, and I lost sight of them for a minute.

When the wall-that-walks-like-a-man finally moved, Harmon was gone and Jake was sitting down, looking winded. I dropped the cone of silence and used my Affinity to say, "What happened?"

"He's gone," Jake said.

I glanced toward the door and saw Harmon's back—he must have been running to get there so quickly.

"Then we're good?" I asked, but for some reason, I felt the power of the curse spike. Voices were suddenly higher pitched, people were breathing in panicked gasps, and I could tell we were on the edge of pandemonium.

"Shit!" I said. "The curse is peaking!"

"Harmon must have spooked people. You've got to distract them!"

"How?"

"I don't know. Make some noise!"

I couldn't seem to think. Laughter had held the curse back before, but as I'd seen with Foley, it could go either way. What else would calm people or make them happy? If YouTube was any judge, I needed cute cat videos or a soldier surprising his kids on his return home, or . . . or a proposal.

I grabbed an empty water bottle and strode out into the middle of lane six, way past where I should have been without proper shoes.

"Ladies and gentlemen," I said with Affinity-fueled amplification, my hand wrapped around that water bottle in hopes everybody would think it was a microphone. "Give it up for Will Foley. He's made Candle-pin Castle history by making three end-of-game strikes during league championship play." I had no idea if it was history-making or not, but it was enough to get people clapping.

"For another piece of Castle history, I would like Rob Klipsch to please come up here."

Klipsch looked startled when I called his name, but when his buddies started pushing him, he gave up and came over.

I put my hand over the water bottle and shut off amplification to say, "Have you got the ring with you?"

"Yeah, but how—?"

"What's her name?"

"Whose name?"

"The one you're proposing to. What's her name?"

"Deb. Deborah Benoit."

I went back to my water bottle. "Deborah Benoit, this gentleman has something he would like to say to you."

A cute brunette wearing a Quiet Willow Nursery polo shirt came up, looking nervous and confused. I was eighty percent sure it was the same woman I'd heard bemoaning the fact that her boyfriend was com-mitment phobic, but if I was wrong, things were about to get worse.

"Take it away, Rob." I held the phony microphone under his mouth.

"Um, Deb. Deborah. There's something I've been meaning— Something I've been wanting to—" He fumbled at his pants pocket and pulled out a ring box covered in soft gray velvet. "Will you marry me?" He even dropped to one knee, though it might have been because his legs buckled.

Deb pressed her hands to her mouth in time-honored fashion, then nodded furiously.

"You will?" he said incredulously.

Before he could queer the deal, I announced, "She said yes!"

The crowd cheered, and as a tide of well-wishers surged forward to pat Klipsch on the back and hug the bride-to-be, I played salmon-swimming-upstream to get to Jake. Except he was gone, and I saw something I hadn't seen from a distance. There was blood on the chair where Jake had been sitting. Harmon had shot him!

Now everybody else was happy, but I was panicking as I listened for Jake. From the staff bathroom I heard a horrendous assortment of noises—popping, cracking, panting. I ran, pushing people out of my way like a fast ball through pins. If I'd needed any more confirmation that the curse's power was broken, I got it when nobody pushed back.

There was more blood on the bathroom door, and I was almost afraid of what I'd hear when I went inside. "Jake? Are you . . . ?"

There was a wolf on the tile floor, surrounded by a pile of Jake's clothes. He was looking at me, and if it's possible for a wolf to smile, he was smiling.

"Can you talk?"

He gave me a look that was pure Jake.

So no talking. "He shot you?"

He nodded his muzzle, and nosed the bloody shirt on the floor. There was a hole in one sleeve. Then he lifted his right hand . . . paw.

"You changed. Did you lose control?"

A shake of the head.

"Then why . . . Did changing help you heal?"

A nod.

"And you're all better now?"

A particularly emphatic nod.

"Jeez, Jake, you scared the hell out of me!" I'd known that werewolves were tough, but I hadn't realized that they could heal from a freaking bullet wound within minutes.

He shrugged.

I stopped to listen to the goings-on in the Castle. Friends were congratulating the happy couple, and if Foley was peeved that his historical game was no longer in the spotlight, he wasn't saying so. Most people were packing up and leaving.

As for the curse, I could still feel it, but it was about as dangerous as a kitten. It might make somebody annoyed, but only if they were halfway annoyed already. "I think the worst of it is over."

He held up one paw.

"Fist bump?"

He nodded.

I went with it, and said, "Shouldn't you change back?"

He looked pointedly at the clothes.

"You think you've got anything I haven't seen before?"

He stood and stalked toward me, growling deep in his throat.

"Okay, okay," I said. "I'll go see if I can find you a clean shirt." After the door was safely shut, I threw my voice into the room to add, "And some kibble."

Amar finally emerged from his office, looking embarrassed, and told me to take a break while he herded the rest of the people out the door and locked up. Belle and Rayleigh were as thick as thieves again, and happy to oblige with Cokes and a fresh batch of onion rings for Jake and me.

While I was waiting for Jake to do whatever it was he had to do, I called Aunt Hester.

"Hello, dear. You have had an exciting evening, haven't you?"

"Aunt Hester, you lied to me."

"Elspeth Allaway, I did no such thing."

"You told me I couldn't break the curse!"

"I did not. I said *I* couldn't break a curse. And I can't. Seeing the future doesn't do a thing against curses."

"But you knew what I thought you meant."

"I can't tell you everything, dear. You have to learn some things for yourself."

"Aunt Hester, Jake got shot! That's a lesson I could have done without."

"I am sorry about that, but I knew he'd be all right. And that man who shot him threw his gun into the lake and then went straight to his therapist—he'll be fine, too. So no hard feelings?"

I was trying to think of what I could say that wouldn't get me in hot water with my mother when she added, "Let me make it up to you by explaining something else you might have misunderstood."

"Okay," I said, not sure if I wanted to hear what she wanted to tell me.

"Remember how you asked me if the curse had anything to do with the Law of Return, and I said it did?"

"Right, because of the prank I pulled."

"How is it you'd put it? Self-centered much? The sprained ankle was the boy's own fault—he shouldn't have been out that night and he certainly shouldn't have jumped out a window. No, the curse was brought on by your boss's actions."

"Amar?" I thought back to something Jake had told me. "Because of firing Theresa?"

"He handled that very badly, and something was bound to happen. It turns out that girl's aunt is a practitioner, and frankly, not a nice woman. She cursed the Castle."

"So it was nothing to do with me?"

"That's right."

"And I don't have to worry about anything happening because of the prank?"

"Oh, no, you're going to have misfortune because of that. And very soon, too."

"Great."

"Don't fret. It'll be far overshadowed by the good fortune because of the people you helped tonight. You know the Law of Return doesn't run on a schedule, or you would know if you'd pay more attention to your mother, but this time you'll get both punishment and reward right away."

"Aunt Hester, you seriously creep me out."

"I know, dear."

She hung up just as Jake joined me, which she had no doubt foreseen. The two of us chowed down, and then helped clean up the unusually messy Castle before clocking out and heading for the parking lot.

"Crap!" I said, looking at my car's front end. "I've got a flat tire."

"You want me to help change it?"

"Thanks, but I can do it." Except that when I went toward the trunk, I saw another flat. "Jeez! Another? I've only got one spare."

"Have you got Triple A?"

"Yeah. Let me find my card." Only it wasn't in my wallet. "The Law of Return strikes!" I muttered. Having two flat tires was worlds better than a curse, but it was a pain just the same.

"Why don't I give you a ride home?" Jake said in an all-too-casual way. "I don't have classes tomorrow, so I can help you get squared away in the morning."

"You wouldn't mind?"

"No, it's no big." As we were getting into his car, he said, "You know, I was thinking about hitting the Sonic for something else to eat. Changing and healing take it out of me. You want to come?"

I was pretty sure the Law of Return had struck again. It was the best thing I'd heard all night.

COPYRIGHTS

HOME IMPROVEMENT
CHARLAINE HARRIS & TONI L.P. KELNER

There's nothing like home renovation for finding skeletons in the closet or otherworldly portals in the attic. Now here's the perfect treat for any homeowner who's ever wondered, 'What's that creaking sound?' (just before the ceiling comes crashing down!). Editors Charlaine Harris and Toni L. P. Kelner return with an all-new collection, this time on the paranormal perils of Do-It-Yourself.

As well as a brand-new Sookie Stackhouse story by the Number 1 Sunday Times bestselling author Charlaine Harris, there are 13 more cautionary tales of home renovation by bestselling authors Patricia Briggs, James Grady, Heather Graham, Melissa Marr, amongst others. This is an outstanding line-up of frightening and funny fixer-upper tales guaranteed to shake foundations and rattle readers' pipes.

Jo Fletcher
BOOKS

www.jofletcherbooks.co.uk